A Baleful Godmother

Novel

Violet

and the

BOW STREET RUNNER

EMILY LARKIN

www.emilylarkin.com

Violet and the Bow Street Runner / Emily Larkin. – 1st ed.

ISBN 978-0-9951436-4-7

Cover Design: JD Smith Design

It is a truth universally acknowledged, that Faerie godmothers do not exist.

CHAPTER ONE

*V*iolet Garland enjoyed the bustle and busyness of the Season—the evenings at Vauxhall, the routs and soirées, the performances at the opera and the theater, the balloon ascensions and the picnics, the multitude of entertainments that London had to offer.

Two of the pastimes she particularly enjoyed were dancing and flirting. She was dancing now, performing a reel with a rather dashing duke's grandson. They went through the figures energetically, enjoyed an extravagant flirtation, and parted ways happy in the knowledge that they didn't wish to marry one another. The duke's grandson preferred wealthy young widows and while he was rather dashing, Violet wanted someone even more dashing. Someone with an adventurous spirit. Someone who liked to ride fast and dance fast and live fast. Someone exciting.

Someone quite unlike the gentleman standing in the nearest corner, who was so nondescript as to be almost invisible. Violet eyed him while she sipped a glass of orgeat. The man was blandness personified, everything about him unremarkable, from his brown hair to his navy-blue tailcoat to the tips of his black shoes. It wasn't that he was unattractive, more that he was profoundly uninteresting to the eye. If he wished to catch an heiress, he needed to exert himself rather more.

But it appeared that the bland man had no wish to catch an heiress. Violet glimpsed him several times during the course of the evening, and each time he was standing in a corner, observing the other guests, as unexciting as a piece of furniture.

Violet danced and flirted with an earl's son, a marquis's son, two fortune hunters, and a rather rakish viscount. Her dashing and adventurous husband-to-be would stroll into a ballroom one evening, she was certain of it, but tonight wasn't the night. She danced one more set and left the ball early, along with her brother, Rhodes, and her younger sister, Aster. Rhodes left early because he didn't much care for balls now that he was a widower. Aster left early because she liked peace and quiet more than she liked noise and crowds. But Violet left early because as much as she enjoyed dancing and flirting, there was something she enjoyed doing far more. Something secret and thrilling that she could only do in the dead of night.

Accordingly, she allowed her maid to remove the delicate ball gown, with its pretty silk rosebuds and its spangled gauze. The pearl necklace and matching earbobs went back in their case. Her hair was unpinned, brushed out, and plaited in a tidy braid.

Violet climbed into bed—and once the maid had gone, she climbed out again and latched her door. She danced across to her dresser and unlocked the bottom drawer. The clothes Rhodes had bought for her lay folded there: long pantaloons, half a dozen shirts, neckcloths, a snug coat, a pair of sturdy shoes.

Everything was black, even the neckcloths.

Violet dressed quickly—shirt, stockings, pantaloons, shoes. The coat had a clever little pocket into which Rhodes had tucked a house key and a penknife. Just in case, he'd said, but there'd never yet been a just in case.

Violet wrapped one of the unstarched neckcloths around

2

her throat like a muffler, tucked the ends down the front of the coat, and put on the mask she'd sewn. It wasn't the sort of mask one wore to a masquerade; it was the sort of mask a hangman wore, covering her face completely.

She tied the mask tightly so it couldn't blow off, wiggled her fingers into a pair of black kidskin gloves, and examined herself in the mirror. Not one scrap of pale skin showed.

As well as men's clothes, Rhodes had bought her a dark lantern. Violet lit it and set it on the hearth, adjusting the metal shades so that only the merest glimmer of light showed. Then she blew out her candles. Her bedroom became almost, but not quite, pitch black.

She parted her curtains, opened her window, and climbed up onto the broad sill, high above the ground. At her back was her bedchamber, quiet and safe. In front of her was . . . adventure.

Violet leaped off the windowsill—and flew, diving up into the night sky. High, higher, even higher. When the lights of London were no bigger than the merest pinpricks, she halted, hovering above the city. The air was thin and chilly. An almost-full moon hung overhead, as bright as mother-of-pearl. London looked beautiful from this vantage point, mysterious and otherworldly, a place of secretive dark spaces and twinkling golden lights.

A familiar medley of emotions swelled in Violet's breast, wonder and awe and elation, tempered by a faint feeling of loneliness.

She was the only person who would ever see this view.

Violet's Faerie godmother was a closely guarded secret. No one outside the family knew of Baletongue's existence, just as no one outside the family received her grudging wishes. Violet was the only person in England who could do this, the only person in the world, and it was exciting and thrilling and she loved it, but sometimes she did wish she could share it with someone else.

But Violet wasn't prone to melancholy, she preferred action

to contemplation, so she gave a loud whoop, high above the city where no one could hear her, and arrowed down again.

Faster and faster she went, exulting in the speed. Wind tore at her clothes and whipped her laughter away as fast as she uttered it. London's rooftops came closer and closer—closer—and then she soared up again, tracing a vast, exuberant somersault in the sky.

When she was tired of soaring and plummeting, Violet drifted, a furlong above the rooftops. Contentment hummed in her veins. She loved these nighttime excursions for the thrill of flying, the unrestrained freedom, the exhilarating speed, but she also loved them for the silence and the solitude, the sense of being apart from the rest of the world.

London was hustle and bustle, it was noise and crowds, carriages and pedestrians. But not up here. It was a different world, high above the rooftops. Here, she was alone. Here, she saw things that no one ordinarily saw.

Here, she saw London's secrets.

Grosvenor Square lay beneath her. In fact, she was drifting above the very house where she'd danced earlier that evening.

Violet glided lower, until she could see the house clearly: the tall façade with its glittering rows of windows, the flambeaux flaring in their brackets, the guests descending the stairs to the flagway, the carriage that had just pulled away.

But tall townhouses in Grosvenor Square weren't very interesting, even if balls were taking place inside them. In fact, Mayfair as a whole wasn't very interesting. Violet preferred to explore further afield. There were so many unexpected places in London, so many curious sights.

One of her favorite things to do was to follow people and see where they led her—and there, descending the marble steps below her, was a man. She'd follow him and see where he took her.

Most likely, he'd lead her to one of the clubs where gentlemen liked to spend their time, drinking and playing at cards, but he might take her to his home or to a gaming hell or to one of the brothels near Covent Garden.

Not that she actually knew that the buildings men visited near Covent Gardens were brothels. She'd never looked in windows to check.

Which wasn't to say that she hadn't been tempted. She had. But Violet had standards. She was a duke's daughter, and dukes' daughters didn't peek in windows.

They did follow people, though. And this man was headed briskly in the direction of Piccadilly, the soles of his shoes making faint slapping sounds on the flagway. He turned onto Charles Street and then Mount Street. As he passed beneath a streetlamp, Violet saw that he was the earl's son she'd danced with earlier. Freddy Stanhope.

She paused in midair. She didn't like to follow people she knew. It made her feel like a snoop.

Someone else walked along the street below. His shoes didn't make the slapping sounds that Freddy's did. He moved as silently as a shadow.

Freddy Stanhope turned into Berkeley Square. So did the man behind him.

Violet drifted after them.

Ahead of her, Stanhope crossed the top of the square and turned into Bruton Street. Violet decided to follow the man who walked so silently, except that he turned into Bruton Street, too.

In fact, every turn that Freddy Stanhope made for the next ten minutes, the silent and shadowy man made, too.

Was Freddy being followed?

Was he about to be robbed?

Violet picked up her pace, drawing ahead of the silent man. She flew low, much lower than she ordinarily did, and landed on a colonnaded portico and crouched there. As the man passed under a streetlamp, she glimpsed his face.

It was the bland man from the ball. The man who had as much presence as a stick of furniture.

Violet stared after him in astonishment.

Mr. Bland was following Freddy Stanhope?

It was so inconceivable that she flew ahead for another look at his face.

Yes, it was Mr. Bland.

Mr. Bland followed Freddy Stanhope all the way to a house on Soho Square.

Violet had seen men enter that particular house before. It was either a gaming hell or an upmarket brothel, she wasn't certain which—and she wasn't going to peek in the upstairs windows to find out.

Freddy Stanhope was admitted into the building.

Mr. Bland didn't follow him inside. He paused in the mouth of an alleyway where shadows gathered deeply. Violet could barely see him.

Two men crossed the square. They were loud and laughing, steadying one another as they walked.

Violet had seen many drunken men in her nighttime explorations. They held no interest for her. She returned her attention to Mr. Bland in his patch of shadows—and discovered that he'd vanished.

She sped along the square at rooftop level, searching for him, afraid that she'd lost the most interesting person she'd ever followed—and caught movement out of the corner of her eye. It was Mr. Bland. He ducked into Frith Street, hugging the shadows, walking briskly and silently.

Violet darted hastily after him.

Usually when she followed someone, she stayed above the rooftops, but Mr. Bland was so determined not to be noticed that Violet had to fly lower. She almost lost him when he navigated a series of alleyways, and again when he ducked into Newport Street. He kept checking over his shoulder as if he thought he was being followed, but she couldn't see anyone behind him.

Mr. Bland headed purposefully southeast. Violet hoped his destination wasn't Covent Garden. If he set foot in a brothel—or worse, decided to take his pleasure in an alleyway with one of the cheaper ladies of the night—she would have to stop following him.

He turned into Hart Street, which meant that Covent Garden was his destination.

Violet used a word that Rhodes sometimes used when he thought he couldn't be overheard: "Damnation."

But Mr. Bland surprised her yet again. He continued along Hart Street to its end, where he left the shadows and strode up the steps of a building on Bow Street. A building that had a watchman at the door. A building that most definitely was not a brothel.

A building that was in fact the Bow Street Magistrates' Court.

Violet watched open-mouthed as the watchman greeted Mr. Bland and opened the door for him. Mr. Bland went inside.

Half a minute later, lamplight flickered in one of the upstairs rooms. Violet flew closer than was prudent and peered in through the window. If the watchman looked up, he might possibly see her, but right now she didn't care. She wanted to know what Mr. Bland was going to do next.

What Mr. Bland did next was peel off his gloves and set his hat on a desk. He sat. He opened a drawer and took out a notebook. He trimmed a quill, dipped it in ink, and began writing.

There was only one conclusion to be drawn. That was Mr. Bland's desk, his chair, his notebook, his inkwell.

Violet stared at him through the windowpane. He looked so *ordinary*.

But he clearly wasn't ordinary.

Magistrates didn't follow suspects, and neither did law clerks or secretaries.

Which meant that Mr. Bland was a Bow Street Runner.

CHAPTER TWO

*V*iolet knew that she'd stumbled upon an adventure, but she didn't know exactly what the adventure was or how to participate in it. Mr. Bland didn't give her any clues. He wrote in his notebook for several minutes, returned it to its drawer, picked up his hat and gloves, and departed.

Violet followed, gliding forty feet above his head.

Mr. Bland walked for five minutes, glancing over his shoulder multiple times and pausing once to scan the street in every direction. Then, he turned into a lane behind High Holborn and let himself into a house with a latchkey. The house was tall and narrow, with dirty brickwork and lopsided shutters. Some of the windows were lit, most were not. Violet darted from window to window, trying to see inside. She caught glimpses through the crooked shutters, enough to tell her that it was a lodging house.

Candlelight bloomed in the attic window. Violet swooped upwards for a closer look.

The window stood open, allowing her to see into a cramped little room with a sloping ceiling. There was a bed, a washstand, and a wooden chair. The floorboards were scuffed and unpainted, the whitewash on the walls flaking, the ceiling water stained.

For the second time that evening, Violet watched Mr. Bland remove his hat and gloves. His tailcoat and breeches had looked plain at the ball; here in this shabby little room they were positively sumptuous.

Mr. Bland peeled out of his coat—and Violet abruptly felt uncomfortable. If she stayed any longer, she'd be a Peeping Tom.

She turned away from the window and sped towards St. James's Square and home.

Why was a Bow Street Runner following Freddy Stanhope?

That question occupied Violet's mind until she fell asleep and was the first thing she thought about when she woke. She pondered it while she dressed and ruminated on it while she ate a very late breakfast. Her parents, the Duke and Duchess of Sevenash, set off to visit friends in Surrey in the early afternoon. Violet stood on the marble steps with Aster and Rhodes and Rhodes's children, three-year-old Hyacinth, five-year-old Jessamy, and seven-year-old Melrose. She waved her parents good-bye and wondered what on earth Freddy Stanhope had done to attract the attention of a Bow Street Runner. The traveling carriage clattered briskly across the square and disappeared from view. Hyacinth looked ready to cry, but Rhodes had brought a ball down from the nursery, so they trooped through the house and went out into the garden at the back to play a game with the children. Violet speculated about Bow Street Runners and earls' sons while she caught the ball and dropped the ball and ran after the ball, and she cogitated on it further when they went indoors again. The children ran upstairs to the nursery where refreshments awaited. Violet changed from her morning dress to a carriage dress.

Her parents had gone into Surrey for a fortnight; Violet only went as far as Hyde Park with her sister, Aster, and her cousins Clematis and Daphne. Aster and Clem and Daffy discussed the latest fashion in bonnets while they took a turn around the park in the open-topped landaulet. Violet paid them no heed; she was too busy puzzling over earl's sons and Bow Street Runners to have any interest in whether brims were getting shorter or longer. On their way back, the coachman took them to Berkeley Square, halting under the maple trees in the middle of the square so that they might partake of ices from Gunter's Tea Shop. A waiter brought menus across to the carriage, but Violet was unable to concentrate on the delights described therein. The choice between *neige de pistachio* and *glacé d'épine-vinette* was inconsequential when one was on the edge of a mystery.

But what was the mystery?

She chose at random. The waiter scurried back across the street. Aster and Clematis and Daphne had stopped discussing fashion and were now talking about Violet's older sister, Primrose, who lived on Berkeley Square and whom they would ordinarily visit when they stopped for ices. But Primrose was in Brighton right now, with her husband Oliver. "I wonder if they'll go sea-bathing?" Aster said, to which Clematis replied, "Oliver will!" and Daphne said, "He'll splash about like a walrus and make everyone wet."

Violet stopped listening. Mr. Bland had followed Freddy Stanhope through Berkeley Square. He had walked past this very spot.

Why?

The waiter trotted across to the carriage carrying a tray of ices in pretty goblets. Aster and Clematis and Daphne accepted theirs with Oohs and Aahs of delight. Violet took the remaining goblet absently.

Had Freddy murdered someone?

No, that was impossible. Freddy Stanhope might be a mad rattle, but he wasn't a murderer.

10

Had he fought a duel?

If he'd done that, everyone in the ton would be talking of it, and they weren't, so it wasn't a duel.

Had he stolen something?

That was as impossible to believe as murder was. Freddy might not be his father's heir, but his horses were expensive and his clothes the height of fashion.

Although . . . he did still reside with his parents on Manchester Square, so perhaps he wasn't as flush in the pocket as he appeared? And he did have six younger siblings. Had his allowance been reduced? Had he lost heavily at the gambling tables? Had he fallen into debt and decided to steal something to replenish his funds?

Violet tabled that as possible but extremely unlikely, and tried to think of other reasons a Bow Street Runner might follow Freddy Stanhope, but every reason she came up with was more preposterous than the last.

Was Freddy planning to abduct an heiress?

Was he selling secrets to French agents?

Was he blackmailing someone?

Violet cogitated on that latter possibility for a few moments and decided that blackmail was as unlikely as theft and murder, because Freddy was an earl's son and earls' sons just didn't do things like that.

Or did they?

She scraped the bottom of her goblet, licked the spoon, and belatedly realized that the ice she'd eaten had been lemon.

Was Freddy conducting an adulterous liaison with someone? That, she could believe. In which case, who was the wife . . . and who the husband who'd hired the Runner?

Violet frowned across the square. People passed by on the flagway: gentlemen sauntering, the ladies strolling, servants hurrying about their errands.

One of the gentlemen caught her eye.

Someone nudged her elbow. "Violet," her cousin Clematis said, in a tone that indicated she'd been saying "Violet" for quite some time.

11

"What?"

Clematis waved a paper bag under her nose. "Would you like one?"

"What are they?"

"Sugar drops."

Violet looked past her cousin, trying to spot the man who'd caught her attention. Something about him was oddly familiar.

"Violet," Clematis said.

Violet found the man. There was nothing remarkable about him at all. He wore a nondescript hat, a nondescript tailcoat, a nondescript—

She suddenly realized why he was familiar. She thrust her empty goblet at Clematis and sprang down from the carriage. "Don't wait for me!" she cried, and pelted in pursuit of Mr. Bland.

Running in Berkeley Square wasn't at all convenable, but Violet didn't care. Fortunately, by the time Mr. Bland turned into Davies Street, she'd almost caught up to him.

They proceeded along Davies Street, twenty yards apart, Mr. Bland walking in that unremarkable way of his, Violet lurking behind.

Mr. Bland paused at Oxford Street. Violet surreptitiously shaded her face with the brim of her bonnet, so that he couldn't see her features. She waited for him to cross, and then followed. As they walked, she tried to be as unremarkable as he was, which was difficult when one's carriage dress was the height of fashion and one's bonnet was a gay confection of ribbons and flowers.

Mr. Bland led her to Manchester Square, where the Stanhope family had their residence, but he didn't pause to observe that edifice. In fact, he didn't so much as glance at it. He walked briskly west and took a turn around Portman Square; then he crossed Oxford Street again and walked all the way around Grosvenor Square. Violet was quite baffled. Why would someone walk around Manchester Square *and* Portman Square *and* Grosvenor Square?

Mr. Bland turned into Charles Street, presumably heading for Berkeley Square, which he was going to walk around, too. Violet followed, still twenty paces behind, feeling hot, sweaty, confused, and frustrated. There was absolutely no logical reason for Mr. Bland to take such a route.

She turned the corner into Charles Street and discovered that Mr. Bland had vanished.

Violet looked left and right. She even looked up, as if he could fly, but Mr. Bland was nowhere to be seen.

Charles Street was very short. Halfway along it, mews opened on either side. If Mr. Bland was in the mews, he would have had to have run to reach them so fast, but there was no earthly reason for him to have run, which meant he must have entered one of the houses.

Violet walked along Charles Street, trying to determine which building Mr. Bland had entered. Did one of them belong to whoever had hired him? She reached the mews, peered around the corner—and came face to face with Mr. Bland.

"Oh," she cried, leaping back, pressing both hands to her chest, where her heart was trying to batter its way out of her ribcage.

Mr. Bland didn't apologize for startling her. He stared at her through narrowed eyes. "Who are you? Why are you following me?"

"Me?" Violet's voice squeaked. She cleared her throat. "I don't know what you mean. I'm not following you."

Mr. Bland crossed his arms. His expression was sardonic. "Manchester Square. Portman Square. Grosvenor Square."

Violet felt her face become red. "I like to walk. For my constitution."

Mr. Bland had the breeding not to roll his eyes at her, but his eyebrows rose a good half inch in disbelief. "In a carriage dress? Without a servant?"

Mr. Bland's appearance might be nondescript, but his vowels weren't. He sounded like Rhodes and Freddy Stanhope

13

and all the other men Violet knew. Which was intriguing. "Who are you?" she asked.

"Who are you?" he countered.

"Violet Garland," she said, omitting the *Lady*.

His gray eyes narrowed further. "Any relation to the Duke of Sevenash?"

"He's my father," Violet admitted.

Mr. Bland didn't bow, which was what most men did when they learned she was a duke's daughter. He looked her up and down. His frown deepened, as if she was a puzzle he couldn't solve.

Violet wasn't used to being looked up and down like that. "Who are you?" she demanded imperiously.

"My name is Wintersmith."

"Any relation to Viscount Wintersmith?" Violet asked, mimicking his earlier question.

"Uncle," he said shortly. "Why were you following me?"

Violet debated her answers. This was an adventure, after all. Why not take hold of it by the horns? "Because I know you're a Bow Street Runner and I want to see what you're doing. You're investigating Freddy Stanhope, aren't you? What's he done?"

Wintersmith's frown became thunderous. "Who told you that?"

"No one." Violet couldn't tell him that she'd followed him across London last night, so she said, "I saw you watching him at the Montlakes' ball."

That answer didn't please Wintersmith. His mouth tightened.

"What's Freddy done? I can help you investigate! One of his sisters is friends with one of my sisters, so I'm invited there all the time. I can search Freddy's room or—"

"No."

"But I want to," Violet said enthusiastically. "Just think! I might see something or hear something—"

"No," Wintersmith repeated. "Absolutely not." He

uncrossed his arms and took a step back, turning away from her.

Violet saw her chance of an adventure slipping through her fingers. "Oh, but please! I'll be such an asset! No one will guess that I'm helping a Bow Street Runner!"

"No," he said again. "And it's Principal Officer, not Bow Street Runner."

Violet knew that, but Bow Street Runner sounded better. Runners ran and followed and investigated and were active and daring. Principal Officers sat and wrote and were boringly officious. She ignored his remark. "If it's murder or theft, then I'm certain Freddy didn't do it. I can find proof for you! I can clear his name!"

"Go home, Miss Garland," Wintersmith said forbiddingly, and then he corrected himself: "Lady Violet." He paused and glanced at the mews, taking in their surroundings. His expression tightened, as if he suppressed a grimace, and then he said, very stiffly, "Allow me to escort you home, Lady Violet."

"I don't wish to be escorted home. I wish to investigate. What is it that you think Freddy's done?"

Wintersmith folded his arms again. "Go home."

Violet folded her arms, too, and matched him glare for glare. A whole minute passed, and then another one. Violet decided that Mr. Wintersmith wasn't nondescript and dull, he was aggravating and annoying. And disobliging. And odious.

A carriage turned into the mews, forcing them both to step aside.

"Very well!" Violet said. "I'll go home, but you're missing a singular opportunity. I can go places you can't."

She turned and strode crossly down Charles Street, muttering about odious Principal Officers under her breath. When she reached Mount Street, she discovered that Wintersmith was following a discreet twenty paces behind, which irritated her even further.

He followed her to Berkeley Square. Violet marched all the way around the square. Wintersmith trailed after her.

When she'd completed the circuit, she looked back and bestowed a dagger-like glance upon him. His expression was unimpressed. Violet was tempted to march around the square a second time, just to teach him a lesson, but she'd already done a lot of walking, so she headed briskly for Piccadilly.

Wintersmith followed her all the way home to St. James's Square. Violet climbed the gleaming marble stairs to Sevenash House. A footman opened the huge door for her. If he thought it was odd that she had left in the landaulet with her sister and cousins but was coming home on foot alone, he didn't show it. His expression was perfectly blank. Mr. Wintersmith's face, when she glanced back, wasn't blank. He wore a good riddance expression.

Violet sniffed, and stalked inside. If the footman hadn't been there, she would have slammed the door.

She climbed the stairs to her room and threw her bonnet on the bed. What a detestable man, to follow her across Mayfair as if he didn't trust her to know her own way home! As if he thought she might follow him if he didn't follow her. And then it occurred to her that Wintersmith might have followed her to make certain she was safe. A duke's daughter, alone and unattended in England's biggest city . . .

Violet didn't know whether to be cross with him or not—and then she remembered their conversation in the mews. Cross. Definitely cross.

"Wherever did you get to?" Aster demanded, when Violet went downstairs to the garden parlor, so named because it looked out over the garden at the back of the house. "We drove around Mayfair forever, looking for you!"

"I saw someone I knew. Where's Rhodes?"

"You could have told us," Aster said, sounding very put out, which was unlike her. "We were worried!"

"Sorry," Violet said, contritely. "Do you know where Rhodes is?"

"Up in the nursery." Aster put down the book she was reading. "Who was it?"

"Oh, just someone." Violet left the parlor and hurried upstairs to the nursery. Childish laughter spilled out through the open door.

Rhodes was sitting on the floor with the children, surrounded by a vast expanse of toppled dominoes.

"Rhodes?" Violet said. "Do you have a minute?"

Rhodes looked up, and for a moment Violet stopped thinking about odious Bow Street Runners and thought instead that she hadn't seen him smile like that, with pure joy, since Evelyn had died in childbirth two years ago, mother and infant both perishing during that long, dreadful night.

"Again! Again!" young Jessamy cried, clapping his hands gleefully.

Rhodes looked from Violet to Jessamy and back again.

"I'll come back later," Violet said.

"No, it's all right," Rhodes said. "We need to gather up all the tiles again."

Melrose and Jessamy set eagerly to work, collecting up the scattered dominoes. Hyacinth stayed where she was, in Rhodes's lap. Rhodes stayed where he was, too, on the floor. He cocked his head and looked up at Violet. "What is it?"

"You were friends with a Wintersmith at school, weren't you?"

Rhodes lost the last of his smile. "Endymion Wintersmith, yes."

"Is Viscount Wintersmith his uncle?"

"He was. Endymion died at Seringapatam."

"Oh."

"Why do you want to know?"

"I met someone today. He said he's Wintersmith's nephew."

Rhodes's brow creased. "Is it Perry? Periander?"

"I don't know."

"I can't see who else it could be. Endymion and Alexander both died in India. What's Perry doing here? I didn't know he was back."

"Back from where?"

"India. They all went into the army. Bit of a scandal at the time. Their father lost his fortune at cards and then had an accident with his gun." Rhodes's tone told her exactly how accidental he thought that mishap had been.

"Oh," Violet said, inadequately.

"The viscount shoved the boys into the army, told them he didn't want to see their faces in England again." Rhodes, who was normally the most placid of men, looked as if he wanted to spit. "Close-fisted son of a . . . hmm." He glanced at his children, and then back at Violet. "Are you certain it's Perry? I would have thought I'd've heard if he were back in England."

Violet was tempted to tell him that Wintersmith had been at last night's ball, doing an imitation of a stick of furniture, but she didn't. "It might not be him. It could be another nephew."

"Not unless there's a branch of the family I don't know about."

"Perhaps there is. Have fun with the dominoes. Thank you!"

Violet went back downstairs and into one of the parlors at the front of the house. She peered out a window. No odious Bow Street Runners loitered in the square.

She ought to have felt relieved, not disappointed.

CHAPTER THREE

*P*erry stood discreetly in an alcove, an untouched glass of champagne in his hand, watching first one suspect, then another. Giles Abbishaw was making his way through a quadrille with a young lady who looked to be in her first season. She was paying painstaking attention to her steps. Giles didn't need to worry about his steps. His execution was easy, if unenthusiastic. He gave the impression of a man who would much rather be somewhere else—which was exactly the impression he'd given two nights ago, before leaving the ball early and giving Perry the slip in the vicinity of South Audley Street.

Giles Abbishaw was currently at the top of Perry's list of suspects.

Giles's brother, Saintbridge, was at the bottom. Lord Abbishaw didn't suspect Saintbridge at all, but Perry was investigating the thefts and he'd placed Saintbridge on the list, because Saintbridge had had as much opportunity as Giles.

Although why would Saintbridge steal clocks from his father? Saintbridge was the heir, pampered and indulged and in possession of a handsome fortune. He had no need for money, no grudge to bear against a doting father, and—as far as Perry could determine—absolutely no interest in clocks, automatous or otherwise.

Giles apparently had no interest in clocks either, but he did have need for money. The viscount was as tightfisted towards his middle son as he was open-handed towards his oldest. A grudge was a possibility, too. Perhaps Giles resented Lord Abbishaw's unequal treatment of his offspring?

Perry's gaze drifted from one brother to the other. The set of their eyes and the shapes of mouth and nose were very similar, but there the resemblance ended. Giles was shorter, darker, and stockier than his brother. And the differences went deeper than height and coloring. Saintbridge looked down his nose with the arrogance of a man who would one day be a viscount; Giles didn't. If Perry were to use one word to describe Giles Abbishaw, it would be diffident. If he were to use a second, it would be anxious. Diffident and anxious were not adjectives that anyone would use to describe Saintbridge.

Saintbridge was on the dance floor, too. His partner was an heiress. Saintbridge's face bore a faintly disdainful expression, not because the heiress didn't meet with his standards—although it was entirely possible that she didn't—but because a little sneer seemed to sit permanently on his upper lip.

The disdain was why Saintbridge was at the bottom of Perry's list. If Saintbridge was too fastidious to visit brothels or to consort with opera dancers and actresses, then it was highly unlikely that he'd steal automatous clocks with amorous scenes painted on their dials.

Unless he'd stolen them because he wished to remove such vulgarities from his father's collection?

Perry didn't think that was likely, but Saintbridge had a key to the cabinet, and was therefore on Perry's list. If not Lord Abbishaw's list.

Perry's gaze roamed further. He located his next suspect: Devereux Abbishaw, the viscount's nephew. Devereux stood in a knot of men near the card room, a glass dangling negligently in one hand, his head thrown back in a laugh.

Perry had spent ten years at school with Devereux—and been best friends with him for most of that time. The boy he remembered had always been up for a lark, and maybe stealing pornographic automatous clocks was a lark?

Devereux had never been given a key to the cabinet, but he'd been a visitor at Lord Abbishaw's residence on Hanover Square. And he'd been friends with Wilton Abbishaw, the viscount's disgraced youngest son. Had Wilton given Devereux a key to the cabinet before he'd been bundled off to America?

It was possible—or rather, it wasn't *im*possible.

It was also possible that if Perry asked, Devereux would tell him the truth. Devereux had always been full of mischief, but he'd never been a liar.

But Perry would prefer to solve this case without coming face to face with Devereux. He'd rule out all the other suspects first—starting with Giles, because men who crept away from balls and took circuitous routes through London often had mistresses, and automatous clocks that featured explicit acts of lovemaking were exactly the sort of gifts that men bestowed upon their lovers.

And if Giles proved to be innocent, he'd move on to Frederick Stanhope, because Stanhope had been a close friend of Wilton's and might have Wilton's key, and because he owned a pocket watch painted with an erotic scene, and what were clocks but overlarge and elaborate watches?

Perry scanned the ballroom again. His gaze skipped over matrons with nodding feathers in their headdresses and débutantes in pale gowns, footmen in livery, musicians playing their instruments—and jerked to a halt. Someone stood in the alcove across from him. A young lady.

He recognized her instantly.

Lady Violet Garland.

Perry managed not to scowl at her, although his fingers tightened on the glass of champagne. He looked away and checked that Giles hadn't somehow vanished from the dance floor. Then he checked the whereabouts of Saintbridge, Devereux, and Frederick Stanhope. When he looked back at the alcove, it was empty.

"It's something to do with the Abbishaws, isn't it?" a voice hissed in his ear.

Perry couldn't conceal a start. Champagne slopped from his glass.

Lady Violet stood alongside him, looking rather smug. She also looked, at this proximity, quite stunning. Her hair was swept up in an elaborate confection of braids and ringlets, with pearls woven through it. More pearls dangled from her earlobes. There were pearls at her throat and yet more pearls stitched onto the delicate fabric of her ball gown. Her cheeks were pink, her lips rosy, her hair black and lustrous.

She dazzled the eye.

Perry was abruptly aware that not only had his ensemble been hired from a secondhand shop, but that it was too tight at the shoulders, too loose at the waist, and rather shabby at the elbows.

"You were watching Giles Abbishaw," Lady Violet declared. "And both Devil and Saint."

Perry stopped being dazzled and started being annoyed. "No, I wasn't."

"Yes, you were." Lady Violet squeezed closer to him in the alcove. The gleam in her eyes was bright and alarmingly enthusiastic. "Is it to do with Wilton? Was Jasper Flint's death not an accident after all? Was it murder?"

"This has nothing to do with Jasper Flint."

"Then why are you watching Saint and Devil and Giles? They were all at Abbishaw Park when it happened."

"This is completely unrelated."

"So you *are* investigating the Abbishaws!"

"I didn't say that."

"But you didn't say that you're *not* investigating them."

"I'm not going to tell you who I'm investigating."

Her mouth opened.

Perry rushed to forestall her. "And I do *not* need any assistance."

Lady Violet closed her mouth. Her expression became faintly mutinous.

Perry looked around for somewhere to place his sticky glass and found a ledge behind him.

"Freddy wasn't there when Jasper died, so why did you follow him yesterday?"

"This has nothing to do with Flint!" Perry said, exasperated.

"Then why have you spent the last hour watching Saint and Devil and Giles?"

"That's none of your business," he said curtly, and then he remembered that she was a duke's daughter. "Thank you for your offer of assistance, Lady Violet, but I must decline it."

"But—"

Perry gave her the briefest of bows and escaped from the alcove. He spent a few minutes discreetly strolling the perimeter of the ballroom, avoiding anyone who might possibly recognize him, although it was highly unlikely that anyone would. He'd been a scrawny little runt when he'd been packed off to India ten years ago. He was a foot taller now and fifty pounds heavier and his hair had darkened from blond to brown. His uncle had looked at him two nights ago and failed to recognize him.

There was only one person who reliably *would* recognize him, a fellow who'd been a classmate of Perry's oldest brother and who'd served in India. Oliver Dasenby had been in a different regiment to Perry, but they'd known each other. Dasenby was now Duke of Westfell, and according to the newspapers he and his new wife were out of town. If Dasenby—Westfell—made an appearance at the ball, Perry would be gone like a shot, but for now the ballroom was empty of dragoons-turned-dukes, so he installed himself in another alcove. A new set was forming. Lady Violet took a place on the dance floor alongside Giles Abbishaw.

Perry watched in horror as the dance unfolded. Lady Violet said something; Giles replied. Lady Violet said something else; Giles replied to that, too. Dread curdled in Perry's belly. He waited for Lady Violet to point at him, for Giles to stare at him, astonished and angry.

It didn't happen.

Lady Violet danced and chatted politely with Giles Abbishaw. Then she danced and flirted extravagantly with Devereux Abbishaw. Then she danced and exchanged a few decorous comments with Saintbridge Abbishaw. None of the Abbishaws swung around to glare at Perry, or worse, abandoned the dance and strode over to demand to know why he was investigating them.

Perry's jaw ached from clenching by the time Saintbridge Abbishaw and Lady Violet finally left the dance floor. Damn the woman. She was the most infuriating person it had ever been his misfortune to meet.

Lady Violet didn't stand up in the next dance. After twenty minutes of keeping a wary eye out for her, Perry acknowledged that she must have left the ball early. This circumstance ought to have relieved him; perversely, it only annoyed him further.

Giles left half an hour after Lady Violet. He departed as surreptitiously as he had two nights ago, not saying his good-byes, just slipping quietly away.

Perry followed him.

Giles strolled along Brook Street, then turned north onto James Street. He picked up his pace, turning in swift succession into Chandlers, Hart, and George Streets. Perry only just managed to keep him in sight. Next, Giles hurried along Green Street, glancing furtively over his shoulder.

Perry kept to the shadows and glanced back over his own shoulder. A prickling across his scalp told him that he was being followed. The street appeared empty behind him, but his scalp never lied. That pins-and-needles sensation had saved his life more than once. Someone was following him. He knew it.

Ahead, Giles strode fast. His reflection strode fast, too, flickering across the panes of a darkened bow window. Perry's reflection crossed those same dark windowpanes a few moments later.

Perry glanced at Giles, then at the windows on either side

of the street. Some were lit behind closely-shut curtains, but most were dark and mirror-like. He saw Giles's reflection, his own reflection, and behind him . . . That was someone, wasn't it? A stealthy flicker of movement across the panes of a bay window, a distorted and wavering shape.

The person didn't appear to be walking, though. In fact, it almost looked as if . . .

The person was gliding through the air.

Every hair on Perry's body stood on end. He experienced two immediate and conflicting urges. One was to turn and attack, to leap at the person and wrestle him from the sky. The other was to flee.

Perry kept walking. The bay window fell behind him. The next two windows were lit, but the one after that was dark . . .

Yes, there was definitely someone following him. Someone dressed in black. Flying.

Perry watched that unnerving reflection slide across the windowpanes and shivered. His heart was beating hard in his chest.

Ahead, Giles Abbishaw vanished into South Audley Street, but Perry had more important things to do than follow a nobleman's son who may or may not have stolen two automatous clocks. Someone was flying behind him.

How were they doing it? Did the person have a balloon attached to his back? Was it some fiendish new brand of thievery? Villains skulking overhead and descending to rob the unwary?

There was only one way to find out—catch the man—and to do that, Perry needed height. Not a lot of height, the man looked to be six feet or so above him. All he needed was a handy fence . . .

Perry turned left at the next corner. He resisted the urge to look over his shoulder; his scalp told him that he was still being followed.

A chapel came into view, a squat building with a short bell tower and a shoulder-high iron fence topped with decorative spikes.

The fence halted to allow a flight of steps up to the door.

Perry burst into motion, taking three strides up the steps, turning and leaping for the top of the wrought iron fence.

If he'd slipped, he would have skewered himself, but he didn't slip. His foot came down between the decorative spikes and he launched himself into the air, arms outstretched.

He collided with the villain and grabbed hold tightly.

The man gave a frightened screech. Whatever held him up broke. Together they tumbled to the ground with a bone-jarring thud.

CHAPTER FOUR

They rolled on the flagstones, wrestling for dominance. The man Perry had captured kicked and thrashed wildly, trying to break free, but Perry was larger and stronger. He subdued his captive swiftly, pinned him to the ground face down, and revised his assessment; this was a youth, not a man. "Who are you?" he demanded, leaning heavily on the lad, crushing him flat. "Why are you following me?"

His captive struggled weakly and said something in a breathless, inaudible voice.

Perry pulled the fellow's mask off. "Who are you?" he demanded again.

"Get off me!" his captive said, still breathless, but more audible this time.

The voice rang alarm bells in Perry's head. It almost sounded . . . feminine?

He eased off a little more and the ruffian he'd caught said forcefully, "Get off me, you great beast!"

Perry recognized that voice. He hastily released his captive and scrambled to his feet. "Lady Violet?"

Lady Violet rolled over and sat up. Perry couldn't see her face clearly, but he knew it was her. He'd heard her speak twice today—once in Charles Street and once at the Peckhams' ball.

Her voice was cataloged in his brain under "annoying, but beautiful." This was exactly the sort of stunt she would pull. She'd followed him in daylight, why not follow him at night? And why not dangle beneath a balloon while she did so?

She was as fearless as she was nosy—and he could have injured her, damn it.

"Are you all right?" he asked belatedly. "Any broken bones?"

"No thanks to you," Lady Violet said crossly. She made as if to stand.

Perry extended a hand and helped her to her feet. "Are you certain you're all right?" he asked again, and took the opportunity to pat her back, searching for the ropes that he knew must be there.

There were no ropes.

Perry patted her back more thoroughly, from nape to waist.

Lady Violet pulled away. "Stop that."

Perry looked up at the sky, but the balloon was gone—and so was whatever had tethered it to her body.

"That was a very dangerous thing to do," he told her severely.

"It wasn't dangerous until you jumped on me."

"Not dangerous? A gently reared female, alone at night, dangling beneath a balloon, and—" He examined her more closely. "Wearing pantaloons? It's not just dangerous, it's harebrained!"

So many things could have gone wrong, starting with broken bones and ending with death, with a frightful detour into abduction for ransom—or worse—in the middle.

"Harebrained?" Lady Violet said, in a tone that suggested she was deeply offended.

Perry picked up his hat, jammed it on his head, and took her elbow. "Let's get you home."

Lady Violet jerked free of his grip. "I'm not going anywhere with you."

"You're not going anywhere *without* me," Perry corrected. "I'm taking you home, even if I have to throw you over my shoulder and carry you."

Lady Violet crossed her arms tightly over her chest. He couldn't quite make out her features, but he knew she was glaring at him. "You wouldn't dare."

Perry crossed his arms and glared back at her. "Wouldn't I?"

The stare-down lasted almost a full minute, before Lady Violet tossed her head. "Very well," she said haughtily. "You may escort me home."

They kept to the alleyways and mews. Perry didn't want anyone to see Lady Violet. She might be a duke's daughter, but not even a duke's daughter would survive the scandal of being caught wandering London at night while wearing pantaloons.

Despite the late hour, there was traffic on Piccadilly. They waited in an alleyway while several farm carts rumbled past, piled high with produce for the morning markets. While they waited, Perry asked Lady Violet how she'd tied the balloon to herself; she countered by asking why he was following Giles Abbishaw.

Perry didn't answer.

After the carts came a carriage with a crest on the door. While it passed, Perry asked Lady Violet how she'd steered the balloon. Instead of telling him, she asked why he'd followed Freddy Stanhope last night.

A stagecoach hove into view next, with passengers perched on the roof and luggage strapped to the back. It lumbered past with a jingling of harnesses and clopping of hooves. Perry asked Lady Violet how she'd inflated her balloon and she asked him why he was watching Saint and Devil Abbishaw.

They were both frustrated with each other by the time they crossed Piccadilly and slipped down an alleyway into St. James's Square. Sevenash House was in darkness, but lights were on in many of the other great houses around the square. "You have a latchkey?" Perry asked.

Lady Violet flourished something in her hand. It glinted dully. "May I have my mask back, please?"

"I don't have it."

"Well, I don't have it."

It was probably still lying in front of the chapel. "Sorry," Perry said, but he wasn't sorry. Without the mask, Lady Violet would be less likely to repeat such a reckless stunt.

He halted at the foot of the steps leading up to Sevenash House. He couldn't see Lady Violet's face clearly, but her demeanor wasn't chastened or cowed.

Her balloon was probably halfway to the moon by now, but what if she had access to another one? What if she broke her neck?

"Lady Violet . . . you must promise not to attempt that again. I don't think you realize how dangerous it was."

Lady Violet huffed out a breath and crossed her arms. "It wasn't dangerous until you—"

"What if I'd been a ruffian? Or if you'd flown too high and fallen?"

She said nothing. If silences could have a mood, this one was mutinous.

"You put me in a very difficult position," Perry told her. "I can't allow you to take such risks. I must speak with your father."

"What?" she said, an alarmed note in her voice.

If he called on the Duke of Sevenash tomorrow and told him that his daughter had been flying around London . . .

The duke would rightfully think he was mad.

But if he banged on the door now, roused Sevenash from his bed, showed the man his daughter dressed in pantaloons . . .

Perry sighed and squared his shoulders and climbed the steps. He raised his hand to the knocker.

Lady Violet caught his wrist. "My father isn't in London at the moment."

"Your brother is, though, isn't he? He was at the ball tonight." Perry twisted his wrist free and reached for the knocker, even though speaking with Rhodes Garland was the last thing he wanted to do.

She caught his arm again. "I won't fly using a balloon! You have my word of honor as a Garland."

Perry looked at her. "That's not the only dangerous thing you've done tonight."

Lady Violet released his wrist and huffed again. "I won't walk around London alone at night. You have my word."

Perry debated the wisdom of believing her. Violet Garland was reckless and foolhardy, headstrong and spoiled, but as a duke's daughter she would have been brought up to believe in honoring her word.

If Rhodes Garland made such a promise, Perry would trust him implicitly. He ought to extend that trust to Rhodes's sister.

"Very well." He lowered his hand and stepped away from the door, wondering if he was making an enormous mistake.

"No balloons," Lady Violet said. "And no walking alone at night. I promise not to do either of those things."

She sounded sincere.

Perry watched her unlock the door. "Thank you for escorting me home," she said politely.

"You're welcome," he replied, equally politely.

Perry waited until he heard the latch fasten again, then headed in the direction of the Peckhams' ball. He'd loiter outside for a while, and see if Saintbridge or Devereux Abbishaw made their departures.

But it wasn't Lord Abbishaw's stolen clocks that he thought about as he walked, it was Lady Violet and her balloon. Where had she obtained it? How the devil did she steer it? She must have attached herself to it with a harness. He wished the balloon hadn't broken free when he'd caught her and that he'd been able to see both it and the harness.

Perry winced, remembering how he'd flattened her to the ground. He could have seriously injured her.

A prickling sensation grew across the back of his scalp as he made his way along Albemarle Street. Someone else was following him. A footpad, most likely. Perry glanced at the windows up ahead. He saw his reflection, but no one else's.

Although . . .

Was that someone? Not in the lowest window, but in the one two stories above?

Perry resisted the urge to turn around and peer at the sky. He peered at the windows instead. Yes, damn it, it was someone, thirty feet above him. An elongated dark shape moved across the windowpanes like a fish swimming through water.

It couldn't possibly be Lady Violet. She hadn't had time to attach another balloon to herself.

Was London populated by people who flew using miniature hot air balloons? Was it all the rage among the aristocracy and he just hadn't heard about it?

Perry scrutinized that wavering and distorted reflection. He couldn't distinguish a harness or ropes or a balloon in the windowpanes, but there was a house up ahead with a tall flight of steps, so he trod up the steps and paused under the dark portico as if fishing for his latchkey—and turned his head and stared intently at the spot where the person must shortly appear. If he was lucky, he'd see the balloon silhouetted against the brightly lit windows of the house opposite.

No one appeared.

Was he dreaming? Was he going mad? Had he fallen and hit his head and didn't realize it?

Perry sidled out from under the portico and peered upwards—and almost yelped in shock when a face peered back down at him.

He recognized that face.

It was Lady Violet, crouched on the portico roof.

Shock turned to anger. He strode down the steps to the street, where he folded his arms and glared up at her. So much for the word of a duke's daughter. She had promised not to fly with a balloon.

Although . . .

Where was the balloon? He couldn't see one.

Perry uncrossed his arms and pointed peremptorily at the flagway.

A long moment passed. He didn't need to hear it to know that Lady Violet had huffed out a breath.

She flew down from the portico. Flew. Without a balloon.

Perry crossed his arms again. "You promised—"

"I promised not to walk alone at night, and I haven't," Lady Violet said, folding her own arms. "And I promised not to fly using a balloon, and I haven't."

Perry walked all the way around her, looking for anything that might account for her ability to fly. A harness, or ropes, or . . . wings? But there was nothing.

"How are you flying?" he demanded, when he was facing her again.

"Why are you investigating the Abbishaws and Freddy Stanhope?" Lady Violet countered.

A linkboy turned into the street, followed by two gentlemen. Perry caught Lady Violet's arm and hurried her in the opposite direction, around the corner and into the dimly lit mouth of an alleyway. "You shouldn't be out at night. Someone might see you."

"No one ever sees me."

"I saw you."

Lady Violet pulled free from his grip and crossed her arms again. "You're the only person who's ever seen me, and I've been doing this for years."

Years? She'd been flying around London at night for years?

"How are you flying?" Perry demanded again. "What magic is it?"

"Why are you investigating the Abbishaws and Freddy Stanhope?"

Perry scowled at her.

He couldn't see Lady Violet's face clearly, but he had no doubt that she scowled back.

Silence grew between them. Half a minute. A full minute. Perry gritted his teeth, then unwillingly said, "I'll tell you why I'm investigating them if you'll tell me how you're flying."

"We have an agreement."

Lady Violet held out her gloved hand. Perry reluctantly shook it.

That done, they both crossed their arms again. "You first," Perry said.

Something rustled in the gutter.

"Is that a rat?" Lady Violet asked.

It was almost definitely a rat, but Perry didn't want her to scream, so he said, "No."

"It *is* a rat," Lady Violet said, and hastily retreated to the street.

Perry looked left, and saw someone with a lantern approaching. Damn, was that a watchman? "We can't talk here." He took her by the elbow and hurried away from that lantern. Ahead, a door opened. Lamplight spilled out onto the street. Several gentlemen emerged.

"Up in the air," Perry said. "Quickly."

For once, Lady Violet didn't argue. She simply rose upwards, her elbow slipping free from his grip.

How the devil did she do that?

Perry resisted the urge to look up and see if he could spot her. He dodged around the men—it was a card party breaking up, judging from their conversation—and headed briskly in the direction of St. James's Square, but when he reached the next corner, a voice above his head said, "Let's go to your place."

"My place?"

"Yes. It's more private than Sevenash House. You wouldn't believe how many servants we have."

Perry might not have any servants, but his tiny attic bedroom wasn't something he wanted anyone to see, least of all a duke's daughter. "We can't go to my place."

"Why not?"

"Because it wouldn't be at all the thing!"

"I don't think you'll compromise me. You seem very prudish."

"Compromise you?" Perry said, stung by the word *prudish*. "I should think not!"

"Men have tried, you know. I'm very wealthy."

"You're the last woman I'd ever want to marry!" Perry said furiously. "You're spoiled and headstrong and *dangerous*."

"At least I'm not an officious stick-in-the-mud," Lady Violet retorted.

Officious? Stick-in-the-mud?

Perry opened his mouth to inform her that he was neither officious nor a stick-in-the-mud—or prudish, for that matter—but Lady Violet continued: "I shall meet you at your place. I know where it is. I followed you last night."

"You what?" He craned his neck, trying to see her.

"Followed you last night." Lady Violet was the vaguest of shadows overhead. "I'll wait on the roof. Don't take too long."

CHAPTER FIVE

*V*iolet sat on the roof for almost half an hour, perched on the low parapet outside Wintersmith's window. The window was open. She could have climbed in if she'd wanted to, but climbing into a man's bedchamber seemed a rather foolish thing to do. She'd already done too many foolish things tonight.

Wintersmith had spotted her. Twice! No one had seen her in more than two years of flying, and this man had caught sight of her twice in one night. And he hadn't merely caught sight of her, he'd *caught* her.

She was going to have to tell her parents. And Rhodes.

Violet knew that she was lucky in her family. Not the status and wealth and the magic, although she was very lucky in those, too, but lucky in what her parents let her do. She was allowed to wait for a love match. She was allowed to fly at night. That didn't mean her parents wouldn't scold her for tonight's misadventure, though. They would. And she deserved to be scolded. She'd been careless and overconfident and had allowed curiosity to overcome good sense—and she'd been caught *twice*. In one night!

Violet sat on the roof and castigated herself, but there were only so many ways to call oneself a fool and only so many promises one could make to be more careful in the future.

After castigation came worry. Should she have agreed to tell Wintersmith the truth? Her family's great secret, revealed to a stranger?

But Wintersmith had seen her. He knew she could fly. He'd already used the word *magic*. And he was a Bow Street Runner, a man used to ferreting out secrets. Far better that she tell him the truth under oath of secrecy than that he start asking questions about the Garlands.

But perhaps she ought to have taken him back to St. James's Square and woken Rhodes? Rhodes always knew what to do, what to say, how to fix things.

Violet chewed on her lip, and decided that it didn't matter. She needed to speak with Wintersmith and she needed to tell Rhodes what had happened. Both things had to be done, but they didn't have to be done at the same time. She might as well salvage what she could from tonight's disaster. Information received for information given.

Finally, candlelight illuminated the attic window, spilling out onto the grubby parapet. Violet turned and saw Wintersmith close the door. He crossed to the window. "Lady Violet," he said, with stiff politeness.

"Mr. Wintersmith."

He hesitated, and then said, "Please come in," and retreated to stand by the door, gesturing that she take the chair, a rickety thing beside the window.

The chair had been draped with clothes when Violet had peeked in yesterday; now those clothes lay on the trunk crammed into the narrow space at the end of the bed.

She clambered in through the window, sat, and realized that she hadn't appreciated how awkward this conversation would be. Her presence in Wintersmith's chamber felt invasive, and not just invasive but uncomfortably intimate.

Perhaps this hadn't been the best idea. True, there were no servants who might hear voices and decide to investigate, but there was a bed close enough to lay her hand on.

Violet fastened her gaze firmly on Wintersmith. *Don't*

think about the bed, she told herself. *Don't even look at it.* But it was impossible not to see the bed when it took up most of the tiny attic room. Its head was by the window, the sole pillow within touching distance.

Wintersmith felt the awkwardness, too. Violet deduced this from the very determined way in which he was not looking at either the bed or at her. His gaze went past her shoulder, to the window frame.

The sense of invading his private space grew even stronger. This had not been one of her better ideas.

"My brother went to the same school as you," Violet blurted.

Wintersmith stopped looking past her and looked at her instead. After a moment, he said, "Yes, he did."

That connection, acknowledged out loud, seemed to ease some of the tension in the room. Wintersmith didn't look away. He frowned at her. "How do you fly? What magic is it?"

Violet pulled a face before she could stop herself. If her parents knew she was revealing the family secret to a stranger . . .

Not quite a stranger. A man who'd been at school with Rhodes.

"You must promise not to tell anyone."

His frown deepened. "Does your family not know?"

"Of course they know. But no one else does, and you must promise not to tell anyone."

"Your brother knows? And your parents?"

"Yes."

"Very well. You have my word."

Violet eyed him. He looked trustworthy and honest and upright and dependable—and if she didn't think he was all of those things, she wouldn't be here, would she?

She took a deep breath and said, "My family has a Faerie godmother."

Wintersmith's frown transformed into an expression of incredulity, eyebrows rising, mouth crimping in disbelief.

"It's true! We have a Faerie godmother and we each get one wish when we turn twenty-three. Each of us girls, that is. I chose flying."

Wintersmith's frown returned. He looked quite affronted. "You expect me to believe such a ludicrous—"

"You said yourself that it was magic!"

"But a Faerie godmother? That's . . ." He sought a word, and flung it at her when he found it: "Impossible!"

"More impossible than a magic potion or powder?"

"Yes!"

Violet shrugged. "Well, it's true. I have a Faerie godmother and she gave me a wish on my twenty-third birthday and I chose flying." She cocked her head at him. "How did you see me? I've been flying for more than two years and no one has ever spotted me."

"I saw your reflection in the windows." Wintersmith folded his arms across what was rather a broad chest. He subjected her to a frowning stare. He seemed much bigger in this tiny room than he had at the Peckhams' ball. "A Faerie godmother?"

"Yes."

"How did your family acquire this Faerie godmother?" His tone was skeptical, almost scoffing.

The skepticism annoyed her, even though it was perfectly justified. "We don't know," Violet admitted. "It happened centuries ago."

Wintersmith's eyebrows once again signaled his disbelief.

Violet felt herself flush with annoyance. "Her name is Baletongue. She's the only Faerie left in England, and we're the only family she grants wishes to."

Wintersmith looked even more skeptical.

"I can't prove it to you. I can't summon her and show her to you—so you'll just have to take my word for it!" She spoiled this grand statement by giving an involuntary shiver. "Believe me, you don't want to meet her. She's not nice."

Wintersmith's eyebrows rearranged themselves into an attitude of bewilderment. "Not nice?"

"Baleful," Violet clarified, with another involuntary shiver. "Dangerous."

The furrows across Wintersmith's brow grew deeper. He looked quite nonplussed.

Violet smiled brightly at him. "So, that's my story. What's yours? Why are you investigating the Abbishaws?"

Wintersmith blinked at this change of subject, then narrowed his eyes suspiciously. He looked as if he thought he'd just been fed a cock-and-bull story.

"If you don't believe me, you can ask Rhodes. He knows I go flying at night. He's the one who bought these clothes for me."

Wintersmith's gaze flicked to the black coat and pantaloons that she wore, then back to her face.

"I don't usually fly so low," Violet said, hoping that if she was open and frank, he would be, too. "I was curious." She leaned forward on the chair and it wobbled slightly. One of its legs was shorter than the others. "Why were you following Giles Abbishaw?"

Wintersmith eyed her for several seconds, clearly not quite believing her, and then equally clearly decided to let the matter rest. "I must have your word not to disclose anything I tell you."

"You have it," Violet said promptly. "My word as a Garland."

Wintersmith pressed his lips together, visibly debating the wisdom of admitting her into his confidence.

Violet held her breath and tried to look trustworthy.

It must have worked, for Wintersmith's expression and stance changed, as if he'd given an internal shrug. The frown vanished and his mouth relaxed. He stepped back until his shoulders were resting against the door.

Violet resisted the urge to wriggle delightedly on the chair.

"It's a private commission," Wintersmith said. "From Lord Abbishaw."

Lord Abbishaw was having his own sons investigated?

Then it had to be about Jasper Flint's death. Violet opened her mouth to make this observation, and hastily closed it. She didn't want to interrupt Wintersmith now that he was finally divulging the details of his investigation.

"Abbishaw collects automatous clocks. Last Wednesday, one of them went missing. It was in a locked cabinet. The only people who have keys are Abbishaw and his sons."

Violet tried not to look hugely disappointed, but it was difficult not to. Automatous clocks? That wasn't exciting at all.

"Giles lives with his father. Abbishaw searched his room while he was out, but the clock wasn't there."

Violet felt quite affronted on Giles's behalf. "Giles wouldn't steal!"

Wintersmith shrugged. "Abbishaw felt he was the most likely suspect. His allowance is . . . very modest."

Violet frowned at him. "Did Abbishaw search Saint's house?"

Wintersmith shook his head. He continued with his tale: "Abbishaw removed Giles's key, but on Friday a second clock went missing."

"So, it wasn't Giles!"

"Wilton's key is unaccounted for. He might have taken it to America. He might have thrown it out. He might have given it to his brother. Or to someone else."

"That's why you're following Freddy! He was Wilton's friend. And so was Devil!"

"Yes."

"But neither of them would steal a clock."

"They're not ordinary clocks. They're, ah, . . ."

"Automatous. Yes, you said. But Freddy and Devil wouldn't steal automatous clocks!"

Wintersmith shifted his shoulders against the door. "They're not ordinary automatous clocks. They're, um . . . You know what an automatous clock is?"

Violet nodded. "Rhodes bought one for the nursery. The face is painted with waves and there's a ship that rocks when the pendulum swings. It's very clever."

"Well, the scenes on the missing clocks are amorous in nature."

"Oh." Violet was suddenly aware of the bed again. "You mean . . . like those Meissen figurines where the shepherd is about to kiss the shepherdess?"

Wintersmith's cheeks flushed almost imperceptibly. "A great deal more explicit than that."

"But . . . Lord Abbishaw is so . . . so proper and so upright."

"Abbishaw collects automatous clocks, and these particular clocks are exceedingly rare." Wintersmith shrugged, as if that explained why someone as straitlaced as Abbishaw had lewd clocks in his house.

"But why would anyone steal them? Although I suppose . . . Freddy is a younger son, and so is Giles, and neither of them is swimming in lard, but . . . isn't it more likely that a servant took them?"

"It's possible. But Giles is behaving rather furtively. Abbishaw says he's rarely home at night. I think it's possible he has a chère-amie and that he gave the clocks to her."

"But Giles is so nice. I can't imagine him stealing anything!" In fact, she couldn't imagine any of Wintersmith's suspects stooping to theft. Giles, because he was so mild and inoffensive. Saint, because he was even more sanctimonious than his father. Devil, because he was playful and fun-loving and not at all the miscreant his nickname would suggest. And Freddy Stanhope because . . .

Actually, she could imagine Freddy purloining a lewd clock.

When Devil flirted with her, it was light-hearted and entirely frivolous, but occasionally something darker ran through Freddy's comments, something a little dangerous, a hint that if she wanted an extracurricular adventure, he was her man. "It might be Freddy," Violet admitted reluctantly.

Wintersmith cocked his head. "Why do you say that?"

"Sometimes he says things that are a little naughty."

"Naughty?" Wintersmith looked as if he was suppressing a laugh at her choice of word.

Violet felt herself flush. "Inappropriate," she amended sharply, cross at him for his amusement and at herself for blushing because of it.

Wintersmith shrugged. "That does corroborate what I've heard about him."

"What have you heard?"

"That he has a pocket watch that's exceedingly, ah, inappropriate."

"Freddy does?"

"Yes. I've confirmed it with the watchmaker."

Violet considered this statement, and decided that it wasn't at all surprising. "Then Freddy stole the clocks. He must have Wilton's key."

"Stanhope purchased the watch. Why would he steal a clock? And besides, it's Giles who's behaving furtively, not Stanhope."

"Giles isn't furtive."

"Did you not notice the route he took tonight?"

Violet hadn't, but now that she thought about it, it had been rather circuitous.

"When I discover where he's spending the nights, I believe I'll find the clocks."

"I can help! I'll follow him tomorrow night."

"No."

"But—"

"No."

"But I can look in upstairs windows and—"

"No," Wintersmith repeated sternly. "Absolutely not. I forbid it."

Violet sat speechless for a moment, her mouth still open, and then she said, "You *forbid* it?"

"I'm a Principal Officer and you're not. *I* have authority to investigate these thefts. You do not."

Violet looked at him with strong disfavor. Who knew that Bow Street Runners could be so stuffy? "Very well," she said, standing. "I wish you luck solving your case. Good night."

It would have been nice to sweep out a door and close it, not with a slam but with very pointed politeness. As it was, she had to climb out Wintersmith's window, knowing that the pantaloons hugged her legs with embarrassing snugness. Although Wintersmith was such a stuffy stick-in-the-mud that he probably averted his gaze.

Violet launched herself crossly into the air. That interview had been a complete waste of her time. She'd thought Wintersmith was investigating the death of Baron Flint's youngest son, but instead he was looking for a couple of silly clocks. It was a piffling little case—and he wouldn't let her help!

It would serve Wintersmith right if she solved his mystery for him.

With that thought in mind, Violet headed for the Stanhope residence on Manchester Square.

CHAPTER SIX

*V*iolet had been a guest of the Stanhopes on numerous occasions. She'd attended dinners and Venetian breakfasts, balls, soirées, musicales. She'd also visited on less formal occasions and been upstairs to the family rooms, and she'd even been in one of the bedchambers, when she and Aster and Freddy's sister had dressed each other's hair with artificial flowers.

Violet hadn't been into Freddy's bedroom, but she knew it was at the front of the house, overlooking the square. It had a narrow little balcony with a wrought iron railing and a statue of a faun playing a pan flute. When he was younger, Freddy had several times used the balcony to tip water on the heads of his siblings, to their wrath and his amusement.

Freddy hadn't tipped water on anyone for years, but Violet knew that he sometimes smoked cigars on the balcony at night. She'd seen him on her nocturnal explorations: a sliver of candlelight shining through not-quite-shut curtains, the shadowy statue of the faun playing the flute, and alongside the statue, lounging with his shoulders against the stonework, Freddy, the glow of a cigar faintly illuminating his face when he inhaled, the scent of tobacco wafting in the air.

Violet approached the Stanhope residence cautiously.

Freddy's curtains were drawn, but faint light shone behind them, as if a few candles still burned. He could be on the balcony . . . but no, he wasn't. The only figure lurking there was the stone faun.

Violet hovered just above the wrought iron railing and wished that the curtains were open a crack. Perhaps she'd see the clocks hanging on Freddy's wall! And then she immediately dismissed that notion as preposterous. Freddy wouldn't hang lewd automatous clocks where his family might see them.

Which begged the question, why was she here?

There was no point peeking in Freddy's window, even if the curtains were open, because the clocks wouldn't be on his walls.

"Idiot," Violet told herself.

She'd wanted to prove to Wintersmith that she could go places he couldn't and find clues he'd never find—and she'd come to the one place where Freddy would never hang the stolen clocks. If indeed he'd taken them.

"Idiot," she muttered again. Behind the curtains, Freddy's room went dark.

Violet rose upwards—which was the only reason that Freddy Stanhope, when he flung his curtains open, didn't see her hovering on his balcony.

Violet froze in midair, barely above the top of the window. To be spotted by Wintersmith was bad enough. To be spotted by Freddy Stanhope would be beyond dreadful!

She was making far too many mistakes tonight. Dangerous mistakes. Mistakes that could expose her family's secret. It was bad enough that Wintersmith now knew, but at least he was discreet and trustworthy. Freddy Stanhope was *not* discreet.

Beneath her, the window opened. A dark figure leaned out.

Violet pressed herself against the wall. She heard the gritty sound of stone against stone, and then a rustle and a dull thump, and then the gritty sound again. Freddy withdrew into his room, closed the window, shut the curtains.

Now was the time to flee—but Violet stayed where she was, torn between caution and curiosity.

What had Freddy been doing?

Had he been hiding something on his balcony? An automatous clock, perhaps?

Violet silently counted to one hundred, then drifted warily down. The only thing on the little balcony was the statue of the faun.

Had Freddy hidden something beneath it?

She floated ever so gently down to stand alongside the statue. Its jaunty head came up to her shoulder.

The faun stood on a cylindrical stone plinth, two feet high and two feet wide. Violet crouched and tried to lift the plinth. It didn't move so much as an inch, which was vastly annoying. This was *her* find. She'd solved Mr. Officious Stick-in-the-mud's little puzzle and she was dashed if she was going to ask him for help lifting a statue.

She stood and grasped the faun by his child-sized elbows and tried again—and lost her balance when he lifted off the plinth with a gritty stone-on-stone sound. She and the faun almost toppled over.

Fortunately, the statue wasn't as heavy as Wintersmith had been. Violet managed to stay standing—barely. She braced herself against the side of the house and held her breath. Had Freddy heard that gritty little sound?

The faun leaned heavily against her. His flute dug into her ribs. Violet ignored that pain and listened tensely. A minute passed, then two minutes, then three.

Violet began to breathe more easily. With utmost care, she propped the faun against the wall. He stood on a round, flat base that had fitted into the plinth like a lid on a sugar bowl.

When she was satisfied he wasn't going to fall over, Violet knelt to investigate her find. The plinth was hollow. There was something inside. It felt like . . . a bandbox?

Below, a carriage rattled into the square and halted at a house opposite. The sound of hooves and wheels and harnesses easily covered the slight noise Violet made easing her find from its hiding place. Yes, it was a bandbox. Not something her most extravagant hats with their wide brims and high, curling feathers would fit into, but large enough for a pretty little bonnet.

The bandbox was rather heavy. It definitely held something weightier than a mere hat. Such as an automatous clock. Or two.

Violet found the clasp, but the bandbox refused to open. Not that it mattered. She knew exactly what was inside.

Across the square, the clatter of the departing carriage swallowed the sound she made fitting the faun back into place. Violet hugged the bandbox to her chest and leaped into the air. She was tempted to fly home and peek at the clocks—just how lewd were they?—but assuaging her curiosity came a very distant second to showing Wintersmith that she'd solved his mystery for him. Less than an hour after he'd dismissed her.

Oxford Street flashed past beneath her, Hanover Square, Bedford Square, and there was High Holborn, curving towards Ludgate and St. Paul's Cathedral. Violet glided down to land on Wintersmith's parapet. His room was in darkness, but the window was open a few inches.

Violet rapped on the panes. "Mr. Wintersmith? Wake up! I have your clocks."

No sound came from within.

Violet rapped more peremptorily on the windowpanes. "Mr. Wintersmith! Wake up!"

This time she heard someone stirring, the rustle of sheets.

She rapped again, to encourage Wintersmith towards wakefulness. A moment later, the window opened fully. Wintersmith peered out. She couldn't see him clearly, but she could make out the pale oval of his face, the darker mop of his hair, and a ghostly white nightshirt.

"What is it?" Wintersmith said, sounding rather cross.

"I have your clocks for you," Violet told him smugly. "See?"

"It's the middle of the night. I can't see a thing."

48

"It's a bandbox. Freddy hid it on his balcony. It's heavy."
She jiggled the bandbox. Something weighty slid inside with
a dull *thump*.

Wintersmith exhaled an exasperated sigh. "Wait here," he
said, and closed the window.

A couple of minutes passed while Wintersmith kindled a
spark in a tinderbox, lit a candle, and donned a dressing gown.
He opened the window again.

The smug sense of triumph that had sped her flight across
London evaporated. Violet began to doubt the wisdom of
coming here. Wintersmith had just climbed out of bed. He
was wearing only a nightshirt and a dressing gown. She'd
invaded his private space—his very privacy—for the second
time tonight.

Plus, it wasn't very nice to rub his nose in her success.
Finding the clocks wasn't a contest. She wasn't the victor in
some great fight. A nicer person—a better person—wouldn't
have come here to gloat; they'd have quietly given him the
clocks tomorrow.

Wintersmith placed the candle on the windowsill and
held out his hand. "Give it here."

Violet handed over the bandbox. She felt rather ashamed
of herself.

Wintersmith didn't step back and invite her inside. He
stood at the window and examined the bandbox, turning
it around before trying the clasp. It didn't open, but in the
candlelight Violet could see that the box was old and rather
battered and that the clasp had twisted sideways. She opened
her mouth to point this out, but Wintersmith had already
seen. A flick of his thumb and the clasp opened.

Violet craned her neck to see inside the bandbox. "Are
they both there?"

The box was filled to the brim. At the top was a stack of
illustrations, the sort of thing one found in magazines, ink
sketches tinted with color. She couldn't see any clocks, ribald
or otherwise.

"Are they under those pictures?"

Wintersmith made a strangled sound and slammed the lid shut.

"What is it?" Violet asked.

Wintersmith retreated into the room, clutching the bandbox tightly. "Stay where you are."

Violet had no intention of entering his bedchamber when he was so scantily clad. She stayed where she was, balanced on the parapet, and watched him rifle through the illustrations in the bandbox. Mr. Bland. Mr. Stick-in-the-mud. Although he didn't look very bland right now. Or stick-in-the-muddish. He looked . . . well, if Violet were perfectly honest, he looked slightly debauched. And if she were even more honest, he also looked rather attractive.

How intriguing.

Violet cocked her head to one side and observed him. Why was Wintersmith suddenly attractive? Was it the uncombed hair? The glimpse of his bare throat? The fact that he was *déshabillé*?

It was those things and more, she decided. His simple, uncontrived maleness, combined with the rumpled bedclothes and soft glow of candlelight. It tempted her and alarmed her at the same time. The temptation overpowered the alarm. She was aware of a fleeting pang of *want*, a visceral tug in her belly. She hardly knew this man, didn't particularly like him, but she wouldn't mind touching him right now, wouldn't mind feeling the texture of his skin, its heat, the prickliness of the stubble shading his jaw.

Wintersmith stopped rummaging in the bandbox. He looked up and caught her staring at him. To her annoyance, Violet felt herself blush. She hoped it was too dark for him to notice.

Wintersmith closed the lid and refastened the clasp.

"Are the clocks there?" Violet asked.

"No."

"But it's so heavy!"

"It's all paper. At least two hundred sheets. Where did you say you'd found this?"

"On the balcony outside Freddy's bedroom. Are you *certain* the clocks aren't there? Perhaps there's a false bottom—"

"There's no false bottom."

"But why would he hide a bandbox full of illustrations on his balcony? It makes no sense!"

"They're . . . rather specialized illustrations."

Violet stared at him without comprehension—and then she realized what he meant. "Oh," she said, as heat flooded her face.

This blush he couldn't not see, but Wintersmith had the good manners to pretend not to. He put the bandbox on the floor by his door. "I'll dispose of this in the morning."

Violet felt quite mortified. She'd woken Wintersmith up, dragged him from his bed, practically crowed her triumph over him—all for a bandbox full of naughty drawings.

Drawings that Freddy would notice were gone.

"I should take it back. If I don't, he'll think someone stole it." Which she had done. She'd thought she was retrieving something that had been stolen, but what she'd actually been doing was stealing. "What if he dismisses one of his servants because of it?"

Wintersmith thought this over—and didn't disagree. He brought the bandbox back to the window, but didn't hand it to her. "I know I can't forbid you to look inside, but I strongly advise you not to."

As soon as he uttered the words, there was nothing Violet wanted more than to look at the illustrations.

Wintersmith gave her the bandbox. "Good night—and for heaven's sake, be careful when you put it back!"

If Wintersmith hadn't advised her not to look inside the bandbox, it was possible Violet would have returned it directly, but now all she could think about was the drawings. Ribald drawings. Lewd drawings. Drawings that weren't meant to be viewed by well-bred young ladies.

She flew slowly towards Mayfair and Marylebone, hugging the bandbox to her chest. If there was one lesson she'd learned tonight, it was that she needed to think before she acted. Everything that had happened—being caught by Wintersmith not just once but twice, almost being spotted by Freddy Stanhope, dragging Wintersmith from his bed for a triumph that wasn't a triumph—all those things had happened because she was too impetuous, because she'd not taken the time to think things through.

So, she took the time to think. She thought, as Broad Street became High Street and High Street became Oxford Street. She thought about the bandbox and she thought about the illustrations it contained and she thought about Wintersmith's warning. And then she stopped flying towards Manchester Square and headed instead for St. James's Square and home.

But it wasn't a rash and impetuous decision; it was a reasoned one.

CHAPTER SEVEN

*V*iolet closed her window, drew the curtains, and opened the shades on the dark lantern she'd left on the hearth. It became much easier to see. She looked at the bandbox sitting so temptingly on the floor and then glanced at the clock. The hour hand was pointing to 4.

Wintersmith had said there were more than two hundred drawings in the box. She didn't intend to flick through them, as he'd done; she intended to scrutinize them thoroughly. All two hundred and more of them. If she started now, she'd still be up at dawn.

That thought triggered a yawn—and a decision. Arguably the first sensible decision she'd made that night. Lord, what an idiot she'd been, letting Wintersmith catch her not once, but twice!

Violet screwed her face up in a grimace. She needed to tell Rhodes that Wintersmith knew the family secret. And she'd have to tell her parents when they returned from Surrey. It was something she dared not conceal from them.

But she wasn't going to tell anyone right at this instant. She was going to hide the bandbox and go to sleep.

Violet didn't have a statue with a cunningly concealed cavity in its base. The locked drawer in her dresser wasn't deep enough for the bandbox, even if the drawer weren't already crammed with things she didn't want her maid to find. She did, however, possess a window seat that was filled with odds and ends. Violet opened it and tossed old magazines, dried corsages, frayed ribbons, tatty feathers, and broken fans to the floor.

She slid the bandbox in and hesitated. The window seat had no lock. What if the children played hide-and-seek tomorrow? What if they found the bandbox? What if they opened it?

That was why Freddy hid it on his balcony, she realized. To keep it safe from childish eyes. His inappropriate pocket watch could be locked away in a drawer, just as her men's clothes were locked away, but a bandbox was too large for that.

There was nowhere else she could hide it, though. Violet pushed it to the very back of the window seat and piled all the tatty feathers, dried corsages, broken fans, frayed ribbons, and old magazines on top, then she changed out of her flying clothes and climbed into bed, but she couldn't sleep. The house was quiet, her bed was cozy . . . and all she could think about was Wintersmith advising her not to look in the bandbox.

She knew exactly how Pandora had felt, and Persephone and Orpheus. They'd all looked at what they'd been told not to look at, admittedly with disastrous consequences, but she wasn't someone from legend and nothing calamitous would occur if she opened the bandbox.

Violet sat up and threw back her covers.

She lit a candelabrum, made certain that her door was latched, and hauled the bandbox from its hiding place. It really was quite heavy. It must have taken Freddy months to assemble such a collection.

She laid the box on the floor, knelt alongside it, and wrestled with the clasp. After a moment, it surrendered.

Violet raised the lid and prepared to be scandalized. But the topmost image wasn't that scandalous, merely two long rows of female statues . . .

Oh.

They weren't statues. They were women. Naked women posing for a man who lounged in the foreground.

The Harem, read the caption.

Violet examined the image. She saw lots of plump bosoms, fleshy buttocks, and bare pudenda.

Judging by his avid expression, the man in the foreground liked the display of female bodies. Freddy obviously liked it, too, otherwise the illustration wouldn't have been at the very top of the pile. Violet didn't exactly like it, but she didn't dislike it either. She felt ambivalent, and a little disappointed. She'd expected something more shocking than dozens of breasts and buttocks and pudenda.

But perhaps it wasn't the breasts that were so shocking, but the scene? All those plump beauties baring themselves for their master's delectation, waiting for him to select one of them.

Put like that, the image became repugnant, as if women were objects and not people at all.

Violet laid it distastefully to one side—and discovered that she'd been wrong in her interpretation of the previous scene. The master hadn't merely chosen one lady from his harem, he'd chosen five, and there they all were, cavorting in his bed.

The Pasha, this drawing was titled, and the eponymous potentate was wearing his hat and his slippers and very little else. Violet studied the drawing, paying particular attention to the pasha's groin. He had an upstanding red appendage with round little balls underneath. Dogs had testicles, and stallions and bulls. Men apparently had them, too.

Violet put that image thoughtfully aside.

Beneath it was an illustration that appeared, at first glance, to portray a ball. At second glance, it was unlike any ball Violet had ever attended. The women were half naked. A glance at the caption told her why: The Courtesans' Ball, the image was titled.

Men ogled the courtesans through pince-nez and fondled

their buttocks and groped their breasts and . . . Violet peered more closely at the picture. What was that couple in the corner doing?

She couldn't tell. The figures were too small, the picture too busy.

Violet put that illustration aside, too. She had no difficulty making sense of the next image: a room with a four-poster bed, a naked woman reclining, a man with his breeches pulled down to his knees. The appendage poking out from his groin was long and pink, with a scarlet tip.

The door to the room was ajar. Through it, three people were watching the couple.

She laid the image aside and delved further into the bandbox. People fornicated in meadows, in beds, in carriages. On tables. Standing up. Lying down. The box contained a plethora of drawings, so many that they all blurred together. Violet revised her estimation of the time it had taken Freddy to collect them from months to years.

She stacked the images in the order in which she removed them, but mentally she began grouping them. Freddy had a great many illustrations of women displaying themselves, legs spread wide, while either one man or many men ogled them. He also had lots of pictures of Peeping Toms. People spied through doors, windows, keyholes, hedges, curtains.

It appeared that Freddy had a penchant for voyeurism.

Some of the images were confusing. Was it possible for a man's appendage to grow that long? And was it possible to balance a candelabrum upon it if it was that long?

Others were frankly bizarre. Why on earth would Freddy have purchased a picture of three women urinating?

Violet studied the drawing, trying to understand what the attraction was. And then she realized. Voyeurism, again. The ladies were almost naked, baring their pudenda, bottoms, and for some incomprehensible reason their breasts, while they peed, all the while observed by a man who stood off to one side.

Violet tutted and shook her head. Freddy, Freddy, Freddy.

Very few of the drawings were actually titillating. That was the point of a collection such as this, wasn't it? Titillation? In which case, Wintersmith had been correct: the drawings weren't for her eyes.

Or rather, they mostly weren't for her eyes, because she did find one image that made her feel warm and tingly inside, and another one that gave her a strong and unexpected pang of something she could only label as lust. Or perhaps, desire. Desire to be that woman with that man. Desire to be held like that, touched like that.

The feeling was similar to what she'd felt when looking at Wintersmith in his nightclothes. The man in the drawing looked a lot like Wintersmith, which possibly explained it, but Violet thought that the lust—or desire—was mostly to do with the nature of the image. There were no Peeping Toms, no voyeurs, no one on display. Just two lovers half naked on a sofa, laughing with one another.

She wanted to be that woman, and she didn't want it just a little bit; she wanted it a lot. The pang of desire was strong and visceral, something she felt in her chest and her belly and even in her loins.

The intensity of that sensation was rather disconcerting.

The two drawings Violet liked were near the bottom of the bandbox. She took that to mean that Freddy liked them the least. After some hesitation, she set them to one side. Freddy wouldn't notice their absence, would he?

It was past five o'clock by the time she removed the very last illustration. Violet checked for a hidden compartment. There wasn't one.

She sat back and yawned, feeling rather disappointed. Fornication, as depicted in the majority of the images in Freddy's collection, didn't look very appealing. It looked awkward and uncomfortable, sometimes grotesque, often ridiculous, and—after viewing so many illustrations—a little boring.

Violet yawned again, so widely that her jaw creaked, and

began repacking the bandbox, replacing the drawings in the order she'd removed them. When she came to one of the more puzzling illustrations, she hesitated. Dare she show it to her married sister, Primrose, and ask if such antics were possible?

She chewed on her lip for a moment, and decided that she might possibly dare. That drawing went to one side, as did two others that were equally puzzling. Surely Freddy wouldn't notice their absence? Not when he had so many others.

Illustration after illustration went back into the bandbox, fifty, sixty, seventy. One hundred. Two hundred. Two hundred and twenty. Lastly, Violet replaced *The Courtesans' Ball*, *The Pasha*, and *The Harem*. She yawned. And yawned again.

She stowed the bandbox in the window seat, with the magazines and everything else piled haphazardly on top. She'd return it to Freddy's balcony tomorrow night. Or rather, tonight, given that it was now dawn.

The servants would shortly be stirring.

Violet hastily unlocked the bottom drawer of her dresser, slid the five drawings she'd selected on top of her black clothes, and locked the drawer again.

She unlatched her door so her maid could enter, climbed into bed, and pulled the covers up over her head. Her body ached with weariness—and with the bruises she'd collected when Wintersmith had captured her. She'd have to tell Rhodes about that today, but even that daunting thought couldn't keep her from falling almost instantly asleep.

CHAPTER EIGHT

Rhodes was understandably horrified when Violet told him that Wintersmith was a Bow Street Runner and that he'd captured her. His face paled, something she'd read about in novels but never actually seen happen in real life.

"He thought you were using a balloon? Thank heavens he didn't realize the truth. That would have been a disaster!"

Violet had found her brother in the library, where he was reading the newspapers. She shifted her weight uncomfortably and said, "He escorted me home, and I used the just-in-case latchkey you gave me, and then . . . I followed him again, I'm sorry, and he saw me."

Rhodes didn't grow paler, but he did wince with his whole face.

She ought not to have followed Wintersmith that second time, but Rhodes didn't point out that very obvious truth. It was one of the many good things about her brother; he didn't rub people's noses in their mistakes.

"He could see I wasn't using a balloon. He guessed it was magic, so . . . I told him about Baletongue. I swore him to secrecy first! He won't tell anyone. He promised!"

Rhodes shut his eyes and rubbed them, as if they hurt.

Violet debated whether to tell her brother about the third

59

she'd seen Wintersmith last night, when she'd brought ɩm the bandbox.

She decided it was best not to.

Rhodes opened his eyes and stood. "I need to speak with Wintersmith."

"He won't tell anyone. He gave his word."

"You don't even know he's who he says he is!"

"He was at school with you. He said so."

"Anyone can claim to have been at school with me."

Violet wished she could refute this statement, but unfortunately it was correct. She bit her lip.

"If your Wintersmith is Periander, why did he leave the army? Did he sell out or was he kicked out?"

"I don't know," Violet admitted. "I didn't ask."

"Well, I shall ask. He's at Bow Street, you said?"

"He wouldn't be hired on at Bow Street if he'd been dishonorably discharged, would he?"

"He might be if he'd lied," Rhodes said grimly.

"I'm sure he hasn't! He's quite stuffy and staid."

Rhodes's frown deepened. "That doesn't sound like Periander at all. What does he look like? Short, skinny, blond?"

". . . No? His hair is brown and he's almost as tall as you and he's rather strapping."

Rhodes's frown grew fierce. "He told you his name was Periander?"

"No. He just said Wintersmith." Violet knew she sounded like an idiot, knew she had been an idiot, but . . . "I trust him. I do!"

"Well, I don't trust him at all. I need to speak with him."

"Oh, but—"

"Father will want to speak with him, too, once he's back."

Rhodes was correct. Their father would wish to speak with Wintersmith. Baletongue's existence was a dangerous secret, one that no one outside the family was supposed to know— and she had revealed it to someone who was essentially a stranger.

"I'm sorry," Violet said contritely. "I know I've made a dreadful mull of things. I didn't mean to."

"I know you didn't." Rhodes gripped her shoulder briefly, then headed for the door. "Don't worry. I'll sort this out."

Violet wished he didn't have to. She crossed to the tall windows and stared disconsolately out at the square. Head-strong, Wintersmith had called her. And harebrained. As insulting as those two epithets were, he wasn't wholly wrong.

Outside, Rhodes came into view, striding briskly. He hadn't gone upstairs to change his clothes, just jammed a hat on his head and departed.

Guilt was an uncomfortable emotion. One that Violet didn't like at all. She felt it now, as she watched Rhodes head in the direction of the nearest hackney stand.

She'd made a grievous mistake last night, one that impacted her entire family.

She hoped Wintersmith was as trustworthy as he appeared to be.

CHAPTER NINE

$\mathcal{P}$erry spent the morning visiting pawnshops and dropping hints of a reward if the stolen clocks were recovered. A number of clocks were produced for his perusal. Some were automatous and others had erotic scenes painted upon their faces, but none were the ones he was looking for.

He headed back to Bow Street, but as he was about to set foot inside the door, someone said, "Wintersmith?"

Perry swung around—and halted.

The man who'd spoken came closer. His eyes were narrow and assessing, his expression one of almost-but-not-quite recognition. "Wintersmith?" he said again.

"Lord Thane," Perry acknowledged reluctantly.

The marquis stared at him. "You look different."

Perry shrugged. "Ten years."

Thane looked him up and down, a perplexed crease to his brow, as if he couldn't quite reconcile the boy Perry had been with the man he was now.

People pushed past them, buffeting Perry, buffeting Thane.

"I need a word with you," the marquis said.

"There's a coffeehouse around the corner."

The coffeehouse catered to the theater crowd and was nearly empty at this time of day. It smelled of coffee, bitter and bracing, and beneath that, of last night's patrons: cologne and sweat and the cheap perfume worn by Covent Garden nuns. Perry chose a table in the darkest corner. Theater bills were pasted atop one another on the walls.

"I can guess why you're here," he said. "But you needn't worry. I'm not going to tell anyone. I give you my word."

Thane's lips folded together tightly. He gave a brusque nod. "Thank you."

"I'm surprised she told you. I hadn't thought she would."

"My sister always meets her fences head on."

"She seems . . . rather intrepid."

Thane snorted. "Intrepid? Yes."

A serving man brought them two cups of coffee. Thane waited until he'd gone to say, "I didn't know you were in London."

"No one does."

Thane's eyes narrowed. "Were you cashiered?"

Cashiered? Kicked out of the army? Affront stiffened Perry's spine. "Of course not!"

"Then why haven't you told anyone you're back?"

"Because I'm obliged to work for my living," Perry told him curtly. "I move in different circles now."

Thane's gaze flicked down. He examined Perry's neck-cloth, his waistcoat, his tailcoat, and no doubt came to a very accurate assessment of Perry's financial circumstances. His face lost its tightness. "I shan't tell anyone you're in London, if that's what you wish."

"It is," Perry said, even more curtly.

They sat in silence for a moment, the untouched cups of coffee steaming between them.

"You work at Bow Street?" Thane's voice was almost, but not quite, neutral. Perry's ears detected a note of disapproval.

His spine stiffened again. "Yes."

Thane gave another of his brusque nods. He stood. "Then I know where to find you."

Perry watched the marquis thread his way between the

tables and step out onto the street. He couldn't decide whether that last comment had been a threat or not. Then he shrugged. Thane might be a marquis, but he was unimportant.

Perry drank his coffee. Then he drank Thane's untouched coffee, too. He went back to Bow Street and climbed the stairs to the room where the secretaries worked, because that's what he was when he wasn't investigating missing clocks—a secretary—and once he found the clocks, he'd go back to being one. Until then, though, Perry's desk was occupied by Mr. Tolly, a raw-boned red-headed man who'd been temporarily elevated from the ranks of the clerks.

Tolly seemed to like sitting behind Perry's desk almost as much as Perry hated it. He scowled when he saw Perry.

"Any messages for me?" Perry asked.

"No."

Tolly's posture, the jut of his chin, the way his hands curved possessively around the papers on the desk, seemed to say "This is *my* desk. *My* chair. *My* job."

He looked like a dog bristling over a bone, but it was a bone Perry didn't want. Tolly could have the joy of that pile of paperwork. He bade the man good day and went back to visiting pawnshops and dropping hints of a reward.

His afternoon's search was as fruitless as his morning's had been. Perry bought a mutton pie from a street vendor and ate as he walked home. He let himself into his lodging house, climbed the stairs to the attic, unlocked his door—and saw a mouse dart under his bed.

It wasn't the first mouse Perry had found in his room and it would undoubtedly not be the last. He clattered down the stairs again and out into the narrow backyard, with its disgusting privy and its discarded bottles and its pile of crumbling bricks.

He fetched up a brick, barricaded the mouse hole, and checked to see what damage the creature had done. There were no droppings in his shoes this time, but—

Curse it. The navy-blue tails of the coat he'd hired were

dangling over the edge of his trunk, well within reach of an enterprising mouse.

Perry examined the tailcoat in trepidation. He couldn't afford to replace the damned thing.

The mouse didn't appear to have done any damage. Perry bundled the coat up, along with the waistcoat he'd hired, and returned them to the secondhand clothing shop on Drury Lane. Tonight, he'd observe from the street—and he'd be damned if he let Giles Abbishaw give him the slip again.

Chapter Ten

*V*iolet restored Freddy's bandbox to its hiding place as soon as darkness fell. The streets were busy, London's inhabitants heading out to indulge in an evening of pleasures. Violet's brother and sister were among those pleasure seekers, invited to make up a party at Vauxhall Gardens with their cousins, but Violet had pleaded tiredness. Her eyes were gritty, her head ached, and now that Freddy's collection was back in its place, all she wanted was to go to bed. She flew back across Mayfair, passing over Hanover Square, where Lord Abbishaw resided.

A man walked down Abbishaw's steps and set off across the square. As he passed beneath a streetlamp, Violet caught a glimpse of his face.

It was Giles Abbishaw.

Violet stopped thinking quite so much about her headache. When Giles turned into Grosvenor Street, she followed him.

So did someone else. Someone who walked stealthily in the shadows. Someone who was either a footpad or a Bow Street Runner.

Violet's pulse gave a little skip of excitement. Her headache retreated. Her tiredness fell away.

Giles strolled as far as Grosvenor Square, walked all the

way down South Audley Street, then reversed direction and walked up Park Street. He picked up his pace, navigating the Reeves Mews so quickly that Violet almost lost him, but she didn't dare fly lower. She was acutely aware of Wintersmith below her. She did not want him to see her reflection tonight. He seemed to be looking for it, though. She saw him scan the windows several times.

Giles vanished into an alley, emerged on Mount Street, turned left, and ducked into another alley. Violet almost lost him again, catching him only when he crossed Chapel Street. Another alleyway, a mews, and . . .

She lost him.

Violet backtracked. Where was he? There! No, that was Wintersmith. He'd lost Giles Abbishaw, too.

She rose higher, circled, spotted another alley and followed it—and saw a man let himself into a house on Portugal Street. Lamplight fell briefly on him before the door closed.

Had that been Giles Abbishaw?

Violet circled the house. It was tall and elegant. With the exception of two windows at the back, overlooking the garden, all the curtains were drawn. Violet drifted closer and peeked into the lower uncurtained window. She saw a parlor and four gentlemen and a table upon which cards, guineas, and wine glasses were scattered.

The second uncurtained window was on the topmost floor. Through it, she saw another gentleman. He lounged on a sofa, reading a book. His shirtsleeves were rolled up, his neckcloth was gone, and he had only stockings on his feet.

Violet ducked away, feeling uncomfortably like a Peeping Tom. She perched on the roof ridge for a moment. The building was obviously a lodging house for well-to-do gentlemen, each man having his own set of rooms. No woman would reside there. If Giles Abbishaw had let himself in the door—and she wasn't certain that he had—then he wasn't visiting a mistress.

She flew back down to see whether Giles had joined the card party, but he hadn't.

Violet became aware of her headache again. She rubbed her temples—and remembered that she'd lost her mask the night before. She really oughtn't fly until she'd sewn herself a new one.

It was definitely time to go home.

She rose upwards, and as she passed the topmost window she saw that the gentleman had left his sofa and was admitting a guest into his room—and that the guest was none other than Giles Abbishaw.

The two men embraced, and then they kissed one another.

Violet hung in midair for a moment, open-mouthed, frozen with shock, then she ducked down below the windowsill, her thoughts in a whirl.

Giles did have a lover.

A man!

No wonder he took such pains to hide his trail. If his secret became known, he'd be ruined. Both men would be.

Had Giles gifted the automatous clocks to his lover?

Were the clocks in this house? In this very room?

Violet peeped above the windowsill. Giles and his lover had stopped kissing, but they stood close, smiling at one another. The man brushed a lock of hair tenderly back from Giles's brow.

Violet glanced swiftly around the room, saw only a carriage clock, and ducked down again, but Giles's expression stayed with her. He'd looked lit from within with happiness.

This wasn't a throwaway affair for him. It was love.

Violet's throat constricted with emotion. Her heart did, too.

The adjacent window was dark, its curtains closed except for an inch-wide crack. Violet cupped her hands against the glass and squinted inside. Was that a bed, looming in the shadows? She thought it might be. She couldn't make out anything else, though. Washstand, dresser, mirror, armoire—if this was a bedroom then those things would be there, but she couldn't see them. It was too dark. There could be a dozen clocks on display in the room, but she wouldn't be able to see those either.

She flew around to the front of the house, where there were two more windows. These windows were lit, but the curtains were pulled tightly shut. She decided that the back two rooms belonged to Giles's lover, and the front two to someone else.

Violet sat on the roof ridge and pondered what to do.

Giles was being furtive and mysterious because he was in love with a man . . . but also possibly because he'd stolen two of his father's clocks and given them to his lover. She didn't think he was a thief, but she couldn't be certain of it. Not unless she searched those rooms—which she wasn't going to do.

Violet chewed on her lip, thinking about Giles and his lover and the contents of Freddy's bandbox. Would a man who loved another man give that man two clocks with naked women on them?

It seemed unlikely.

Although . . . Wintersmith hadn't said that the clocks had women on them. She'd assumed it, but perhaps she'd been wrong? Perhaps the clocks depicted men in erotic poses?

Would Wintersmith tell her if she asked?

Violet circled up into the sky. She ought to go home, but instead she went hunting for a Bow Street Runner.

CHAPTER ELEVEN

*D*amn it. How had he lost Giles Abbishaw yet again? Perry retraced the route for a third time—alleyway, alleyway, mews . . . and then where? Had Giles turned left or right? And did it even matter at this point? He wasn't going to find the man tonight. He'd be tucked up in his mistress's bed by now.

Damn it all to perdition.

A pins-and-needles sensation crawled across his scalp. It wasn't the first time Perry had felt it this evening, but he'd not caught sight of anyone following him.

He glanced around, saw nothing, and headed back towards Grosvenor Square. The prickling sensation grew more intense with each step that he took, more urgent. Perry halted and raised his fists, scanning the shadows, alert for ambush.

"Psst," someone hissed above him. "Wintersmith."

Two nights ago, Perry would have leaped out of his skin if he'd been hailed from the sky. Tonight, he only jumped a little bit. He lowered his fists, looked up, and saw only darkness. "Did you see where he went?"

"Meet me at the Grosvenor Chapel."

Perry hurried back the way he'd come. Two minutes later, he climbed the steps to the chapel's portico. "Lady Violet?"

"Mr. Wintersmith."

She was above him somewhere, tucked into the shadows. He peered up, but couldn't spot her. "Did you see where Giles Abbishaw went?"

"I have a question for you."

Perry heaved a sigh. Why couldn't this be simple? "What is it?" he said, in a tone that he never would have used with dukes' daughters prior to meeting Lady Violet.

"What's on the clocks?"

She'd called him prudish last night, and perhaps he was, because he was surprised by the question, even a little shocked. "I beg your pardon?"

"What's on the clocks? Did Lord Abbishaw tell you?"

"He did. But I can't discuss the particulars of the case with you."

Lady Violet gave a little huff of annoyance. "I don't want the particulars, I just want to know what's on the clocks."

"Why?" An answer to that question presented itself: Lady Violet was asking because she'd *seen* the clocks. "You've found them? Where are they?"

"I haven't found them, but in case I should, I'd like to know what's on them. Is it men or women or both?"

"Both, and I must ask you not to look for the clocks. This case is none of your—"

"Men *and* women? Together?"

Perry huffed out an annoyed breath of his own. "Yes. Men and women together."

"On both clocks?"

"Yes."

"Thank you. Good night."

A dark shape detached itself from the shadows above him.

"Wait!" Perry called out.

The shape halted.

"Did you see where Giles Abbishaw went?"

"I can't tell you that."

Perry took a step towards her. "I answered your question; I

must ask you to do me the courtesy of answering mine." His voice was too curt for speaking with dukes' daughters, so he amended his request with a polite: "Please."

Lady Violet was silent for a long moment, so long a moment that Perry thought she'd slipped out of the portico and that the shadow he was staring up at was just a shadow. He almost jumped when she said, "I saw where he went, but I can't tell you where it is. What I *can* tell you is that he didn't steal the clocks. I'm quite certain of it."

Perry stared up at her, baffled. How the devil could she be certain? And why had she dragged him to Grosvenor Chapel to ask such strange questions?

Men *and* women? Why the emphasis on the "and"?

His brain made a sudden leap of intuition. It was such an unexpected leap, such a shocking one, that he actually pressed his hand to his forehead. "By thunder. Giles is meeting a *man.*"

"No, he's not," Lady Violet said quickly.

Perry heard the lie in her voice. "Who is it?" he demanded.

"He's not meeting a man!"

"I can hear that you're lying. Tell me who it is."

"No. Giles is not your thief!"

Perry gritted his teeth. Lady Violet had to be the most uncooperative, most stubborn, most *annoying* person in the whole of England. And then he realized why she was refusing to tell him.

She was protecting Giles Abbishaw. From him.

That stung.

Perry had been to boarding school and he'd been in the army. He knew that men sometimes fell in love with other men. It happened. He wasn't going to ruin Giles's life just because he'd had the misfortune to fall in love with a man, not a woman.

Lady Violet clearly believed that he would.

Perry looked up at where he thought she was. "If there's no connection between the man Giles is seeing and the clocks, I'll say nothing of the matter to anyone. You have my word on it. But I have to know who the man is. I must rule him out."

"Giles doesn't have anything to do with the clocks. I know he doesn't!"

"I need to be the judge of that," Perry told her, trying not to let annoyance leak into his voice. "What if the fellow is a clockmaker? Or a dealer in clocks?"

"If he was, he'd have lots of clocks, and he doesn't!" she retorted. "I looked in the window and there's only a carriage clock."

Perry held on to his temper. "Lady Violet, I give you my word of honor that if Giles isn't the thief, I won't expose the affair."

There was a long beat of silence.

"My *word* on it," he repeated. "Who Giles Abbishaw spends his nights with is his own business. Not mine, not yours, not anyone else's."

There was another beat of silence, and then Lady Violet grudgingly said, "Very well."

The shadow he was staring up at detached itself from all the other shadows. Lady Violet glided down until she was standing in front of him. She wasn't wearing a mask tonight. Her face was a pale oval. Perry couldn't be entirely certain, but he thought that her arms were crossed and her chin tilted up, defensive, protective.

He admired her for that protectiveness.

"Say it," she demanded.

"I won't tell anyone about Giles's lover," Perry said. "Not unless Giles stole the clocks for him."

"And you won't write about it in that notebook of yours."

"I won't make note of it either," Perry said, and then wondered how she knew he had a notebook.

"All right." Lady Violet didn't sound happy, and she didn't make any move to leave the chapel portico.

"I'm not going to expose him," Perry told her. "Not unless he's the thief. I promise."

She must have heard the truth in his voice, just as he'd heard the lie in hers earlier. She sighed, and Perry imagined her deflating slightly. "All right," she said again. "The house is in Portugal Street."

"What number?"

"I don't know."

"Will you show me?"

Portugal Street was just around the corner from the chapel. It was short, only a dozen houses. Perry halted where the shadows were deepest. He couldn't see Lady Violet, but his scalp told him she was close by. "Which house is it?"

"The second on the left. It's a lodging house. He's on the top floor, at the back."

Perry located the lodging house and observed it for a moment. It was a very different establishment from the one in which he lived, elegant and well-kept.

"What does he look like?"

"Taller than Giles. Dark hair."

"Age?"

"Maybe thirty?"

"Thank you. I promise I'll be discreet in my enquiries." Perry turned and headed back the way he'd come.

"Where are you going now?" Lady Violet asked.

"Home."

Mount Street was wide and well-lit. He saw no sign of Lady Violet while he strode along it, not even her reflection ghosting across the topmost windows. Once past Berkeley Square, he took to the smaller lanes, mews, and alleyways. His scalp prickled with pins-and-needles again. He wasn't at all surprised when a voice said out of the air above him, "I don't think it was either Freddy or Giles. Do you?"

Perry had come to that conclusion himself. "No."

"And it's hardly likely to be Saint."

"No."

"Which leaves Devil, but I don't think it's him, either."

Perry didn't think it was Devereux either. Or rather, he hoped it wasn't. But he doubted his reasons were the same as Lady Violet's. "Why don't you think it's him?"

"Because he inherited a very comfortable fortune. Why would he steal anything?"

Why indeed?

"It must be someone else. Perhaps one of the servants has Wilton's key? I know! It's his valet."

"Wilton's valet went with him to America."

Lady Violet was silent while they navigated the tangle of streets and alleys near Golden Square. He knew she was nearby though—his scalp told him. At the corner of Cambridge and Pulteney, Lady Violet suddenly said from above his left shoulder: "There are shops that give people money in exchange for their belongings."

"Pawnbrokers," Perry said. "I've checked them already."

"All of them?"

"All of them."

"I'll follow Saint tomorrow night," she said, once he'd crossed Hopkins Street. "Or Devil. Whichever one I see first."

Perry halted and looked upwards. He couldn't spot her. "Lady Violet," he began sternly.

"I helped tonight, didn't I?"

Perry spun on his heel. Where was she, damn it? "Yes, but—"

"I'm better at following people than you are. Not that you could help losing Giles! I lost him for a while, too. He was very tricky. But the point is, I found him again and you didn't."

Perry tried not to take offense, because it was true: Lady Violet *was* better at following people than he was.

"So, may I assist with your investigation? Please?"

He opened his mouth to say *No,* and closed it again. If he'd learned anything these past two nights, it was that Lady Violet was going to involve herself regardless of what he said, in which case he should say *Yes*. That way, he'd have a chance of setting ground rules. "On one condition," he said. "No, three conditions."

There was a long moment of silence, and then: "What are they?"

"The first is that you don't do anything dangerous, and the second is that you don't let anyone see you flying."

Lady Violet made a scoffing sound above him. "I already do that."

"*I* saw you."

"Well, of course you did. I might be better at following people than you are, but you're better at seeing them. Better than anyone in London!"

Perry ignored the tiny flicker of gratification this statement afforded him. "And the third condition is that you mustn't go anywhere or follow anyone without telling me first."

"I'm not a child," Lady Violet said indignantly.

"You're a female, alone at night, which is extremely dangerous." Perry suddenly thought of a fourth condition. "And you mustn't land. Ever. That's a condition, too."

"I never land," Lady Violet retorted. "I promised my parents I wouldn't, and I don't."

"You landed on Stanhope's balcony," Perry pointed out. "And on my roof."

"But not on the ground. I never land on the ground!"

She'd landed on the ground when Perry had caught her, but that contact hadn't been voluntary. It made him shiver to think of it. What if a ruffian had captured her last night? Or if one caught her in the future?

He wanted to forbid her to ever fly again—but he could guess how that would be received. If Lady Violet wanted to roam London at night, there was absolutely nothing he could do to stop her. If she wanted to poke her nose into his investigation and follow people, he couldn't prevent that either.

But he could keep tabs on her. He could limit the risks she took.

"If you wish to help me with this case, then I need to know your movements. If you follow any of the suspects or go anywhere connected to them, you must inform me."

She huffed. "That's ridiculous."

"If one of the foot patrol officers was assisting me, I'd require it of him."

That statement hung in the air for a long moment and then Lady Violet said, grudgingly, "If I accept your conditions, what do I get in exchange?"

Perry hesitated. Technically, he shouldn't tell her anything about the case, but he'd already crossed that line. "I'll share what I know—as long as you keep what I tell you in the strictest confidence."

"Of course I'll keep it secret!"

"Then we have an agreement." His scalp prickled warningly. Perry glanced behind him and spotted movement. Two men approached, stealthy, keeping to the shadows. He decided it would be prudent to move before they reached him.

He ducked down an alleyway and then another, left onto Berwick, along Edward, through St. Anne's Court.

Lady Violet didn't speak until he'd crossed Soho Square. "The Honeywells' ball is tomorrow night," she announced. "Both Devil and Saint will be there."

"Good," Perry said, glancing over his shoulder. He couldn't see the two men, but his scalp was still tingling its warning.

"You'll be there, too, I take it?"

"No."

"What will you be doing?"

Perry looked back again, too distracted to answer. He couldn't see anyone, but the prickling sensation was crawling down the nape of his neck, telling him to be very careful.

"What will you be doing?" Lady Violet asked again.

"Sitting in a cupboard," Perry said. "Can you see someone behind me? I know I'm being followed."

She was silent, and he guessed she was doing as he'd asked, and then: "There are two of them! And they have cudgels!"

Perry lengthened his stride and took the next corner at a run. The men behind him undoubtedly knew this part of London well, but so did he. Two streets and an alleyway later, he eased to a jog and then, when his scalp didn't prickle, a brisk walk.

He crossed High Holborn and turned into the narrow, down-at-heels lane where he lived, fishing the latchkey from his pocket while his gaze skipped ahead, checking each dark doorway before he came to it.

"How did you know you were being followed if you couldn't see them?" Lady Violet asked, when he halted.

"Magic," Perry said, fitting his key into the lock.

"What?"

He laughed at the sharp curiosity in her voice, stepped inside, and closed the door.

CHAPTER TWELVE

*P*erry lit a chamberstick from the lamp that had been left in the entranceway and climbed the narrow staircase. The usual medley of smells assaulted his nose: sweat and tobacco and chamber pots, cabbage and onions and pickles, the mutton smell of tallow candles. It was a relief to reach his room, where his window stood open and the air smelled only of coal smoke and tallow. Lady Violet was perched on his windowsill, her black-clad legs crossed at the ankle. In the candlelight her skin was luminously pale, her eyes dark and mysterious. She looked beautiful and otherworldly, as beguiling and dangerous as one of the nymphs who'd enticed Hylas to his doom.

"What do you mean magic?" she demanded once he'd closed his door.

Any resemblance she had to a naiad was snuffed out. The female on his windowsill was no dangerously alluring nymph, but rather an extremely nosy duke's daughter.

"I was joking," Perry said, setting the candle down on his washstand. "It's not magic. It's . . ." How to describe it? He took off his hat and laid it on his old army trunk. "My scalp tingles whenever someone follows me. I don't know why." He shrugged. "My grandmother had something like it. She swore she could feel when ghosts were nearby. I've never felt a ghost, but I know if someone's following me."

"By the pricking of my thumbs, something wicked this way comes?"

"Exactly. Except that it's not my thumbs." He pulled off his gloves and tossed them alongside his hat. "It's saved my life several times. Saved my whole regiment twice."

Her eyebrows shot up. "Truly?"

"Raiding parties set to ambush us." Perry rubbed the top of his head, remembering the urgency of the pins-and-needles, how they'd stabbed into his skin like claws. "It's how I knew you were following me last night."

"You said you saw my reflection."

"I did, but only because I was looking for it. I knew you were behind me, but I was dashed if I could see you."

She made one of her huffing sounds, then said, "I wonder if it is magic? Does everyone in your family have it?"

"I don't know. I never told anyone."

"Why on earth not?"

"Because everyone thought my grandmother was crazy, and I didn't want to be thought crazy, too."

"Perhaps all the Wintersmiths have it and you're all keeping it a secret from each other!"

"It was my mother's side of the family and they're all dead now, so no."

"Well, that's disappointing." Her mouth folded into a frown.

Perry reached up to loosen his neckcloth—then lowered his hand. Best not to do things like loosening neckcloths when there was a duke's daughter sitting on one's windowsill.

Lady Violet lost her frown. "Why will you be in a cupboard tomorrow? Is it another case? Can I help with it?" Her gaze was bright and eager and the set of her chin was purposeful and he could tell, just by looking at her, that she was determined to interrogate him until she'd ferreted out every last scrap of information.

Awareness of her flooded through him. Lady Violet might be as persistent as a terrier and she might be the last woman in

England he'd wish to marry, but that didn't mean he couldn't notice how attractive she was. Her breasts filled out her coat in a way that coats were not meant to be filled out and the pantaloons did nothing to conceal the shapely curve of her legs.

Perry looked away.

Lady Violet trusted him to be a gentleman and part of being a gentleman was not undressing her in his head.

He took a step back and rested his shoulders against the closed door, resolving to get this inquisition over as quickly as possible. "The cupboard is in Lord Abbishaw's clock room. I'll be in it because there's a chance the thief will attempt to steal another clock."

Lady Violet opened her mouth to ask a question.

Perry held up a hand to forestall her.

"Abbishaw is reclusive and rarely ventures from home—except on Wednesday and Friday evenings, when he dines at his club. It's the only time he's guaranteed to be from home, apparently."

Lady Violet closed her mouth.

"The first clock was stolen on Wednesday last week and the second on Friday. It's possible the thief will try again this week. Hence, the cupboard."

"No one would be foolish enough to risk it again! They'll know watch is being kept."

"Abbishaw hasn't told anyone about the thefts. The thief may well think he's got away with it."

Her brow creased as she considered that nugget of information. "Giles must know. Abbishaw searched his room and took his key to the cabinet."

"He searched the room when Giles wasn't there and took the key without telling him. Giles probably hasn't noticed it's gone."

"By Jove, that's rather shabby!"

Perry couldn't help laughing.

"What? It *is* shabby."

"I agree."

"Then why did you laugh?"

"I've never heard a lady say 'by Jove' before."

Lady Violet's cheeks became a little pink. She lifted her chin. "Well, now you have."

Perry almost laughed again. He managed to suppress it.

Lady Violet leaned forward on the windowsill. The way that she sat, her hands on the sill, her shoulders back, made her breasts rather prominent.

Perry lifted his gaze and looked past her left ear.

"Why didn't Lord Abbishaw raise a hue and cry? Does he not want anyone to know he collects naughty clocks?"

He looked at her face again. "That would be my guess."

"But he displays the clocks in a cabinet!"

"That particular cabinet doesn't have glass doors."

"So, they're not on display?"

"No."

"Then why collect them in the first place?" She looked quite baffled.

Perry shrugged. "Your guess is as good as mine." His personal guess was that the viscount found the clocks titillating, but that he didn't want anyone to know he possessed them.

"If no one can see into the cabinet, how does Abbishaw know when the clocks went missing? They could have been stolen weeks ago. Months, even!" Her eyes widened dramatically. "Perhaps Wilton took them to America with him, or—no! Jasper Flint stole them, and that's why Wilton killed him!"

"Flint's death was an accident," Perry said, squashing this sensational line of thought. "And the clocks only went missing last week. Lord Abbishaw checks the clocks in the cabinet every day."

The viscount said it was to wind the clocks and make certain all the movements were working properly, but Perry thought Abbishaw rather enjoyed watching all those little pricks slotting themselves into all those little quims.

Which was something he really ought not to think about while Lady Violet was sitting on his windowsill, close enough to his bed that she could touch it if she wished.

His thoughts leaped there anyway: Lady Violet, the bed.

Perry didn't dare look at her. Or at his bed. He stared at the top of the window frame instead. The paint was flaking away. An old water stain tracked its way down from the ceiling.

"Lord Abbishaw keeps naughty clocks in a cabinet and looks at them every day? *And* he gives his sons keys so that they may look at them, too? I must say, I wouldn't have thought it of him at all."

Perry risked a glance at her face. She was frowning. "It's not like that," he told her. "The cabinet's one of a pair. The other one's in the library and has family memorabilia in it. The keys fit both cabinets."

"Oh." Her frown cleared. "That makes more sense. I can imagine Wilton sneaking in to look at naughty clocks, but not Saint or Giles."

Perry had never met Wilton Abbishaw, but from what he'd heard it was entirely likely that Wilton had sneaked in to look at the clocks. It was also possible that he'd showed the clocks to his friends. And possibly given his key to one of them. But which friend?

"So, you'll watch from a cupboard while Lord Abbishaw is dining at his club?"

"Yes."

"You might catch the thief!"

"I hope so," Perry said.

Lady Violet leaned forward and peppered him with questions. How big was the cupboard? What was in it? What was its position in the room? Would Perry leave the door open a crack or peer through a keyhole? What time did Lord Abbishaw leave for his club? What time did he get home? What would Perry do if the thief attempted to steal a clock?

"I'll confront him. Possibly arrest him. It depends who it is."

"You won't follow him?"

"It depends who it is," Perry said again. "If anyone comes at all."

"I wager it's a servant."

Perry hoped it was. He didn't want to have to arrest Devereux Abbishaw.

"Do you have a tipstaff?"

Perry fished the tipstaff from his pocket. It was quite short, with a small brass crown at one end and a slim wooden handle.

Her eyes lit up. "May I?"

Perry crossed the room, something he accomplished in only four steps, and gave it to her.

Lady Violet examined the tipstaff curiously. "It's not very heavy."

"No."

"And it's not at all fearsome."

"If you're a criminal, it is."

She made a little moue and handed him the tipstaff, clearly disappointed by its lack of weighty menace. Perry tucked it back in his pocket and retreated the four steps to the door. The tipstaff might be small, but it had gravitas and authority. It was equivalent to the braiding he'd worn when he was an officer. He liked its inconspicuousness. The braiding had been there for all to see, but the tipstaff was invisible until he chose to bring it out.

"How many people have you arrested?" Lady Violet asked. "What were their crimes? Have any of your cases been written up in the newspapers?"

"This is my first case," Perry admitted.

"Your first?" Her eagerness evaporated. It was obvious that he'd disappointed her again.

"When Abbishaw came to Bow Street, all the Principal Officers were busy with other investigations. Sir Mortimer deputized me. He thought I had the right background for the case."

"Sir Mortimer?"

"Sir Mortimer Treadwell, one of the magistrates at Bow Street. I generally work as his secretary."

Her eyebrows went up. "You're a secretary?" Perry heard surprise in her voice, and something that sounded like disdain, as if being a secretary was a very lowly occupation—which it was, seen through the eyes of a duke's daughter. Although given what he knew of Lady Violet, the disdain was probably because she thought secretaries were more boring than Principal Officers.

Perry agreed with that sentiment. Secretaries might make more than Principal Officers, but he'd far rather earn his shillings hunting down criminals than pushing sheets of paper across a desk. Which was why, when Sir Mortimer had asked, he'd said yes.

"If you don't solve this case, will you have to be a secretary again?" Lady Violet asked.

"I shall have to be a secretary again either way. This position is temporary."

Her nose wrinkled. "That's a shame."

Perry couldn't help but laugh again.

She frowned at him. "What?"

"Most people consider secretaries to be superior to Principal Officers."

"Oh." Her nose wrinkled a second time. She said cautiously, "Would you prefer to be a secretary?"

A secretary would earn his way out of this attic room more quickly than a Principal Officer and a secretary wouldn't have to hide in a cupboard or lurk in a ballroom trying not to be noticed by people he'd been to school with, but Perry had never wanted to be a secretary and the thought of sitting behind a desk for the rest of his life made him feel the way a bird caught in a cage must feel.

"No." What he'd prefer was to go back to his regiment, but he'd promised his mother on her deathbed that he wouldn't do that.

Lady Violet pursed her lips, and then thankfully abandoned

that line of discussion. "Did Lord Abbishaw procure your invitations to those balls?" she asked.

"No."

"Then who invited you?"

"No one."

"Did you *sneak* in?"

"Yes."

Lady Violet didn't appear outraged by this admission; if anything, she seemed impressed. "No wonder you were trying to look like a piece of furniture." She swung one leg slightly. Her heel bumped against the wall. "What did you think you'd see? It's not as if anyone would bring a clock to a ball."

"I wanted to observe the main suspects, see who they spoke with, how they interacted with one another, where they went afterwards."

She nodded, and bumped her heel against the wall again. "I wish I could hide in the cupboard with you."

Perry was very glad that she couldn't. Lady Violet was distracting enough seated on his windowsill. In the closeness of a cupboard, there'd be no barrage of questions, just barely heard breaths. It would be shadowy and quiet and intimate. In such circumstances, Lady Violet would be more than distracting; she'd be damned near irresistible—and heaven forbid that he ever step over that line.

"What if I sneak in and—"

"No."

"But—"

"What did you say about Sevenash House last night? That there were too many servants? The same applies to Abbishaw House."

Lady Violet huffed out a breath and subsided. Her pout was rather comical.

"And besides," Perry said. "It's even odds the thief won't come."

"Do you think so?"

"Yes."

86

"Why?"

Perry shrugged. "Just a feeling." He fished out his pocket watch and checked the time, a hint that Lady Violet fortunately took.

"I must be going," she said.

Perry restored the watch to its pocket. "Good night, Lady Violet."

She drew her legs up and turned to clamber out the window. The pantaloons did extremely enticing things to her *derrière*.

Perry examined the water stains on his ceiling.

"I'll watch Abbishaw House tomorrow night."

Perry glanced at her. She was perched on his parapet, an amorphous black shape except for the pale oval of her face.

He crossed to the window. "You'll probably be watching in vain."

"But perhaps not. Imagine if the thief should come!" Lady Violet grinned.

The grin transformed her from beautiful to breathtaking. Perry experienced a rather strong urge to reach out and pull her close enough to kiss. He took a step back from the window. "Good night," he said again.

"Good night."

When he was certain that Lady Violet had gone, Perry ventured back to the window. A faint scent lingered in the air. Orange blossom.

Perry breathed that scent into his lungs and thought about the last time he'd touched a woman. It had been more than a year ago. He'd been a veritable monk since returning to England. Perhaps he ought to do something about it.

But not tonight.

He'd wait until he'd solved this case.

CHAPTER THIRTEEN

*T*he next morning, Violet found her brother in the library with an encyclopedia laid out on the table. "Rhodes? I won't be attending the Honeywells' ball tonight."

"No?"

"I'm going to help Wintersmith watch for a thief."

Rhodes looked up from the encyclopedia. "Violet," he said, in the sort of voice he used when he told his children not to do something.

"I'm an adult," she reminded him. "I can do what I wish."

"Within reason."

"This is within reason. There's no danger at all. I'll be observing from a distance."

Rhodes did not look convinced.

"And anyway, Wintersmith thinks there's a good chance the thief won't come."

Her brother sighed and rubbed above his right eyebrow, as if he had a headache. "Violet, involving yourself in something like this isn't good ton."

"The victim and the thief are both noblemen!"

"That's not what I meant, and you know it."

Rhodes was frowning now, beginning to become cross, which matched Violet's mood perfectly. "I'm considerably more than seven!" The very fact that she had to say it made her sound like a child, which made her crosser. She folded her arms. "I cut my eye teeth years ago."

Rhodes leaned one hip against the table and crossed his own arms. "What would Mother and Father say?"

Violet's indignation faltered. If her parents were in town, she'd be having this conversation with them—and they'd be no happier than Rhodes currently was.

She unfolded her arms and huffed out a breath. "Father would probably forbid it, and Mother would say that I could help Wintersmith as long as I kept them apprised of any happenings."

Rhodes considered this answer, and nodded his agreement.

She eyed him hopefully. "May I help Wintersmith as long as I keep you apprised of any happenings? I'll be very careful. I promise!"

Rhodes sighed, and rubbed his eyebrow again, and then said, "Did you see Wintersmith last night?"

"Yes. But that isn't why I stayed home from Vauxhall. I really was tired! I only went out for a little while. But I saw one of the suspects and followed him, and Wintersmith followed him, too, but then he lost him and I didn't, so . . ." She trailed to a halt, not sure how to describe the tangle of last night's events.

Rhodes was frowning again.

"I helped him, and we talked, that's all. I'd really like to see this case to its end. It's a puzzling little mystery." And it was an adventure. The only adventure she'd likely ever have.

Rhodes pressed his lips together the way their father did when he was making difficult decisions. Then he sighed. "All right, but I expect you to tell me what happens."

"Some of it's confidential."

"I don't need to know who's stolen what, but I do need to

know where you are and what you're doing. I need to know that you're safe, Vi."

She wanted to protest again that she was an adult, but it wasn't just her safety that was at stake. The Garland name was, too, and the Garland secret, and while their parents were away it was Rhodes's duty to protect those things.

"All right."

They eyed one another; then Rhodes gave a nod and returned to his perusal of the encyclopedia.

Violet bit her lip, and took a step closer. She didn't like being almost at outs with her brother. "What are you looking up?"

"Hot air balloons. Miniature ones made of paper. I thought I might make one for the children. There are instructions here."

"That sounds exciting. May I see?"

Rhodes shifted sideways and angled the book towards her. There were indeed instructions for making miniature hot air balloons, complete with drawings and measurements.

"It looks rather complicated."

"It is, but I think we can do it. Would you like to help?"

"Yes, I should. Very much!"

CHAPTER
FOURTEEN

*N*umber 4 Portugal Street was an upmarket lodging house catering to gentlemen who were well-heeled but not affluent. The inhabitants of the topmost floor were a Mr. Brockmole and a Mr. Guthrie. Brockmole was a little Jack Sprat of a man who'd been valet to a baron, according to the kitchen maid Perry spoke to. He descended the stairs every day to stroll in Hyde Park wearing an elaborate wig and carrying a gold-topped cane that the baron had gifted him upon his retirement.

Guthrie was younger and worked at one of the banks. Very quiet he was, the kitchen maid said, and never caused a mite of trouble.

Perry spent the rest of the day trying to find some connection between Guthrie and clocks. He failed, but he did find a connection between Guthrie and Giles Abbishaw: tea. Both men were frequent customers of the Twinings Tea Shop on the Strand. If he had to guess, that was where the men had met. The viscount's son and the banker had become friends over cups of tea, and then taken the dangerous step of becoming lovers.

At dusk, Perry presented himself at Lord Abbishaw's residence on Hanover Square.

The cupboard in the room where Abbishaw housed his collection of clocks was quite spacious. Several men could have hidden in it. Perry didn't suggest that the viscount join him. Abbishaw was proud and fastidious and very jealous of his dignity. Not a man who'd ever hide in a cupboard.

"If it is my son Giles, you do not have my permission to arrest him." Abbishaw had a way of speaking to Perry without actually looking at him, as if this distasteful matter could be ignored if he didn't meet Perry's eye. "Don't let him see you. I'll deal with it personally."

As the victim of this crime, Lord Abbishaw had the right to decide whether or not to proceed with an arrest, so Perry merely said, "Yes, sir. And if it's your nephew?"

Abbishaw's gaze almost flickered to Perry's face. "No arrest. But you may show yourself and request the return of my clocks."

"And if it's one of Wilton's friends?"

Abbishaw's thin lips pursed. Perry could see that he wanted to say *arrest*, but Wilton's friends were the sons of Abbishaw's friends, so he wasn't surprised when the viscount said, "You may show yourself and request the clocks back, but no arrest."

"If it's a servant, I have your permission to arrest them?"

"Of course."

"Shall I send word to your club if the thief does come?"

"No," Abbishaw said sharply. "Absolutely not!"

Perry wondered what the viscount feared so much. That his cronies would discover he collected smutty clocks? Or that they'd learn Abbishaw had been the victim of something as vulgar as theft? "Shall I wait for your return then, sir? To apprise you of what happens?"

Abbishaw hesitated. It was clear that he didn't want to speak to Perry at all, not now, and not at midnight or whenever he returned from his club. He wished that the problem of his missing clocks would simply go away.

"Or I can report to you in person tomorrow, if you prefer?"

Abbishaw considered this suggestion, and then said, "Tomorrow morning. Eleven o'clock."

If Perry were the viscount, he'd want to know what had happened before he went to bed, but Abbishaw was paying for the investigation, so he said, "Very good, sir." He stepped into the cupboard, set the candlestick he was holding down on one of the shelves, and drew the door almost shut.

"Can you see the cabinet?" Abbishaw asked.

"Yes, sir."

Abbishaw departed without a *Good-night*, taking the other candle with him. The room beyond the cupboard plunged into darkness.

Perry acquainted himself with his immediate surroundings. The cupboard was roomy, its shelves mostly empty. There were cloths for cleaning clocks, oil to lubricate their inner workings, various polishes, an array of little keys on hooks, and not much else.

Perry blew out his candle.

Cupboards were generally silent, but this one wasn't. The sound of ticking crept in through the inch-wide gap between door and frame. It was surprisingly loud, louder than his breathing, louder than the rustle of clothing when he shifted his weight.

Perry leaned back against the shelves and waited for the thief. Twenty minutes later, the clocks announced the hour. They didn't all do it at exactly the same time. The medley of chimes lasted for more than a minute, each clock briefly adding its voice to the chorus.

The last of the *dings* died away. Perry realized that the cupboard was no longer completely dark. The clocks' chiming had masked the sound of someone entering the room.

He straightened away from the shelves and leaned sideways, peering out through the gap.

He saw a sliver of wall upon which two clocks hung and part of the cabinet that contained the viscount's collection of erotic clocks. A lamp sat on the floor, with a small valise alongside it. The door to the cabinet was open. Someone was rifling through its contents. A man. Perry could only see his back, but he clearly wasn't a servant. No servant would wear a tailcoat that elegant.

The man bent and tucked something into the valise, then stood and locked the cabinet, presenting his back to Perry again. He was too tall to be Giles or Frederick Stanhope.

Dread clenched in Perry's stomach. *Please don't be Devereux*, he prayed, even as he rested his fingertips on the door, ready to fling it open and confront the thief.

The man turned.

It wasn't Devereux, it was Saintbridge.

His face was clearly visible in the lamplight. For once, he didn't look disdainful. A scowl contorted his eyebrows and twisted his mouth. He looked angry. Furious. Consumed with rage.

Saintbridge dug in his pocket and flung something on the floor. He picked up the lamp and the valise and headed for the door.

Perry watched through the crack as Saintbridge Abbishaw, heir to the Abbishaw viscountcy, made off with one of his father's erotic automatous clocks.

The door shut. The room became dark.

Perry slipped out of the cupboard and crossed the room. He fumbled for the door handle, found it, turned it cautiously. The corridor was empty but he heard stealthy footsteps to his right, heading away from the front of the house.

He followed the footsteps, peering around a corner in time to see Saintbridge deposit the lamp on a table and exit his father's townhouse through a side door.

Perry counted to 10, then slipped out through the same door.

Saintbridge was crossing the lamplit square. He moved fast, a scuttling, scurrying stride, head ducked, shoulders hunched, the valise tucked close to his body.

Perry followed at a discreet distance, slipping from shadow to shadow.

Saintbridge had a house on Conduit Street, its lease paid for by his father. Conduit Street was two minutes' walk from Hanover Square, directly down George Street, but instead of going down that wide thoroughfare, Saintbridge chose a circuitous route, along Pollen Street, Maddox Street, and Mill Street.

At the corner of Mill and Conduit, Saintbridge paused to look furtively around; then he crossed the street swiftly and ran up the steps to his house.

Perry glanced upwards. He couldn't see Lady Violet, but his scalp told him she was somewhere above him. Either that, or he was about to be set on by footpads.

"Give me half an hour," he announced to the dark sky, and then he headed back to Hanover Square. He wanted to see what Saintbridge had dropped in the clock room.

The side door to Lord Abbishaw's house was unlocked and the lamp Saintbridge had used still sat on the table.

Was the door always unlocked? Was the lamp always there? Or did Saintbridge have an accomplice in the house?

Those questions were secondary to far more important ones, namely why the blazes was Saintbridge stealing from his father, and why was he so angry about it?

Perry took the lamp and retraced his steps to the clock room. He didn't meet a single servant. Was Abbishaw's house always this quiet on nights when he went to his club?

It was another question worth asking.

The clock room was dark, but not silent. The automatous clocks ticked and tocked industriously. Ships sailed across heaving seas and moons rose in star-studded skies. Fiddlers fiddled and dancers danced and a milkmaid milked a cow.

Without the key, Perry couldn't open the cabinet that housed the erotic clocks, but he could see what Saintbridge had dropped on the floor.

A tiepin.

Perry picked it up. As tiepins went, this one was distinctive, a ruby set within a ring of pearls.

Saintbridge had left it deliberately. Therefore, it probably didn't belong to him.

Perry tucked the tiepin into his pocket. He had a feeling Lord Abbishaw would recognize it.

CHAPTER FIFTEEN

Perry crossed Hanover Square briskly and turned into the nearest alleyway. Within seconds, a voice came out of the air above him. "It was *Saint*?"

"Yes."

"But that's impossible! He's so . . . He would never . . ."

Perry kept walking, along the alley and then across a wide, lamplit street. He cut through a mews, where glossy horses were being harnessed to a coach. His scalp prickled faintly, telling him that Lady Violet was following him, high above the light and the bustle.

Emerging from the mews, he had a choice of another wide street or an alleyway. He chose the alley. The prickling sensation intensified.

"Tell me," Lady Violet demanded from somewhere not too far above his right shoulder.

Perry told her what he'd witnessed.

She wanted to see the tiepin, of course.

"Not here," Perry said, as he picked his way along the alley. "It's too dark." The moon was full, casting enough light for him to see where to place his feet, but not enough for anyone to look at a tiepin.

Lady Violet didn't argue, instead she said, "And he was

angry?"

"Furious."

"I wonder why? Do you think . . . was it a righteous anger? Is he ridding his father's house of vulgar clocks?"

Perry paused and considered this for a moment, shook his head, realized she couldn't see that gesture, and said, "No. He didn't look righteous."

"How do you know?"

Did she have to doubt everything he said? Perry almost huffed out a breath. He stopped himself in time. Heaven forbid that he adopt Lady Violet's mannerisms for his own. "You know the way he puts back his head so that he can look down his nose at people? And the way he pinches his mouth disdainfully? It would be that, but angry."

"Yes, that's it exactly!" Lady Violet gave a delighted laugh, and Perry realized that she hadn't questioned him because she'd doubted him; she'd been curious.

"I'm better than everyone else," Lady Violet announced, in a deep, pompous voice. If she was trying to mimic Saintbridge Abbishaw, she was doing a dreadful job. "I'm more virtuous than you and you and you." She returned to her normal voice: "Except that he's not more virtuous. Not if he's stealing his father's clocks." There came a thoughtful pause, and then, "I would have sworn he'd be the last person to steal . . ."

Perry would have sworn it, too.

The alleyway ended. He crossed a street, turned a corner, found another alley.

"Spite," Lady Violet announced above him. "He's angry at his father, so he's punishing him."

"I don't think so. Spite is . . . gleeful? He didn't look gleeful. And what does Saintbridge have to be angry at his father for? I can imagine Giles being angry, but not Saintbridge."

"True. Abbishaw has always favored Saint above the others." She gave a disparaging sniff. "Awful man!"

"A lot of noble families do that," Perry said neutrally.

"Well, they ought not to! They should be like the Duke of Linwood, treating all his sons the same."

Perry agreed. His father had been a younger son—a least son—disregarded by his parents, looked down upon by his brother. When he'd become a father himself, he'd made certain to treat his sons equally—the same schooling, the same allowances. Not that it had made any difference. They'd all been equally penniless in the end.

"If Saint's angry, but it's not righteousness or spite, what is it?" Lady Violet asked.

Perry had no answer to that.

They parted ways while he crossed Long Acre. "Was it a hot anger or a cold anger?" Lady Violet asked again, the moment he was safely in another alleyway.

"Hot. He looked ready to burst with it, like a child about to have a tantrum."

"A tantrum," Lady Violet said musingly. "Why do children have tantrums?"

Perry halted. He should be at his desk by now, making a start on his notes, but instead he was standing in a dark, malodorous alley, answering a duke's daughter's questions while rats scuttled nearby. The astonishing thing was, he didn't mind. He didn't mind the smell, he didn't mind the rats, he didn't even mind the questions, because the questions were helping. They sent his thoughts on tangents they might not ordinarily have taken.

"Children have tantrums because they're hungry," he said. "Or tired. Or because their will has been thwarted. Because they're not allowed to do or have what they want."

"Or . . . because they have to do something they don't want to do?"

Her suggestion hung in the air for a long moment. Perry wanted to dismiss it, but he couldn't. "It's possible," he admitted. Saintbridge's rage could have been the rage of a man forced to steal against his will.

But why?

"Blackmail?" Perry said, trying the word out.

"But he's *Saint*. He'd never do anything worthy of

99

blackmail."

"Threat, then. Someone's threatening him with harm?" He shook his head as soon as he'd uttered the words. "No. It's not that. He didn't look scared."

They were both silent, both stumped. Perry started walking again.

"Will you talk with him tomorrow? Saint, I mean."

"I doubt Abbishaw will want me there for that conversation."

"But Abbishaw will tell you what Saint says, won't he? You need to know in order to close the case."

"The case closes when Abbishaw says it does. He's the one paying for it."

"But . . . that means we may never know why Saint stole the clocks!"

"Most likely not."

"But that's not fair! To do all this work and not find out *why*."

"I was hired to find out who was stealing the clocks, not why they were being stolen." But he did agree with her. He wanted to know why Saintbridge Abbishaw was making off with his father's clocks.

"It's still not fair," Lady Violet muttered. "I wish I'd chosen invisibility. Then I could be there when Abbishaw confronts Saint. Oh! My sister can do it! I'll ask her to—"

"No," Perry said.

"No," she agreed, her tone somewhat regretful. "Eaves-dropping isn't good *ton*."

He was nearly at the end of the alley, nearly at Bow Street, but Perry found his steps growing slower. He wanted to continue talking to Lady Violet. He wanted to see whether they could come up with a reason that accounted for Saintbridge's anger and his thieving.

"Do you think Abbishaw will recognize the tiepin?" Lady Violet asked.

"I'm certain of it, but I'm not sure he'll tell me whose it is."

"Why wouldn't he?"

Perry was getting better at interpreting the tone of her voice, better at interpreting *her*. She wasn't questioning because she disparaged his reasoning; she was questioning because she was curious. She was inviting him to keep talking, to share ideas.

Perry halted. "I think Saintbridge is trying to cast suspicion on someone else. If that's the case, Abbishaw won't want me to know it."

"Why not?" Lady Violet asked, and he heard curiosity, not criticism, in her voice.

"Because I think he'd rather die than admit his heir has done something so underhand." Perry shrugged, even though she couldn't see it. "But I could be wrong."

"No, I think you're right."

"I'll ask him if he recognizes the tiepin *before* I tell him where I found it—and who left it there."

Lady Violet clapped her hands together. "Brilliant!"

Perry felt a foolish blush rise in his cheeks. Fortunately, it wasn't visible in the dark. "It might not work."

"I'm sure it will! May I see the tiepin?"

"It's too dark—"

"There's a lit window up ahead. I'll take care that no one sees me. I promise!"

Perry reluctantly took the pin from his pocket. "For heaven's sake, don't drop it."

"I won't."

He held the tiepin up.

He couldn't see Lady Violet, but he could *feel* her, hovering close. His scalp tingled, but whatever it was that caused the tingling no longer interpreted her as a threat. The pins-and-needles didn't stab urgently.

Her hand bumped his hand. Her fingers slid over his fingers. She plucked the tiepin from his grasp. "I'll only be a minute."

"Don't drop it," Perry said again, stupidly, and was

unsurprised when Lady Violet didn't deign to reply.

She'd gone, but she'd left a whisper of orange blossom in the air. Perry inhaled it, and wondered when he'd come to enjoy talking with Lady Violet.

Something ran across the toe of his boot. He managed not to yelp. On the heels of that brief moment of excitement, his scalp tingled, telling him that Lady Violet had returned.

"Wintersmith? Where are you?"

"Here." He raised one arm.

Lady Violet's hand fumbled over his. Orange blossom teased his nose. He felt an urge to pluck her from the sky and kiss her.

Perry jerked his hand back and nearly dropped the tiepin. "Do you recognize it?" His voice came out sounding slightly strangled.

"No. But I'll know it if I see it again. Even if Abbishaw won't tell you whose it is, we can figure it out."

We. The case would be closed by then, but Lady Violet was still talking of "we."

Perry tucked the pin back in his pocket. He set off down the alley.

"You're meeting Abbishaw at eleven o'clock tomorrow?" Lady Violet asked.

"Yes."

"I wish I could be there. I'll have to wait until nightfall to find out what he says!" She gave a little huff of frustration.

Perry wondered when he'd begun to find those huffs rather adorable.

"Will you be at home tomorrow night? I'll come as soon as it's dark."

Perry halted again. It would be better if they didn't meet at his lodging house. Better, in fact, if they didn't meet at all. Lady Violet would agree, if she knew that he wanted to kiss her.

"Will you not be at home tomorrow?" she asked, a thread of anxiety in her voice.

"I'm not sure," Perry said. Perhaps they should meet in an

alleyway? This one, for example, with its filth and its rats and its possible footpads.

No. His room was safer than any alleyway in London. He might want to kiss Lady Violet, but he wasn't going to act on that urge. A brief conversation, she on his windowsill, himself over by the door, and then he'd send her on her way. "I'll be home tomorrow evening," he told her.

"Excellent! I'll come as soon as it's dark. Even if it rains!"

"I'll be there," Perry said. He took a step towards the mouth of the alley. "Good night."

"Good night. And good luck tomorrow!"

By the time he reached the street, Perry's scalp no longer tingled.

He looked up at the sky, vast and limitless overhead. What a strange life Lady Violet led. A double life. Pampered and protected and with servants all around, slipping free only for a few hours at night.

Did it vex her, to be so curbed and constrained during the day?

He thought it probably did. Lady Violet didn't give the impression of someone who wanted to be pampered and protected. She wanted adventure. It was why she'd shoehorned herself into his investigation.

Well, he'd give her this adventure, mild though it was.

Perry touched his pocket to make certain the tiepin was still there. He had a feeling Lord Abbishaw was going to be very displeased when he learned of tonight's events.

CHAPTER SIXTEEN

$\mathscr{A}$bbishaw was more than displeased; he was disbelieving. "Nonsense!" he snapped. "You've confused my sons. It was Giles whom you saw."

"I know what your sons look like, sir. It was Saintbridge."

"Don't be ridiculous!" Abbishaw made a sharp gesture that swept several papers off his desk. He thrust his chair back angrily and stood. "If this is the best you can do—fabrication and falsehood!—then you may consider yourself dismissed!"

"It was Saintbridge," Perry repeated. "He's taller than Giles, and his hair is fairer."

Abbishaw inhaled an irate breath.

"I saw his face quite clearly, sir."

Abbishaw's color heightened, not just his cheeks, but also the wattle under his chin. He shook a fist at Perry. The fist that was clenched around the ruby-and-pearl tiepin. "This belongs to Giles. I gave it to him myself!"

"And it was left in your clock room by Saintbridge."

"I don't believe you! If you repeat this slander to anyone, I'll see you ruined!"

Perry held on to his temper. "He may not be acting of his own volition, sir. He looked . . . unwilling." *Unwilling* wasn't an accurate description of Saintbridge's expression last night, but it served to deflect Abbishaw slightly.

"Unwilling? What the devil do you mean?"

"Perhaps he's been threatened?" He didn't mention black-mail as a possibility; it would set Abbishaw off on another rant about his heir's unimpeachable virtue.

"Threatened? By whom?"

"I suggest you discuss that with him, sir."

"Discuss it with him? I might as well accuse him of theft to his face!" Abbishaw threw the tiepin on his desk. It skittered across the polished surface and fell to the floor, where the carpet swallowed the tiny sound of its impact.

They were at an impasse, then. One that left Saintbridge blameless and Giles the target of his father's wrath—something that Perry wasn't prepared to meekly accept.

"If you can't bring yourself to believe my testimony, sir, perhaps you'd like to watch with me tomorrow night. It's possible the thief will return."

"Watch with you? From a *cupboard*?" The wattle beneath the viscount's chin proclaimed his outrage. Behind him, a man gazed down from a portrait. The man's face was broader than Abbishaw's, his nose shorter, but his upper lip curled in the same supercilious manner. He was clearly one of Abbishaw's forebears.

"Yes, sir. That way you can see for yourself who the thief is."

"I don't have to see it; I know!"

"Respectfully, sir, you do not."

Abbishaw inhaled, his nostrils flaring in umbrage.

"I doubt you'd have to wait long, sir. The thief came less than an hour after your departure."

That rider did nothing to pacify the viscount. He opened his mouth to utter what was clearly going to be an excoriating rake-down, but Perry spoke first: "Or if you wish, I can confront the thief tomorrow night. Hold him until you return home. That way there can be no mistaking who he is."

Abbishaw froze with his mouth open.

"Naturally you wish to be certain of the thief's identity before you act. A painful task, but not one that a man of your lordship's caliber would shirk." Perry spoke the words with as much deference and respect as he could muster, which wasn't much, because his opinion of the viscount was not high.

Abbishaw closed his mouth with a snap, and then opened it again to say, "You forget your place!"

"Begging your pardon, sir," Perry said stiffly.

He stood at parade rest and waited for the viscount to decide on a course of action, the most likely being that Giles Abbishaw would be accused of something he hadn't done. It took effort to keep his expression wooden. He wanted to glare at the viscount as balefully as the man was glaring at him. Abbishaw might be a nobleman, but he was a puffed-up pigeon-hearted fool, preferring to sidestep his problems rather than meet them head-on.

"I shall watch for one hour only," Abbishaw announced.

Perry blinked his astonishment.

"But if you'd managed things better last night, it wouldn't be necessary!"

Perry refrained from pointing out that he'd done exactly as the viscount had instructed. He maintained his wooden expression.

"Dismissed," Abbishaw said curtly.

Perry felt his nostrils flare, as the viscount's nostrils had flared earlier. He turned on his heel and left the man's study. Damn, but he was going to enjoy proving Abbishaw wrong tomorrow night.

If Saintbridge reprised his rôle as thief.

One of the viscount's footmen opened the front door for him. Perry marched down the steps and set off across Hanover Square. He'd wished for many things in his life, but he'd never wished for anything quite as fervently as he wished for Saintbridge Abbishaw to steal another clock while his father watched from a cupboard.

CHAPTER SEVENTEEN

*A*fter luncheon, Aster said, "I'm going to Hatchards with Daphne and Clem. Would you like to come?"

"I can't," Violet said regretfully. She needed to finish sewing her new mask. The one she'd stitched together so hastily yesterday had barely held together last night.

Half an hour later, Rhodes looked into the blue parlor. "I'm going to start making that balloon now. Would you like to help?"

"I'd love to, but I can't right now. I'll come as soon as I can!"

Rhodes came into the room and closed the door. "How did it go with your thief last night?"

"We know who he is! Wintersmith is informing the victim today, to see what he wishes to do." Violet hesitated, and then said, "I'm going to see him tonight. Wintersmith, I mean. To find out how it went."

Rhodes looked as if he'd like to tell her not to, but he said nothing.

"I shan't go the Olvestons' musicale. Can you please give them my apologies?"

"Not go?" His eyebrows drew together. "But—"

"I shouldn't be able to sit still. I want to know what happened with Wintersmith's case!"

Rhodes sighed, then said, "Very well. I'll make your apologies."

"Thank you."

He nodded and turned to leave.

"May I still help with the balloon?"

"Of course." He turned back to face her. "I'm not angry, Vi. I'm just worried."

"I shan't do anything foolish. I promise!"

Violet sewed as fast as she could, but it was almost two o'clock by the time she was done. She locked the mask away in her drawer and ran upstairs to the nursery.

The pattern Rhodes had found required thirteen panels that were called gores. Pasted together, the gores would make a balloon. In the time it had taken her to finish sewing the mask, Rhodes had copied the pattern from the encyclopedia and started tracing the shapes onto silver paper.

"But the paper's not silver," Jessamy was saying when Violet entered the room.

"It's called silver paper because silversmiths use it," Violet said, crossing to the table.

"They make silver from paper?"

"No, they use the paper to wrap their silverware." She bent to ruffle Jessamy's hair. "Are you excited to be making a balloon? I am!"

"My balloon," young Hyacinth said, watching as her father outlined another gore. The silver paper was white and as thin as chiffon, almost translucent.

"*Our* balloon," Melrose corrected her.

Hyacinth pouted. Sharing was a concept that she hadn't quite learned.

"You can each have a balloon," Rhodes said. "There's more than enough paper."

"What about Aunt Violet? Can she have one too?"

Rhodes glanced up at her.

"I should like a balloon of my own," Violet confessed.

"And you must have one, too, Papa!"

"Very well, balloons for us all."

Six balloons—one for each of them, including Aster—required a lot of gores. Violet helped Rhodes trace the shapes and together they cut them out. The children made piles, one for each balloon. By the time they'd finished, the nursery was littered with paper and the afternoon was almost over. Rhodes put down his scissors and shook out his hand. "That's enough for one day. Who'd like to play ball out in the garden?"

The nursery clock chimed from its place in the corner as he spoke. Rhodes had bought the clock especially for the children. It had cunning little waves on its face and a ship that rocked to and fro.

Violet watched the ship move and wondered if Wintersmith had discovered why Saint was stealing his father's clocks—and then she went out to play ball with the children, a happy half hour of sunshine and grass stains and laughter.

CHAPTER EIGHTEEN

*P*erry sat at his window as night fell. The setting sun painted the haze of coal smoke above London an intense, burning orange that faded slowly into gray and then black. He lit a candle, opened the book he was reading—a gothic novel from the circulating library—and waited for Lady Violet to appear.

If his scalp gave him warning, he didn't notice it. He was deep in a scene involving a dungeon and a sinister monk when something loomed at his window. He almost fell off his chair. He did drop the book.

"I beg your pardon," Lady Violet said, while he fumbled on the floor for the novel. She perched on the windowsill and removed her mask. "What happened? What did Lord Abbishaw say?"

"He didn't believe me." Perry assured himself that none of the pages were torn and put the book safely on his bed. "He thinks I mistook Giles for Saintbridge."

"But you didn't! It *was* Saint!"

"Abbishaw doesn't want it to be him. He wants it to be

Giles. The tiepin was his. Giles's. Abbishaw thinks that clinches the matter."

"It doesn't at all!"

"No."

"We must do something!"

"I've persuaded Abbishaw to watch with me tomorrow night."

Her eyes grew wide. "Watch? From the cupboard?"

"Yes. For one hour."

Lady Violet clapped her hands together. "Capital!"

"I hope Saintbridge comes."

She mulled over the implications of Saintbridge not making an appearance, and pulled a face. She shouldn't be attractive with her nose wrinkled like that and her mouth scrunched up, but she was. Very attractive—and very kissable.

Perry took a step away from the window. "I'm tempted to search Saintbridge's house," he told her. "Not just for the clocks, but for some indication why he's doing it."

"Search it? You mean, sneak in? Like a housebreaker."

"Not precisely like a housebreaker." Perry retreated to the door. "When Abbishaw hired me, he gave me permission to search his property for the clocks. He pays the lease on Saintbridge's house, so one could argue I have permission to search it, too."

"I don't think you'd win that argument," Lady Violet informed him.

"No." Perry leaned his shoulders against the door.

Why was Saintbridge stealing the clocks, and what the devil was he doing with them once he'd taken them?

If he looked for clues in the man's house, he might just find out.

"You're thinking of doing it!"

"Of course I'm not."

Lady Violet cocked her head at him. "The Olvestons' musicale is tonight. Saint will certainly be there."

Perry folded his lips together and considered the consequences of creeping into Saintbridge's house.

Lady Violet watched him, her head still cocked to one side. "What are you thinking?"

Perry was thinking that if he were discovered in Saintbridge's house, he'd lose his job at Bow Street, and not merely his temporary appointment as a Principal Officer, but his position as secretary to Sir Mortimer.

He didn't enjoy being a secretary, but it kept food in his belly and a roof over his head.

"If Saintbridge steals another clock tomorrow," he said, "while Lord Abbishaw is watching—"

"His guilt would be irrefutable and the case will be closed."

"Yes. But if he doesn't make an appearance, or if he comes after the viscount's gone—"

"Abbishaw will believe that he's right and you're wrong, and that it's Giles who's the thief." Lady Violet scowled and kicked one heel against his wall. She looked even more kissable than she had before, damn it.

"Yes."

"Do you think Saint knows about Giles's lover? Is that why he's doing this? To punish him?"

Perry shook his head. "No. If Saintbridge knew, he'd go straight to Abbishaw and have the poor devil shipped off to America. This thing with the clocks . . . it's something else."

They both pondered that statement, and then Lady Violet said, "You should look for clues in Saint's house."

Perry wanted to, but . . . consequences.

"Ten o'clock would be the perfect time. Saint will be out and most of his servants will be in bed." She leaned forward on the windowsill, her eyes shining, her lips slightly parted.

Perry's gaze caught on those lips. They really were the most tempting lips he'd ever seen. The softest, the rosiest.

There was a long moment when neither of them spoke, neither of them moved, and then Lady Violet moistened her lips.

Perry found himself mimicking that movement. He wrenched his gaze upwards, away from her mouth, and discovered that Lady Violet was staring at him. Her expression was oddly intent, oddly expectant.

She leaned a little further into the room and moistened her lips again.

Perry only just managed not to copy her. He tried not to imagine what kissing her would be like, and failed. He could almost feel her lips under his—warm, soft, eager. The imagined taste of her blossomed on his tongue.

Perry's brain jammed to a halt. He couldn't think of a single thing to say.

Lady Violet appeared to have run out of words, too. The silence between them grew until it was almost a presence in the room, taut with possibility, humming with expectancy, as if the idea of him kissing her and her kissing him was real and tangible and alive.

It was absurdly difficult to stop staring at her. Perry dragged his gaze away, shook his head to clear it, and tried to take a step back, but he was already pressed against the door. He cleared his throat and spoke in the general direction of the window. "Uh, yes, uh, ten o'clock."

Lady Violet didn't say anything.

Perry risked a glance at her. She was no longer leaning eagerly forward. Her lips weren't parted. She wore the faintest of pouts.

It was an extremely kissable pout.

He looked away again, cleared his throat again.

Another silence grew. This one was awkward, not alive and expectant. Lady Violet broke it. "So, you'll search Saint's house tonight?" Her voice sounded flat.

"I don't know." It came down to consequences. The consequences to himself. The consequences to Giles Abbishaw.

Lady Violet sniffed. "Well, if you don't, *I* shall."

His gaze snapped back to her.

"Someone has to," she said, a hint of challenge in her voice.

"No one has to," Perry corrected her. "And if anyone does, it will be me."

"It'll be easier for me to get inside."

"Easier for you to be caught, you mean." And the consequences would be dreadful. Duke's daughter or not, she'd be ruined. "I absolutely forbid it."

Her eyebrows rose. "You *forbid* it?"

Perry was aware that he'd misstepped, but he wasn't going to back down. Not on this. He crossed his arms. "Yes."

Lady Violet tossed her head. "You're not my father." She pulled her mask out of her pocket and started putting it on.

Perry uncrossed his arms. "Wait!" he said urgently. "You must promise not to search Saintbridge's house."

She lowered the mask. "Are you going to search it?"

"I don't know."

"Then I don't know whether I will or not either."

He strode to the window. "Damn it—I mean, dash it—it's too dangerous!" He wanted to reach out and shake her. He wanted to reach out and kiss her.

Their eyes caught. He saw her pupils dilate slightly. Her lips parted. She leaned towards him.

Perry hurriedly stepped back. "I forbid you to enter his house."

Lady Violet recoiled. Anger kindled on her face. "You can't tell me what to do. I'm an adult, not a child." She sprang up off the windowsill, mask clutched in one hand. In the blink of an eye, she was gone.

Perry turned away from the window and flung his arms up in exasperation. "She's the most infuriating person I've ever met!" he told his ceiling.

CHAPTER NINETEEN

Violet had no intention of sneaking into Saint Abbishaw's house. She was a Garland, and Garlands weren't voyeurs or eavesdroppers or housebreakers. They didn't poke through other people's belongings, even if those people were thieves. Although . . . she *had* looked at Freddy Stanhope's collection, and she *had* kept five illustrations, so didn't that make her someone who went through other people's belongings? And didn't it also make her a thief?

The answer to both those questions was, of course, yes.

Violet perched on a rooftop across from Saint Abbishaw's house on Conduit Street and ruminated on the unwelcome realization that she was a thief.

She couldn't undo the poking through Freddy's belongings, but she could return the five drawings. She decided to do that. Just as soon as she'd copied them.

That dilemma resolved, she settled in to wait for Saint to depart for the Olvestons' musicale. Not because she was going to sneak into his house, but because she was hoping she'd see Wintersmith do so. If Wintersmith was waiting for

Saint to depart, she couldn't spot him. He'd be tucked into the shadows somewhere, just as she was tucked into the shadows alongside a rough, warm chimney.

In the next half hour, Violet saw numerous pedestrians on the street below, most of them gentlemen heading out for an evening of entertainment, but also footmen running errands and linkboys carrying torches. A sedan chair passed by, as did several carriages, but she didn't see any Bow Street Runners. Voices drifted up, the clatter of horses' hooves, the jingle of harnesses. A breeze plucked at her mask. Every breath she inhaled carried a faint whiff of coal smoke.

The Olvestons lived in Bruton Street, barely two minutes' walk from Saint's house; therefore Violet was unsurprised to see Saint descend his stairs and set off for the musicale on foot. He didn't look like the man who'd scuttled home yesterday via the back streets, clutching a stolen clock. He was sauntering, his nose in the air, a haughty strut to his stride.

"Loathsome man," Violet muttered. She crept closer to the roof edge and watched intently for Wintersmith.

Ten minutes after Saintbridge sauntered down his front steps, an urchin scampered up them. He plied the knocker vigorously and handed a letter to the servant who answered.

Violet watched the boy run back along Conduit Street, torn between following him and waiting for Wintersmith to appear.

Had she just witnessed a blackmail note being delivered?

She hesitated, decided that she ought to follow the urchin, and sped after him. But her five-second delay had been five seconds too many. The boy had vanished.

Violet returned to her perch on the roof opposite Saintbridge's house, muttering remonstrations at herself, annoyed that she'd let a potential clue slip through her fingers.

In the next ten minutes she saw two more footmen and one more linkboy, a trio of rowdy gentlemen, another sedan chair, another carriage. No Bow Street Runners emerged from the shadows to stealthily enter Saint Abbishaw's house. Although . . . perhaps he'd slink in via the back door?

Violet sprang lightly off the roof, flew over Conduit Street, flew over Saint's house, and drifted to a halt above the back-yards and the mews.

Conduit Street was busier at its rear than at its front. Housemaids and scullery maids let themselves in and out of back doors, grooms readied a carriage for departure, and in the yard next to Saint's, someone scurried to use the outdoor privy.

Violet decided that a prudent Bow Street Runner would avoid all that bustle. She returned to her former rooftop perch, with its view of Saint's front door. But wouldn't a prudent Bow Street Runner avoid the front door, too, bathed in lamplight as it was? In fact, wouldn't a prudent Bow Street Runner avoid creeping into a nobleman's house at all? If Wintersmith were caught searching Saint's house, he'd lose his job. He might even find himself in gaol.

Wintersmith was cautious and conscientious. He might *talk* about sneaking into Saint's house, but he'd never do it.

Violet huffed out a breath. She'd just wasted an hour sitting on a roof, waiting for a Bow Street Runner who wasn't going to come. Worse than that, she'd failed to follow an urchin who might be relevant to the case.

She tried out a word she'd overheard Rhodes use once: "Bollocks."

Violet liked the sound of the *b* popping and the hiss of the *s*, so she said it again. "Bollocks."

Below her, a man came into view. He was neither slinking in the shadows like Wintersmith nor strutting like Saintbridge. His pace was strolling but purposeful. He wasn't wearing a hat, which was rather odd. Most gentlemen out for a night on the town wore hats.

The man's trajectory took him to Saint's front door. He didn't knock, just opened the door and entered as if the house were his own.

Violet stared, another *Bollocks* sitting unuttered on her tongue.

Had that been Wintersmith, walking boldly into Saint-bridge Abbishaw's house?

CHAPTER TWENTY

*P*erry closed the door quietly behind him. If there'd been a servant in the entrance hall, he would have clapped a hand to his forehead and exclaimed that he'd entered the wrong house, but the entrance hall was empty—which was his second piece of luck. His first was that the door had been unlocked.

He stood for a moment listening intently, but there were no distant voices, no half-heard rustles or footsteps. If Saintbridge's servants were engaged in their evening chores, those chores kept them busy elsewhere in the house.

Perry slipped a black halfpenny loo mask over his face, appropriated a lamp from the pier table, and swiftly reconnoitered the ground floor. He peeped into a dark parlor, a dark dining room, and a dark drawing room. None of those seemed likely places to find clues as to why Saintbridge was stealing clocks from his father.

He went to the foot of the stairs and listened. Silence met his ears.

Perry tiptoed upwards.

Saintbridge's bedroom occupied most of the next floor. Its door stood open. The bed was a grandiose four-poster with blue and silver hangings. Two tall cheval mirrors stood at angles to each other and another mirror hung over the fireplace. Beyond the bed were a lavish washstand and dressing table, and beyond that was an open door through which he glimpsed an armoire and yet another mirror. Abbishaw's dressing room.

Lamplight cast a welcoming glow over polished wood and silver thread, issuing an invitation, beckoning him inside, but Perry didn't enter. Bedrooms were frequented not just by valets but also by housemaids. In his opinion they weren't good places to hide stolen clocks. But there were two more doors on this floor. Two more possibilities.

One door opened into a servants' staircase, narrow and uncarpeted. A broom was tucked behind the door. It wanted to tip over, but Perry caught it before it could and carefully propped it back against the wall. No sound drifted up those cramped wooden stairs, but he closed the door extremely quietly.

He tiptoed to the final door, turned the handle, and found himself gazing into Abbishaw's study.

Perry stepped inside and closed the door. A desk dominated the room. It was a handsome piece of furniture, ebonized wood inlaid with mother-of-pearl.

He crossed to it.

The desktop was bare except for a silver writing set—inkwell, sand shaker, wax jack for melting sealing wax—and an unopened letter.

The letter was addressed to "Saint" Abbishaw.

The quotation marks around the word Saint looked ironic to Perry's eye, as if the writer was implying that Saintbridge wasn't saintly at all.

Perry set down the lamp and examined the letter. There was no postmark, no indication of who'd sent it, or when or why. It was sealed with a wafer, which was as interesting as the quotation marks. One used wafers when corresponding with one's social inferiors—which meant that this wafer was an insult, something intended to sting Saintbridge's pride.

Perry scrutinized the writing. It was round and looping, a little clumsy. Deliberately round? Deliberately clumsy? An attempt to disguise handwriting that Saintbridge might recognize?

The letter was feather-light, and yet heavy with clues. Irony in those quotation marks, an insult in the wafer. If it wasn't a blackmail letter, then it was something close, something that would tell him why Saintbridge had begun stealing his father's clocks.

His fingers flexed, itching to peel off the wafer and read the letter, but Saintbridge couldn't fail to notice such tampering.

Perry reluctantly put the letter back where it had lain. With any luck one of the drawers in the desk held earlier missives, already opened and brimming with clues.

The top right-hand drawer held no such letters. Instead, Perry found an ebony and silver hand mirror, an embossed silver hairbrush, and a silver comb with ivory teeth.

He stared at those items, and then glanced around the study. Belatedly, he realized that there were several mirrors in the room. Three, if he counted the mirror built into the sideboard. Four, counting the hand mirror.

Perry slid the drawer closed and investigated further. The next drawer contained half a dozen unused quills, a penknife for trimming them, a taper of sealing wax, two bottles of ink, and a letter knife, all meticulously arranged according to size. The bottom drawer held sheets of hot-pressed paper, their edges aligned with scrupulous precision.

The left-hand drawers contained, from top to bottom, letters, receipts, and a collection of visiting cards. The letters were all quite ordinary, nothing to do with clocks or blackmail or burglary. Perry carefully lined their edges up again before closing the drawer.

Next, he investigated the sideboard. Usually one found a clutter of decanters and glasses atop a sideboard, but Saintbridge's sideboard was bare except for one silver candelabrum. Perry put the lamp down beside it and opened the left-hand cupboard. It contained glasses of various sizes and shapes, arranged with military precision. The right-hand cupboard held an array of cut-glass decanters, each one perfectly aligned with its fellows.

Perry crouched and moved two of the decanters aside—and found a clock hidden behind them.

He eased the clock from its hiding place and stood to examine it in the lamplight. According to Lord Abbishaw, the clock stolen last night had been in the Egyptian style, with gilded cartouches and a scene depicting Antony and Cleopatra. What he hadn't said was that Cleopatra was wearing nothing but her headdress and that Antony had lost his toga. Nor had he said that Cleopatra was on her knees with her mouth wide open, ready to suck Antony's little red prick.

Perry set the clock on the sideboard and crouched again. He moved the rest of the decanters quietly aside, but found no more clocks.

He sat back on his heels and looked around the room. Where might letters be hidden? His gaze alighted on the bookshelf. Perhaps Saintbridge had slipped something between the pages of an account book or ledger?

A faint prickling sensation ran over Perry's scalp. He cocked his head and listened.

Footsteps reverberated in the corridor, brisk and angry. They were accompanied by a peevish voice. "Stupid bitch spilled ratafia on me. Ruined my waistcoat. First time I've worn it!"

"It might not be ruined, sir."

"Well, I'm not going to wear it again. Not after that. You may throw it away."

"Yes, sir."

"I'll change into the green and ivory. Fetch it out for me."

Perry decided it would be prudent to hide while Abbishaw was in the house. He picked up the lamp and scanned the room. Could he conceal himself behind the tall curtains?

"A letter came for me? Why didn't you say so immediately?"

Perry had no time to hide behind any curtains. He barely had time to snuff out the lamp and cram himself into the gap beside the sideboard. He crouched low as the study door opened.

Footsteps stalked across to the desk, accompanied by flickering candlelight. Perry heard a sharp hiss of breath, a tiny scratch of sound that was probably the wafer being torn, and the brisk rustle of a letter being unfolded.

Abbishaw swore, a short, ugly, and decidedly unsaintly word. On the heels of that utterance came another sound that Perry's ears recognized: paper being screwed up.

Candlelight bobbed, painting the walls with spiky shadows. Saintbridge crossed to the fireplace, crouched, held the crumpled letter to the candle flame, and set it alight. Seen in profile, he looked furious: a scowl knotted his forehead, a snarl pulled his lips back from his teeth.

Perry stayed very still in his dark corner, scarcely daring to breathe. If Saintbridge turned his head he'd see him.

Saintbridge didn't turn his head. He tossed the last burning scrap of paper into the grate and stood. Candlelight headed for the door, then paused and veered toward the sideboard. "What the devil?"

Perry could guess what had happened: Abbishaw had cast a final glance around his study—and seen the automatous clock standing out in full view.

He shifted his weight forward, preparing to leap to his feet, run down the stairs, and escape out onto the street.

Saintbridge set his candlestick down on the sideboard, reached for the clock—and saw Perry.

For the space of a heartbeat they were motionless—Abbishaw letting go of the candlestick with one hand and reaching for the clock with the other; Perry poised on the brink of motion.

Perry lunged to his feet and made for the door.

Saintbridge tackled him with a wild grab and a clash of shoulders. Their legs tangled. Perry's momentum took them to the floor with a bone-jarring thud. They rolled, wrestling for supremacy. Abbishaw's mouth was open in a shout, but no sound emerged. A tiny part of Perry's brain realized that as long as the clock was on the sideboard where servants might see it, Saintbridge wasn't going to yell for help. The rest of his brain was occupied with stopping Abbishaw ripping off the loo mask and with keeping the man's hands from around his throat.

They grappled with silent intensity, panting and snarling, jabbing with elbows and knees. Perry didn't begrudge Saintbridge his vigorous attempt to subdue him. If he'd come home to find a thief going through his belongings, he'd have flung himself at the man quite as ferociously as Abbishaw had flung himself at Perry—but that didn't mean he was going to let the man win this battle.

It did mean that he was going to try not to injure Saintbridge, though.

They rolled again, wrestling furiously, and collided with the desk. The writing set tumbled to the floor, the inkwell spilling its ink, the sand shaker spilling its sand. Abbishaw snatched up the silver wax jack and wielded it as a weapon, hammering at Perry's temple.

Perry jerked his head aside and jabbed Saintbridge's nose with an elbow, not hard enough to break it, but hard enough to make the man recoil. He heaved Abbishaw aside and scrambled to his feet, heading for the open door. Saintbridge didn't shout for his valet. He hurled himself at Perry, tackling him wildly, bringing him crashing to the floor with enough force to drive all the air from Perry's lungs. He rolled instinctively, kicking out, struggling to breathe, fending off Abbishaw's attempts to snatch the mask from his face.

They grappled and rolled, flailing across the floor—and still Perry couldn't breathe. The fact that Saintbridge was trying to wrap his hands around Perry's throat didn't help. The fury on the man's face eclipsed last night's rage. He looked savage enough to kill, but Saintbridge was a viscount's son

124

who'd never done anything more violent than gentlemanly sparring matches at Cribb's Parlour, whereas Perry had been a soldier for ten years. He might be winded, but he knew how to fight and he knew how to kill.

He could have bashed Saintbridge's head against the desk, could have broken his nose or punched him in the throat, even gouged out an eye, but Perry didn't want to injure him too badly, so he kneed him in the groin, hard enough to make Abbishaw cry out and release him, but not so hard as to destroy the family jewels.

"Sir? I've laid out your new clothes." A man stepped into the open doorway. He took the situation in with a glance. "Housebreaker!" he cried.

Perry's lungs started working again. He inhaled a great wheezing breath, rolled to his feet, and barreled for the door.

The valet put up his fists in a manner that was valiant but unscientific. "Housebreaker!" he cried again, ringingly.

Perry shoved him aside, hard enough to knock the man off his feet, but not so violently that he'd be hurt. He had no beef with the valet, other than his bad timing and his loud voice.

Heavy footsteps thundered up the main staircase. A footman with a wig and an astonished expression charged into view.

Perry veered in the opposite direction. He wrenched open the door to the servants' stairs. A broom toppled at him for the second time that evening. He caught it, slammed the door shut, and jammed the broom between the third step up and the door.

That should hold off his pursuers.

He plunged down the stairs—and caught himself at the half-landing. Soft voices were echoing upwards. Female voices. Housemaids on their way up to bed?

Knocking down a far-too-loud valet was one thing. Knocking down housemaids was something else entirely.

Perry turned and fled back up the stairs. Someone pounded on the door he'd jammed shut.

Up one flight, past what were probably guest bedrooms. Up another flight, with muffled yells and thumps filling the stairwell behind him. The stairs came to an end. Perry found himself in servants' territory, the floorboards bare, the ceiling low and sloping. His brain was in the hyper-alert state it went into whenever he was in battle, weighing up options in the blink of an eye, making decisions that would save him. Not that door—it was on the wrong side of the house—not that one either—but that one, standing a few inches ajar and with lamplight shining through the gap.

Perry set his fingertips to the door and pushed it gently open. He saw a bedchamber as small as his own, a lamp on a table, a dormer window facing out over the mews.

The room was empty.

Perry stepped inside, closed the door quietly, and crossed to the window. He wrestled with it for a few nerve-racking seconds before it grudgingly surrendered. There was a foot-wide gap between windowsill and parapet. He climbed out.

The parapet came up to his knees. Beyond it was a four-story drop into Abbishaw's backyard.

Perry tried to shut the window, but it closed even more grudgingly than it had opened. He gave up. Falling off a roof was not how he wanted to die.

He scrambled up the slate roof on hands and knees, pausing once he was above the window to let his eyes adjust to the darkness.

A clamor of voices rose from the bedchamber he'd so rudely entered, but no one emerged to follow him. Perry didn't blame them. He wouldn't have wanted to pursue a masked man on a dark rooftop either.

His eyes became accustomed to the gloom. Pitch black became gray. He could see the sloping roof, see the chimneys, see the golden glow of London's lights.

Perry peeled off his gloves for a better grip and shoved them in his pocket. He cautiously made his way up to the roof's crest. The ridge was broad enough to stand on if he dared to, but he didn't, so he crouched there, one hand flat to the slates, the other on the warm bricks of a chimney. He wished he could fly like Lady Violet, spring up into the air and cross Conduit Street in one giant leap, but he needed a more mundane route out of this predicament.

Several houses along from Saintbridge's, the roofs intersected with the mews. From there he ought to be able to find his way into the stables and down onto the street.

Perry inched his way around the chimney.

"Halt!" someone cried.

He gripped the chimney and turned to look.

A man had climbed out onto the roof. He crouched in the gap between window and parapet. Lamplight illuminated his face—and the dueling pistol he held.

Saintbridge Abbishaw.

In other circumstances, Perry would have admired the man's persistence. Right now, he damned him to perdition.

He doubted Saintbridge could see him well enough to hit, not with the lamp hindering his night vision, but a wildly aimed bullet could kill just as easily as a precisely aimed one. Perry had seen it happen more than once.

He edged his way around the chimney, keen to put it between himself and Saintbridge—and froze as a prickling sensation crawled over his scalp.

Lady Violet was nearby.

CHAPTER
TWENTY-ONE

*C*old horror swept through him. Lady Violet couldn't be here. Not while Saintbridge had a pistol in his hand.

"Go away!" Perry cried loudly.

Saintbridge fired. The bullet struck not far from Perry's face. Chips of brick went flying. One collided stingingly with his temple.

Perry flinched and almost lost his grip on the chimney. He grabbed hold more tightly. "Go away!" he cried again, shouting up at the sky.

His eyes caught movement, a dark shape skimming low over the rooftops.

"Pass me the other one," Saintbridge snapped to someone in the bedchamber.

"He has a gun!" Perry cried desperately. "Get out of here!"

Lady Violet ignored him. She suddenly doubled in size— then equally suddenly split in half. Before his brain could understand what had happened, something dark swallowed Saintbridge's crouching shape.

Saintbridge gave a muffled shout of frightened fury.

Lady Violet swooped towards Perry. She looked like a dark avenging angel, silhouetted against the night sky. "I threw a horse blanket over him. Hurry!"

Perry hesitated, torn between the urge to flee and a terrible fear that Saintbridge could plummet to his death. "He might fall!"

"He won't. He has something tied around his waist."

Perry relinquished his grip on the chimney and set off along the ridgeline on all fours. "Get out of here before he shoots again!"

Lady Violet flew closer. Her arms were spread wide to catch him if he slipped.

Perry didn't dare glare at her for fear of falling off the roof. "If you're going to stay, for God's sake get on the street side," he snapped. "He has pistols."

"You should get on the street side, too."

"It's too steep," he said, between gritted teeth.

For a moment it seemed as if Lady Violet was going to ignore his command, but then she flitted up and over the ridgeline.

Perry's eyes followed that movement and he almost lost his balance. He halted, clamping the ridgeline between his knees, gripping with hands and feet. His heartbeat thundered in his ears. He took a deep breath, blew it out, and set his focus on the chimneys ahead, not on the duke's daughter floating alongside him or the viscount's son trying to shoot him.

He set off again, moving with careful, awkward haste. It took an eternity to reach the row of tall chimneys.

"You'll be faster if I help," Lady Violet said while he carefully navigated the chimneys.

"I don't need any help." This next ridgeline was wider— wide enough to walk on if he dared. He straightened to his full height, gathering his willpower.

"He has another pistol," Lady Violet observed.

Perry glanced back between the chimney pots. Saintbridge had fought his way free of the blanket. His arm was outstretched and inhumanly long in the lamplight.

He didn't appear to be aiming in the right direction.

Perry turned his back on the man and focused on the rooftop ahead, not on the pistol behind him. He took a deep breath and fixed his gaze on the next chimney, which seemed very far away.

"Let me help," Lady Violet said.

"I don't need any help." Perry raised his arms for balance and took a careful step. Took another careful step. His gaze was fixed on the chimney ahead. He was not thinking about the street far below. He was *not*.

"I'm going to touch you," Lady Violet said quietly from behind him, and then she did, laying her fingertips lightly on his shoulder.

Perry gave a little start and lost his balance. He teetered, and as he teetered two arms slid around him from behind, a pair of hands linked firmly over his breastbone, and a chin came to rest on his right shoulder.

Perry froze in mid-teeter. He didn't have eyes in the back of his head, but he knew that Lady Violet was lying in the air behind him.

Her grip tightened, hands knotting more firmly over his sternum. "Walk. I promise I won't let you fall."

It seemed to Perry that it was a promise she couldn't make. He weighed more than she did. "I don't think—"

"Walk!"

Perry set his jaw, fixed his eyes on the chimneys again, and took a tentative step. His balance was off-kilter. That chin on his shoulder, those arms around him—they made him less steady, not more. He wobbled, tried to catch himself, wobbled more wildly.

Lady Violet's arms locked around him, as tight as a vise.

Perry stopped wobbling, but he was too tense to take a step, almost too tense to breathe. He was aware of the roof sloping steeply on either side and of the very long drop to the street.

He decided he'd prefer to navigate this ridgeline on hands

and knees. As he opened his mouth to tell Lady Violet, a shot rang out.

"Run!" she said urgently in his ear.

Perry stopped worrying about his balance and ran—if it could be called running. He lurched from side to side, almost falling with each step, held up only by Lady Violet's arms— and then, for a few seconds, he found his balance—found *their* balance—and instead of being on the verge of falling, he was on the verge of flying. The ridgeline flashed past beneath his feet.

They reached the next chimney. Perry made his way around it and set off again, more confident this time, no longer so afraid of the steeply pitched roof and the hard street four stories below. It took a few heartbeats to find that magical sense of combined balance again, but once he did running became effortless. Lady Violet propelled him upwards and forwards with each step, and when he lengthened his stride and pushed off harder with his feet, he wasn't almost airborne with each stride, he *was* airborne.

A row of chimneys loomed ahead, chest-high, separating one house from the next.

"Want to jump them?" Lady Violet asked.

"Yes!"

Perry pushed off with all his might. Together they sailed over the tall chimneypots. His feet slapped down on the next roof and he was off again, running like the wind. He found not just balance, but rhythm. A rhythm of deep, easy breathing and long, soaring strides. With rhythm came the feeling that he'd never tire, that he could do this forever. More chimneys loomed. "Jump!" Lady Violet cried, and Perry leaped right over them. A wild laugh came from his throat.

Ahead, the rooftops parted for an alleyway.

"Want to jump it?" Lady Violet said in his ear.

"Yes!" Perry stretched his legs further, pushed off harder . . . and leaped right over the alley.

He stumbled slightly when he landed. For a heartbeat

they lost their joint balance—they lurched together, wobbled together—and then balance and rhythm returned and they were off again. Perry ran harder, ran faster, came even closer to flying. From the moment one foot left the rooftop to the moment the other foot touched down, he was almost weightless. He was no longer fleeing Saintbridge's pistol, he was running for the exhilaration of almost flying. He leaped over a row of tall chimneypots, ran, leaped over another. The end of Conduit Street came closer, but he didn't want to stop, wanted to keep running. He cast prudence and caution to the wind. "Let's jump over Swallow Street!"

Lady Violet didn't tell him it was too risky, too dangerous, that he might kill himself; she simply tightened her arms until they felt like iron bands around his sternum.

Perry hurdled another chimney, pelted down the ridgeline—and leaped right over Swallow Street.

This time, when he landed, he stumbled to one knee, but he still wasn't afraid. "Again!" he cried, and pushed off the roof with both hands and a knee, propelling himself along this new ridgeline, building up speed again for a soaring leap across King Street.

He could have run forever, but once he'd cleared King Street he forced himself to slow to a jog, then a walk. They halted in the middle of the row of townhouses on Tyler Street. Perry slung one arm around a warm chimney pot, panting and laughing in equal measure.

Lady Violet released him and drifted over to lean on the other side of the chimney.

"Your arms must be just about falling off," Perry said, once he'd caught his breath. "I'm no lightweight."

"You're not as heavy as Rhodes."

Perry did a double take. "You've done this with your brother?"

"Not on rooftops—he doesn't like heights—but on summer nights we run across the lake at Manifold Park." Lady Violet paused, and then said, "I drop him in sometimes."

"I bet you do," Perry said, and then he put back his head and laughed again. He didn't think he'd ever felt so alive as he did right now. Every part of him felt energized and elated, even his fingernails, even his hair follicles.

Lady Violet laughed, too, and Perry wished they could spend the rest of the night like this, high on London's roofs. He didn't want to descend back to streets and gutters and the small, gritty problems of everyday life.

He looked around, trying to determine the best route to the ground. "I should be able to get down over there."

"Or we could stay on the rooftops," Lady Violet said.

"But your arms—"

"I'll stop if you get too heavy."

Perry considered his choices. He wanted to run across the rooftops because it was the most exhilarating thing he'd ever done in his life, but not only was it dangerous, he was in closer physical contact with a duke's daughter than any man ought to be.

A gentleman would descend to the ground at this point. So would a cautious man. But he might never get this chance again.

"Which would you prefer?" he asked. "To stay up here or—"

"Stay up here."

CHAPTER
TWENTY-TWO

*I*t wasn't much more than a mile from Tyler Street to the lane behind High Holborn where Perry lived, twenty minutes' brisk walking, but it took them over an hour to get there, partly because their route was rather circuitous, and partly because they stopped a lot. Perry had hoped to approach High Holborn from the north, but Oxford Street and Broad Street were too wide to leap across, even with Lady Violet's assistance. They had to skirt around St. Giles's Churchyard, which brought them uncomfortably close to the Seven Dials rookery. At street level, neither of them would have been safe in such a neighborhood, but on the rooftops they were. Which wasn't to say that they didn't have some alarming moments, just that those moments had nothing to do with footpads or bully boys.

The first time Perry startled pigeons into flight, it almost killed him. The panicked birds flew in all directions, buffeting him with their bodies, and for a disorienting moment, he thought he was being attacked by demons. He reared back and flung his arms over his face, and if Lady Violet had thrown her arms over her face, too, he would have plummeted to his death. Fortunately, she didn't. She held on tightly while his feet flailed for purchase. In his fright, the night was suddenly pitch black and he didn't know which direction was up and which down, let alone what was attacking them, but then the last pigeon flapped away and the world slowly righted itself. His night vision returned. Perry found his balance again, planted both feet firmly on the crest of the roof and pressed his hands over Lady Violet's, where they were knotted together over his chest. He stood there for a full minute, while his heart careened wildly.

"Do you want to climb down?" Lady Violet asked, once his breathing had steadied.

"No." But he ran more cautiously after that—fast, but not hell-for-leather fast—which was probably why they survived the second fright, when he leaped over a row of chimneys only to discover that the roof on the other side was a full story lower than its neighbors. Perry's stomach swooped up into his throat and if he hadn't lost all his breath, he would have screamed.

He landed on hands and knees, hugging the ridgeline.

"I'm sorry!" Lady Violet said, her arms crushingly tight around his chest. "I didn't see—"

"Not your fault," Perry said, his voice thin and high-pitched.

"Do you want to stop?"

Perry cleared his throat. "No." His voice sounded rather more like his own. He didn't try to stand, though. Not yet. Not while his stomach was still settling back into place and his heart was galloping as madly as a runaway horse.

Lady Violet was a barely-felt warm weight against his back, her arms around his chest, her grip strong and reassuring.

He wasn't going to fall to his death, not while she held him.

His heartbeat steadied. His breathing steadied. "I'm going to stand."

"All right." Her grip tightened fractionally.

Perry slowly stood. His balance might not be perfect on this narrow ridgeline, but *their* balance was. There was no nearby chimney for him to grab hold of, but he still felt safe—and that was something he needed to think about. When had he come to trust Lady Violet with his life? Because he did. Trust her with his life.

It needed pondering, but not now, not while he was on a roof with no chimney to hold onto.

This particular house had only three stories, but the next one had four. "Think we can climb that?" he asked.

"We can try," Lady Violet said, and then, "I won't drop you, I promise."

"I know," Perry said, and it was true: he did know.

With the help of a window ledge and a flying duke's daughter, Perry scaled the side of the next house. When he was up on the ridgeline, Lady Violet said, "Onwards?"

"Yes. But first, you need to scout ahead."

Lady Violet didn't call him a stick-in-the-mud. In fact, she didn't protest his cautiousness at all. She left him leaning against a chimney and flew ahead to survey the upcoming roofs.

They traversed London in short bursts. Lady Violet's repeated reconnaissance slowed them down, but there were no more heart-stopping falls. The running was exciting, thrilling, exhilarating—so many words he could use to describe it and none of them catching the sheer magic of it. Pelting along London's rooftops, vaulting over chimneys, leaping across streets and lanes, was more fun than anything Perry had ever done. He laughed while he ran, and he heard Lady Violet laugh, too.

Waiting for her to reconnoiter their route wasn't thrilling, but it had its own magic. He liked being up on the rooftops alone, just himself and whatever chimney he was holding onto. The London he knew was dirty and crime-ridden, an unfriendly, every-man-for-himself place. This nighttime, rooftop London was a different city entirely. From this perspective it was a place of a thousand cozy firesides, mysterious and oddly welcoming, dark but not hostile, dangerous but not threatening.

Perry liked this London.

He leaned against a chimney above New Compton Street and gazed out over the city. There was more to London than he'd thought, just as there was more to Lady Violet than he'd given her credit for. She'd proven herself to be coolheaded and courageous tonight, not to mention resourceful, fetching a horse blanket from the mews to smother Saintbridge.

A faint prickling sensation crept over his scalp. He lifted his gaze, searching the sky until he found a dark shape skimming towards him. He straightened away from the chimney.

"There are some pigeons a few roofs ahead," Lady Violet announced, gliding to a halt alongside him. "I scared them off, but they may have settled again. I'll slow down when we get there." Her arms slid around him. Her hands laced together over his sternum. Her chin settled on his shoulder. Perry caught the faint scent of orange blossom.

His brain found intimacy in what they were doing—her arms around him, her masked cheek pressed against his masked cheek. Perry gave himself a mental shake. *Do not make this into something it isn't*, he told himself sternly.

What they were doing was no more intimate than someone riding a horse, although he was uncertain whether he was the horse or whether Lady Violet was. Perhaps they were both the horse. But then which of them was the rider?

Perry took a deep breath, inhaling the mingled scents of coal smoke and orange blossom. He found his balance, released the chimney, and set off. His focus was on the ridgeline and on his feet, but now that he'd noticed Lady Violet's scent, he couldn't *un*-notice it. Nor could he un-notice the way that her chin was tucked snugly on his shoulder. He heard every breath she took, just as she undoubtedly heard each of his breaths.

It should have been distracting, but it wasn't. It made him

137

feel safer. They weren't two people right now, they were one. It didn't matter that sometimes he didn't land quite right or that sometimes his feet slipped, because Lady Violet's magic was his magic and falling wasn't possible. He was her legs and she was his wings and together they were one.

The pigeons *had* landed again. This time Perry didn't almost fall. He shielded their faces and waited, poised on the ridgeline, until the chaos of wings abated and the last bird had flapped indignantly away. Then he set off again.

All too soon they came to the narrowest point of High Holborn. He leaped over the street. Two minutes after that, he was running along the rooftops above his own lane. Perry didn't want to stop, didn't want their mad journey across London to end. He wanted to hurdle the next alleyway and keep going.

Reluctantly, he slowed. He came to a halt alongside one of the chimneys jutting up from his rooftop and took hold of it.

Lady Violet released him. "Did you leave your window open?"

"Yes," Perry said, and sighed quietly.

Perhaps Lady Violet's ears caught that sigh, or perhaps she didn't want the night to end either, for instead of offering to help him scramble down to his window, she said, "Shall we sit up here for a while?"

"Yes, let's." Perry crouched and then sat, keeping one arm slung around the chimney.

Lady Violet perched alongside him. She was little more than a dark blur, but he thought she removed her mask.

After a moment, Perry took off his mask, too. It seemed to signal the end of their journey. Exultation fizzed in his veins. He wanted to stand up and run again, and if he couldn't run, then he wanted to do something equally mad and reckless, such as throw an arm around Lady Violet's shoulders and kiss her soundly.

Which he was not going to do.

Once the notion had taken seed in his brain, though, it

was impossible to uproot. He wanted to know whether her lips were as soft as they looked. He wanted to know what she tasted like. He wanted to know whether she would slap him or kiss him back. Either response seemed equally likely. Lady Violet was a risk taker. Kissing someone on a rooftop might very well take her fancy.

But he didn't merely want to kiss her. He wanted to invite her in through his window and then indulge in some very athletic sex.

Which was not going to happen.

Perry cleared his throat. "It's getting late. You'd better go. Thank you for your help tonight."

"Did you find anything in Saint's house?"

Perry had forgotten about the letter and the clock. He had a moment of startled surprise, of startled memory. "I found one clock. And what might have been a clue. A letter." He described it to her, the quotation marks, the wafer.

"It's a blackmail letter!" Lady Violet declared.

"That's my guess."

"I think I saw it being delivered. Not long before you arrived."

"By a footman?"

"No, an urchin. I tried to follow him, but he was too fast for me—but that was a good thing perhaps, because it meant I saw you go in. I got such a fright when Saint came back! I wonder why he returned so early?"

"Someone spilled ratafia on his waistcoat."

"Oh." Lady Violet pondered this answer, then thumped one heel against the roof. "That was bad luck."

"Yes."

"But good luck that I was there and could help."

"Thank you for that," Perry said. "But you should have flown straight home. Pistols are—"

"And leave you there? Never!"

"Pistols are dangerous."

Lady Violet ignored this statement and said, "Do you

think Saint suspects I was flying when I dropped the blanket on him?"

"He'll think I had an accomplice on the roof."

"You think so?"

"I'm certain of it. Magic's the last thing he'll think of. Trust me."

"I hope you're right." Lady Violet thumped her heel softly against the roof once, twice, and then said: "At least you weren't shot!"

"At least neither of us was." Perry shuddered, still appalled by the risk she'd taken.

"I hope Saint tries to steal another clock tomorrow night. And I hope you catch him red-handed!"

Her vehemence made Perry laugh. It also made him want to kiss her, to taste her vibrancy and her passion. The urge was so strong that he actually reached out towards her.

Perry hastily retracted his hand. "It's late. You ought to go home." He released the chimney and moved sideways until he was above his window, then turned to lie belly-down over the ridgeline. He groped for the top of the dormer with his feet. It was beyond his reach.

"Wait. Let me help."

"I'm fine." He gripped the ridge with both hands and eased cautiously lower.

"Slates come lose sometimes," Lady Violet informed him imperiously. "And what would you do then?"

Plunge to his death, most likely.

Her presence was suddenly close. Very close. He smelled her scent, felt her pat his back, pat his waist—and then she took firm hold of the waistband of his breeches.

Perry slid slowly down the roof until his feet hit the cornice over his window. He shuffled sideways and slid down further, his arms at their fullest extent. His balls were being strangled in his breeches, but he was glad for Lady Violet's grip on his waistband. He had to let go of the ridgeline before his feet came to rest in the narrow gap between roof and parapet.

Perry crouched low, hands splayed over the slates, sand-wiched between Lady Violet and the roof. When he'd been sitting on the ridge, her proximity had made him want to kiss her. She was even closer now, but his brain was making an entirely different connection. Her presence at his back, her hands gripping his breeches, her breath in his ear, equated to safety. If a slate came away, if the parapet crumbled under his weight, he wouldn't fall. Probably.

Perry moved carefully sideways, aware that Lady Violet was the only thing between him and a four-story drop to the lane. He grabbed the window frame. "You can let go now."

She did.

Perry scrambled into the sanctuary of his bedroom. He blew out a gusty breath and tugged down his breeches. Blood flow returned to his balls.

The room was dark. He groped for his tinderbox and attempted to light a candle. Finally, the wick caught. Light blossomed in the room. The attic looked almost cozy. It felt like safety and home, and for the first time since he'd moved in six months ago, he was glad to be there.

He turned to the window, where Lady Violet crouched. Her expression transformed into one of horror. "You're bleeding!"

CHAPTER TWENTY-THREE

*P*erry touched his forehead and found his skin tacky with dried blood. How the devil had that happened? And then he remembered: Saintbridge's first shot striking the chimney and spraying chips of brick. "It's nothing."

"There's blood all over your face!"

He turned to peer in the little mirror propped up on his washstand and discovered that she wasn't exaggerating. He had a cut on his forehead, but also one at his temple. He stared at that second cut blankly—and remembered Saintbridge hitting him with the wax jack. Neither cut was large, but they'd both bled profusely. Rivulets of dried blood tracked over his brow, his cheeks, even his chin. How had he not noticed?

Because he'd had more important things to concentrate on—namely, running across London's rooftops without falling off.

"It's nothing," Perry said again. "It'll wash off in a trice." He fished his handkerchief from his pocket, dipped it in the ewer on the washstand, and dabbed at his forehead.

"Wait!" Lady Violet commanded, climbing in through his window. "Your hands are absolutely filthy."

Perry looked down and discovered that she was correct. His hands were black with soot and whatever else one found on rooftops. "A little dirt never hurt anyone."

Lady Violet gave an unladylike snort and proceeded to take charge. She removed her gloves, washed her hands, washed his, then sat him on the bed and meticulously cleaned the blood from his face, using every handkerchief he possessed, plus two of his neckcloths and all of the water in the ewer. "There," she said finally, subjecting both wounds to narrow-eyed scrutiny. "I don't think they need stitches."

"Of course they don't need stitches. They're just scratches." Perry reached up to finger the cut on his temple.

Lady Violet batted his hand away. "Don't touch it. You'll make it bleed again."

Her bossiness made him want to laugh—which in turn made him want to kiss her. Lady Violet didn't look as if she wanted to laugh, though. Her expression was sober as she folded the last of the bloodstained cloths, her eyebrows crimped together in something that wasn't quite a frown.

"Are you all right?" Perry asked.

Her lips quivered. Her eyes were suddenly bright with tears. "You could have been killed."

Perry had seen it happen before: heroism in the face of danger, and then afterwards the reaction, the shaking, the inadvertent tears.

"But I wasn't." He reached for her—hesitated, because he really *ought* not to touch her—then condemned propriety to perdition. She'd risked her life to rescue him. If she needed comfort, he'd damned well give it to her.

Perry took her hand and drew her to sit alongside him; then he condemned propriety even further to perdition and put his arm around her. Platonically. "You were there to stop me falling off any roofs. And as for my fight with Saintbridge, it was nothing. You would have laughed to have seen us rolling around on the floor. He hit me with a wax jack, you know."

"A wax jack?" It wasn't amusement he heard in Lady Violet's voice, but dismay.

Perry stole a glance at her. Tears sparkled like diamonds on her lashes. The tip of her nose was pink. Damn, but she was beautiful.

He looked away. "Wax jacks aren't dangerous," he informed her.

"You had blood all over your face!"

"From the merest of scratches. Now, if he'd stabbed me with a letter knife, that would have been something to worry about."

Lady Violet's shoulders tensed. "Letter knife?"

Perry realized his mistake. "There wasn't one out on the desk," he said. "It was tucked away in a drawer. Trust me when I say I was in no danger. It was a trifling scuffle, that's all."

Lady Violet was silent for a long moment; then she gave one of her huffs. The tension in her shoulders eased slightly.

"The valet was my undoing," Perry told her. "He found us and set up a loud hue and cry. I couldn't go down the main staircase, so I went up the servants' stairs instead, and out onto the roof—at which point a guardian angel flew in to save me. I'm very grateful, you know, but you must promise never to do anything like that again. It was exceedingly dangerous."

Lady Violet fixed him with a damp and indignant stare. "Of course I'd do it again. He was shooting at you!"

"He wouldn't have hit me. He couldn't see well enough."

"He might have hit you," she said, setting her chin defiantly.

Much as Perry would have liked to refute this point, she was actually correct. "He might have hit me," he conceded. "But I need you to promise that if you ever again encounter someone with a pistol, you won't go near them. Pistols are dangerous."

"I have a pistol," Lady Violet said, her chin still defiant. "Rhodes taught me how to use it. I can shoot pips from playing cards at twenty paces."

Perry opened his mouth to tell her that pistols weren't toys, and then closed it again. He chose his words with care: "Then you're obviously a very good shot. Just be careful. Please. Accidents happen."

"Of course I'm careful. Especially after what happened to poor Jasper Flint." She looked away. A shudder ran through her. "I would never shoot at a card someone else was holding! What on earth was Wilton thinking?"

"People do stupid things when they're drunk."

Lady Violet considered this statement, and nodded. Then she said, "Saint was there when it happened. Do you think that's why he's being blackmailed?"

"Saintbridge didn't shoot Flint."

"Then why is he being blackmailed?"

"I wish I knew," Perry said, and damn it, he *did* wish he knew. It was why he'd sneaked into Saintbridge's house—and that in itself was proof that people could do stupid things even when they weren't drunk.

"I hope Saint steals another clock tomorrow," Lady Violet said, with the same vehemence she'd had on the roof. "And I hope Lord Abbishaw sees him!" She kicked her heel against his bed frame as punctuation to this sentiment; then her expression faltered, becoming dismayed. "What if he *doesn't* steal a clock tomorrow because of what happened tonight? That would be worse than anything!"

"Worse than getting shot?"

She huffed. "No."

"It's possible it'll scare him off, but there's nothing we can do about it now. What's done is done."

She wrinkled her nose at him in disfavor. "You're so sensible."

"Not always," Perry said, remembering his skirmish in Saintbridge's study.

Lady Violet reflected on this answer, and then nodded. "It wasn't sensible to jump over King Street."

Perry laughed. "No. It wasn't." But it had been fun. Exhilaratingly, dangerously fun. Just thinking about it made his heart beat faster.

Their eyes caught. Perry was suddenly breathless.

He wanted to kiss Lady Violet.

He wanted to kiss her more than he'd ever wanted anything in his life.

Her eyes were no longer tear-filled, but they were still bright in the candlelight. Bright with everything that made her so unique. Her recklessness. Her passion. Her determination. Her courage.

He saw her pupils dilate. Saw her moisten her lips with the tip of her tongue.

They were breathing in time with one another. Short, shallow, anticipatory breaths.

Lady Violet's lips parted.

His own lips parted in response.

Perry jerked his gaze away. He hastily removed his arm from her shoulders. He practically leaped off the bed. "You'd best be going."

Lady Violet didn't move.

Perry backed towards the door. He risked a glance at her.

Lady Violet's face was flushed and her expression stormy. She was angry with him—furious—and he deserved that. He knew he did. They shouldn't have sat on his bed. He shouldn't have put his arm around her. And he most definitely should not have almost kissed her.

He fixed his gaze on the floor. "Good night, Lady Violet."

Lady Violet stood, but she didn't head for the window. She marched to where he stood, grabbed hold of his lapels, hauled him closer, and kissed him.

CHAPTER
TWENTY-FOUR

*P*erry tried to resist Lady Violet's kiss—for all of one second, and then he surrendered, because her mouth tasted even more intoxicating than he'd imagined, sweet and spicy, hot and wild.

Her kiss wasn't shy or demure; it was a forceful collision of lips and tongues and teeth. Perry had never been kissed so fiercely. It wasn't at all what one would expect of a duke's daughter.

Realization hit him like a bucket of ice-cold water. Perry jerked his head back. "Lady Violet," he said, trying to detach her hands from his coat. "We mustn't do this. I can't marry you!"

Lady Violet frowned and released her grip on his lapels. "I don't wish to marry you."

Perry frowned, too. "Then why did you kiss me?"

"Because I wanted to. Don't you want to?"

Perry felt himself flush. "Well, yes, but . . . but I can't marry you, so it was very wrong of me to do so." He avoided that bright accusatory gaze and stared at her left earlobe. "I must beg your forgiveness."

In his peripheral vision he saw her cross her arms. "Do you feel obliged to marry every woman you kiss?"

"Of course not," he told her earlobe.

"Then why must you propose marriage to me if we kiss?"

His gaze jumped to her face. "Because you're a duke's daughter!"

Her lips pursed and her eyebrows drew together. "So if I were a flower seller, you'd kiss me and *not* propose marriage?"

It didn't sound very honorable, phrased like that. Perry crossed his own arms. "I don't want to kiss any flower sellers."

"Some of them are very pretty."

"That's not the point. The point is that you're a duke's daughter and I'm a penniless nothing. You shouldn't be in this room, let alone kiss me!"

Lady Violet uncrossed her arms and put her hands on her hips. "You're not a nothing. And if I *want* to be in this room and if I *want* to kiss you, then I don't see any reason why I shouldn't!"

"Your reputation—"

She made a dismissive sound. "No one's going to find out."

"They could."

"How? Are you going to tell someone?"

"Of course not," Perry said, affronted.

"And *I'm* not going to tell anyone, so unless there's someone else in London who can fly up to peek in this window, no one will ever know." She lifted her chin at him, challengingly. "Will they?"

"No, but—"

"I want to kiss you and you want to kiss me, and I don't see why we shouldn't do it."

"Because I'm—"

"Don't say you're a nothing, because you know that's not true! You're a viscount's nephew *and* an officer *and* a Bow Street Runner—and all of those things mean that you're a very respectable person!"

"Principal Officer," Perry corrected her. "And I'm not

respectable at all. Look where I live!" His gesture encompassed the flaking whitewash, the water stains, the scuffed floorboards.

Lady Violet glanced around the room. Her shoulders lifted in a shrug. "It is a little shabby, but who cares?"

"*I* care. You shouldn't be here!"

Her head tipped to one side. She looked him up and down, a swift head-to-toe survey. "You are *very* respectable, aren't you?" She smiled at him, an expression that was as wild and brilliant as it was unexpected. "It's one of the reasons you should kiss me."

Perry was transfixed by that dazzling smile . . . and then his brain caught up with his ears. "I beg your pardon?"

"You're very honorable. You'd never try to ravish me, would you? Or trap me into marriage."

"Of course not!"

"Which is why we should kiss," Lady Violet said, in the manner of someone stating an irrefutable truth.

"No, it's not."

"Of course, it is. You're the safest person in London for me to kiss."

"The safest person for you to kiss is *no one.*"

It sounded pompous even to his own ears, so he was unsurprised when Lady Violet rolled her eyes in response. "Well, I don't want to kiss *no one.* I want to kiss you, and you want to kiss me—and I don't see why we're arguing about it. Where's the harm in a kiss?"

"There's a great deal of harm in it."

"If you were someone else, yes. But you're you. You're respectable and honorable and *safe.*"

In different circumstances, he could imagine her flinging those words at him as pejoratives. Right now, though, it was clear that she meant them as compliments. She truly did think he was respectable and honorable, and that both of those things made him a safe person to kiss.

Perry wasn't certain that Lady Violet's reasoning was

sound, but he was gratified that she trusted him so much.

"Please?" She stepped closer and took hold of his lapels again and tilted her face invitingly.

Perry stood immobile, torn between the urge to kiss her and the knowledge that he shouldn't. No such dilemma immobilized Lady Violet. She stood up on tiptoe and pressed her lips to his—and there was only one response he could make to that: he kissed her back.

He *was* the safest person for her to kiss, damn it. If Lady Violet was going to kiss anyone, it would be *him*. And if he was going to be the person kissing her, then he was going to give her the best damned kiss she'd ever have. Which wasn't going to happen while she was standing on tiptoe.

Perry broke the kiss.

Lady Violet inhaled an indignant breath—which turned into a squeak as he swept her up in his arms. Perry crossed to the bed and set her gently on it. "Kneel," he said.

She did, rising up on her knees. Now they were eye to eye. The perfect height for kissing. Lady Violet took hold of his lapels again and tugged him closer. "Much better," she whispered against his mouth.

Perry set his hands at her waist and kissed her—lips, tongues, teeth—a deep and intimate clash of mouths.

He was panting when they paused to catch their breaths—at which point he discovered that his hands were no longer decorously at her waist. Without realizing it, he'd wrapped his arms around her and hauled her close.

He eased his grip, trying to put some space between their bodies, but Lady Violet was having none of it. She put his hands back exactly where they had been, then slid her arms around his neck again. "More."

Perry reasoned that the best kisses did require a certain proximity, so instead of arguing with her, he gave her what she wanted: more heated, heady, fierce, urgent kisses.

"Don't stop," Lady Violet said, the next time they paused for breath.

He felt the softness of her breasts pressed against his chest, felt the curve of her buttocks under his hands, but he didn't try to pull away this time.

"Don't stop," she repeated.

It wasn't a request; it was a command. A command that Perry was happy to obey. He lost himself in another kiss, a kiss that was deep and forceful, intoxicating, carnal.

He was dizzy by the time he drew back. Dizzy from lack of breath. Dizzy with lust. He dragged air into his lungs and tried to think past the hot, imperative pulse of blood in his veins. He loosened his hold on her. "I think we should stop."

"I don't," Lady Violet said, and she tightened her arms around his neck and tipped over backwards on the bed.

Perry, perforce, went with her. He barely managed to fling out his hands and stop himself from crushing her. "Lady Violet—"

She didn't relinquish her tight hold on his neck. She laughed up at him, her eyes alight with mischief. "Kiss me," she demanded.

He wanted to, with every fiber of his being, but being on the bed with her like this was dangerous. It was too much like sex. He didn't think he could lie on top of her and kiss her without rutting against her—which he was *not* going to do.

When she raised her head and pressed her lips to his, it was impossible not to kiss her back, but Perry retained enough self-preservation to scoop one arm under her and roll them both sideways before the kiss grew too deep.

They lay like that for several minutes, side by side on the bed, devouring each other's mouths in a kiss that was dangerous and perfect, yielding and bold. Perry didn't want it to end, but finally the moment came when it did. Their lips clung together, and then parted. They lay inches from one another, panting, staring into each other's eyes. Her breath was his breath. Her heat was his heat.

It took him several seconds to realize that their legs had become entwined and that his cock was plump in his breeches.

There was a line between kissing and sexual congress and they were perilously close to it.

"More," Lady Violet whispered huskily.

There was nothing in the world that Perry wanted more than to give her what they were both craving. "No," he said, untangling their legs.

Lady Violet tried to kiss him again, but Perry placed a hand between them, holding her off.

She recoiled as if he'd slapped her. Emotions flickered across her face: surprise, hurt, umbrage.

"You chose me because I'm safe, remember? Well, if we kiss any more, it'll stop being safe."

Lady Violet regarded him silently. Her frown faded. Her perusal became thoughtful, not angry. "You *are* safe. Thank you, Periander." She gave him a startlingly sweet smile, reached out and touched his cheek, a swift and tender brush of fingertips, then hopped off the bed. Two quick steps and she was gone, flitting through the open window like a bird taking flight.

Perry blinked at his suddenly empty room. He sat up slowly. He felt disoriented, a little dizzy.

A dark figure settled on the parapet outside his window. Lady Violet. She crouched and looked at him. Candlelight softly touched her face. She looked luminous, otherworldly, beautiful. "Good night."

Perry cleared his throat, but his voice was still husky: "Good night."

CHAPTER
TWENTY-FIVE

*V*iolet's first task of the day was to speak with Rhodes. She traced him up to the nursery, where he'd eaten breakfast with the children, then down to the mews. He'd gone for a canter in Hyde Park. Usually, he read the newspapers after that, so she retreated to the library.

She didn't have to wait long. "Good morning," her brother said, entering the room. He looked rather windswept, his cheeks pink with color.

"Good morning. Do you have a moment? I'd like to tell you about last night."

"Something happened?"

"Yes."

Rhodes sat in his usual armchair, with the newspapers laid out on the table alongside. "Tell me."

"Wintersmith searched the thief's house and he came home early—the thief, that is—and almost caught him. He had to escape via the roof. I was afraid he'd fall off, so I helped him."

"I take it he got down all right?"

"Yes."

Violet decided not to tell him that Wintersmith had run across London's rooftops for more than a mile before climbing down. As Wintersmith had said last night, what was done was done.

She wasn't going to tell her brother about the kiss, either—that was private, between Wintersmith and herself—but she knew Rhodes would want to know about the pistols. "The thief fired at Wintersmith while he was on the roof."

Rhodes had been reaching for the newspapers. He halted, hand outstretched. He looked thunderstruck. "Those shots were at Wintersmith?"

"You heard them?"

"I heard about them."

Violet leaned forward. "What did you hear?"

"That shots were fired from a rooftop in Conduit Street."

"Did anyone mention a housebreaker?"

"No. I heard it was someone trying to shoot a pigeon off a chimney pot."

"A pigeon?" Violet considered that information. It sounded as if Saint was attempting to keep last night's events a secret.

She didn't think he'd succeed. His servants knew there'd been an intruder in the house and that Saint had fired upon him. It was too exciting a tale not to spread.

Unless Saint paid them not to.

Rhodes was observing her, narrowed-eyed. "Who fired at Wintersmith? Whose house was it?"

Violet chewed on her lip briefly. "I don't think I can tell you. Who was it who said someone was shooting at pigeons?"

"I don't know. Does it matter?"

"It might."

Rhodes knitted his eyebrows together while he thought, then shook his head. "I heard the story from half a dozen people over supper. You know how these things spread."

Violet wanted to ask whether Saint had returned to the musicale, but she didn't dare. Instead, she said, "Who stayed to supper at the Olvestons? Were any of them residents of Conduit Street?"

"Several. Let me see . . . The Beebys were at supper, and Colonel Colthorp. Saintbridge. The Van Diemens. Molyneux." Rhodes cocked his head at her. "Was it one of their houses?"

"Yes, but I can't tell you which one."

Violet tapped her chin with a fingertip. How intriguing. Saint hadn't called for a watchman or the foot patrol. He'd returned to the musicale and stayed for supper, starting a rumor that someone had been shooting at pigeons.

What did that mean for Wintersmith's case? Was Saint more or less likely to steal another clock from his father?

Rhodes frowned. "I don't like this, Vi. It sounds dangerous."

"Last night was a little dangerous," she admitted. "But Wintersmith was all right."

"I'm not worried about him! I'm worried about you. If someone was firing pistols—"

"That won't happen again. The case is almost over. Wintersmith won't be searching any more houses, so there'll be no more pistols and no more escapes over roofs."

Rhodes looked unconvinced. "How do you know the case is almost over?"

"Because the victim has decided who he wants the thief to be—but he's picked the wrong person."

Her brother's eyebrows rose.

"Tonight will be the last night. Wintersmith's going to watch for the thief. I hope he comes, because otherwise the wrong person will be blamed!"

"Watch for a thief? That sounds rather dangerous."

"It's not," she hastened to assure him. "Wintersmith will be hiding in a cupboard. No one will shoot any pistols."

"I take it you intend to speak with him afterwards? Find out how it went?"

"Yes, but I'll watch the house, too."

Rhodes frowned. "Watch it?"

"To see whether the thief comes."

Her brother's frown deepened.

"It'll be quite safe. I'll be high above the square."

"Which square?"

Violet hesitated, decided there was no harm in telling him, and said, "Hanover."

Rhodes rubbed his forehead. Was he thinking how safe Hanover Square was? How unlikely it was that anyone would fire a pistol there?

"It's no different to what I normally do," Violet pointed out. "I fly above London and watch people. I've been doing it for years now."

Rhodes rubbed his forehead again, and then sighed. "I'll make your apologies to the Heriots tonight. But for heaven's sake, be careful. Keep your distance."

"I will." Violet rose to her feet, crossed to where he sat, and dropped a kiss on his cheek. "I promise I'll be careful."

Rhodes picked up the topmost newspaper. "Want to help me with the balloons after lunch? There'll be a lot of pasting."

There was indeed a lot of pasting. More pasting than could be done in one afternoon, or even two. As tended to happen when paste and children were in close proximity, the paste found its way onto more things than just brushes and strips of silver paper. The children required a wash and change of clothing afterwards. Violet did, too. She had paste under her fingernails and on her gown and she even had paste in her hair.

By the time she was clean, it was almost time for the Grand Strut in Hyde Park, but Violet didn't change into her promenade dress and her new bonnet with the cluster of cherries on it. Instead, she ordered a pot of tea sent up to her room. While she had Freddy Stanhope's illustrations tucked away in her drawer, she was a thief, and she'd prefer not to be a thief after tonight.

She locked her door and sat at the escritoire with a sketchbook and some pencils and Freddy's drawings. Violet poured herself a cup of tea and sipped it. She examined the topmost drawing. It showed two performers at a fair, a man and a woman, neither of whom wore many clothes. The man's appendage stretched out in front of him, as long as an arm. Balanced on its tip was a candelabrum.

The candelabrum, Violet dismissed as an absurdity. She wanted to dismiss the appendage as absurd, too. No man could possibly possess one that long. Could he?

But the woman's pudendum was to scale and her breasts were of modest size, so perhaps appendages did grow that long?

It was a question Violet wanted to know the answer to, but she didn't know who to ask. Definitely not Rhodes. Dare she ask Primrose when she returned from Brighton?

She decided she probably did dare ask her sister.

Violet copied the drawing and set it to one side.

Next was an illustration that bore the title "Feats of Horsemanship." In it, a man and a woman were astride a galloping horse. The woman's dress was up around her waist and the man's breeches were open. They were engaged in the act of copulation.

Was it possible to do that on horseback? It looked rather precarious.

Violet copied that drawing, too, and put it aside to ask Primrose.

The next illustration was titled "The Merry Whipster" and featured another couple—or possibly the same couple. They were in a curricle. The woman was driving, reins in one hand, whip in the other, while the man knelt on the footboards and plied his appendage energetically between her legs. The lady's ankles were crossed around his waist and she waved the whip in a most jolly manner.

Violet doubted that anyone could drive a curricle while being the subject of energetic amorous attention, but perhaps it was possible?

She copied the illustration, then poured herself another cup of tea.

Those three drawings comprised one part of her little hoard. Presumably Freddy Stanhope had purchased them because he found them titillating. Violet didn't find them titillating; she found them perplexing. Was she naïve to think that the scenarios were implausible, or naïve to think that they weren't?

The last two illustrations she'd kept were different.

Violet laid them side by side on the escritoire. These scenes weren't implausible or ridiculous; they were realistic. Two parlors, two sofas, two couples engaged in lovemaking.

In one, the man was uppermost. In the other, the woman was.

These drawings were titillating. A whisper of heat unfurled beneath her skin when she looked at them—and with the heat came longing.

She wanted to be those women, and she especially wanted to be the woman in the right-hand drawing, not only because she was uppermost, but because the lovers were laughing while they kissed.

Violet stared at the illustration. She had a burning desire to be kissed like that, to be made love to like that.

Would her kiss with Wintersmith have turned into some-thing like this if he hadn't called a halt?

She rather thought it might have—which ought to have horrified her, but didn't. Instead, she felt a pang of regret.

Violet sipped her tea thoughtfully.

She'd been kissed before, three times. Swift, silly kisses. Throwaway kisses. Pecks on the mouth that were meaningless and forgettable. Last night's kiss had definitely not been for-gettable, and Periander Wintersmith was also not forgettable.

He hadn't been stuffy or stick-in-the-muddish. Not

before their kiss, when he'd been running along the rooftops, and definitely not afterwards. He'd looked disheveled and disreputable and dangerous after they'd kissed. Deliciously dangerous, with his hot, bright eyes and his bare throat and that hectic flush in his cheeks.

Violet set her cup back in its saucer and studied the right-hand illustration. What if Wintersmith were the man reclining on the sofa and she was the woman on top of him?

She felt a tingling rush of heat, as if blood surged through her body and reached every one of her extremities. The sensation was imperative and carnal.

Violet rather liked it. It was almost as exciting as flying.

She sharpened her pencils with a penknife and bent her attention to copying the two illustrations, and as she copied them she came to several conclusions.

One: that she apparently liked Wintersmith rather more than she'd realized.

Two: that she wanted to experience the sort of lovemaking the two drawings depicted.

Three: she wanted to experience it with Wintersmith.

But wanting and doing were two very different things. She wanted to fly in daylight, but she didn't, because it would bring ruin upon her family.

Being caught having an affair would be almost as bad, but she'd kept her flying secret for two years. If she could do that, surely she could keep an affair secret too?

Violet sketched in the last of the details—a chair leg, a footstool, the buckle on a shoe—and once she'd done that she went to her dresser and unlocked the bottom drawer. Buried underneath her black clothing was a little jewelry box. She fished it out. Inside the box was a golden charm on a chain. The charm was a clover leaf, pretty and simple and imbued with magic, one of a dozen such charms handed down from mother to daughter to granddaughter, protection not against ill health or ill luck, but against pregnancy.

As Faerie wishes went, it was one of the more unusual ones

Violet's ancestresses had chosen, but the woman who'd made that particular wish had been blessed with six children by the age of twenty-three. She'd wanted to choose whether she had any more, and the charms she'd gifted to her descendants had allowed them to choose, too.

Violet had received her charm on her twenty-first birthday. There were a great many things her mother could have said when she'd handed it over, stipulations and conditions and provisos, but all she'd said was, "Use it wisely."

The gift hadn't been encouragement towards licentious behavior—Violet was a Garland, and Garlands did *not* engage in licentious behavior—but it had been tacit permission to walk her own path. Discreetly. Or at least that was how she'd interpreted it.

Violet was *almost* certain that her mother had tiptoed down that path before her marriage. Not after it, of course—the Duke and Duchess of Sevenash only had eyes for each other—but hadn't the gift been her mother's way of saying *I needed this when I was your age, so perhaps you'll need it too*?

Violet returned to her escritoire. Drawings lay spread across it. Freddy's illustrations, her copies.

She didn't want to *look* at drawings of women with their lovers; she wanted to *be* one of those women. She wanted to experience the thrill of making love, the excitement, the intimacy.

And she wanted to experience it with Periander Wintersmith.

She'd called him a stick-in-the-mud, but he wasn't. Nor was he stuffy and staid and boring.

He wasn't a prude either.

But he *was* safe, and he was the man she wanted to walk down this path with.

If he was willing.

CHAPTER
TWENTY-SIX

*P*erry strode along King Street on his way to Hanover Square. His gaze was drawn upwards. He looked from one side of the street to the other, gauging the distance between those lofty rooftops. Had he really run along that ridgeline? Dared to make that leap?

It was so far beyond belief that his mind couldn't comprehend it. No one could possibly make that jump and survive—and yet he knew he had, fueled by recklessness, euphoria, and magic.

He turned into Conduit Street, glancing up at the high, steep roofs—and remembered the moment when Saintbridge had fired his pistol. Being shot at seemed insignificant compared to what had happened afterwards. The rooftop run. Kissing Lady Violet.

Perry made an impatient sound and shook his head sharply—as if shaking his head could shake that kiss from his memory. It didn't work. It hadn't worked all day.

He strode past Saintbridge's house, turned into George Street, and forced himself to think about clocks.

Saintbridge knew that someone had been in his house. He knew one of the stolen clocks had been discovered. He'd be wary, on edge, more than a little suspicious—and he definitely wouldn't steal another clock tonight. No one with an ounce of sense would. Which meant that lying in wait for him was a fool's errand. It would serve no purpose except to enrage Lord Abbishaw.

Hanover Square opened out before him. Prominent on one corner was Abbishaw House. Dusk was closing in. The lamplighters were at work with ladders and wick trimmers and oil.

Perry's pace slowed. Damnation. He really shouldn't have searched Saintbridge's house. Not only had he put the wind up the man, he'd failed to find anything to deflect suspicion from Giles Abbishaw—and now he was going to have to endure an hour in a cupboard with a displeased viscount, followed by wrath heaped upon his head when no one came to steal a clock.

Given that he'd known he ought not enter Saintbridge's house, it was no less than he deserved. But Giles Abbishaw didn't deserve the fate that was in store for him.

Perry squared his shoulders. He might not be able to prove Giles's innocence tonight, but he *would* prove it, regardless of whether Lord Abbishaw declared the case closed or not. He was damned if he was going to let Saintbridge get away with his deceit and his spite.

He strode across Hanover Square, up the steps to Abbishaw House, and rapped on the door. Two minutes later, he was in Lord Abbishaw's study, trying to convince the viscount that there was no need for them both to keep watch.

But Abbishaw was as obstinate as he was proud. He'd decided he was going to sit in the cupboard to prove Perry wrong, and nothing would sway him from that course. "A pointless exercise," he said, while he supervised the placement of the chair he'd chosen. "Completely unnecessary. I shall complain to Sir Mortimer about your incompetence when this is over, mark my words! Not there, you dolt. There."

Perry maintained a wooden countenance, obeyed that peremptory finger, and moved the chair two inches sideways.

The clocks in the room began proclaiming the half hour. Shortly after that hubbub died away, the Abbishaw carriage drew up at the front door, ready to convey the viscount to his club. Tonight, it was empty when it departed, setting out across the dusky square with a *clip-clop* of hooves and brisk jingle of harnesses.

In less than a minute, it would pass Saintbridge's house on Conduit Street.

The butler closed the front door. He must have been wildly curious, but his expression was as wooden as Perry's. "Sir?" he enquired of his employer.

Abbishaw waved a hand in curt dismissal. "Out of my sight."

The butler and two footmen hastily retreated.

Lord Abbishaw marched into his clock room and halted at the cupboard. He sneered at the doorknob.

Perry gritted his teeth and opened the door for him.

Abbishaw sniffed and pushed past and lowered his bottom onto the chair he'd chosen, a giltwood armchair with a plump upholstered seat. He fussed for almost half a minute, crossing first one leg and then the other. "Well?" he said, when he'd finally settled. "What are you waiting for? Put out the candles." He shot Perry a glance filled with triumph and malice—a glance that told Perry he wasn't just going to end his stint as a Principal Officer in ignominy, he was probably going to lose his job as a secretary, too.

Perry closed the door all but a crack and snuffed the candles in the candelabrum. Fuck. Why had he crept into Saintbridge's house last night?

Because he was an idiot, that's why.

He regretted that decision, but he couldn't find it in himself to regret the mad run across London's rooftops. Or the kisses that had followed.

Those were the sorts of memories that lit up one's life. He would remember that rooftop run until he died, and he'd remember the kisses, too, and if he lost his position with Sir Mortimer, then damn it, it had been worth it. He could always rejoin his regiment. He'd much rather be a soldier than a secretary, anyway.

His heart lightened at the thought of returning to his regiment. A soldier's life was bedbugs and saddle sores and lice, hardship and boredom, danger and death—but it was also camaraderie and the friendship of men who didn't care whether one barely had two pennies to rub together. It was fellowship and brotherhood and belonging.

He missed it. Even the saddle sores. Even the boredom.

Lord Abbishaw was a noisy breather. His nose whistled with every exhalation. Perry listened to that noise and wondered how soon he could be back in India. He couldn't leave London immediately, not even if Sir Mortimer tossed him out on his ear. He needed to prove Giles's innocence and Saintbridge's guilt, if not to the world at large, then at least to the sanctimonious nose-whistler sitting beside him.

It would be difficult to solve the case without the authority the tipstaff gave him, but by hedge or by stile he'd do it. He was damned if he'd let Giles Abbishaw be branded a thief. With Lady Violet's help, he'd expose Saintbridge for what he was. He was certain they could do it. Together, they were practically invincible.

His thoughts veered sideways. To Lady Violet. To that run, those kiss.

Perry went through the rooftop journey in his head, from his mad scramble out of Saintbridge's window to his much more sedate scramble in through his own, remembering every street he'd leaped over, every lane, every alleyway, remembering, too, the times he'd almost fallen.

He remembered Lady Violet's orange blossom scent. And the smell of blood when she'd bathed his face. He remembered her tear-shiny eyes. He remembered her grabbing his lapels and pulling him into a kiss.

The door to the clock room opened. Perry gave a convulsive start. Beside him, Lord Abbishaw uttered a whistling snort. "Wha—"

"Shhh," Perry hissed.

Faint lamplight leaked into the cupboard. Perry angled his head to see better through the gap between door and frame. Someone came into view.

Saintbridge Abbishaw.

Perry stared in utter disbelief. Saintbridge didn't look insane, but he had to be. No one but a lunatic would steal another clock after last night's events.

Unless Saintbridge was returning the clocks he'd stolen?

Perry plucked at Lord Abbishaw's sleeve. The viscount rose from his chair and peered through the gap, elbowing Perry in the stomach as he did so.

Perry crammed himself back against the shelves and stood on tiptoe to see over Abbishaw's head. Saintbridge's back was to them as he unlocked the cabinet, but not even the viscount could mistake him for Giles. He was too tall, too narrow-shouldered, the hair visible beneath the brim of his hat too blond.

Saintbridge turned and crouched and shoved a clock into the valise at his feet. His face was plainly visible.

The viscount gasped. Saintbridge didn't hear that tiny sound. He closed the valise and stood. In place of his habitual sneer was a scowl. He dug something from his pocket and cast it on the floor. Undoubtedly another piece of evidence to incriminate his brother.

Perry reached past the viscount to push the cupboard door open—but Abbishaw caught his arm.

Saintbridge locked the cabinet, picked up the valise and lamp, and headed for the door.

Perry tried to shove the cupboard door open, but Abbishaw clutched his arm more tightly. "No."

The door to the corridor closed. The clock room plunged into darkness. Saintbridge was gone.

After a moment, the viscount eased his grip on Perry's arm. His breath was hoarse, wheezing.

"Sir?"

Abbishaw's hand shook where it lay on Perry's arm.

"I think you should sit, sir." He groped for the chair, found it, helped the viscount to sit. "I'll fetch some light."

The corridor was empty. Perry heard no furtive footsteps; Saintbridge would be halfway across the square by now.

He took a candle from a sconce and returned to the cupboard in the clock room. The candle illuminated the containers of wax and oil, the cloths, the keys on their hooks. It illuminated Abbishaw's face, too. He was pasty white. He fumbled a handkerchief from his pocket and pressed it to his mouth. He didn't look pompous and starched-up; he looked like a man who'd suffered a profound shock.

The candelabrum sat on one of the shelves. Perry lit the three candles and decided to give the viscount a moment to recover his composure. He crossed to the cabinet and scoured the floor, looking for whatever it was that Saintbridge had dropped. He found a cuff link, agate set in silver.

Perry picked it up and brought it to the viscount. "Do you recognize this, sir?"

Abbishaw lowered his handkerchief. He took the cuff link with trembling fingers.

"Do you recognize it?" Perry asked again.

"It belongs to my son Giles." The cuff link slipped through his fingers, rolled off his silk-clad knee, and fell to the floor.

Perry bent to pick it up. "Are you all right, sir?"

It was a stupid question; the man was wheezing again, clearly struggling for breath.

"I'll fetch someone for you."

It was like knocking over an ants' nest; one moment the house was silent, the servants below stairs—the next, people ran in all directions. Lord Abbishaw was tenderly helped to his bedchamber by the butler, three footmen, and his valet, while housemaids turned back his bedcovers and chased after hartshorn and lavender water. "Don't go," the viscount commanded querulously, so Perry cooled his heels in the library for almost an hour.

Finally, a footman came to fetch him. Perry was admitted to Abbishaw's bedchamber by his valet. The man's expression was somber, his footsteps hushed as he trod across the carpet, his manner as funereal as if the viscount lay at death's door, but Abbishaw's cheeks weren't as pale as they'd been and he was no longer wheezing.

"Leave us," Abbishaw told his valet. He waited until the door had closed, then said, "I forbid you to arrest my son. Do you hear me? I forbid it!"

It was Abbishaw's right, as victim of this crime, to decide whether or not to proceed with an arrest. Perry might not like it, but there was nothing he could do about it. "Yes, sir. I understand."

He waited for the viscount to tell him that the case was now closed, but no such announcement came. Instead, Abbishaw fretfully said, "Go away. Tell my valet I want him."

Perry obeyed both those commands.

The ants' nest had settled. He had to summon a footman to unlock the front door and let him out into the square. Perry paused on the flagway and looked up at the dark sky, waiting for pins-and-needles to prickle over his scalp, announcing Lady Violet's presence.

They didn't come.

CHAPTER
TWENTY-SEVEN

*V*iolet fastened the necklace and tucked the charm inside her shirt. It wasn't the only thing tucked inside her shirt tonight. Freddy Stanhope's drawings were there, too, hopefully not getting too creased.

She wound the black neckcloth around her throat, shoved the ends down the front of her coat, and checked the sky. Almost fully dark.

Ten minutes later, Violet slipped out of her window. She flew over St. James's Square, over Piccadilly, and swooped down to land on a roof high above Hanover Square.

She leaned against a chimney and waited to see whether Saint Abbishaw would creep into his father's house, but what she saw instead was him slipping out through a side door. He hurried across the square, a valise clasped to his chest.

Violet waited for Wintersmith to emerge, too, but the door remained firmly closed.

Saint vanished into Pollen Street.

Violet abandoned her perch on the roof and sped after him. She expected him to take the same indirect route home that he'd taken two nights ago, but instead he hastened to the hackney stand in Swallow Street and climbed into a carriage.

Violet glanced back at Hanover Square, hoping Wintersmith had appeared. He hadn't.

Saint's hackney made its way down Swallow Street and onto Piccadilly. Violet glided in its wake, high above the rooftops. Where was Saint taking the clock? To a co-conspirator? A blackmailer? A *chère-amie*? Was he going out of London? Perhaps even as far as Richmond?

But the hackney turned left at the next corner and then left again, into Jermyn Street. It halted in front of St. James's Church.

Saint paid off the jarvey, peered furtively around, and scurried into the church, the valise tucked under his arm.

St. James's Church had a lofty nave, with galleries on three sides and windows all around. Violet wondered whether she dared look in those windows.

The hackney was in motion again, trotting away. Jermyn Street was quiet and dark.

Violet glanced left, glanced right, and decided that she did dare look into the church. She flitted across to one tall window and cupped her hands against the glass, trying to see where Saint was and what he was doing, but the church was poorly lit and the gallery she was looking down on was deep in shadow.

She muttered a forbidden word and tried the next window, with similar lack of success. Where the devil were Bow Street Runners when one needed them? If Wintersmith were here, he could creep inside the church and see what Saint was doing.

She was halfway through muttering "Damnation" again when she spotted movement in the opposite gallery. A shadowy figure prowled between the pews.

Was it Saint?

Violet peered and peered, but she couldn't make out who the person was or what he was doing. Was he sitting on a pew? Crawling on the floor? No, he was doing neither. He was standing, walking, gone.

Violet turned her attention to the entrance and sure enough, Saint emerged. He still carried the valise, but his manner was no longer furtive. He strolled in the direction of Piccadilly.

Violet deduced that he had rid himself of the clock he'd stolen. Further, she deduced that someone else would come to retrieve it—and that person probably wouldn't be a *chère-amie*. Saint would have given the clock to a *chère-amie* in person, surely?

Which left a co-conspirator or a blackmailer.

Violet decided that it was more important to see who collected the clock than to follow Saint back to Conduit Street.

The steeple tower made a good place to sit while one waited for criminals to retrieve stolen clocks. Violet perched at the top and waited.

And waited.

And waited.

Dare she slip inside and see what Saint had left?

She wanted nothing more than to do so, but St. James's Church was a public place. Even if she managed to get inside unobserved, there was no guarantee she'd be able get out again without being seen.

Better to be bored but safe up on the steeple than to take such a risk.

An hour passed with glacial slowness before someone approached the door, lantern in hand.

Violet perked up—and then slumped when she recognized the man as the rector. Unless the rector was Saint's co-conspirator?

It seemed unlikely, but she glided across to the windows to observe what happened.

What happened was that the lamps in the church were extinguished. The rector emerged again and locked the door with a jingle-jangle of keys. Violet watched him depart, lantern in one hand, keys in the other; then she headed for Manchester Square. She had five drawings to return and then she had a Bow Street Runner to visit.

CHAPTER
TWENTY-EIGHT

*P*erry set the chamberstick down on his washstand and removed his coat and his boots. In the corner where he kept his boots was a scattering of mouse droppings. Perry pretended he hadn't seen them. He emptied his pockets and locked the tipstaff in his trunk.

He'd left the window open. The room smelled faintly of coal smoke.

Perry leaned on the windowsill and stared out over the lane. He could see lit windows below him, candlelight leaking between crooked shutters, but the rooftops were indistinct shapes against a fathomless sky. He couldn't even make out the chimneys. If someone sat on those roofs looking back at him, he couldn't see them. If someone ran along that ridgeline, he'd never know.

He wished he was on a roof, wished he was running along it.

For a fleeting moment, he smelled orange blossom. He lifted his head, scanning the sky, looking for movement, waiting for a telltale prickle across his scalp, but the prickling didn't come. The hint of orange blossom was only in his memory.

Lady Violet wasn't coming tonight. Perhaps she was busy—or more likely, the kiss they'd shared had scared her off. She'd wanted more last night, but today she must have realized that what they'd done had in fact been far too much.

Perry grimaced and turned away from the window and picked up the book he'd borrowed from the circulating library.

It took him a while to fall into the story, but once he did, he forgot about rooftops and dukes' daughters, querulous viscounts and pilfering heirs. He lounged on the rickety wooden chair with his stockinged feet up on the bed, lost in a world of catacombs and secret passages and ghostly portents.

When someone landed on the parapet outside his window, his heart gave a great leap of fright—followed by an equally great leap of delight.

"Lady Violet." He sat up and fumbled for the scrap of paper he'd been using to mark his place. "I didn't expect to see you tonight."

Lady Violet pulled off her mask. Her face was aglow with excitement. "I followed Saint! You'll never guess where he went!"

Perry stopped looking for the scrap of paper and snapped the book shut. "Come in and tell me!"

Lady Violet glided in through the window and settled on the edge of his bed, her legs crossed like a Turk. "He took a hackney to Jermyn Street," she said, practically bouncing with excitement. "And then he *hid the clock!*"

Perry felt his eyes grow wide. "Where?"

"In St. James's Church, up in one of the galleries. I waited until the rector locked up for the night, but no one came. I wager someone will collect the clock tomorrow!"

"Where exactly did he hide it?" Perry listened carefully and then declared: "I'll watch to see who it is."

"So will I!"

They stared at each other. Perry wondered if he looked as excited as she did, eyes sparkling, cheeks flushed.

"Why didn't you follow him?" Lady Violet asked. "Weren't you at Abbishaw's house?"

"I was. But Abbishaw had a bit of a turn—couldn't catch his breath. By the time he'd recovered, Saintbridge was long gone. I'm devilish glad you followed him."

Lady Violet gave a very unladylike grin. "So am I!"

Perry remembered what else he'd witnessed. "Saintbridge left one of Giles's cuff links on the floor."

Lady Violet lost her grin. "Lord Abbishaw saw everything, though? He knows it was Saint?"

"He knows. I don't know what's going to come of this, but at least he can't accuse Giles of stealing the clocks."

"It must have been a blackmail letter," Lady Violet declared. She uncrossed her legs and dangled them over the side of his bed. "The one that was delivered last night."

Perry nodded. Nothing else made sense. Only a desperate man would have attempted another theft after last night's events.

"What can he have done? Something worse than stealing clocks. Something *bad.*" She kicked one heel against his bedframe, then said with relish in her voice: "Murder. He killed Jasper Flint!"

"He did not kill Flint," Perry said, and as he said it he became aware that Lady Violet was sitting on his bed. The bed upon which he'd kissed her last night.

Heat flushed beneath his skin.

"We'll find out who's blackmailing him." Lady Violet kicked her heel against his bedframe again to punctuate this statement. "And once we know that, we should be able to figure out why."

"With any luck."

"You'll stop being a Bow Street Runner then, won't you? Once the case is solved."

"Principal Officer," Perry corrected her.

She rolled her eyes in a very unladylike manner. "Won't you?"

"Yes."

Her nose wrinkled. "How boring."

Perry agreed. He didn't want to go back to being a secretary. He'd much rather return to his regiment. There was nothing he'd miss in London. Nothing at all.

Except for the person sitting on his bed. She was refreshing and invigorating and quite unlike anyone he'd ever met. The hour he'd spent running along London's rooftops had been the best hour of his life, with the exception of the minutes he'd spent kissing her.

But there'd be no more running along rooftops. No more kisses. Once he became a secretary again, Lady Violet would stop visiting him.

"I'm going to re-enlist," Perry blurted. It was shocking to hear that statement come from his mouth—had he actually said it?—but on the heels of that utterance came a sweeping sense of relief. Leaving England was the right decision.

She frowned. "Re-enlist? Why?"

"It's a better fit for me than London is."

"When will you leave?"

"Once we've solved this case."

Lady Violet unwound the neckcloth she wore as a muffler, reached inside her shirt, and pulled out a necklace. A golden charm dangled on the slender chain. "Do you know what this is?"

Perry leaned closer to see. "A clover leaf?"

"A *magic* clover leaf."

"How so?"

"My great-great-grandmother asked for it to be enchanted. It was what she wished for when Baletongue came."

"What sort of enchantment?"

Lady Violet released the charm. It lay gleaming on the lapel of her black coat. "She had six children by the time she was twenty-three. She almost died giving birth to the last one. She decided she didn't want any more, so she asked Baletongue to enchant the charms on a necklace. This is one of them."

Perry worked his way through that explanation and came to what he thought was the correct conclusion. "Wearing the charms made her barren?"

"Yes."

"Forever?"

"No. Only when she wore them."

Perry eyed the charm with interest. It was like a magical cundum, only made from gold, not sheep's intestines. And worn by the woman, not the man.

Somewhat belatedly, he came to another conclusion.

"Why are you telling me this?" he asked cautiously.

"Because I want to kiss you again," Lady Violet said.

Perry's throat was suddenly very tight.

"And perhaps after that we could do something more."

Perry's mind instantly supplied him with ideas as to what that something more might be. Many ideas, all of them as thrilling as they were forbidden.

"No," he said, his voice sounding very far away. "That's not something we should—"

"Why not? No one will ever find out."

Perry could remember having a similar argument last night. Lady Violet had won that one—and while part of him wanted her to win this one, too, the rest of him knew that he couldn't allow it. "I think it's best if you wait until your wedding night. You may not think so now, but—"

"Mother gave me this charm when I turned twenty-one and Father knows she gave it to me, so if that's not tacit permission to use it when I want to, I don't know what is!"

Perry pondered that information—and decided that the Garlands were a very odd family. "Have you used the charm before?"

"Of course not."

"Then why do you wish to use it now?"

"Because I like kissing you. You're safe. And because you're leaving soon."

"I'm not sure those are good reasons to—"

175

"And because I want to know what it's like, and you're the person I want to do it with."

That statement rendered Perry speechless.

"But only if you want to, of course. You don't have to decide now. First, we should kiss." Lady Violet tucked the golden clover leaf back inside her shirt and looked at him, bright-eyed and expectant, as if anticipating he'd kiss her immediately.

Perry was too discombobulated to kiss anyone right at that moment. He tried to put his bemusement into words: "You're being very businesslike about this."

"I think it's best, don't you? Otherwise you'll get stick-in-the-muddish halfway through and stop. Best to lay it all out on the table from the start."

"Stick-in-the-muddish?"

Lady Violet nodded. "Stick-in-the-muddish." She gave him an impish grin. "I don't mind. It's part of your charm."

Perry uttered an involuntary laugh, and then sobered. He rubbed his face with both hands. "Lady Violet . . ."

"May I show you what I want us to do?"

He lowered his hands.

Lady Violet took a folded piece of paper from inside her coat and held it out. "This."

CHAPTER
TWENTY-NINE

*P*erry knew he would probably regret his curiosity, but he took the paper she held out and unfolded it, revealing a pencil sketch of a man and woman upon a sofa. Mid-coitus.

He winced and hastily refolded the paper. Which was a very stick-in-the-muddish thing to do.

"It's from Freddy's collection," Lady Violet informed him. "I copied some of the drawings."

Of course she had. Perry couldn't find it in himself to be surprised.

"Do you know how to do it like that?"

Perry unfolded the drawing and looked at it again, even though the scene was etched onto his eyeballs. The man lay sprawled on the sofa, his breeches about his ankles, while his scantily-clad inamorata rode them both towards pleasure.

He imagined doing that with Lady Violet.

Heat rushed through him. His cock began to stiffen. He hastily refolded the paper.

"Do you know how to do it like that?" Lady Violet asked again.

Perry had to clear his throat before he could speak. "Yes."

"Do you want to do it?"

"Do you?" he hedged.

"Maybe. I won't know until after we've kissed." Lady Violet plucked the drawing from his hand and tucked it back inside her coat. She tilted her head and gave him a smile that was as inviting as it was wicked. "Shall we begin?"

Perry found himself unable to speak. His vocal cords were frozen, as was his tongue. He stared at her, torn between kissing her and bundling her out of his window as fast as was physically possible.

Lady Violet solved his dilemma by slipping off the bed and bending to kiss him in the chair. As kisses went, it was brief and lopsided, but she captured his face in her hands and laid a second kiss on his mouth, one that was neither lopsided nor brief, but was instead fierce and insistent. She nipped at his lips, demanding a response from him.

Perry's tongue had abandoned speech, but his mouth proved itself capable of communication nonetheless. *Yes*, his lips silently said, as they parted for Lady Violet. *Yes*, as she delved into his mouth. *Yes*, as their tongues touched.

It was a feverish kiss, as mad and headlong as running over London's rooftops had been. Perry leaned into it, reaching up to hold her in place while they plundered one another's mouths, tongues dueling, teeth clashing.

Lady Violet drew back. They stared at each other, panting heavily. Her eyes were almost black, her cheeks wildly flushed, her lips ripe and swollen.

Perry stood. Not to bundle Lady Violet out of the window, but to sweep her up in his arms. There was no need to pick her up, the bed was directly behind her, but some possessive, primitive part of him needed to lift her up and then place her on the coverlet. *His* coverlet. *His* bed.

He followed her down onto the bed, leaning over her, forearms braced on either side of her head, knees bracketing her hips. Lady Violet gave a breathless laugh, a breathless gasp, and tilted her face up to meet his kiss.

The plundering of mouths resumed.

The last time they'd lain on this bed, Perry had had a line he'd refused to cross. Tonight, he crossed it without even realizing. When they finally stopped to catch their breaths, he discovered that he was practically lying on top of her. He also discovered that his cock was doing its damnedest to burst through his breeches.

He rolled away from her, onto his back, but Lady Violet followed, slinging one leg swiftly over him, straddling him on hands and knees. She took hold of his wrists, pinning them down.

Her dominance was only an illusion. Perry was bigger than her, stronger than her. He could flip her off in an instant if he chose to—but he didn't. Those tight hands at his wrists, her weight pressing them down, made his cock leap in his breeches.

"Where do you think you're going, Bow Street Runner?" Her eyes were narrow, her voice teasing.

"Principal Officer," Perry growled.

Laughter flared on her face. She leaned closer, her lips almost touching his. "Are you running away, Runner?" she whispered.

"No."

"Do you want to stop?"

"No." Blood thrummed in his veins, thrummed in his cock. "Do you?"

"No." Lady Violet grinned fiercely, kissed him fiercely. Her teeth nipped his lips, her tongue invaded his mouth.

Time ceased to have meaning. Perry had no idea how long the kiss lasted. It could have been minutes, it could have been hours. All he knew was that kissing had never been this good before. Her hands tight at his wrists, her weight pressing down, her mouth devouring his so forcefully—it lit a fire in him that had never been lit before.

They broke for breath, dragging air into their lungs. Lady Violet sat up, still straddling him, still holding his wrists. Her *derrière* brushed his cock, imprisoned in breeches that were far too tight. Pleasure jolted through him. His breath caught in his throat. Lady Violet shifted her weight, repeating the move, brushing against his hard cock, watching his face closely.

Perry's whole body shuddered.

"You like that, don't you?" She laughed and did it again. Her smile was delightfully wicked.

Perry pulled his wrists free and set his hands at her waist. Holding her in place, he pressed up with slow deliberation.

This time it was Lady Violet who caught her breath.

Perry stilled. Had that gasp been from shock or pleasure?

Lady Violet's expression changed, no longer laughing but instead intent, curious. She shifted a few inches until their loins were perfectly aligned, then settled her weight on him.

This time, they both shuddered. A groan rose in Perry's throat. He clenched his jaw, holding it in.

Layers of clothing separated them, but Perry could feel the warmth and welcoming softness of her quim, just as she could undoubtedly feel the heat and hardness of his cock.

Lady Violet's gaze was focused inwards. She was absorbed in the newness of it, absorbed in the sensations. She shifted her weight slightly, and gave a delicious little wiggle that made them both shudder. Perry's hips moved without his bidding, rocking upwards, trying to press their bodies more closely together.

Lady Violet hummed in her throat. He watched her pupils dilate even further. "I want to do it," she whispered, her voice so low and breathless that his ears barely caught the words.

This line was far bigger than the one he'd refused to cross yesterday, but Perry was beyond thinking about lines and whether he ought to cross them or not. His whole body was shouting that yes, he wanted to do it, too.

Lady Violet gave him a wide, wild grin and yanked at the buttons fastening her coat. In a matter of seconds, she cast the garment onto the floor. She set to work on her shirt. She wasn't wearing stays. Perry saw her nipples pressing against the cambric.

His brain kicked into action. He sat up, lifted her off him, set her to one side on the bed, and began shucking his clothes as fast as he could. It was a race, both of them breathless, both of them laughing. A button pinged to the floor. Shirts went flying, stockings, his breeches, her pantaloons.

The race ended with them kneeling on the coverlet, chests heaving with laughter, naked. Perry's gaze was transfixed. He couldn't look away. He'd never seen anything as breathtaking as Lady Violet. Everything about her was perfect: the creamy skin, the rosy nipples, the glossy black hair slipping free from her braid.

She was slender, not voluptuous, a Diana rather than a Venus, but even that was perfect.

Perry stopped laughing, but he couldn't stop staring. He watched her breasts rise and fall. The golden charm dangled between them, the clover leaf glinting in the candlelight.

Lady Violet stopped laughing, too. Her gaze was riveted on his cock. "May I?" She reached out and wrapped a curious hand around him.

His cock jerked in her grip. His whole body jerked.

Perry held still while her hand accustomed itself to his heat and his hardness, his girth, his weight. Breathing was impossible.

Lady Violet released him. "Lie down, I want to look at you."

Perry wanted to fling her down on the bed and kiss his way across her body; instead, he lay back and let her look at him. Lady Violet might be adventurous and bold, but she was also a virgin, and she was only doing this because she felt safe with him.

He tucked his hands behind his head so he wouldn't be tempted to reach for her.

Fortunately, when Lady Violet had said *look* she'd actually meant *touch*. And while she might be a virgin, there was nothing hesitant in the way she explored his body. She was intrigued by the hair on his chest, intrigued by his muscles, running her hands over them greedily. Perry let her investigate, watching her face, watching her breasts. It was torture to lie still, to not kiss that mouth, not kiss those breasts. Lady Violet traced a figure eight across his pectorals with a fingertip, which tickled pleasantly, but when she did it again with the edge of a well-manicured fingernail, all Perry's nerves flamed alight and he shivered with arousal. Lady Violet laughed. "You like that?"

Perry nodded, his throat too tight for speech.

She did it again, scoring a path across his skin, making him twitch and shiver, and then she shifted her attention to his nipples. She stroked them, which tickled, and plucked at them, which was pleasant, and then, to Perry's delight, she pinched one. His whole body gave a jolt of arousal.

"You like that, too," she said with satisfaction, pinching his other nipple.

Yes, he did like that tiny stinging pain.

She pinched again, harder, and laughed at his helpless response, sending him a glance filled with mischief, looking so tempting and wicked that it took all Perry's self-control not to haul her into a ravishing kiss. He clenched his hands tightly behind his head. If she did it again . . .

But she didn't. Having acquainted herself with his nipples, Lady Violet turned her attention further south. Her fingers followed the trail of hair from his chest to his groin, tugging lightly on the strands, making him shiver and twitch. Every muscle in his body was taut with anticipation, but when she reached for his cock, standing eagerly to attention, Perry managed to say, "Careful." His voice was a hoarse croak.

Lady Violet paused, her gaze rising to meet his, a question on her face.

"I know it looks robust, sticking up like that, but it's actually not." Perry raised himself up on one elbow and took her hand. He fitted her fingers around his shaft and squeezed until it was almost uncomfortable. "No tighter than this, and no pinching or scratching. And as for down there . . ." He released her hand and gestured to his balls. "Be careful with them, or we won't be doing anything more tonight."

Her eyebrows rose. "Truly?"

"Truly."

She released his cock. "How careful?"

Perry sat up further, took her hand again, and cupped her fingers around his balls. "This careful."

He hesitated, then released her hand. He felt very vulnerable, half reclining on the bed with his balls in someone else's hand. He wasn't sure if Lady Violet realized how great an act of trust it was, but perhaps she did, because her expression was thoughtful, almost serious. Her thumb brushed over his skin, a light, cautious, tickling touch.

Perry shivered with his whole body.

She let go of his balls abruptly and sat back on her heels, wide-eyed. "Did that hurt?"

"No," he hastened to reassure her. "It felt good."

She looked as if she didn't quite believe him.

"Let me show you what it felt like. Lie down." He patted the coverlet.

They matched stares for a moment, and then Lady Violet lay down. She didn't look quite as bold and confident as she had before. In fact, she looked a little shy. Her legs weren't tightly pressed together, but neither were they spread brazenly wide.

Shy wasn't a word that Perry had ever associated with Lady Violet. Assertive, yes. Daring. Spirited. Plucky. Intrepid. Adventurous. Reckless. But even though she was all those things, she was also a virgin, and right now she probably felt as vulnerable as he had when she'd held his balls. More vulnerable, most likely.

Perry moved back slightly, trying not to loom over her. "It felt like this," he said, and he trailed his fingertips very lightly up her inner thigh.

She shivered.

"Good, isn't it?" He did it again, tracing tickling paths with his fingers. Such smooth skin. Like silk.

Lady Violet made a wordless noise. Her hips shifted on the bed. Her legs spread a little wider.

Perry obeyed that unspoken invitation. He slid his hand higher, until his fingers almost touched that tempting thatch of dark hair, then dared to bend his head and press an open-mouthed kiss to her inner thigh.

He heard her breath catch in a gasp. Encouraged, he tasted her skin with his tongue.

Her breath caught again. She shivered convulsively.

Perry hummed in his throat and bent his attention to the pleasurable task of showing Lady Violet just what it felt like to have someone lay a damp and tickling path across extremely sensitive skin. He used his lips, his tongue, his teeth, kissing and licking and occasionally nipping. She appeared to enjoy it prodigiously. Her hips shifted restlessly on the bed and her hands clutched the coverlet.

If Lady Violet's fingers had led her south, his mouth led him north. Perry inched his way higher, then lifted his head. "If you want me to stop just say—"

"Don't stop!"

Perry laughed at that imperative command and nipped her thigh lightly, then soothed that sting with his tongue. He was so close to her quim that her curls tickled his cheek. Her scent enticed him even closer, musky and feminine and incredibly arousing. His cock was so hard that it almost hurt. He kissed her thigh again and delved into those fragrant curls with gentle fingers, finding her delicate nether lips, learning their shape. If Lady Violet had been shy earlier, she wasn't now. She arched against his hand, urging him on. Perry slipped a finger into her soft, slick, tight heat. The muscles in his groin contracted in sharp need.

Lady Violet didn't protest his invasion; she spread her legs wider. Perry slipped a second finger inside, then he dipped his head and tasted her, filling his nose with her scent and his mouth with her sweet, salty flavor.

Lady Violet gave a gasp of surprise. "Oh!" she said, and then, "Oh, that feels good. Don't stop!"

It was another command that Perry was glad to obey. He

explored with his tongue, with his fingers, while Lady Violet urged him on, the sounds she was making breathless and eager and uninhibited.

She climaxed surprisingly fast—although perhaps it wasn't surprising; Lady Violet wasn't one to hang back and wait.

Perry almost climaxed, too. He wanted to be inside her, wanted to feel those sleek contractions around his cock.

He slid his fingers free, raised himself up on his elbow, and looked at her. Was it over now? Was she done with him?

Lady Violet's cheeks were flushed, her eyes as bright as stars. She sat up, but instead of climbing off the bed and starting to dress, she reached for him, impatient and eager, clearly wanting more.

They tumbled across the bed in a mad, fierce embrace, limbs tangling, hands roaming, mouths clashing. Lady Violet explored him greedily, boldly, and Perry was equally greedy, equally bold. Her breasts were like plump fruit, smooth and soft and luscious, fitting perfectly into his hands. Her buttocks fitted his hands perfectly, too, and her waist. Everything about her was perfect. Her taste, her scent, her silky hair, her soft skin. Her bold mouth, her bold hands. Her bold nature.

Twice they rolled so that he lay on top of her, and twice Lady Violet pushed him back on the bed so that she was on top. The second time, she rose up on hands and knees and said, "I want to do it now."

Her breasts were too tantalizing to ignore when she was astride him like that. Perry reached up and cupped them in his hands, brushing his thumbs over taut, rosy nipples, making her shiver.

The enchanted charm dangled from her throat, glinting in the candlelight.

Perry reluctantly released her breasts. "Are you certain this will work?" He flicked the charm with one finger, setting it spinning on its chain.

"As certain as I am that I can fly!"

CHAPTER THIRTY

$\mathcal{P}$erry captured the charm and stopped it spinning. He looked at the little four-leafed clover and then at her candlelit face. Violet Garland. Impatient and impetuous, quick-witted, bossy, stubborn, inquisitive. The duke's daughter in his bed whom he desperately wanted to swive.

He really ought not to.

But he wanted to—and more importantly, *she* wanted to.

Perry looked at the charm, and decided that some things you just had to take on faith. "Very well."

"I want to be on top," Lady Violet announced—and that was another thing Perry liked about her. She asked for what she wanted.

"All right." He released the charm and put his hands at her waist, helping guide her into position. "It might hurt at first," he cautioned, and then the sensitive head of his cock brushed the entrance to her body and he lost the ability to breathe for a moment, let alone speak.

Lady Violet took firm grip of his shaft and lowered herself onto him. Perry's hips wanted to lunge upward into that soft, tight heat. He clenched his jaw, struggling to hold himself still.

Lady Violet's gaze was focused inwards and she was

186

frowning ever so slightly, but he didn't think the frown was because she was in pain. She was concentrating on the newness of the sensation—and then she did wince.

Perry unclenched his jaw. "We can stop if it hurts too much," he managed to say, although he thought it might kill him if that was what she decided to do.

Lady Violet didn't stop. She gritted her teeth and sank fully onto him.

Perry uttered an involuntary groan of pleasure.

Lady Violet didn't groan. She was wincing again—but even as he watched, the tension eased from her face. Her expression changed from pained to curious. "Mmm, that feels . . ." She rocked cautiously, then leaned forward to brace her hands on his shoulders and rocked again, a little more boldly.

Perry bit back another groan.

"Is this all it is?" Lady Violet asked, sounding rather disappointed.

"No. Now, you ride me."

It took a minute for her to get the knack of riding him à la St. George, but once she did, she set a fast, fierce rhythm. She leaned over him, hands pressing his shoulders into the bed, an exultant grin on her face, glorying in holding him down, glorying in riding him. She looked untamed and beautiful and carnal, like one of the dangerously seductive nymphs who'd enticed Hylas to his doom. Perry held her waist and dug his heels into the mattress and arched his hips to meet her.

Their mad, wild, magical gallop came abruptly to its end, cresting in a paroxysm of bliss that involved every muscle Perry possessed. He pumped his pleasure into her while she bucked in the throes of her own ecstasy, gasping and laughing, digging her fingers into his shoulders.

When the intensity of their climaxes had ebbed, Lady Violet didn't climb off him. Instead, she eased down to lie on him.

Perry put his arms around her. His heart was thundering madly. Her heart no doubt was, too, but he couldn't hear it, couldn't hear anything except his own harsh panting and the deafening pounding in his ears.

It became easier to breathe. His pulse slowed its headlong pace. Lady Violet was on top of him, cradled in his arms, smelling of sex and orange blossom. He heard his own soft breathing, heard her soft breathing. His cock was still inside her, warm and replete.

Lady Violet crossed her hands over his breastbone and rested her chin on them. Her face was so close that Perry couldn't quite focus on it.

"That was good," she said.

It had been a damned sight better than good, in Perry's opinion.

"I want to do it again."

"Now?" He wasn't sure he could carry off a repeat performance immediately, however much he might wish to.

Lady Violet shook her head. "Tomorrow?"

"Tomorrow," Perry agreed.

She leaned forward and pressed a brief kiss to his mouth, then sat up. The golden charm peeled off his skin. Perry sent up a prayer of thanks for Faerie godmothers and magical wishes and for dukes' daughters who were bold enough to ask for what they wanted, even if what they wanted was scandalous.

It hadn't felt scandalous, though, making love to her. Wild, frenzied, and unreal, yes, but not scandalous, not wrong, not something to be ashamed of. It had felt like something to be celebrated.

Lady Violet climbed off him. "Oh, bother," she said, and picked up a discarded shirt and dabbed at her thighs.

Perry took the shirt when she handed it to him and wiped himself off, too. The shirt was his, not hers, he was relieved to note. He didn't know who washed the clothing she wore when she flew, but whoever it was would probably recognize the smell of sex.

There was no blood on the crumpled fabric. She'd been a virgin, but she hadn't bled.

Lady Violet dressed almost as fast as she'd stripped, pulling on stockings, pantaloons, shirt. She bent to tie her shoelaces, then thrust her arms into the sleeves of her black coat. She bounced on her toes while she buttoned it, her fingers dancing down the placket. She looked euphoric, almost manic, her eyes bright, her grin wide. "I'll see you tomorrow morning? At the church?"

It took him more than a few seconds to remember that Saintbridge Abbishaw had stolen a clock from his father and hidden it in St. James's Church. Perry gave himself a sharp mental shake. Lord, what was wrong with his wits? "Yes," he said, climbing off the bed. "I'll be there."

Lady Violet wound the black neckcloth around her throat, then stretched up on tiptoe to give him a brief and exuberant kiss. She put on her mask, pulled on her gloves. "Good-bye!" She took two quick steps to the window and launched herself into the night sky.

Perry crossed to the window and peered out.

Lady Violet was gone.

He leaned against the sill, feeling a little dazed, a little dizzy, as if someone had picked up his life, shaken it vigorously, and put it back upside down.

CHAPTER
THIRTY-ONE

*P*erry was outside St. James's Church before dawn. He loitered discreetly as London came awake, sleepy servants throwing open shutters and unlocking doors. A man dressed in ecclesiastical attire performed the same service at the church, unlocking the main entrance with a jangle of keys.

Perry waited to see whether anyone would dart in that open door to retrieve the stolen clock. Half an hour passed. He peeled himself away from the wall he was leaning against and ambled across to the church, slipping inside. He paused in the shadows for a moment, listening, then climbed the staircase to the north gallery.

The gallery had three stepped rows of pews. Perry counted off the windows and the pews until he came to where Lady Violet had seen Saintbridge Abbishaw.

He went down on one knee to peer under the pew. There was nothing there.

He looked under the next pew. Also nothing.

He knelt on the hard wooden floor and cast a frowning glance around. Lady Violet had said the north gallery, hadn't she? The third window along? The pew nearest the wall?

As he knelt, a sound came faintly to his ears.

Tick tick tick.

Perry tilted his head and followed that ticking . . . and discovered two clock-sized bundles tucked behind the next pew.

He glanced around, listened intently, assured himself that no one else was up in the gallery, then fished one of the bundles from its hiding place.

It was wrapped in oiled cloth. Perry unwound the cloth. The *tick tick tick* became louder. Yes, it was one of Lord Abbishaw's automatous clocks, a half-clad soldier plying his cock between the legs of a nubile young lady.

He rewrapped the clock and retrieved the second bundle from behind the pew. It was a clock, too, but no longer ticking, the participants caught in mid-act.

Antony and Cleopatra.

"May I see it?" someone whispered in his ear.

Perry almost leaped out of his skin. He dropped the clock. It was only by sheer luck that he managed to catch it before it struck the floor. He spun round on his knees, clutching the clock to his chest.

Lady Violet stood there, hovering an inch off the floor— which would be why he'd not heard any footsteps. "Sorry," she said, wrinkling her nose contritely. "May I see it?"

Perry hesitated, then realized how idiotic it was to refuse to let her see it. Lady Violet had looked through Frederick Stanhope's collection. The act depicted on the clock was nothing she hadn't seen before.

Plus, she'd seen him naked. Had ridden him à la St. George.

Perry's brain stuttered to a halt as memory of last night washed over him. He froze, kneeling between the pews, the clock clutched to his chest.

Lady Violet's eyebrows twitched together. "You won't let me?"

Dumbly, Perry handed her the clock.

Lady Violet examined it, lips pursed, eyebrows arched.

Perry unwrapped the clock that was still ticking and gave that to her, too.

"Oh." Her eyebrows arched higher. She gave a little laugh. "This is rather comical, isn't it?"

"Yes." He took the first clock, rewrapped it, and stashed it behind the pew again. Lady Violet was still watching the soldier plunge his little red prick in and out of his inamorata, her expression highly amused.

"I can't imagine Lord Abbishaw owning something like this. He's so priggish." She handed back the clock. "Mind you, I thought you were a prude and you're not, are you?"

Memory of last night blazed between them. He was thinking about it, and he knew she was, too.

Perry's face heated. He managed to rewrap the clock without dropping it, but it wasn't easy. The salty-sweet taste of her was on his tongue and he could smell the scent of their lovemaking.

He fumbled the clock back into its hiding place and stood. He had to clear his throat before he could speak. "I'll watch from over there." He gestured at the south gallery.

Lady Violet nodded. "I have to go home now, but I'll be back. I'll bring my sketchbook and pretend to be drawing."

Perry cast a frowning glance around. "Are you here alone?"

"My maid is downstairs."

"Good." It seemed silly to worry about her walking the few hundred yards between the church and her family's mansion on St. James's Square when she roamed London's night sky alone, but it was daylight now and she couldn't fly. Both her reputation and her person were at risk.

Lady Violet departed, treading briskly along the gallery. At the staircase she paused and waved, then descended out of sight.

Perry crossed to the balcony and looked over. He caught a brief glimpse of her before she vanished into the vestibule, a maid trailing at her heels.

He waited two minutes, then made his way down the

stairs, across the width of the church, and up to the south gallery. He prowled between the pews before selecting the spot where he'd be least likely to be seen.

He sat and stared across at where the clocks were hidden. Lady Violet was gone, but she occupied his thoughts. He could think of nothing else.

He knew he ought to feel guilty and ashamed. He'd bedded a duke's daughter. Taken her innocence. Deflowered her. It was a dreadful thing to have done, but the emotions in Perry's breast weren't guilt and shame. Last night he'd felt dazed and euphoric, and he still felt a little dazed. He definitely still felt euphoric. But most of all, he felt lucky. Lucky that he'd caught Lady Violet following him all those nights ago. Lucky that she'd badgered him into assisting with the investigation. Lucky that she'd been there on Saintbridge Abbishaw's roof. And above all else, lucky that she'd chosen him to be her lover.

He wanted to do it all again. He wanted to run along rooftops with her, kiss her, make love to her. And he wanted to do more than that. He wanted to fall asleep with her in his bed. He wanted to wake in the darkest hours of the night and hear her soft breathing, wanted her to be there in the morning sunshine, wanted to lie in bed with her and talk and laugh together, and probably argue, too. He wanted to hold her and cherish her and make love to her and—

His thoughts came to an abrupt halt, like one of Abbishaw's clocks with its cogs jammed. He wanted to *what*?

Perry rewound his thoughts, ticking back through them, and winced.

"Don't be a beetle-head," he told himself out loud. He might want to have sex with Lady Violet, but he most definitely didn't want to cherish her or anything equally foolish or lovelorn. "Beetle-head," he said again, under his breath. Was it so long since he'd had sex that his wits had been addled by last night? He was confusing physical intimacy with something else. Something that could never be.

Dukes' daughters didn't fall in love with Principal Officers.

Or with secretaries. And Principal Officers and secretaries most definitely did *not* fall in love with dukes' daughters. Not if they had any common sense. Not if they knew what was good for them.

Lady Violet inhabited a completely different world to him, one that should never have intersected with his, and the sooner things returned to the way they ought to be, the better.

Perry stared across at the north gallery and wondered how soon he could leave London. First he had to solve this case, then he'd hand in his notice, and once that was done, he'd apply to rejoin his regiment. There'd be paperwork, of course, but the approval would be a formality.

All going well, he might be able to depart London as early as next month.

Perry sat through a morning service. It was sparsely attended. No one came up to the galleries. The church bell tolled the hour. Not long after that, Lady Violet returned with her maid. She selected a pew at some distance from Perry, laid out her pencils, and opened a sketchbook.

"You may go, Carter. Come back in two hours."

The maid bobbed a curtsy and scurried off.

Lady Violet gathered up her sketchbook and pencils and came to sit alongside Perry.

"Are you sure it's wise to sit next to me?"

"No one comes up here during the day."

The next two hours proved her correct. No worshippers climbed the stairs to the south gallery. Nor did anyone climb the stairs to the north gallery and retrieve the hidden clocks.

Lady Violet occupied herself by sketching the church. She had a good eye and a quick hand. Perry was impressed, but given the competence of the drawing she'd shown him last night, he probably shouldn't have been.

Thinking of that drawing brought a vivid surge of memory.

His tongue remembered her taste. His shoulders remembered how her fingers had dug into them.

Perry shook his head, shook away the memory. It seemed wrong to be sitting in a church and thinking of sexual congress.

He examined the barrel-vaulted nave, the pulpit, the altarpiece, the font . . . and then his gaze wandered back to Lady Violet. She looked very different from the person he'd become acquainted with during the past week—the villain he'd wrestled from the air, the guardian angel who'd smothered Saintbridge in a horse blanket, the uninhibited lover who'd been in his bed last night. The Lady Violet he was familiar with didn't dress her hair in ringlets. Nor did she wear pretty muslin dresses. She pulled her hair back in a braid and wore men's clothing of severest black.

Which was the real Violet? The one he'd come to know during the past few nights, or the one seated alongside him now?

The one seated beside him was a great deal more feminine than he was used to. She looked demure and sedate—two things he knew she wasn't. His Violet smelled of orange blossom, as this one did, but also a little of coal smoke. She was daring and adventurous, bold, bossy, nosy, persistent, and most of all, she was unique. The woman alongside him didn't look unique. She looked interchangeable with any number of pretty, well-bred young ladies.

"Finished," Lady Violet declared, putting down her pencil and closing her sketchbook. "What shall we discuss?"

Her gaze was bright and challenging, her manner confident, and she was both the person he was familiar with and a stranger. It was extremely disconcerting.

"Have you been here all morning?" she asked.

"Yes."

"Do you not need to . . ." Her brow wrinkled as she searched for a word. "Pluck a rose," she said finally.

It took Perry several seconds to understand what she meant. "I'm all right, thank you."

"Are you certain?"

"Yes."

Lady Violet swung one foot to and fro. She scanned the church, from the vestibule to the altarpiece and back again. "What's it like being a soldier?"

Perry recounted some of his more daring exploits, some of the more humorous ones. He didn't tell her about killing people. Some stories didn't need to be told.

"It sounds prodigiously exciting," Lady Violet said when he'd finished. He heard envy in her voice, saw it on her face. "No wonder you want to return."

"Mostly my regiment's been on garrison duty," Perry admitted.

"Is that why you sold out?"

"No. I sold out because my mother begged me to. She didn't want all her sons to die in India. The irony is that she died herself, not two months after I got back."

"Oh." Lady Violet's expression was grave, somber. "I'm very sorry."

"At least I got to see her again." It was something neither of his brothers had had the chance to do.

They sat in silence for a while, side by side on the pew; then Lady Violet said quietly, "Your brothers both died in action?"

"Yes." Chances were he would too, eventually. His regiment wouldn't be on garrison duty forever. But it was better to die quickly on a battlefield than to rot away in an attic in Holborn.

Lady Violet caught her upper lip meditatively between her teeth. Several seconds passed, and then she said tentatively, "Must you re-enlist?"

"Yes." Sometimes you needed to take risks in order to make the most of life. It was something Lady Violet would understand.

He opened his mouth to tell her this, but at that instant the church bells began tolling the hour. Lady Violet hastily gathered up her sketchbook and pencils. "My maid will be here any minute. I'll come back after luncheon."

She returned to her former seat. Scarcely two minutes later, her maid returned.

Lady Violet departed.

Time passed. No one came to remove the clocks.

Lady Violet returned in the afternoon with her maid and her sketchbook. Everything went as before, except that this time, when Lady Violet relocated to sit alongside him, she handed him something wrapped in a napkin.

Perry took it, and discovered that she'd brought him two thick sandwiches.

The bread was fresh, the ham succulent, the mustard spicy. He ate every last morsel. "Thank you."

"Do you need to pluck a rose now?"

Perry's need was rather urgent, but he hesitated.

"Go." She waved in the direction of the staircase. "If someone should come for the clocks, stay out of sight!"

He took the stairs two at a time down to the vestibule and hurried outside. The sunshine was bright after so many hours in the cool gloom of the church.

Perry relieved himself in the nearest alleyway and hurried back. Lady Violet was sitting precisely where he'd left her.

He slid into place on the pew alongside her.

No one came to retrieve the clocks during the next two hours. Lady Violet drew another sketch and then they both sat through the afternoon service. "Does your brother know you're here?" Perry thought to ask, rather belatedly.

"Of course."

"Does he know why?"

"Yes."

"And he's . . . all right with that?"

"Only because it's a church and it's so close to home. He knows I'm safe here." She wrinkled her nose. "Plus, he made me promise I wouldn't leave the church, even if we *did* see someone. I have to let you do the following." Her tone perfectly expressed her disgruntlement.

Perry was relieved that Thane had made that stipulation.

He didn't want Lady Violet following their mysterious clock collector in daylight, not when she might be seen and recognized.

No one came, though.

"I wish whoever it is would hurry up!" Lady Violet said crossly, when it was time for her to leave again.

"He'll probably wait until after dark."

Lady Violet stopped looking so aggrieved. "If he does that, I'll be able to follow him." She gathered up her sketchbook and pencils. "I'll come back as soon as it's dark. I'll sit up on the steeple and watch."

"He might come before then," Perry cautioned.

"I hope he doesn't! I know it's boring for you to wait all day, but I want to be here when he comes!"

Lady Violet got her wish. It was dark before someone came to retrieve the clocks. Perry didn't hear the man enter the church, nor did he hear anyone climb the stairs, but he saw a figure emerge into the north gallery. A man, dressed in dark clothing and carrying a valise.

Perry stayed very still, a shadow among many other shadows in the south gallery.

The man walked swiftly and silently to the pew where the clocks were hidden. He glanced around, his gaze passing over Perry, and then knelt. Half a minute passed—enough time to shove two clocks into a valise—and then the man climbed to his feet. He headed for the stairwell. Lamplight illuminated his face briefly, causing his nose and chin to cast long shadows, but even so, Perry recognized him.

CHAPTER
THIRTY-TWO

A man carrying a valise exited the church. Wintersmith followed a few seconds later.

Violet gave a gleeful little skip in the air and set off after the man, skimming above the rooftops, keeping pace as he strode along Jermyn Street. The man looked over his shoulder before turning into St. James's Street. He didn't see Wintersmith. Violet had to look twice to see him herself; he was slipping stealthily from shadow to shadow.

The man led them to the nearest hackney stand, where several carriages waited. He climbed into one. The jarvey flicked the reins and the hackney trundled off.

Wintersmith ran to the next carriage. His voice floated up to her: "Follow that hackney!"

Violet gave chase, east along Piccadilly and then north, up Old Bond Street. The hackney crossed Oxford Street, then turned right. Its destination proved to be Cavendish Square, barely five minutes' walk from Lord Abbishaw's house, which begged the question: Why hadn't the clocks been hidden in St. Margaret's Chapel? It would have been much closer.

The answer came immediately upon the heels of the question: Whoever was in the hackney didn't want Saint to guess his identity.

The hackney rattled around Cavendish Square and halted outside a tall townhouse. A second hackney stopped on the opposite side of the square. Violet hoped it was the one bearing Wintersmith.

The man with the valise paid off the jarvey, trod up the steps to the townhouse, and let himself in with a latchkey. Violet didn't dare fly low enough to see his face, but she thought she knew whose house it was.

Devil Abbishaw's.

She hovered at roof height, struck with uncertainty. Devil was someone she called a friend. She'd laughed and flirted with him for years. He couldn't possibly be involved in something like this.

Whatever this was.

She drifted lower. The house was definitely Devil's. It was a little taller than its neighbors and had an arched fanlight above the front door.

Her confusion grew. Saint and Devil cordially loathed one another. They'd never plot to steal clocks together. And as for blackmail, Devil wouldn't stoop to such a thing! He wasn't evil, despite his nickname. He was dashing and devil-may-care, frank and funny and open, not sly and deceitful.

But she'd never thought that Saint could be a thief, so perhaps she was wrong about Devil?

It occurred to her that the man who'd entered Devil's house could be someone else. His valet, perhaps, indulging in a spot of extortion?

No. A valet would have used the servants' entrance.

The hackneys had both departed. Wintersmith was crossing the square on foot, skirting the fenced garden in the middle. Violet swooped toward him. She doubted he'd seen her, but he looked up anyway, his face a pale blur in the gloom.

"Was that who I think it is?" she asked.

"Yes."

"But *why?*"

"That's what I'm going to find out."

"Are you going to sneak in and search for clues?"

"No. I'm going to speak with him face-to-face."

Violet trailed Wintersmith across the square, gaining height as she flew, until she was level with the rooftops again.

Wintersmith rapped on Devil's front door. After a moment, someone opened it. Violet couldn't hear what Wintersmith said, but whatever it was gained him entry. He stepped inside. The door closed.

Violet settled on the edge of the roof to wait.

CHAPTER
THIRTY-THREE

*T*he footman showed Perry to a sitting room and asked him to wait while he fetched his master. Perry stayed standing, bracing himself for what was to come. His jaw kept wanting to clench. He examined the room, trying to find clues as to its owner's character. There were no ladies' magazines on the side tables, no pretty china figurines on the mantelpiece. The armchairs were sturdy, upholstered with dark leather, and a row of decanters was openly displayed on the sideboard. A bachelor's room.

He turned on his heel, trying to reconcile the sitting room with the schoolboy he'd known. The Devereux of ten years ago would never have blackmailed anyone. The Devil of today clearly did.

But why?

Devereux's father had caught himself an heiress, just as Perry's father had done, but Devereux's father hadn't run through that fortune; he'd stewarded it carefully. Devereux should have no need to replenish his coffers, through blackmail or marriage or any other means.

Or rather, he shouldn't need to.

Was Devereux a gambler, hurtling towards ruin, just as Perry's father had?

The door flung open. Devereux stood in the doorway. "Perry? Is it really you?"

Perry managed a stiff smile. "Yes."

Devereux stared at him intently, searching his face, then closed the door and crossed the room with long strides. "Lord, I never would have recognized you!" He caught Perry in a mighty hug, then stepped back, hands on Perry's shoulders. "Look at you! You were such a scrawny little thing and now you're a regular Gollumpus!"

Perry gave an awkward shrug. "Ten years."

Devereux hadn't changed much. He was still lanky and loose-limbed, with a shock of dark hair and a lively face. He laughed and delivered another fierce hug. "It's devilish good to see you. Sit, sit! What would you like? Brandy? Claret?"

"Brandy," Perry said.

Devereux crossed to the sideboard and poured two healthy measures, talking all the while. "When did you get here? Where are you staying? You can stay with me, if you like. I've more than enough space! I'm rattling around in this house all by myself." He turned back towards Perry, a glass in either hand, his expression suddenly somber. "I'm very sorry about Alexander and Endymion."

"Thank you." Perry said. Those losses had hurt. They still did. They probably always would.

"And your mother," Devereux said, still solemn, handing him a glass. "My condolences. Is that why you're back? Dealing with her estate?"

"Not exactly."

"Sit," Devereux said, taking the armchair opposite Perry. "Are you on leave, or have you sold out?"

"I sold out."

Devereux's face lit with delight. "Excellent! That means you're back in England for good!" He held his glass up. "To friendship renewed!"

That delighted smile, that intention to embrace their friendship again, was precisely why Perry hadn't informed Devereux of his return. His own smile felt ghastly on his face. He raised his glass and took a great gulp. The brandy burned its way down his throat, potent and warming. Heat spread in his belly. Dutch courage. Which was what he needed right now.

"Dev, we need to talk."

Devereux's eyebrows rose. "Sounds serious."

"It is." Perry took a deep breath—and then let it out without saying anything. He couldn't lead with St. James's Church and the clocks. He needed to start the tale earlier.

Fuck. He was such a coward.

He took another gulp of brandy, and in the wake of that rush of belly-warming, courage-fueling heat, said, "I've been in England for eight months, London for the last six."

Devereux's face had always been expressive, broadcasting his emotions. Laughter, usually. Mischief. Glee. Amusement. None of those emotions were visible now. His smile vanished. His face became oddly blank. "Six months?"

"Yes."

"Why didn't you tell me?"

That note in Devereux's voice, that look on his face . . . it wasn't anger. Devereux was hurt. Which was why Perry hadn't wanted to have this conversation. He took another swallow of Dutch courage.

"Why, Perry?" There was an edge to Devereux's voice.

"Because I have no money. We can't be friends anymore."

Devereux looked affronted. "Why not?"

Perry took a breath to spew it all out, and then caught himself. "I didn't come here to talk about this."

Devereux subjected him to a hard, narrow-eyed stare. "Then why are you here?"

Perry drank another mouthful of brandy. His belly was feeling nicely warm. The rest of him was cold and tense. "I'm working for Sir Mortimer Treadwell. He's one of the magistrates at Bow Street. I'm his secretary."

There was nothing wrong with being a secretary—thousands of men across England were secretaries—but Perry felt shame admitting he was one. It was the sort of career he and Devereux had scorned when they were boys, safe and sedentary and unexciting.

"Week before last, someone came to Sir Mortimer with a case that needed investigation. A private commission. Sir Mortimer deputized me." Perry dug the tipstaff from his pocket and displayed it. He wasn't sure why. To prove he was telling the truth? To show off?

Devereux's eyebrows had been pinched together. Now, they arched upwards. "You're a Bow Street Runner?"

"Principal Officer, yes. Temporarily." He stuffed the tipstaff back in his pocket. "I'm investigating on behalf of Lord Abbishaw. He wants to know who's stealing his clocks."

Devereux became perfectly motionless.

"I followed you from St. James's Church tonight." Perry put his glass of Dutch courage aside and leaned forward. "What the devil's going on?"

Devereux said nothing. His expression was guarded, his eyes wary.

A clock on the mantelpiece ticked the seconds away. "Why is Saintbridge stealing clocks for you?" Perry asked, after ten seconds had passed.

Devereux's lips pressed together. He looked on the brink of speech, or perhaps on the brink of ordering Perry from his house.

"Saintbridge left one of Giles's cuff links by the clock cabinet last night."

Devereux's nostrils flared. His hand clenched tightly around the brandy glass. "Of course he did!" he burst out. "That venomous son of a bitch!"

"What's going on, Dev? Tell me."

Devereux's knuckles were white, but his face was flushed with fury. "What's going on is that Saint killed Jasper Flint—and he put the blame on Wilton!"

It was a wildly improbable accusation—an impossible accusation—yet there was no doubting Devereux's sincerity. It was in his fierce voice, his harsh breathing, the white-knuckled grip on his glass.

"Tell me it all. From the beginning."

"Saint killed Jasper and he said it was Wilton, and now—"

"How did he kill Flint? How did he lay the blame on Wilton?"

Devereux took a gulp of brandy. "We were at Abbishaw Park. A house party. Christmas cheer and all that." He grimaced, as if house parties at his uncle's seat were the worst of punishments. "After dinner, Wilton and Jasper and I went down to the cellar to shoot pips from playing cards. I got bored, went upstairs again. When I undressed later, I couldn't find one of my cuff links, so I sent my man, Goodlace, down to the cellar to look for it. He saw Saint shoot Jasper. Aiming for a card and got him right here instead." Devereux tapped the middle of his forehead.

"But if Saintbridge shot Flint, why the devil didn't Wilton say so?"

"Because Wilton was as drunk as a wheelbarrow. Out cold. And that's the worst of all this! Wilton thinks he killed his best friend!" Devereux's face was flushed, but the glitter in his eyes looked to be tears as much as rage.

"Why didn't your man say something?"

"Because Saint bribed him. Two hundred pounds."

Two hundred pounds would be more than Devereux's valet earned in a year. It was certainly more than Perry earned. "If Saintbridge bribed him to stay quiet, how do you know about it?"

"Because he told me a couple of weeks ago. His conscience pricked him too much."

"You believe him?"

"Yes."

"Why?"

"Because Goodlace has no reason to lie. None at all.

And this is exactly the sort of thing Saint would do! He's never to blame for anything. Ever! If something's broken, he didn't break it. If something goes missing, he didn't take it. If someone lies, it's not him. If someone cheats at cards, it wasn't him." Devereux's voice was bitter and impassioned. "Butter won't melt in his mouth and shit won't stick to him and he is *scum*."

Perry eyed him for a moment, and then nodded. "Did you confront Saintbridge?"

Devereux shook his head. "If he won't confess to cheating at cards, he's sure as hell not going to admit to killing Flint, is he?"

Perry picked up his glass again. "Explain the clocks to me."

Devereux's mouth twisted. "I went to my uncle, tried to tell him what Saint had done, but he wouldn't listen. Called me a malicious little worm, said I was jealous. Jealous! Of Saint? I wouldn't want to be him for all the money in England!"

"Abbishaw does seem rather shortsighted where his heir is concerned."

Devereux snorted. "Shortsighted? You could say that again."

"Why didn't you go to Bow Street? Tell one of the magistrates what had happened?"

"No point, is there? It's Saint's word against a valet's. No one would believe me. Or Goodlace."

A servant's word against a viscount's heir? Especially an heir with as virtuous a reputation as Saintbridge Abbishaw? Perry gave a reluctant nod of agreement. "So why the clocks?"

Devereux gave a sharklike smile. "I'm punishing Saint."

"How?"

"I'm making him do something he doesn't want to do, over and over again. Do you think it's wrong of me? Because it isn't! What's wrong is Saint strutting around London, acting as if he's purer than driven snow, when he killed Jasper and set his own *brother* up to take the fall! Wilton was banished to America! He thinks he killed Jasper!" Devereux's voice was impassioned again, loud in the room. He looked quite ferocious, teeth bared, eyes blazing. "The clocks are justice. For Wilton and Jasper both!"

"Well, your justice is backfiring. Saintbridge is setting Giles up to take the fall."

Devereux deflated. "Fuck. I should have known he'd do that."

"I still don't understand the clocks. You're blackmailing him?"

"Of course not!" Devereux said indignantly. Then his brow wrinkled. "Maybe?"

"Well, that's as clear as mud." Perry took a sip of brandy.

Devereux leaned back in the armchair, cradling his own glass against his chest, and blew out a noisy breath. "I sent him an anonymous letter, gave him a choice: tell the truth about Jasper or steal a clock. He chose to steal, so I did it again. And again." He shrugged. "It's not my fault he's a liar and a coward and a thief."

"The thieving *is* your fault," Perry pointed out.

"It's Saint's fault for being such a coward."

"And there's no 'maybe' about what you're doing. It *is* blackmail."

Devereux scowled at him. "It's justice," he muttered into his brandy.

"Dev, you have to stop."

Devereux glared at him over the rim of his glass. His expression was mutinous. He looked sixteen, not twenty-six.

The years peeled back and for a moment Perry felt as if he was sixteen, too, and Devereux was still his best friend. Back then, he'd have joined Devereux in this act of revenge without hesitation.

But he was ten years older now. Ten years wiser. "You have to stop with the clocks," he said, and put up a hand to forestall Devereux's protest. "It's made you a blackmailer *and* a thief."

"I'll give the clocks back. Eventually." Devereux's expression underwent a mercurial change, from sullen to gleeful.

"Have you seen Abbishaw's collection? Lord, can you believe he collects such things? Saint hates them. Thinks they're vulgar and obscene." He gave a laugh. His smile became sharklike again. "That's why I chose them. Because they're the *last* thing he'd want to steal."

"Stop with the clocks," Perry said.

Devereux scowled again. "No. I want that smug bastard to regret what he did."

"His soul is clearly black with iniquity," Perry said dryly. "But that doesn't mean *your* soul needs to be, too."

"Maybe it does!" Devereux's voice was harsh with frustration. "He killed Jasper and he's just walking around, with no guilt or remorse! I can't sit back and do nothing!"

Perry eyed him, and decided to try another tack. "Was Goodlace the only witness?"

Devereux gave a short nod.

"Then Saintbridge must think Goodlace is behind the blackmailing."

Devereux smirked. "He does. Came here on the slimmest of pretexts last week, asked me ever so casually about the whereabouts of my valet."

"What did you say?"

"That Goodlace had run off without giving notice."

"Did he?"

"Of course not. He's upstairs."

Perry shook his head. "You're playing with fire, Dev. If Saintbridge pinned Flint's death on Wilton, and he tried to set Giles up for the clocks, you can bet he'll be after Goodlace, too. Your man could find himself accused of something he didn't do. He could be transported, or even hanged!"

Devereux set his jaw mulishly.

"Saintbridge always finds a way to lay the blame on someone else. Isn't that what you said?"

Devereux grimaced, and then sighed and rubbed his brow wearily. "Yes."

"What are you hoping to gain from all this? Even if you

expose Saintbridge, he's not going to go to gaol. Flint's death was an accident, not murder. Abbishaw's not going to banish him to America. Saintbridge will still be the next viscount."

"He might be the next viscount, but I want the world to see him for what he is," Devereux said fiercely. "I want him to confess! I want everyone to know he killed Jasper. I want everyone to know what he did to Wilton." He deflated again, slumping in the armchair. "I know it's impossible."

"The confession, certainly." Perry looked down at his brandy, thinking everything through. When he glanced up, he found Devereux's gaze fixed intently on him. "I think you need to lay all this before Sir Mortimer."

"Your magistrate at Bow Street?"

"Yes."

"He's not going to do anything. It's all hearsay. And Saint's . . . well, he's Saint!"

"Sir Mortimer was not very impressed with Lord Abbishaw," Perry said dryly.

Amusement flashed across Devereux's face. "Came over rather too high-and-mighty, did he?"

"Talked down to him as if he were a servant," Perry said, remembering how affronted the magistrate had been. "I think Sir Mortimer will listen to you. I think he'll even believe you. He might not be able to do anything—that depends on the law—but if there's something that can be done, he'll know what it is."

Devereux eyed him. "That's what you advise?"

"It is. I shouldn't, though. Lord Abbishaw hired me, and I know damned well he wouldn't want this information brought to Sir Mortimer."

"You'll get in trouble?"

Perry shrugged. It didn't matter if he did. His future wasn't at Bow Street or even in England. "I'll see if I can arrange for us to speak with Sir Mortimer on Monday. Until then, no more blackmailing."

"It's not blackmail. It's *justice*."

Perry put up his eyebrows.

"All right. It is blackmail." Devereux hunched his shoulders and slouched sheepishly in the armchair. "I'll stop."

That slouch, that sheepish glance, made it feel as if the years had peeled back again, but they hadn't. He and Devereux weren't boys, and this was far more serious than putting salt in someone's tea or flicking spitballs at their classmates. "Does Wilton know?" Perry asked.

"I wrote to him last week. Heaven only knows when he'll get the letter. Or if he ever will." Devereux expelled another sigh and rubbed his brow again.

"Were you and Wilton close?" Perry asked. "Was Flint a good friend of yours?"

Devereux shook his head. "Not really. We were friends, but not chums." He shrugged, then gave a wry laugh. "I was rather too staid for them, if you can believe it."

"You? Staid?"

Devereux grinned. "I know. Shocking, isn't it?" His grin faded. "But compared to Wilton, I am. He's a regular rakehell. Wild to a fault."

"If you're so staid, why do people call you Devil?" It hadn't been Devereux's nickname back when they were at school.

"Oh, that's from my Oxford days. I ran in the same crowd as Wilton and Jasper, back then. Always ripe for a spree, we were. Lord, the larks we got up to!" Devereux laughed at some memory, then shook his head. "But there's more to life than getting bosky every night. I haven't had much to do with either of 'em the last few years." His smile flattened. "But that doesn't mean I'm going to let Saint get away with this."

"No." Perry put his glass aside and stood. "I must be going."

Devereux stood, too. He took Perry's glass. "Sit."

"But—"

"*Sit*," Devereux said. There was no laughter on his face anymore, no smile in his eyes. He looked almost angry.

Perry hesitated, and then sat.

211

CHAPTER
THIRTY-FOUR

*D*evereux refilled the glass and thrust it into Perry's hand. "Now explain this nonsense about not being friends."

Perry looked away from those hard, angry eyes. He put the glass down on the table. "Dev, I told you, I have no—"

"I understand that you're not flush in the pocket, but I don't understand why that means we can't be friends."

"Because we live in different worlds."

"Nonsense," Devereux scoffed, sitting back down.

"It's not nonsense," Perry said, beginning to grow angry himself. "How much did that waistcoat cost? What about your shoes? That coat you're wearing? I earn eighty pounds a year, Dev, and you're wearing clothes worth three times that!"

"Then let me give you—"

"Don't!" Perry said fiercely. "If you're about to offer me money, don't."

They matched stares, then Devereux flexed his mouth in a rueful smile. "Sorry."

"This is your world," Perry said, less heatedly. He gestured at the comfortable parlor. "Mine is an attic in Holborn."

Devereux leaned forward. "I meant it, Perry. You can live here."

"No." He shook his head sharply. "I don't fit here anymore. And anyway, I'm re-enlisting."

"What? Why?"

"I sold out because Mother begged me to, but she's dead now, so . . ." He shrugged. "I'm going back to India."

"But you could be killed!"

"I'd rather die in battle than rot to death in Holborn."

Devereux frowned and opened his mouth.

"I hate it here, Dev."

Devereux must have heard the truth in his voice. He closed his mouth again.

"We live in different worlds, don't you see? We can't be friends anymore."

"I don't see it. What I see is that if you won't spend time here, I'll spend time in Holborn."

"What?"

"Holborn. Tomorrow." Devereux folded his lips mutinously.

Perry was familiar with that expression. It meant that even if he spent hours arguing—or days— Devereux wasn't going to budge. He sighed. "You always were a stubborn dog." But he wasn't angry. He'd like to be friends with Devereux again, even if it was only for a few weeks. "All right. Tomorrow you're dining in a chop house in Holborn. Four o'clock. Corner of High Holborn and Kingsgate."

"I'll be there," Devereux said.

Perry crossed Cavendish Square, so deep in thought that he didn't notice the prickling sensation across his scalp. When a disembodied voice came from above him, he was startled enough to jump.

"What happened?" Lady Violet asked. "What did he say?"

"A great deal. Too much to tell you here." His thoughts were awhirl, and not merely because Lady Violet had startled him. He needed to separate what Devereux had told him about Flint from everything else he'd said. "Can you meet me at my room in an hour and a half?"

"An hour and a half? Why?"

"Because I need to go back to Bow Street and write up my notes."

"Must you?" There was a pout in her voice.

"Yes, I must." He wanted to commit Devereux's tale to paper while everything was sharp in his memory. With that done, hopefully his thoughts would stop churning so madly and he'd be able to focus on other things.

Lady Violet huffed, and then said, "Can you at least give me a hint?"

Perry looked up. She was a dark blot against the night sky. "A hint?"

"Yes."

He frowned, wracking his brain—and then it came to him. "I know what you'll say when I tell you what's at the root of all this."

"What?"

"I told you so."

"I told you so?"

"That's what you'll say," Perry said, and then he strode in the direction of Bow Street.

CHAPTER
THIRTY-FIVE

Wintersmith refused to elaborate further, which was prodigiously frustrating. When he reached Oxford Street, he turned east. He walked fast, keeping to the main thoroughfares. Violet was forced to follow him at a distance.

The streets became busier, the people frequenting them less affluent. Wintersmith stopped and purchased something from a street vendor. The man's voice drifted up: "Penny pies! Eel, beef, and mutton pies! Pies all hot!"

Wintersmith ate while he walked. Two streets further on, he bought another pie and consumed that, too. Violet had never eaten a pie from a street vendor. She wondered what they tasted like.

At the corner of Bow Street and Long Acre, Wintersmith halted a third time, handing over a coin for what was loudly being advertised as "Lunnon's best Banbury cakes! Two for a penny!" He polished the pastries off in a few bites and ran up the steps to the magistrates' court, exchanging a word with the night watchman before going inside.

Violet took up position on a roof across the street.

Wintersmith entered the same room he'd entered last time. He sat at the same desk, unlocked a drawer, and took out what was probably the same notebook. He trimmed a quill and set to work.

Wintersmith had been telling the truth when he'd said he needed to write his notes. Words spilled from his quill, covering page after page. It was frustrating to watch him and yet not be able to read what he was writing. Questions sprouted in Violet's brain, proliferating madly, until her skull felt crammed with curiosity.

After fifteen minutes of writing, Wintersmith reached the end of his notebook. He read back through what he'd written, struck some sentences out, rewrote others, then took a fresh notebook from his drawer and set to work methodically transferring everything into it.

He was writing a clean copy.

Of course he was. Because he was meticulous and conscientious and if he was given a job he would do it scrupulously.

Violet rolled her eyes at him, but her smile was affectionate. She rather liked Wintersmith's diligence. If more people were as diligent as he was, the world would turn more smoothly.

But it was boring to watch him copy his notes.

She leaped off the roof and arrowed upwards.

Violet followed the Thames as far west as Richmond Park, then glided slowly back to London. This high above the river, its stink didn't reach her. The Thames looked peaceful and mysterious, sprinkled with moonlight and lamplight, a faerie-tale river winding its way through faerie-tale countryside to a faerie-tale city.

Violet drifted to a halt high above St. Paul's Cathedral and let the quiet joy of flying soak into her soul. Her heartbeat slowed. Her breathing slowed. She floated on cool air currents, as light as gossamer, drinking in the beauty of the night. London was a tapestry of shadow and light, glowing jewels laid out on a dark cloth.

The tolling of clocks drifted faintly up. Violet began a slow descent to a lane behind High Holborn.

She was sitting on the parapet outside Wintersmith's window when he at last came home. She suffered through the time it took him to close his door, set down his candlestick, and remove his hat, but when he began peeling off his gloves, she could no longer hold silent. "Why will I say 'I told you so'?" she demanded.

"Because you were right about something."

"What was I right about?"

He crossed to the window, tugging at his neckcloth to loosen it. "Jasper Flint's death is at the root of all this."

"It was murder!" Violet cried. "I knew it!"

Wintersmith shook his head. "It was an accident." He paused, and then said, "Wilton didn't kill Flint. Saintbridge did."

Violet's mouth dropped open.

She listened in astonishment to Wintersmith's tale. When he'd finished, she realized that her mouth was still open. She closed it hastily, and then opened it again to say, "What do we do now?"

Wintersmith leaned one hip against the windowsill. "I'm going to lay everything before Sir Mortimer on Monday. It's gone beyond the scope of what I was hired to do. I can guess how Lord Abbishaw would like me to proceed, but . . ." He pulled a face.

Violet could guess, too. "We can't let Saint get away with it!"

"I don't want him to, but I think he probably will. Saintbridge's word against a valet's?" Wintersmith shook his head. "Even if Abbishaw believes Goodlace—which I doubt—he won't want the truth to get out. He'll try to bury it, and he's a viscount, so he'll probably succeed."

"That's not fair!"

"Life isn't always fair." Wintersmith tugged at his neck-cloth again. Violet was reminded of how he'd looked when she'd arrived last night—sleeves rolled up, boots and neckcloth discarded. High above London the air was fresh and cool, but here, down among the streets and lanes, it was sluggish and warm. Despite the open window, Wintersmith's attic was stuffy. He probably wished he could roll up his sleeves and remove his neckcloth.

"Take it off," she said. "I don't mind."

Wintersmith's hand halted in mid-tug. "I beg your pardon?"

"Your neckcloth. Take it off if you wish."

He hesitated, then unwound the neckcloth. It was a very ordinary thing to do, unwinding a wrinkled strip of muslin, but it also seemed very intimate. Wintersmith was undressing; she was watching.

A frisson of arousal shivered over Violet's skin. "Your coat, too," she said in a low voice.

Wintersmith held her gaze for a moment, then removed his tailcoat and tossed it over the trunk at the end of his bed.

Seeing him in his shirtsleeves and waistcoat, with his shirt open at the throat, gave Violet another one of those exciting little frissons. "Roll up your sleeves."

Wintersmith did.

Violet liked the shape of his wrists and forearms, their sinewy strength. She decided she wanted to see the rest of him similarly exposed. "Waistcoat off."

Wintersmith waited a beat, then unbuttoned his waistcoat and shrugged out of it. He tossed it aside and met her eyes. He said nothing, but there was a hint of challenge in the tilt of his head.

Violet stared at him and listened to her heartbeat thump in her ears. She remembered the way he'd touched her, remembered what his skin had tasted like, what it had felt like to have him inside her.

She wanted to do it again.

Wintersmith wanted to do it again, too, or he wouldn't have taken off his waistcoat. Nor would he be standing there with his head tilted at that precise angle.

Anticipation was taut in the air, like the barely audible hum of a harp string.

Violet opened her mouth to say, "Shirt," and changed it to "Boots," instead.

She thought she saw a flicker of disappointment cross Wintersmith's face. She was certainly disappointed. She'd balked at the last instant, like a horse refusing a jump. "Shirt," she said decisively, as soon as he'd removed his boots.

A tiny smile ticked up one corner of Wintersmith's mouth. He pulled the shirt over his head, tossed it aside, and looked at her. The tilt of his head was even more pronounced. How far dare you go with this game? he was asking her silently.

All the way, was her answer, which he would shortly learn, but first Violet took a moment to drink in the sight of him—the strong bones of his shoulders, the planes of his chest. She'd been blind to think him bland and nondescript when she'd first seen him. Everything about him was rather thrilling, not just the little peaks of his nipples and the exciting line of hair that drew her gaze down towards his breeches, but every single thing. Even his nose. Even his ears.

She wanted to see all of him. The strong, muscular legs. The fascinating organ hidden beneath his breeches. She even wanted to see his toes. But that could wait another minute or two. The way Wintersmith stood, easy and confident, letting her stare at him, was exhilarating. He was waiting, letting her dictate what he did, what *they* did.

Violet knew what they were going to do. "Stockings and breeches," she said, fishing in her pocket for the drawings she'd brought with her.

Wintersmith shed his stockings and breeches. His gaze flicked to the folded pages in her hand, but he didn't say anything. He tossed the breeches on the growing pile of discarded clothing. All he wore now were his drawers.

Violet looked him up and down. She had nothing to compare him with except half-naked heroes immortalized in paint or marble, but in her opinion he was a very fine specimen. Except for those ragged, well-worn drawers. They had to go.

Violet's throat constricted, not with apprehension, but with anticipation. "Drawers," she said huskily.

Wintersmith stripped off his drawers and dropped them on the pile of clothes. He stood, arms relaxed by his sides, lightly balanced on his feet, his eyes meeting hers squarely.

Violet held his stare for a long moment, reading the challenge there, the invitation, and then let her gaze drift down.

Yes, a very fine specimen.

Wintersmith's organ hung engorged from the nest of hair at his groin, although it wasn't as big as she remembered, nor did it jut upwards quite so enthusiastically . . . but even as she watched, it altered, growing before her very eyes.

Violet stared, enthralled. How extraordinary that a man's organ could change like that, could become so plump and stiff and rosy.

When Wintersmith's organ had finished its transformation, she looked him up and down. Every part of him was intriguing, not just that miraculous organ. Her gaze strayed to his groin more than once, but she also spent time looking at his arms, his shoulders, his hands. His mouth. His calves.

Wintersmith didn't tell her to hurry; he simply let her look her fill. But even though he stood patiently, she could see what he wanted. It was in that eager organ, in the way he balanced lightly on his feet, as if ready to spring into action, in the way he held his hands, loosely curled, but not relaxed. It was in the way he watched her with intent, hungry eyes.

A great many of the illustrations in Freddy's bandbox had been of naked women being ogled by men. There hadn't been any scenes like this: a fully clothed woman staring at a naked man, enjoying how he looked, arousal heating her until it felt as if she had a furnace beneath her skin.

When looking was no longer enough, Violet said, "I have a drawing of what I'd like us to do."

Wintersmith didn't move, except for his mouth, which turned up at first one corner and then the other.

"Are you laughing at me?"

"No," he said, but his smile grew wider.

Violet huffed faintly, and unfolded the sketches she'd brought. She found the one she wanted. "This," she said, holding it out. "I want to do this."

Finally, Wintersmith moved. He crossed the floor, halting at the window. He was close enough to pull her in for a kiss, but he didn't; he plucked the drawing from her fingers and looked at it. His gaze flicked to her. "Are you wearing the clover leaf?"

"Yes."

He handed her back the drawing.

Violet didn't bother folding everything neatly; she shoved the pages back in her pocket. She thought Wintersmith might reach for her and pull her into the room, but he didn't. He moved back, silently inviting her inside.

Violet stepped down from the windowsill.

Now, he reached for her. Now, he kissed her.

CHAPTER
THIRTY-SIX

*T*he drawing Lady Violet had chosen was similar to last night's one—a man, a woman, a sofa—but this time the man was uppermost. She appeared to enjoy this variation as much as she'd enjoyed last night's, urging Perry to go faster, and then faster still. She climaxed twice before his own orgasm barreled through him.

Afterwards, Perry ached to take her in his arms and hold her close, but he didn't think she wanted tenderness from their liaison. He reluctantly rolled off her.

They lay side by side on his bed, catching their breath.

"By thunder," Lady Violet said. "I understand now why men visit brothels all the time."

Perry laughed at the "By thunder," because it sounded comical coming from a duke's daughter, and said, "Not all men."

Lady Violet pushed up on one elbow to look at him. Her lips were kiss-swollen, her eyes starry bright. "You don't?"

He shook his head.

"Why not?"

"I prefer it when sex isn't a business transaction."

"By thunder," she said again. "You're a romantic!"

Perry didn't laugh at that "By thunder." He felt himself blush. He pushed up onto one elbow, too. "No, I'm not."

It was a lie. He *was* a romantic—and it was just as well Lady Violet didn't want to be held tenderly, because if he did, it would be impossible not to fall in love with her, for her beauty and her spirit and because she made him feel alive in a way no one else ever had.

"You have other lovers?" Perry wasn't quite sure how to interpret her expression, the way her eyebrows tilted both inwards and upwards. Was she displeased? Curious? Both?

"Not in England."

"In India? While you were on campaign?"

"No, while I was on garrison duty."

He braced himself for questions about the women he'd known in India, but instead Lady Violet sat up. "Would you like to run on the roofs?"

"I'd love to, but it's too dangerous."

She gave a pretty little pout. "It's not that dangerous."

Perry sat up. "If I fall and die, it won't matter to me because I'll be dead. But it might matter to you."

Lady Violet's pout vanished. She stared at him, her eyes wide and shocked.

"My father gambled away a fortune. He didn't think about the consequences of what he was doing until it was too late. And then he went out and shot himself—a purposeful accident—and he didn't think about the consequences of that, either. To my mother, my brothers, me. So my question to you is, if I fall off a roof and die, can you live with that? Because you'll be the one who's left behind. The one who has to deal with it."

Lady Violet didn't answer. Her eyes were still wide, still shocked.

"If you'd be all right—"

"Of course I wouldn't be all right!"

"Then we can't do it again. I'm sorry. I wish we could. It was . . ." He struggled to find words to describe how exhilarating that journey across London had been. "It was the best hour of my life."

Lady Violet looked down at the coverlet and traced a fraying seam with her finger. Her expression was solemn, thoughtful. She glanced at him. "What if we fashion a harness? Then if you lose your footing, you won't fall."

"I'm heavier than you. You'd fall with me."

Lady Violet scrambled off the bed. "Stand up," she said imperiously.

She seemed to neither notice nor care that she was naked, but Perry certainly did. His cock began to express interest in resuming intimate relations.

He obeyed her command, standing alongside her on the bare floorboards.

"Face me."

He did.

Lady Violet stepped close and put her arms around him. Her breasts pressed tantalizingly against him, warm and round. Her nipples teased his skin. Perry's cock became even more interested in what was happening.

Lady Violet tightened her grip until it was almost painful . . . and then Perry found his feet lifting off the floor.

"Whoa!" He clutched at her shoulders. "What are you doing?"

Lady Violet didn't reply. Her arms clamped even more tightly around his ribcage. Perry's head bumped the ceiling. "Ouch."

"Sorry." They lurched an inch or two lower, and stayed there, hovering.

Perry's feet dangled, toes reaching in vain for the floor. He felt as heavy as a carthorse in her arms. "I'm too heavy for you—"

"You're not too heavy for my magic," Lady Violet said. "You're too heavy for my arms, though. I couldn't hold you up for long." They drifted back down. Perry's feet found the floor gratefully.

Lady Violet released him and shook out her arms. "I could hold you up with a harness. Not forever, but long enough to be safe. If you slipped, you wouldn't fall all the way to the street."

"It's too dangerous," Perry said, but his tone was unconvincing.

"No, it's not." She put her hands on her hips and stared at him challengingly.

Perry was distracted by her breasts. And by her waist. By her quim. Her—

"Periander!"

He jerked his gaze up to her face. "I beg your pardon. Yes?"

"With a harness, the risk would be no greater than riding a horse."

Perry frowned. He wasn't certain it was a valid comparison, although it was definitely possible to fall off a horse and break one's neck. People did it every day, a fact that had never stopped him from riding.

But it wasn't the safety of the rider that concerned him in this instance; it was the safety of the horse. If Lady Violet were to be injured, he wouldn't be able to live with himself.

"You said it was the best hour of your life . . ." Lady Violet said coaxingly.

Actually, the best hours of his life were the two he'd spent making love to her, last night and tonight, but the rooftop running came a very close second.

"Please?"

Perry gave in. "If we can fashion a harness, I'll try it."

"Yes!" Lady Violet clapped her hands and gave a little skip and then bounced on her toes to press a kiss to his mouth. She took a step back and looked down at his burgeoning erection. "Does that mean what I think it means?"

"If what you think it means is that I'd like to have congress with you again, then yes, it does. But you don't have to if you don't want to."

"I do!" Her eyes were bright with curiosity. "What shall we do this time?"

"What would you like to do?"

"I don't know."

"Do you have any more pictures?"

Her nose wrinkled. "I don't think they're things that can be done, and even if they are, we can't do them now."

"Show me."

Lady Violet rooted through her discarded clothes, giving him a view of a very enticing derrière as she did so. She produced several sheets of crumpled paper and unfolded them. "Is this possible?"

Perry's startled gaze landed on a sketch of a man and woman copulating while riding a horse that was galloping hell-for-leather. "No," he said emphatically.

Lady Violet gave a satisfied nod. "I didn't think so. What about this one?"

"It's possible, but only if the curricle is at a standstill and the horse tied up."

Lady Violet gave another nod. She held out a third sketch.

Perry took it, and felt his eyebrows climb up to his hairline. "You want me to balance a candelabrum on my, uh . . ." He searched for an inoffensive word for a penis. "My yardstick?"

She chuckled. "No, of course not, but is it possible?"

"No. Nor is it possible for yardstick to be a yard long." He handed the sketch back. "It's nonsense. All three of those are."

"I thought so." Lady Violet didn't look disappointed. She screwed the three sketches up as if they were no more than tinder for a fire, which, in Perry's opinion, was all they were good for.

"That's it? They're the only ones you copied?"

"Yes. I didn't like most of the pictures in Freddy's collection. I wonder . . . could you purchase some for me? Is that possible? Do you know where Freddy bought them?"

Perry didn't frequent the pornographers in Holywell Lane, but he knew where they were. "I can try. But you may not like them any more than you liked most of Stanhope's collection."

"I like ones like this." She laid two sketches on his rumpled bed, last night's image and tonight's.

Perry studied them. He knew why he liked them, but he wasn't sure why Lady Violet did. "What is it about them that you like?"

"No Peeping Toms," she said, without hesitation. "No people spying through keyholes or windows. And no ladies displaying themselves for men to look at."

Perry cast his mind back to the contents of Stanhope's bandbox. Most of the images had fallen into that latter category: women on display for men to look at. "What else?"

She gave a helpless shrug. "I don't know. I just like them."

Perry picked up the drawings and looked for similarities. The most obvious one was that the women were active and enthusiastic participants, not passive receptacles. He liked that, and Lady Violet probably did, too, even if she couldn't articulate it.

But that wasn't the only reason he liked the drawings, or even the main reason.

The images she'd chosen were playful. The couples looked like lovers, people who shared an intimate connection. The drawings were lighthearted, fun, joyful, but more than that, there was a sense of tenderness.

That was what Perry liked most: the tenderness.

If Lady Violet had chosen these two drawings out of all the ones in Stanhope's box, then perhaps she liked tenderness, too?

Perry handed the sketches back. "I'll see what I can do. It won't be until Monday, though."

"Thank you." She looked from one drawing to the other. "Which one would you like to do now?"

"How about we try something different? Have you ever seen a stallion cover a mare?"

"No, but I did see two dogs do it once. Is it like that?" Lady Violet dropped the sketches and scrambled up on the bed. "Like this?"

All the blood in Perry's brain migrated south so abruptly that he felt dizzy. Speech deserted him. He had never in his life seen anything so erotic, so sensual, so arousing, as what was before him.

It wasn't just the lush curve of Lady Violet's buttocks and the way she tilted them invitingly upward, nor was it the globes of her breasts so beautifully defined by gravity, or even the quim enticingly displayed between her parted legs. It was the way she was looking at him, a glance that was roguish, mischievous, provocative.

Perry swallowed. "Yes," he said huskily. "Exactly like that."

He mounted her the way a stallion mounted a mare, but there the resemblance ended. Stallions didn't fondle their mates until they were trembling and breathless, nor did they tease their quims until they were so lost in arousal that all they could utter were guttural moans.

Their coupling, when he finally gave in to Lady Violet's increasingly incoherent urging, was as vigorous and energetic as any stallion's, but Perry didn't release her once the last spasms had shaken their bodies. He snugged one arm around her and eased them down on the coverlet, and then he held her close, his body curling around hers, his face pressed into her sweet-smelling hair, one hand stroking her skin, infinitesimal movements of his thumb and fingers, soothing and gentle, giving her the tenderness he wanted. The tenderness he thought she might want, too.

Lady Violet didn't object. On the contrary, she lay relaxed in his arms. Five minutes passed, or perhaps it was ten, before she said, "I liked that."

"Good."

She sighed, a sound that his ears wanted to interpret as reluctance to leave his embrace, and then stirred as if she wanted to get up.

Perry released her.

Lady Violet sat up, gave another sigh, and stepped down from the bed—then she scrambled back up. "A rat!" she hissed, eyes wide with fright.

"It'll only be a mouse," Perry said, hoping that she wasn't going to scream. He peered over the edge of the bed, and revised his opinion. The creature investigating the discarded clothes was definitely a rat.

Perry wasn't allowed female guests in his room, and if Lady Violet screamed someone would undoubtedly hear, so he said, in a falsely cheerful voice, "Just a mouse," and flicked his hand at the creature, hoping to startle it into flight.

The rat didn't run for whichever hole it had come from. It sniffed at the clothes.

"That is *not* a mouse," Lady Violet whispered fiercely in his ear.

"It's a large mouse," Perry said. He was reluctant to step down from the bed with bare feet. He'd seen rat bites and how putrid they could become.

He reached down to grab one of Lady Violet's shoes.

"It's a *rat*."

"A giant mouse," Perry said, snagging the shoe and casting it at the rat.

The rat bolted.

Perry climbed off the bed and shoved his trunk sideways to cover up the hole—which exposed another hole, but at least that one was only large enough for mice. When he turned back, Lady Violet stood beside the bed. Her arms were folded across her chest. "That was a *rat*," she said accusingly.

"It was," Perry admitted.

"Why didn't you say so?"

"I didn't want you to scream."

"I wouldn't have screamed. I'm not a pudding heart!"

"I beg your pardon. The next time I see a rat, I'll tell you."

"There won't be a next time. Not in this room."

"I've covered up the hole."

Lady Violet's expression informed him that it was too little, too late. She uncrossed her arms and began to dress rapidly.

Perry watched her uneasily. Was this good-bye? Forever?

"I'll make up a harness tomorrow," Lady Violet said, pulling her shirt over her head. "And I'll bring some blankets. Unless you have spares?"

"Blankets?" Perry said, relieved that she intended to return. "Whatever for?"

"To put on a roof."

"Which roof?"

"One that's flat on top. Some of them are, you know."

Perry felt his brow scrunch in confusion. "Why?"

"So we can do that again, of course." Lady Violet gestured at the bed, her meaning clear.

"You want us to swive on a roof?" His voice rose on the last word in disbelief.

"Swive?" Her head tilted inquiringly.

"Uh . . . sexual congress."

"Swive." Lady Violet repeated the word, fixing it in her internal lexicon, then said, "Yes, I want us to swive on a roof— because we're certainly not doing it in here! Not if there are rats."

Perry thought that rats could roam about on roofs almost as easily as they could roam about in attic bedrooms, but he didn't tell Lady Violet that, because he wanted to make love to her again. "I don't have any spare blankets."

"Then I'll bring some." She did up her shoes.

Perry watched, bemused, as Lady Violet shrugged into her coat and buttoned it swiftly. She wound her neckcloth twice around her neck and shoved the ends inside the coat, then caught up her gloves and mask. "Good-bye." A flash of a grin, a wave of her fingers, and she was gone.

CHAPTER
THIRTY-SEVEN

*A*fter Sunday morning service, Violet set to work making a harness for Wintersmith. First, she invaded the mews and appropriated one of her family's carriage harnesses. It was too heavy to carry all by herself, so a stable boy helped her lug it back through the garden and up to the house. He balked at the door, though, indicating the state of his boots, so two footmen took over. Violet led them up the stairs and directed them to lay the harness out on the floor of the blue parlor.

"Thank you," Violet said, once this task had been completed.

"What *are* you doing?" Rhodes asked from the doorway.

"I thought you were going out in the barouche with the children."

Rhodes shook his head. "Aster, Daffy, and Clem have gone with them."

"Excellent!" Violet said. "You can help me."

"Help you with what?"

The footmen had gone, but she gestured for Rhodes to close the door before she told him: "I'm making a person-sized harness."

"Whatever for?"

"Do you remember I told you how I helped Wintersmith down from a roof?"

Rhodes nodded.

"Well, I didn't help him down immediately."

Rhodes eyed her for a long moment, and then shook his head. "Of course you didn't." He sat down on the Egyptian sofa. "Tell me."

Violet told him about holding on to Wintersmith so that he could run along the ridgeline, and how Wintersmith had leaped over the first alleyway—and how after that they'd decided to stay on the rooftops until he was home.

Rhodes winced with his whole face. "How far was this?"

"From Conduit Street to High Holborn."

"And he *jumped* across the streets?"

"Yes."

Rhodes made another whole-face wince. "He's lucky to be alive."

"He did almost fall a couple of times," Violet confessed. "That's what the harness is for. He says he won't go up on the roofs again, because if he falls he doesn't want me to think that I killed him. But if he's tied to me then he can't fall, can he?"

Rhodes frowned and opened his mouth, no doubt to point out that if Wintersmith stayed on the ground, he couldn't fall either.

"He says it's important to think about consequences. The harness is for *my* sake as much as his."

Rhodes closed his mouth. A very peculiar expression crossed his face.

"What?"

"The Periander Wintersmith I knew did not think about consequences."

"Well, he does now, which is why I want to make a harness. Will you help me?"

Rhodes hesitated.

"Please?" Violet clasped her hands together beseechingly. "I'm always alone up there. You have no idea how marvelous it was to have company!"

Rhodes looked as if he was torn between offering to go up on roofs himself or telling her that rooftop jaunts were too dangerous for people who couldn't fly, even if they had harnesses.

"I know you'd come with me if you could, but you don't like heights and Wintersmith does. He said it was the best hour of his life."

Rhodes's expression told her that if he were up on a rooftop it would be the worst hour of his life.

"Please will you help me make a harness?" Violet begged. "I want it to be as safe as can be."

Rhodes sighed. "All right, I'll help—but for heaven's sake don't either of you break your necks, or *I'll* be the one who has to live with the consequences."

"I promise." Violet hugged him exuberantly. "You're the best brother ever!"

They worked on the harness for the rest of the morning. Rhodes was relentless. Violet would have been satisfied with the first iteration, but it took another hour before her brother was. Then he insisted on taking it down to the ballroom to test. Violet donned her part of the harness while Rhodes made certain all the doors were locked. He checked her buckles, his frown easing somewhat when he found them snugly fastened. Next, Violet hovered behind him while he secured not one, not two, but three straps around his chest.

Rhodes double-checked all his buckles.

"Ready?" Violet asked.

"Ready."

Violet allowed her legs to float up behind her until she was lying flat in the air. She put her arms around Rhodes, clasping her hands over his breastbone, resting her chin on his shoulder.

Rhodes took off at a jog across the ballroom.

On the hottest of summer nights, they flew like this across the lake at Manifold Park, Rhodes's feet skimming just above the water. Occasionally her brother reached the other side dry, but more often than not he ended up in the water, sometimes because he became too heavy for her, sometimes because she dropped him on purpose. This was different. Violet couldn't drop him even if she wanted to. The straps dug in across her shoulders and upper back, easing the strain on her arms. Rhodes was still heavy, but holding him up was easy.

Violet flew a little higher, taking more of his weight. Rhodes's toes touched the floor at the beginning and end of each stride, but he was weightless in between.

Her brother ran faster. It was similar to how it had been on the rooftops with Wintersmith. Rhodes was flying as much as running, taking great soaring strides, but she didn't have to hold on tightly. Her shoulders bore the brunt of his weight. Her hands were only loosely clasped.

They made two circuits of the ballroom before Violet slowed to a halt. The harness didn't feel precisely comfortable, but her hands weren't cramping from holding on and her arms didn't ache.

Rhodes was a little out of breath.

"What do you think?" she asked.

"It's rather fun. I can see why Wintersmith enjoyed it."

"Would you like to run on the roofs?" Violet asked, surprised.

"No, thank you," her brother said, very firmly.

"We can use the harness at the lake this summer, if you like?"

Rhodes shook his head again. "I like falling in."

He reached up to undo his buckles, but Violet said, "May I try one more thing?"

"What?"

"I want to see how easy it is to bear your full weight."

"All right."

Violet snugged her arms around her brother again, but this time she lifted him straight up off the floor. She rose two feet, three feet, five, ten. Rhodes was tense with discomfort, but he didn't ask her to put him down.

"Do you mind if I take you even higher?"

His hands clamped over hers. "Do it," he gritted.

Violet floated up until their hair almost brushed the high, ornate ceiling. Her brother's weight pulled her down. He was hugely heavy. The straps strained, biting into her shoulders, but her magic didn't strain.

She could feel Rhodes's tension, his fear. His hands were locked over hers and he sounded as if he was breathing through clenched teeth.

She lowered him back to the floor. He released his breath in a whoosh and hastened to undo the buckles.

"Thank you. I know you hated that."

Rhodes merely grunted.

"We'll be safe, don't you think?" Violet asked, once he'd extricated himself from the harness.

"Yes." Rhodes rubbed under his arms, wincing a little.

"Did it hurt?" she asked, undoing her own buckles.

"Not so much with the running, but that . . ." He tipped his thumb at the ceiling. "Yes."

Violet rubbed her shoulders. She could feel where the straps had bitten in, but it was a mild discomfort. Negligible compared to the consequences, namely that if Wintersmith were to fall off a roof, he'd be safe. Her magic was strong enough for them both.

"So, you and Wintersmith . . ." Rhodes was frowning. "I think perhaps I ought to speak with him again."

Heat flamed in her cheeks. Violet bent hastily and fussed over the harness, laying it out on the floor. "There's no need. He's leaving London soon. We'll probably only run on the roofs once or twice." She rolled the harness up.

"Leaving London?"

"Yes. He's re-enlisting, as soon as the case is closed—which could be tomorrow." She forgot about her hot cheeks and straightened excitedly. "We know the whole of it, now! I wish I could tell you! It's such a story. You'd never believe who the villain is and why he's doing it."

"Tell me," Rhodes invited.

Violet shook her head firmly. "No. I gave my word."

Rhodes didn't look annoyed. She saw curiosity on his face, but also something that might possibly be approval. He tucked the bundled harness under one arm. Together they crossed the ballroom.

"I'll ask Wintersmith if I can tell you it all," Violet said as she unlocked the door. "But I think it's going to be hushed up—and it shouldn't be! Someone you and I both know has done a dreadful thing. I do wish I could tell you. You'd give him a direct cut!"

"You intrigue me," Rhodes said. They climbed the stairs, side by side. At the door to her bedroom, Rhodes handed her the bundle of straps and buckles. "I'm going to finish pasting the balloons together. Want to help?"

"Yes. I'll be there in a moment!"

Violet crammed the harness into her window seat. She had blankets yet to find for tonight, as well as something sturdy and preferably waterproof in which to wrap them, which might require more plundering of the stables, but first, balloons. She ran up to the nursery to help her brother.

CHAPTER THIRTY-EIGHT

*D*evereux Abbishaw was waiting at the corner of Kingsgate and High Holborn at four o'clock. He'd dressed down—drab buckskins, a plain waistcoat—but his clothes still cost more than Perry earned in a year.

"Afternoon," Perry said.

"Afternoon," Devereux replied.

There was a brief, uncomfortable pause. Were they friends who shook hands when they met? Friends who clapped one another on the shoulder? Friends who hugged? Ten years ago, they'd have known. Now, they just stood awkwardly.

"So, a chop house?" Devereux said.

"Yes."

Perry took him round the corner to a chop house where he often ate. To one side was a shop where one could purchase various cuts of meat, at the back was a busy kitchen, and all around were cheap tables where one might sit and dine. Perry didn't care what he ate today, so he merely asked for the ordinary and a tankard of ale. After a moment's hesitation, Devereux did, too.

Perry leaned back in his chair and tried to look relaxed. He didn't feel relaxed, though; he was deeply uncomfortable. He frequently patronized chop houses like this, but it was clear that Devereux had never eaten anywhere so humble. He kept darting glances around, watching as customers brought in beef cheeks and pig trotters to be cooked. The air was thick with the scent of roasting mutton, and beneath that aroma was the ever-present smell of sweat. The people who dined here were not people who tended to wash weekly. Or even monthly.

He glanced at Devereux, only to find that he'd stopped scrutinizing the other patrons and was now staring at Perry.

"Tell me about India."

A serving man wearing a catskin waistcoat brought their ale at that moment. Perry received his tankard gratefully. "India? Well . . ."

It was an easy conversation opener, but the conversation wasn't easy. It was awkward, labored, clumsy. They were striving for something convivial, and failing—until halfway through the tankards, when suddenly the awkwardness melted away and it was as if ten years and a gulf in fortunes didn't stand between them.

The serving man brought them the ordinary, which proved to be pea soup, bread and cheese, and a roasted pig jowl.

Perry dug in heartily. So did Devereux.

They talked as they ate, talked and laughed and ribbed one other. Perry felt like himself for the first time since he'd returned to England. This was what he missed most from India: the camaraderie of his regiment, the feeling of brotherhood. When he'd finished eating, he pushed his plate to one side. "Thank you for your letters. I know I didn't write back very often, but they meant a lot. I, uh, saved them all." He felt himself flush at that admission.

Devereux shrugged. "I saved all yours."

They looked at each other for a long moment. "I missed you, Perry," Devereux said.

"I missed you, too."

"Can you not stay in England?"

"And do what? The jobs my schooling suits me for bore me to death, and the ones that fit my temperament don't pay enough for a roof over my head."

"Will you be able to purchase your captaincy back?"

Perry shook his head. "I'll have to work my way up again, but that's all right. My C.O. will be glad to have me back. He was none too pleased when I left."

Devereux opened his mouth as if to offer to pay for a captaincy, but whatever he saw on Perry's face made him pick up his tankard instead.

The serving man came to collect their plates. Perry asked for fresh tankards for them both and more bread and cheese. While they waited, Devereux said, "What is it you like so much about the army?"

Perry hadn't known the answer to that when he was in India, but he did now. "They're my family."

Devereux's expression altered ever so slightly, a faint compression of his lips, an infinitesimal contraction of his eyebrows. Perry wasn't sure what that change meant. Sympathy? Pity? Fellow feeling? Devereux had an uncle and cousins who acknowledged his existence, but other than that he was as alone in the world as Perry was, parents dead, no siblings.

The bread and cheese and ale arrived. Perry changed the subject. "Do you remember that time we poured milk down the headmaster's chimney?"

Devereux uttered a crack of laughter. "I can't believe we did that. Lord, we were mad."

Perry agreed. "Would have been expelled if they'd caught us. Would've served us right, too."

"I got sent down a few times from Oxford," Devereux confessed. "Drank too much, you know. Bosky nearly every night. Lord, the mischief I got up to!" His smile was nostalgic. "Those were the days."

Perry snorted a laugh. "You sound like an old man."

"Wilton and Jasper thought I'd become one. Heckled me when I went to bed that night." Devereux pulled a face. "I wish I'd stayed."

"What happened wasn't your fault."

"I know. But . . ." He grimaced, shrugged.

Perry sipped his ale, and thought about Jasper Flint's death. "Do you think your man would talk to me?"

"Possibly. Why?"

"I'd like to know exactly what he saw."

It was almost dark by the time they left the chop house. "Best meal I've had in years," Devereux declared.

Perry would have laughed at such blatant hyperbole, except that it had been one of the best meals he'd ever had, too. Not the food, but the company.

They strolled in the direction of the nearest hackney stand. "What are you doing this evening?" Devereux asked. "Want to come back with me? Play some chess? If I recall, you won the last game."

"I can't," Perry said, and even though he was counting the minutes until he met with Lady Violet, part of him regretted not being able to take up Devereux's invitation. "I have a prior engagement."

"Oh?" Devereux cocked an eyebrow and waited for him to elaborate.

"I'm meeting someone, is all."

Devereux's gaze sharpened. "A female someone?"

Perry opened his mouth to say *No*, found himself reluctant to lie, and instead evasively said, "Maybe."

"Got yourself a convenient, have you?"

A faint blush warmed his face. "It's not like that."

"She's inconvenient then, is she?"

His face grew warmer. "Of course not."

Devereux hooted with laughter.

Perry elbowed him in the ribs. Devereux elbowed him back. They were both grinning. It felt as if they were sixteen again, not twenty-six.

All too soon, they came abreast of the hackneys. There was no awkwardness when they parted. They hugged and clapped shoulders, because that's the sort of friends they were.

Perry hurried back to his lodgings, fetched up a ewer of cold water, and washed as best he could. He dressed in clean clothes. The laundrywoman hadn't used enough starch on his neckcloths, but that didn't matter, because the state of one's neckcloths was irrelevant when one was on roofs.

He was tucking a fresh handkerchief into his pocket when he heard a sound at his window.

Perry turned quickly.

A dark figure leaned in over the windowsill, a bulky bundle clasped in its arms.

"Lady Violet."

"Just Violet." She slung the bundle onto the floor, where it landed with a tinkling thud.

"Violet," Perry said. It felt significant to dispense with the honorific, a declaration of intimacy.

Lady Violet didn't follow the bundle in through the window. She sat on the sill and removed her mask. Clearly she'd decided not to set foot in his rodent-plagued room. "Rhodes helped me make it. Go on, try it."

Perry turned his attention to what she'd tossed on the floor.

Lady Violet had said that she'd bring blankets for them to lie on, but the bundle consisted only of leather straps and metal buckles.

241

He felt a sharp pang of disappointment. There'd be no lovemaking tonight.

"You couldn't find any spare blankets?" It took effort to sound neutral rather than deeply disappointed.

"I did," she said cheerfully. "I've already chosen a roof. I left them there. Don't worry; I wrapped them up in oilcloth. They're quite clean."

"Which roof?"

Lady Violet swung one of her legs, bumping her heel against the wall. Mischief was bright in her eyes. Her smile was a little wicked. "Northumberland House."

Perry was struck speechless for several seconds. When he found his voice again, he said, "Underneath the lion?"

"Of course."

He laughed. It was impossible not to.

Lady Violet's smile widened into a grin. "You approve of my choice?"

"I love it," Perry said, almost stumbling on the last word, because his tongue wanted to say *I love you*, not *I love it.*

And it was true. He was in love with her.

He hoped that realization wasn't emblazoned across his face and crouched to hide it if it was, because Lady Violet hadn't come for romance and love; she'd come for excitement.

His love for her was unwanted and unviable, a tiny seedling that would never grow into a tree.

Perry spread the harness out on the floor. There were a lot of straps, a lot of buckles, but both straps and buckles were sturdy. His heart kicked in his chest. Tonight was going to be exceptional.

But when he looked up at Lady Violet, perched on his windowsill, he came to another realization. He didn't need rooftops or lovemaking for tonight to be exceptional. This was all he needed: Violet Garland sitting on his windowsill. He'd be happy with that alone. Her presence. Her conversation.

But conversation wasn't what she was here for, any more than she was here for romance. She wanted the thrill of the rooftops.

"How does this harness work?" he asked.

It took several minutes for them both to get into the harness, but at last all the straps were tight and all the buckles fastened. Perry put on the black loo mask to hide his face and pulled on gloves to keep his hands clean.

Getting out of the window proved rather awkward, but it too was accomplished. Perry stood with his boots wedged precariously in the narrow gap between the parapet and the roof, his hands splayed on the slates.

He scrambled upwards, slipping and sliding but unafraid. The harness was tight around his chest. If he fell, he wouldn't fall far.

Lady Violet tried to help by gripping his tailcoat, but the fabric merely bunched. Undeterred, she took hold of the waistband of his breeches. Perry stopped slipping and sliding. Within seconds, he was standing on the ridgeline. Euphoria rose in him like a tide. He wanted to tip back his head and laugh.

Lady Violet released his waistband and linked her arms around his chest. She lay in the air behind him, her chin resting on his shoulder. He caught the faint scent of orange blossom.

"Ready?" she asked.

"Ready."

Perry began to run.

CHAPTER
THIRTY-NINE

*I*t was even better than it had been last time. The harness wasn't comfortable, but it gave Perry the confidence to run faster, to leap higher and further. He headed towards Charing Cross, pelting along one ridgeline after another, soaring effortlessly over alleyways and streets. When he leaped over a row of chimney pots and discovered that the roof on the other side was a story lower than its neighbor, Lady Violet brought his plunge to a halt. His feet landed lightly on the new ridgeline and the instinctive scream in his throat came out as a wild laugh.

Two chimneys later, the houses became taller again. Lady Violet took hold of his waistband and Perry scaled the side of the building like a monkey. He paused at the top.

"All right?" Lady Violet asked in his ear.

"More than all right. This is capital fun!" And then he thought to ask, "Are you enjoying it?"

"Prodigiously!"

He ran again. Roof after roof, street after street. They reached the Strand and headed west. Charing Cross came into view: the statue of Charles the First astride his horse, the pillory, the Golden Cross Inn. Across from the inn was the huge brick edifice of Northumberland House.

Perry leaped across the Strand opposite Hungerford Market, where the street was at its narrowest. The buildings were uneven in height. Tall, short, tall, taller. The square towers at each end of Northumberland House were the tallest. Perry scrambled up the side of one and climbed over the parapet, high above Charing Cross. His heart was beating hard and he was panting. Lady Violet was a little out of breath, too.

He walked along the lengthy frontage of Northumberland House feeling like a mountaineer traversing a narrow ridge. To his left was the inner courtyard, to his right was Charing Cross. No one was in the pillory at the center of the cross-roads, but the taverns were busy. A stagecoach negotiated the turn into the yard of the Golden Cross.

At the very middle of the frontage, above the central bay with its oriel window, was a mighty arch upon which stood a proud stone lion.

Nestled under the arch was a dark bundle that Perry guessed was blankets.

Anticipation shivered through him. He reached for the buckles that fastened the harness.

"Let's sit on the lion," Lady Violet said, before he had time to loosen the first buckle.

"All right."

Perry clambered up the archway and they sat on the lion's broad back together. Lady Violet leaned snuggly into him.

"Have you sat up here before?" Perry asked.

"Yes."

He wondered which she preferred—to be up here alone, or with company—which led him to wonder whether she ever felt lonely while she flew. Her everyday life brimmed with people and entertainments, but her private nighttime life was solitary.

Lady Violet made no move to climb down from the lion.

Perry sat, soaking in the busyness of Charing Cross and the quietness of night. He smelled orange blossom and coal smoke and a faint, rank whiff from the Thames. The clatter of carriage wheels rose up, distant shouts, a street vendor's cries, a dog barking.

"Are the pies that one buys on the street nice?"

"Some of them."

"What about the Banbury cakes?"

"They're good, but I'm sure your cook makes better."

"We have a pastry cook. He's French. He makes mille-feuille and macarons, but he doesn't make Banbury cakes."

It seemed rather odd to be sitting on a stone lion on top of a mighty house talking about baked goods and French cooks. The street vendor's cries drifted up again, and Perry belatedly realized why they were discussing pastry.

"I'd like to try one of those Banbury cakes," Lady Violet said.

Perry peered down and located the vendor. "Now?"

"No, not now. Right now, I'd like to swive."

The word "swive" sounded incongruous coming from her mouth, a blunt, uncouth piece of slang, but it effectively diverted Perry's thoughts from Banbury cakes.

They climbed down from the lion.

They unfastened the harness.

They unrolled the oilcloth and spread the blankets beneath the arch.

They didn't swive on those blankets, though. At least, not in Perry's opinion. In his opinion they made love. It was laughing and playful, fast, breathless, exuberant, but also tender. Afterwards, they lay entwined in the blankets. None of it felt real. Not the coal-scented breeze feathering over his bare skin. Not the sounds drifting up from the busy crossroads. Not the great arch looming above them with the stone lion standing proudly atop. Not the duke's daughter in his arms.

Perry pressed his face into her hair and breathed in her scent. He wanted the moment to last forever.

It didn't. It couldn't.

They dressed and rolled the blankets back up in the oilcloth, then buckled themselves into the harness and put on their masks. "I'll come back for the blankets later," Lady Violet said, and then, sounding uncharacteristically diffident, she said, "Would you like to do this again tomorrow?"

"Yes. That is . . . if you wish to?"

"I do. How about the roof of Spencer House? Or the Burlington House colonnade?"

"I don't mind. You choose."

"The colonnade," Lady Violet said, checking the last of the buckles. "Is there anywhere you'd like to do it?"

Perry thought for a moment. "The roof of the British Museum?"

Lady Violet gave a little crow of laughter. "Yes! Let's!"

They took a different route back to Holborn, where they climbed in through Perry's window and extricated themselves from the harness. Lady Violet kissed him good-bye. "You'll tell me what Sir Mortimer says tomorrow, won't you?" she said, refastening her mask.

"Of course."

"I hope . . ." She didn't finish that sentence, but Perry knew what she hoped for. He hoped for it, too. For Saintbridge to face reckoning for what he'd done.

He didn't think it would happen, though.

"Oh! I almost forgot." Lady Violet dug into a pocket and produced a banknote. "If you have time, can you buy me some of those pictures? You know the sort I like."

"I'll see what I can do."

"Good night—and good luck tomorrow!"

CHAPTER FORTY

*F*irst thing Monday morning, Perry went to Bow Street to request an audience with Sir Mortimer.

Unfortunately, Sir Mortimer was exceedingly busy. The only time he had available was late in the day. Perry took it.

Next, he went to Cavendish Square, where he and Devereux had a long conversation with the valet, Goodlace. Perry had assumed the valet would be a bumptious, get-ahead type with an eye open for any opportunity that might present itself. Instead, he found himself interviewing a meek, self-effacing little man whom Perry could very well imagine being bullied into accepting a bribe.

Goodlace still had the money Saintbridge had given him. Several of the banknotes looked to be brand new. "Mind if I borrow these for an hour or two?" Perry asked.

"You think you can trace them?" Devereux said.

"Possibly."

When Perry presented himself at Coutts & Co. private bank, along with his Principal Officer's tipstaff, he discovered that some of the banknotes were indeed brand new. An inspection of the ledger confirmed that they'd been issued to Saintbridge Abbishaw shortly before Flint's demise. The manager obligingly wrote out a statement to this effect and stamped it with the bank's seal.

Perry returned to Cavendish Square and gave the notes back to Goodlace, who looked as if he would rather be rid of them. Devereux cocked an eyebrow. "Well?"

"Issued to your cousin."

This news appeared to cheer Devereux immensely. He clapped his hands together. "Excellent! That calls for a toast."

Perry drank a glass of very fine brandy, then appropriated Devereux's study and transcribed the valet's account of Jasper Flint's death onto several sheets of hot-pressed paper.

He ate a late luncheon there at Cavendish Square, then bade his friend farewell and headed across town to where the purveyors of erotic literature and prints sold their wares. A brisk breeze plucked at his coat-tails and hat.

Setting foot on Holywell Street was like stepping back in time. The buildings were tall, crooked, and half-timbered, leaning towards one another over the narrow street. A thin strip of daylight illuminated grimy shop fronts with stacks of books piled high in their windows. More books were displayed outside on trestle tables.

Perry browsed his way up the length of the street, looking for images he thought Lady Violet would like. He wasn't the only customer. Men of all ranks frequented the shops. He even saw several footmen in livery, presumably purchasing the latest publications for their masters. The only women on the street were Covent Garden nuns.

The majority of images for sale were of the sort Stanhope favored, the sort Lady Violet had said she didn't care for—women on display, women exposing themselves to men, couples being spied on through doorways and windows and keyholes—but Perry managed to find half a dozen that showed acts of playful and affectionate lovemaking. He found the two illustrations she'd liked in Stanhope's collection. She'd already copied them, but he bought them in case she wanted the originals. He also came across a number of quite absurd images that he thought would make her laugh. A dozen such were bound into a pamphlet, so he bought that, too.

In one shop, with a low ceiling and crooked floor, he found a drawing that subverted the normal paradigm: a man stood naked while a fully clothed lady looked him over.

The lady admires her stallion, it was titled.

It reminded him of when he'd stripped for Lady Violet and she'd watched with hungry curiosity. Perry bought that one, too. If she didn't like it, he'd keep it for himself.

He still had an hour and a half before his appointment with Sir Mortimer, so he went to the leatherworkers' shops down by the tanneries and purchased several items that he hoped would make their next rooftop excursion easier. He ducked into a secondhand clothing shop on his way home and bought a black neckcloth, a black shirt, black breeches, black stockings. He ran up the stairs to his attic bedroom, stowed the purchases in his trunk, then headed back to Bow Street. A boisterous breeze sped him on his way.

Tolly was still ensconced behind Perry's desk, guarding his little territory of documents, inkpot, quill, and sand shaker.

"Any messages for me?" Perry asked.

"No."

He'd thought Lord Abbishaw would have called him off the case by now, but perhaps Abbishaw was operating under the assumption that if one ignored a problem it would go away.

Which this problem probably would.

Perry unlocked his topmost drawer and took out his earlier notes, while Tolly scowled at him; then he went downstairs to wait for Devereux and Goodlace. They arrived in a hackney. Neither man looked overjoyed to be at Bow Street Magistrates' Court.

Perry led them upstairs. At the door to Sir Mortimer's office, he exchanged a glance with Devereux. For a brief, disorienting moment, it felt as if they'd spun back in time and were at school, standing in front of the headmaster's door, about to be subjected to yet another dressing down and most likely a caning.

They'd once had a ritual for moments like this. One of them would whistle a few jaunty bars under his breath, and the other would say "Time to face the piper," and then they'd square their shoulders and lift their chins and march inside to meet their fate.

This time, no one was at risk of being caned. In all likelihood, Sir Mortimer would listen to their story and tell them to leave best alone.

Perry rapped on the door.

"Enter."

Perry ushered in Devereux and Goodlace and introduced them. They all sat.

Sir Mortimer eyed them from across his behemoth of a desk. He looked like any other aging member of the gentry: a little stout, a little soft, going gray at the edges. He had a bulldog face, with a short nose and heavy jowls, but his gaze was bright and shrewd beneath bristling eyebrows. "What's this about, Wintersmith?"

Perry rested his notes on his knee, took a deep breath, and launched into his tale. He described the accidental death of Baron Flint's youngest son, as witnessed by Goodlace, and Saintbridge Abbishaw's application of bribery to suppress the truth. He touched on Wilton Abbishaw's subsequent exile to America, then recounted what Devereux had done when he'd learned who the real killer was—his failed attempt to inform Lord Abbishaw, his decision to present Saintbridge with the choice of revealing the truth or plundering his father's collection of clocks.

Goodlace hadn't known about that little scheme. Perry wished he could have watched the valet's face when he discovered what his master had been up to. As it was, he could only observe Sir Mortimer, whose expression was steadily growing grimmer.

Perry recounted everything he'd witnessed in the order in which it had happened: Saintbridge's act of theft and his placing of a tiepin to incriminate his brother, Lord Abbishaw's refusal to believe it, the second theft and attempt to incriminate Giles, Lord Abbishaw's refusal to let him confront Saintbridge and his demand that Perry not arrest him.

Given that Goodlace had admitted to receiving a bribe and Devereux to blackmailing his cousin, Perry felt it only right to report his own possibly-not-quite-lawful search of Saintbridge's study, his discovery of the stolen clock, and the scuffle with Saintbridge.

Lastly, and with a silent apology to Lady Violet for concealing her pivotal rôle in the case, he concluded by saying, "I followed Saintbridge to St. James's Church, where he hid the clock. The next night, his cousin retrieved it. I spoke with him and thus learned the full truth. This morning, I interviewed Mr. Goodlace and viewed the banknotes. I have a statement from Coutts & Co. that two of the notes were issued to Saintbridge Abbishaw shortly before Flint's death.

"A grave injustice has occurred, but I don't know whether it can be redressed. Lord Abbishaw commissioned my investigation into the missing clocks, and while he hasn't specifically advised me of his wishes, I believe I can guess how he'd like this matter handled."

Sir Mortimer's nostrils flared ever so slightly. Perry chose to read that as contempt for Abbishaw.

"I've not informed him of my findings yet. I strongly suspect that he won't believe me."

Sir Mortimer's nostrils gave another little flare.

"I'm uncertain how to proceed, sir, so I'm laying the matter before you."

Sir Mortimer said nothing for more than a minute. He directed a daunting glower at Perry, while his legal mind no doubt analyzed everything that had been said. His arms were crossed and he looked particularly bulldoggish, jaw short, jowls set, bristling eyebrows drawn low over his nose.

Finally, he uncrossed his arms and leaned forward. "Tell me what you saw," he demanded of Goodlace. "In precise detail."

The valet shrank back in his seat, but obeyed the command: "I went down to the cellars to see if I could find my master's cuff link," he said in a soft, timid voice. "Mr. Wilton Abbishaw was there, passed out cold in a chair, and Mr. Saintbridge Abbishaw was there, too, and Mr. Jasper Flint. Mr. Flint was holding out a card at arm's length." Goodlace held one arm out to the side in demonstration, finger and thumb pinched together. "And he said, 'I wager you can't shoot out the pips,' but Mr. Abbishaw—Mr. Saintbridge Abbishaw, that is—said it was easy to do. He loaded the pistol and aimed it, and Mr. Flint laughed and said, 'Better yet, do it like this,' and he moved the card half a second before Mr. Abbishaw fired." The valet mimicked this move, holding his pinched thumb and forefinger just above his head. He swallowed audibly. "The bullet went right through his forehead."

"How did Mr. Abbishaw react when this happened?"

"He was horrified, he was. Ran to Mr. Flint and slapped his face several times, but it were no use, sir. He was dead. And then Mr. Abbishaw turned to me and said, 'You didn't see this,' and he pulled out all the guineas he had in his pocket and made me take them." Goodlace hunched his shoulders, gripping his hands tightly together. "He was so fierce. Angry. Maddened, like. So I took the guineas and went back upstairs, and the next morning it was all about the house that Mr. Flint was dead and Mr. Wilton Abbishaw had done it, but I knew he'd slept through the whole thing. I didn't know what to do, but then Mr. Abbishaw—Mr. Saintbridge Abbishaw—he found me and he gave me this." The valet produced the banknotes from his breast pocket and held them out meekly. "He said they were mine if I promised not to tell anyone what I saw. So I promised. But then Wilton Abbishaw was sent off to America and it wasn't him as killed Mr. Flint, and it were all wrong, so I told my master, and he said he'd take care of it."

For the next hour, Sir Mortimer picked his way through their separate tales, not once, but three times, step by painstaking step. It was an interrogation, a cross examination, but

Goodlace's story didn't falter, and neither did Devereux's or Perry's. At long last, Sir Mortimer leaned back in his chair and directed another of his bulldoggish glowers at them.

They waited in silence. Again, Perry had the feeling that he'd gone back in time and was in a headmaster's office awaiting pronouncement of a punishment.

"I don't see a way to prosecuting Saintbridge Abbishaw," Sir Mortimer said finally. "The death was clearly an accident. There was no inquest, so he has not committed perjury."

It was what Perry had expected, but he tried not to show his disappointment.

"However," Sir Mortimer continued. "It is my opinion that Viscount Abbishaw and Baron Flint should both be apprised of the truth. Flint needs to know the exact circumstances of his son's death, and Abbishaw should be given the opportunity to recall his son from America."

Perry was conscious of Devereux stirring slightly in the chair alongside him.

"You say Lord Abbishaw keeps at home mostly?"

"Yes, sir," Perry and Devereux said at the same time.

"You think he'll be home now?"

Perry glanced at Devereux.

Devereux nodded. "Yes, sir. He only ever leaves the house on Wednesday and Friday evenings."

"Well, then." Sir Mortimer slapped his palms on his desk and stood. "No time like the present. Let us inform Lord Abbishaw of his youngest son's innocence." There was a note in the magistrate's voice that indicated he was going to relish the upcoming encounter.

Goodlace blenched and looked as if he'd prefer to stay where he was; Devereux flashed Perry a grin that was fierce and jubilant, almost wolfish.

They put on their hats and trooped down the stairs. Fortuitously, a hackney was disgorging its passengers in front of the Brown Bear tavern. Two minutes later, they were on their way to Hanover Square.

Whatever happened next, Saintbridge would probably avoid public exposure, but that didn't stop hope burgeoning in Perry's chest. Opposite him, Devereux sat tautly, hands clenched, a militant gleam in his eyes, one heel tapping a fast tattoo on the floor.

Goodlace also sat with his hands clenched, but he looked as if he was trying to melt into the seat. Either that, or become invisible.

The hackney halted in front of Lord Abbishaw's mansion. They descended. Devereux said, in a tone that was too casual to actually be casual, "That's Lord Flint's residence across the way."

They all turned to look. There was a beat of silence, and then Sir Mortimer said, "Perhaps we'll start there."

They headed across the square. An open barouche passed them by. Four extremely modish young ladies sat in it. The ribbons on their bonnets danced in the breeze.

Perry did a double take. So did one of the occupants.

Lady Violet turned in her seat, a question written on her face. Their eyes met briefly, and then the carriage swept out of sight.

CHAPTER
Forty-One

*T*heir first stroke of good luck was that Lord Flint was at home. Their second was that he believed the valet's account of what had happened. He insisted on accompanying them to talk with Lord Abbishaw. Perry wasn't sure whether that counted as a third stroke of good luck or not, but he suspected it might.

Baron Flint was thin and stooped and liberally afflicted with liver spots, but despite his apparent frailty his pace was brisk as he marched across the twilit square. Flint was a man on a warpath, if Perry was any judge, and while it was still doubtful that Saintbridge's perfidy would be exposed to the world—noble families liked to hide their shameful secrets—it did look as if Lord Abbishaw would be forced to confront the ugly truth about his heir.

The door to the Abbishaw residence opened as they reached it. Giles Abbishaw stepped out, dressed for an evening on the town.

Devereux snagged his arm. "You need to hear this, cousin."

"Hear what?"

Devereux didn't answer, merely steered him back inside.

"I must speak with his lordship immediately," Baron Flint said, in a tone that sent the servants scurrying.

Less than a minute later, they were ushered into Abbishaw's library. Curtains were drawn against the dusk, candelabra were lit, and a small fire burned in the vast marble hearth. Lord Abbishaw was seated in a giltwood bergère, a newspaper on his lap and a decanter of what looked to be port on the table beside him. Surprise crossed his face when he saw that Lord Flint wasn't alone. The surprise turned to alarm when he recognized Sir Mortimer. Perry thought he saw a flicker of fear before Abbishaw took refuge in peevish hauteur. "What is this?" he demanded.

"Something you need to hear," Flint replied brusquely, taking a seat without being invited. "Sit," he told the rest of them.

They sat. Sir Mortimer chose an armchair, Devereux a sofa, and Goodlace sidled into a wooden chair with a laurel wreath carved into its back. The valet looked as if he wished he was a thousand miles from Hanover Square.

Giles Abbishaw, his expression a study in bafflement, sat alongside Devereux.

Perry stayed standing. He watched Lord Abbishaw's face, seeing unease, anger, and fear beneath that imperious mask.

"Whatever nonsense this is, I don't have time for it now. I must ask you all to leave." Lord Abbishaw made as if to stand.

"You will hear this," Flint said. He was only a baron, but his voice held so much rage and authority that the viscount subsided in his chair. Abbishaw's mouth pinched, making him look more haughty than ever, but his eyes betrayed him, darting from side to side, faintly panicked.

The baron gestured curtly at Perry. "Tell him."

Perry related the tale of Jasper Flint's death and subsequent events. Twice, Abbishaw tried to interrupt with objections and denial, and twice the baron said, "Silence."

"It's not true," Lord Abbishaw protested weakly, when

Perry had finished. "Saintbridge would never do that." He turned to Giles. "Tell them he wouldn't!"

But Giles Abbishaw folded his lips together and said nothing.

"How dare you!" Lord Abbishaw cried, directing his fear and wrath at his middle son—but Baron Flint cut him off: "We should let Saintbridge speak for himself, don't you think?"

"Yes!" Lord Abbishaw grasped at this twig. "He'll tell you he's innocent and that this . . . this . . . this worm here is lying!"

Goodlace shrank even further into his chair.

A footman was dispatched to Conduit Street to fetch Saintbridge urgently to his father's library. They waited in tense silence. After several minutes, Devereux rose and crossed to where a number of decanters sat on a sideboard. He poured two glasses of what looked to be brandy and presented them to Baron Flint and Sir Mortimer.

The viscount, whose library it was and who should have offered the hospitality, compressed his lips more tightly. Judging from his rising color, fear was giving way to outrage.

Devereux poured two more glasses, for himself and Giles. He glanced at Perry and lifted an eyebrow. Perry shook his head minutely. In this room he wasn't a nobleman's nephew; he was barely a step up from a servant.

Five more minutes passed. Perry spent the time praying that the footman had found Saintbridge at home. Lord Flint swallowed his brandy in three quick, angry gulps, but Sir Mortimer sipped his slowly. The magistrate was the only one of the assembled company who appeared to be enjoying himself. The air was so taut with emotion—rage and fear—that Perry's scalp prickled a ghost of a warning.

Footsteps sounded in the corridor. The door to the library opened. "You wished to see me, Father?"

Perry suppressed a triumphant smile. Truly, luck was on their side tonight.

Lord Abbishaw didn't look as if he felt lucky. He looked like a man turned to stone, a gargoyle with his face bent out of shape, mouth half-open to shout at his eldest son to run.

Saintbridge closed the door and advanced into the room. "What's this about, sir?" He glanced around, saw Baron Flint, saw Devereux, saw Giles. Saw Goodlace. He halted, visibly tensing. "What's that man doing here?"

"Well may you ask," Baron Flint said grimly.

Saintbridge correctly interpreted that utterance. "Whatever he's told you is a lie! That man is a criminal of the worst kind!"

"What is it that you believe he's told us?" Sir Mortimer inquired.

Saintbridge looked down his nose at him. "Who are you?"

"This is Sir Mortimer Treadwell," Devereux informed his cousin. "One of the magistrates at Bow Street." His tone wasn't grim; it was affable, with an undertone of glee.

Saintbridge's face stiffened.

Lord Flint gestured at Perry. "Again," he ordered.

Perry began his fourth repetition of the tale. "On the night of December twenty-seventh, Mr. Goodlace went down to the cellars at Abbishaw Park to fetch a cuff link his master had left there."

"Who the devil are you?" Saintbridge demanded. He didn't appear to recognize Perry as his housebreaker. The expression on his face wasn't suspicion; it was hauteur.

Perry displayed his tipstaff. "Bow Street Principal Officer, sir."

To his great pleasure, Saintbridge paled.

He continued with his recitation of events: "When Goodlace entered the cellars, he saw Wilton Abbishaw passed out drunk in a chair, and Jasper Flint and yourself engaged in shooting pips from playing cards."

"That's a lie," Saintbridge snarled.

"Flint held a card out at arm's length for you to shoot at, but an instant before you fired, he placed the card above his head instead."

"Lies!"

"The bullet struck Flint and killed him."

259

"It's not true, I tell you!" Saintbridge rounded on his audience, fists clenched, lips drawn back from his teeth.

"You told Goodlace to say nothing about what had occurred, and the next morning you gave him two hundred pounds in exchange for his silence on the matter."

Saintbridge took a step towards Goodlace. "This man is vermin of the lowest kind! Spreading filthy lies and slander!"

Goodlace cowered in his chair and held out the banknotes in one trembling hand. "I don't want your money, sir. I want to tell the truth."

"That's not my money!" Saintbridge shouted, swinging around to face his father.

"Banknotes are numbered," Perry stated. "The numbers on those notes correspond with banknotes that were issued to you shortly before Jasper Flint's death. I have a statement from Coutts & Co. confirming it."

"I didn't give that man money! He stole it!"

"I never," Goodlace said tearfully.

"*You* are the liar," Devereux said, surging to his feet. He looked almost as enraged as Saintbridge. "A liar and a coward! You killed Jasper and put the blame on Wilton."

"Wilton killed Jasper!"

"No, *you* did!" Devereux roared. "And because of your lies, Wilton thinks he killed his best friend!"

"So?" Saintbridge's voice was thick with rage and contempt. "Who the devil cares? They were useless, the pair of them."

Lord Flint's face quivered as if he'd been slapped, muscles flinching beneath his eyes, around his mouth.

"You lied about Wilton! And then you stole your father's clocks and tried to make it look as if Giles were to blame."

"Lies!" Saintbridge cried again, his voice almost a scream. He didn't look frightened or panicked; he looked murderous.

"Not lies," Devereux said flatly. "A Bow Street Runner saw you do it. Twice."

All eyes in the room turned to Perry. He nodded, and said, "That's correct. I did witness it."

Saintbridge swung to face his father. "It's not true!"

"Lord Abbishaw was with me the second time," Perry said. "He saw you take a clock and leave your brother's cuff link behind. Didn't you, sir?"

The viscount's lips pinched together and his cheeks puffed out. He looked like a man caught between apoplexy and panic. It was clear that he wanted to deny what he'd witnessed.

But he couldn't. Not with Perry there.

He dipped his head in a stiff, reluctant nod.

"How could you do such things?" Devereux demanded. "To your own brothers!"

Saintbridge rounded on him, fists clenched, lips pulled back in a snarl. "Because they're *nothing*. Jasper was nothing! And you're nothing, too!"

Devereux's lips peeled back from his teeth in a matching snarl. He raised his own fists.

Perry took a step forward to stop what would clearly be a brutal brawl, but Sir Mortimer beat him to it. He rose majestically from his chair. "Enough."

Sir Mortimer had the gravitas of a man who had sent many criminals to the gallows. Perry was unsurprised when Saintbridge and Devereux both lowered their fists. After a moment, Devereux sat.

"You may be a nobleman," Sir Mortimer told Saintbridge, "but you have no understanding of integrity, courage, or honor. Deceit and cowardice, however, appear to be concepts with which you're very familiar."

Saintbridge drew himself up in outrage. "How *dare* you."

"I must ask you the same question. How dare you behave so egregiously towards your family? You have done your brothers, your father, your very name, a grave dishonor."

Saintbridge inhaled sharply.

"A man of courage and integrity would have owned to Mr. Flint's death, not laid the blame at a brother's feet."

"How dare you speak to me like this! Don't you know who I am?"

Sir Mortimer smiled thinly. "Yes. You will one day be a viscount, but you will never be a man of honor."

Rage flamed in Saintbridge's cheeks.

"Mr. Flint's death was an accident, but everything that you did afterwards was deliberate. Your behavior has been unconscionable, and yet you show no shame or remorse."

"Who cares who killed Jasper?" Saintbridge flung out. "Good riddance, I say. And good riddance to Wilton, too! Useless wastrels, the pair of them."

"Jasper was my *son*," Baron Flint said, rising from his chair, frail and slight and bristling with fury.

"Perhaps you could apologize to Lord Flint for killing his son," Sir Mortimer suggested, an edge to his voice.

Saintbridge's nostrils dilated. He glared at Sir Mortimer, then swung round and strode for the door, flinging it open, slamming it shut behind himself.

The silence that followed was utter. Perry thought that the clock on the mantelpiece didn't even dare to tick.

Lord Abbishaw's expression was aghast. He appeared to have finally realized that the son he'd valued so highly was a monster.

"Well, that was edifying," Devereux murmured to Giles.

Giles didn't respond. He looked almost as stunned as his father.

Perry's greatest emotion was regret that Lady Violet hadn't been there to witness everything.

Baron Flint turned to the viscount. "If you expect me to remain quiet about this, Abbishaw, you are gravely mistaken."

Lord Abbishaw closed his eyes in acquiescence, or perhaps it was defeat.

Baron Flint departed. He didn't slam the door.

Devereux stood. "I believe I shall dine at my club. Will you join me, Giles?"

Giles glanced at his father.

The viscount had opened his eyes. He was staring bleakly at the coals smoldering in the fireplace.

"Father?" Giles asked tentatively. "Do you [...] with you?"

Abbishaw turned his head wearily. He ga[...] a long moment, and then said, "You're the b[...] tone, faint and disbelieving, made the statem[...] a compliment.

Giles acquired the just-been-slapped look that Baron Flint had worn only a few minutes ago.

Devereux took hold of his cousin's elbow. "Come on, let's go to my club. Your father needs some time alone."

Giles allowed himself to be hauled to his feet and guided from the room.

Sir Mortimer turned to Lord Abbishaw. "Are you all right, sir? Shall I send for your man?"

Abbishaw shook his head. "I wish to be alone."

Sir Mortimer, Perry, and Goodlace retreated from the library. The butler sent a footman to fetch a hackney for them. They waited out on the flagway. It was fully dark, streetlamps holding the night at bay around the edges of the square. Perry's scalp prickled, telling him that someone lurked nearby.

Sir Mortimer clasped his hands behind his back and surveyed the square. "The truth will out," he said, with great satisfaction.

The truth would most definitely be out. Perry had no doubt that Devereux would spread the tale of Saintbridge's perfidy far and wide—and with Baron Flint's corroboration, the Polite World would believe him.

The footman returned at a run. Behind him, a hackney clattered into the square.

"I don't want this," Goodlace said, holding out the banknotes to Sir Mortimer.

"In my opinion, you've earned it," the magistrate said. He subjected the valet to a long, scrutinizing look, then gave an approving nod. "Sometimes it takes courage to do the right thing. Well done."

In the lamplight, Perry saw Goodlace flush. The valet

.red the money back into his pocket and bobbed his head. "Good night, sirs." He scurried off into the dark.

"You did very well in this matter, Wintersmith," Sir Mortimer said, as the hackney drew to a halt.

"Thank you, sir."

The footman opened the carriage door for them.

"I'll walk," Perry said. "Do you wish to have this back now?" He offered Sir Mortimer the tipstaff.

Sir Mortimer gave a negatory wave of his hand. "Tomorrow's soon enough. Come see me in my office." He told the jarvey his address and climbed into the carriage.

The footman closed the door. The hackney rattled off.

Perry headed for the nearest alleyway.

CHAPTER
Forty-Two

Violet pounced on Wintersmith the moment he set foot in the alley. "What happened?" she demanded. "Tell me!"

Wintersmith moved deeper into the shadows and proceeded to narrate the events of the past few hours. Violet listened, agog. "I saw that!" she cried. "Saint came *storming* back across Hanover Square. I've never seen anyone in such a high dudgeon! Go on, go on, tell me what happened next!"

"Very little," Wintersmith said. "Except that the baron declared he won't hold silent."

Violet clapped her hands in delight. "Excellent! What did Lord Abbishaw say to that?"

"Nothing. He was quite overset by it all. Devereux took Giles off to his club. They'll spread the tale, I have no doubt."

"I shall too!" Violet declared. "If I may, that is?"

Wintersmith considered this request, then said, "Say nothing about the clocks, but you may tell anyone you wish about the circumstances of Flint's death. The more people who know, the better."

"May I tell them tonight? It's the Galpins' ball. Everyone will be there!"

Wintersmith gave this request consideration, too. "I don't see why not, as long as you don't say which servant was bribed. And please don't name myself or Sir Mortimer."

"I shan't." Violet floated a little lower. "It'll be all over town by tomorrow, I promise! Saint won't dare to show his face anywhere."

"It's no less than he deserves. I wish you could have seen him. I don't think he possesses a conscience."

"I wish I *had* been there!" Violet huffed out a breath, but she had no time to dwell on such disappointment. She had a ball to attend and a story to spread. "I'll come by later tonight."

"If you're too tired—"

"I shan't be. See you later!" Violet swooped upwards and arrowed across the rooftops. Three minutes later she crawled in through her window. She flung off her clothes willy-nilly, bundled them away, then unlocked her door and tugged urgently on the bellpull for her maid. "Carter, I feel so much better! I believe I'll go to the ball after all. Make haste, make haste! Is everyone still downstairs?"

"Still dining, miss."

"Excellent! Quickly, I'll wear the rose pompadour satin."

Violet completed her toilette so hastily that the covers hadn't been cleared by the time she burst into the dining room. "Can you please give us a few moments?" she requested of the servants who were in attendance on the table.

The butler and footmen withdrew.

Violet closed the door and stood with her back to it.

Nine people looked at her with expressions of mingled surprise, interest, curiosity, and alarm: Rhodes and Aster, three of her cousins, her aunt and uncle, and newly returned from Brighton, her sister Primrose and brother-in-law Oliver.

"I have such a story for you!" Violet cried. "Just listen to this!"

She spilled out the tale: Jasper Flint's death at Saintbridge's hand, the bribery of the only witness, the lie that had seen Wilton shipped off to America, Saint's refusal to acknowledge remorse now that he was found out or to even apologize to Lord Flint. When she finished, everyone at the dinner table wore the same expression: wide-eyed astonishment. "What do you think?" Violet said triumphantly. "Is it not beyond belief?"

"I've never heard of more despicable behavior," her uncle said. "Are you certain it's true?"

"Absolutely certain!"

"Who told you this?" her aunt inquired.

"I can't tell you. He asked me not to say."

The shocked astonishment was slowly transforming into doubt, except on her brother's face.

"Is the person who told you this who I think it is?" Rhodes asked.

"It is."

"Then we may trust it is the truth," he informed the table.

Violet beamed at him. "It most definitely is! And moreover, Lord Flint is going to tell everyone. And so is Devil Abbishaw. Have you finished eating yet? I want us to go to the ball and make sure everyone knows!"

Aster wrinkled her nose distastefully.

"It's not gossip," Violet told her sister. "It's justice!"

Rhodes pushed back his chair and stood. "I agree with Violet. Saintbridge deserves to be seen for what he is."

Violet turned and flung open the door. "You may come in," she told the servants. "And we need the carriages brought around right away!"

❦

The Galpins had transformed their ballroom into a woodland bower. Gauzy green draperies covered the walls, and everywhere were potted palms and ferns and *jardinières* with ivy tumbling down their sides. Chandeliers blazed overhead like great suns. There was barely room to move. The musicians labored to make themselves heard over the hubbub of conversation.

Violet plunged into the crush. "Have you heard?" she cried, to the first person she encountered.

She spilled the tale into as many ears as she could. Rhodes and Oliver were circulating among the younger men, her aunt was surrounded by a bevy of matrons, and her uncle was holding forth to the gentlemen clustered by the card room. As the tale spread, the hubbub changed its tone, gay dissipation giving way to shocked delight at a scandal of such magnitude.

"Outrageous!" someone exclaimed near the refreshment table, where Primrose was talking to a gaggle of ladies, and "Beyond shabby!" asserted one of the young dandies to whom her cousin Carlyle was speaking.

Violet encountered the occasional "Arrant nonsense," and "I refuse to believe it; he's such a virtuous young man," on her circuit of the ballroom, but most people were only too happy to swallow the tale of Saint's iniquity. If he hadn't been such an out-and-out villain, she would have felt guilty. As it was, she felt only triumph. She paused in an alcove clustered with ferns and sipped a much-needed glass of lemonade. The ballroom was aswirl with excited conversations.

"Dreadful!" said one of the ladies dancing past.

"Very scaly behavior," agreed her partner.

Two dowagers with diamonds on their bosoms and ostrich feathers nodding over their heads passed the alcove. "Have you heard?" one of them said to the other. "I have it on most *excellent* authority that it was Saintbridge Abbishaw who killed young Jasper Flint!"

Violet hid a smile against the rim of her glass and counted her work as done. She finished her lemonade and went in search of her brother. She overheard a "Deplorable!" to her left and two steps further on an "Unpardonable!"

She surveyed the ballroom, noting all the busy conversations, the bright eyes and flushed cheeks of people enthralled by the latest scandal. *Truly we're a shallow, frivolous bunch*, she thought. *To be so delighted by gossip is not a thing to be proud of.*

But this gossip wasn't frivolous.

This scandal truly *was* a scandal.

She spotted Rhodes near the entrance to the ballroom, in conversation with her brother-in-law, Oliver, and headed towards them. On the dance floor, couples were assembling for a *contredanse*.

Newcomers were still arriving, fresh ears in which to pour the tale of Saint's wickedness, but Violet was confident that the story had legs of its own and could be left untended. The person she wanted to spend the rest of the evening with was Periander Wintersmith.

Colonel Mountfort and his wife entered the ballroom. Behind them was a familiar figure.

Violet stopped dead.

Colonel and Mrs. Mountfort nodded cordially to Rhodes and Oliver, who nodded cordially back.

Saintbridge Abbishaw stepped into the ballroom, resplendent in formal evening dress. He paused for a moment and glanced around. His face was set in its customary expression of haughty disdain.

Someone gasped behind Violet. "Is that—?"

"Look!" someone else whispered excitedly. "Oh, I say, look!"

A footman approached Saint and offered a tray of crystal glasses filled with champagne.

Saint took a glass.

Shocked gasps and hushed exclamations rippled across the ballroom. Heads turned and conversations halted.

Rhodes and Oliver stopped talking.

Saint accorded them an aristocratic smile and an inclination of his head.

Rhodes looked him up and down, and then very deliberately turned his back. So did Oliver.

They weren't the only ones. The cut direct rippled out across the ballroom. Fabric swished and rustled as person after person turned their back on Saintbridge Abbishaw.

Violet watched, open-mouthed. She didn't turn her back. She wanted to see what Saint did.

The musicians played the opening notes to the *contredanse*, oblivious to the unfolding drama, but only one pair of dancers made their bows to one another. The other couples were too absorbed in the scene at the doorway.

The musicians played half a dozen bars and straggled to a halt, baffled and bewildered.

Saint didn't look baffled or bewildered. If one thing was blindingly obvious, it was that he knew exactly why Rhodes and Oliver had given him the cut direct. The emotion that contorted his face wasn't shame or dismay, but fury. His lips peeled back in a snarl. Rage flushed his face. He looked murderous. He raised his glass and cast it violently on the floor. It smashed to smithereens, a sharp and shocking sound.

Saint turned and shoved the footman aside. The poor man fell head over heels along with his tray. More glass smashed to smithereens.

Saintbridge didn't pause. He roughly elbowed aside the person entering the ballroom—Lady Sefton—and she went head over heels, too.

A flurry of gasps echoed across the ballroom, along with cries of *Oh!* and *Goodness!* and *Did you see?* For the next few minutes, the babble was cacophonous, those whose backs had been turned demanding to know what had happened, and everyone else excitedly telling them.

It took Violet several minutes to push her way through the crush to where Rhodes and Oliver stood. "Well!" she said. "That was thrilling."

"Not for Lady Sefton," Rhodes replied dryly.

Behind him, servants were scurrying to clean up broken glass and spilled champagne. Lady Sefton was nowhere to be seen. She was probably recovering her composure in one of the withdrawing rooms, tenderly assisted by Lady Galpin and her maids.

The musicians began playing again, a melody fighting to be heard above the clamor of voices. "Will you take me home, Rhodes?"

Her brother glanced at Oliver.

"Go," Oliver said. "I'll keep an eye on the ladies."

Rhodes escorted Violet home, but he didn't come inside. "Are you going back to the ball?" she asked.

"To my club. This tale needs spreading further." He paused, and then said, "You're going out, too, if I'm not mistaken."

Violet felt herself blush. She tilted her chin a little defiantly. "I want to tell Wintersmith what happened at the ball. It *is* his case, after all."

"It does seem a shame that he missed it," Rhodes agreed mildly.

Violet stopped tilting her chin at him. "You and Oliver were superb," she said. "That cut direct! I've never seen anything like it!"

"Saintbridge won't be able to show his face in Society after tonight," Rhodes said with satisfaction.

"No." She stood on tiptoe and planted a kiss on his cheek. "Thank you for your help. You were magnificent!"

CHAPTER
FORTY-THREE

*R*ather than fly directly to Holborn, Violet took a detour past Conduit Street. The door to Saint's house stood open, lamplight spilling into the street. A traveling chaise was drawn up. As she watched, a servant ran down the steps and placed a portmanteau in the carriage.

Unless she was mistaken, Saintbridge Abbishaw was leaving London.

Violet gave a gleeful little skip in the air, then sped in the direction of Holborn. Wintersmith's window was open. A lone candle cast faint, flickering light.

Violet peeped inside.

Wintersmith lounged in his chair, his attention wholly captured by the book he was reading. His shirtsleeves were rolled up, neckcloth discarded, his feet up on the bed.

It seemed terribly intimate to observe him like that. His bare throat looked vulnerable, as did his stockinged feet.

Wintersmith's forearms didn't look vulnerable, though. They were brawny and muscular, and his fingers, as they turned the page, were strong and capable.

Violet had the uncomfortable feeling that she was a voyeur, but before she could make her presence known, Wintersmith glanced up. "Hello. I didn't expect you so soon."

"I left the ball early. I wanted to tell you what happened. It was prodigiously exciting!"

"Oh?" He closed the book and put it aside. "Tell me."

Violet looked dubiously at the scarred floorboards. "Are there any rats?"

"Not at this instant, no."

Violet hopped in through the window and up onto the bed, not letting her feet touch the floor. "Well," she said, and launched into an account of everything that had occurred at the Galpins' ball.

"You should have seen Saint's face," she concluded. "He was in the fiend's own temper! He collided with Lady Sefton on his way out the door. She tumbled head over tail—and he didn't even stop to help her or to apologize! He won't be able to show his face anywhere after that. He'll be blackballed." She paused, and wrinkled her brow. "Which will make it very awkward when he succeeds to the viscountcy, come to think of it. Oh! And there's a carriage drawn up at his door and his servants are loading it with luggage. He's leaving London!"

"Good riddance," Wintersmith said.

Violet echoed the sentiment: "Good riddance." Then she grinned. "He rather put the nails in his own coffin, knocking over Lady Sefton like that. I must say, I wonder that he came to the ball. I was astonished to see him!"

"Hubris," Wintersmith said. "His besetting sin. It probably never crossed his mind that the truth would get out. Family secrets and all that. It probably would have been hushed up if he'd shown any remorse, begged Baron Flint's forgiveness; as it was . . ." He shook his head.

"I wish I'd seen it," Violet said. "And I wish you'd been at the ball." She looked down at the coverlet, plucked at a seam, then glanced across at him. "We did well, didn't we?"

"Exceedingly well." Wintersmith gave her a nod that was

oddly formal. "Thank you for your assistance. I couldn't have solved the case without you."

Violet pursed her lips and considered this statement, then shook her head. "You probably would have solved it, but it would have taken you longer. And you might have fallen off Saint's roof."

Wintersmith laughed.

"People were calling him an out-and-out rogue when I left the ball, and they don't even know the whole of it." Violet plucked at the coverlet again, glanced at him again. "May I tell Rhodes about the clocks? He won't tell anyone else, I swear, and he did help tonight. A lot! He's at his club right now, telling everyone about Saint."

Wintersmith considered this request, then nodded. "You may tell him."

"Thank you!" She leaned across the narrow gap between bed and chair and placed a clumsy kiss on his mouth.

Wintersmith raised a hand, cupped her cheek, held her still, and returned the kiss, not clumsily at all.

When he released her, Violet drew back, hot and breathless and deliciously flustered.

They stared at one another. Violet was intensely aware of Wintersmith's bare throat.

She wanted to touch him there. With her fingers. With her lips.

"Rooftops?" Wintersmith suggested.

"Rooftops," she agreed.

"But first, I have something for you."

He reached for some papers that were sitting on his washstand, peeled off the topmost ones, and handed them to her.

"What's this? Oh!" Violet paged hastily through the illustrations, and then a second time more slowly. Five drawings. Five drawings that made her skin tingle and grow warm. Five drawings that made her want.

"Do you like them? I thought you might, but if I'm wrong—"

"I love them," Violet declared. "They're perfect. What else have you there?"

"The two that you liked from Stanhope's collection, and . . . this. It may not be to your taste."

A lady views her stallion was the title of the illustration he handed her.

Violet caught her breath. Heat flared inside her. "Oh," she breathed.

"You like it?"

"Oh, yes."

She lifted her gaze from the drawing and looked at Wintersmith, imagining him standing naked before her—and belatedly noticed that he still held something. A thin pamphlet. "What's that?"

"A collection of rather silly drawings that I thought might amuse you."

The drawings were very silly and they did amuse her, but they weren't to be treasured, not like the precious, perfect pictures he had bought for her. Violet put the pamphlet aside and went through the loose drawings again. Six new ones, plus her two favorites from Freddy's collection. Eight altogether. Eight tantalizing, titillating prints that quickened her pulse and kindled fire in her blood. Eight images that made her long for bare skin and kisses, laughter and passion. She examined them raptly, then hugged them to her chest. "Thank you."

"It was my pleasure." There was heat in Wintersmith's eyes and something a little wicked in the tilt of his smile. "Rooftops?" he suggested again.

"No." Violet wanted to stay right where they were, so that she might see him clearly. "I'd like to do this." She showed him the drawing of the lady viewing her stallion. "And then . . ." She leafed through the precious drawings. "This. If it's all right with you?"

Wintersmith's smile grew wider. "It is very much all right with me."

The next hour was several orders of magnitude better than "all right." She and Wintersmith lay tangled together afterwards, amid the tumbled bedding. Violet didn't care that the mattress was lumpy, the sheets were threadbare, and there were water stains on the ceiling. Everything was perfect just as it was. The temptation to drift off to sleep was almost overwhelming. If she stayed, then they could be lazy together in the morning sunlight, and right at that moment there was nothing she wanted more than to wake in an attic bedroom and to spend the whole day with Wintersmith, talking and laughing and arguing and making love.

But she couldn't.

Violet sighed and sat up and reached for her clothes. "What are your plans for tomorrow?" she asked as she pulled on her shirt.

Wintersmith rolled onto his back and stared up at the ceiling, one arm tucked behind his head. The pose did very distracting things to the muscles in his chest and arm. "I'll go in to Bow Street and give back the tipstaff, tell Sir Mortimer I wish to resign, and then over to the regimental agent to see about a new commission."

Violet's mood plummeted. "Do you think you'll be able to rejoin your regiment?"

"Yes. Although things are heating up in Egypt. They may prefer to send me there."

"Oh." Heating up? That didn't sound reassuring. "Are you certain you don't wish to remain in London?"

Wintersmith sighed, too, and sat up. "Being a soldier suits me better than being a secretary," he said, but he didn't sound particularly happy about it.

Violet climbed off the bed and pulled on her stockings and pantaloons. "How long before you leave England?"

"Maybe a month."

"Oh," she said again. She donned her shoes, then tucked the precious drawings and the ridiculous little pamphlet safely down the front of her shirt. She buttoned her coat and turned to face him.

Wintersmith was watching her. His expression was unsmiling, solemn.

"I must be off," Violet said.

"Yes."

It didn't feel like good-night; it felt like good-bye—and she didn't want it to be good-bye. "May I visit you tomorrow night?" she asked, with a diffidence she was unaccustomed to feeling.

"If you would like to."

"Yes," Violet said firmly. "I would. We'll go to the British Museum."

The solemnity vanished. Wintersmith laughed. He climbed off the bed and kissed her. "Good night."

Violet kissed him back, and then she flew home, hugging the drawings close, hugging the memory of their lovemaking and the sound of Wintersmith's laughter.

CHAPTER
FORTY-FOUR

*S*ir Mortimer expressed regret at Perry's decision to resign. "Are you quite certain? You did a fine job with the Abbishaw case. Bow Street might need your investigative talents again."

"I'm quite certain, sir."

Sir Mortimer didn't press him further; he merely took the tipstaff and locked it away in a drawer.

"How much notice would you like, sir? Tolly seems to be doing a fine job."

Sir Mortimer leaned back in his chair and looked him up and down. "In a hurry to be off, are you?"

Perry decided to be honest. "Yes, sir."

Sir Mortimer grunted. "Very well." He scrawled a note on a piece of paper. "Give that to Mr. Fergus. He'll pay out your wages."

"You'll keep Tolly on in my place?"

"Don't see why not. His handwriting's better than yours." It wasn't a criticism; there was a jovial twinkle in the magistrate's eye.

"And my payment from Lord Abbishaw? When should I expect that?"

"Best if you apply to him directly." Sir Mortimer glanced at his pocket watch. "Now, if that's all, I have to be in court shortly."

"Thank you, sir."

Perry presented Sir Mortimer's note to Mr. Fergus and received several shillings in exchange, then made his way to the office where he'd spent so many tedious hours trapped behind a desk.

Tolly glowered at him, hunching defensively over the documents he was working on.

"Morning," Perry said cheerfully.

Tolly's lips twitched in something that was more grimace than smile. He didn't return the greeting.

Perry unlocked the topmost drawer and removed the notebook that held his old case notes. It was best burned. Other than that, there was nothing in the desk that he wanted.

He gave the key to Tolly. "This is yours now."

Tolly's glower intensified. "What do you mean?"

"I've resigned."

Tolly's expression of disbelief was almost comical.

"It's not a humbug, I assure you."

Tolly didn't look convinced. He glared at Perry, clearly suspecting a joke.

Perry shrugged. Tolly would find out the truth soon enough. He whistled on his way down the stairs, stepped out onto Bow Street—and just like that, he was free.

His first destination was Hanover Square, to request payment for services rendered. The viscount was indisposed, but Abbishaw's man of business bade him return later in the day.

Next, Perry headed for Charing Cross, where the regimental agent had his office.

Ordinarily, applying for one's commission was a lengthy process, but Perry had been mentioned in the dispatches several times and had finished his military career in very good odor. That expedited everything. In fact, the speed with which it was arranged almost made him dizzy. The agent approved his application directly, the Horse Guards granted it without hesitation, and it was done. A process that ordinarily took weeks only took a few hours.

He would depart London within the fortnight.

It was early afternoon when Perry emerged from the agent's office, having completed the last of the paperwork. He paused on the flagway and inhaled a deep, rib-expanding breath. Soon he'd be back with his regiment, shoulder to shoulder with his brother soldiers, his days filled with purpose and activity.

Relief brimmed in his chest like champagne, light and effervescent. Perry felt like throwing his arms wide and laughing up at the sky.

His relief was seasoned with regret, though. He'd miss Devereux. He'd miss Lady Violet.

On the other side of Charing Cross was Northumberland House. The great stone lion gazed down from high above. It seemed wildly impossible that he and Lady Violet had made love up there. The memory of it was like something out of a dream, surreal and fantastical.

Two more weeks and he'd be gone. No more running along rooftops. No more making love beneath the stars. No more Lady Violet.

Relief and regret churned in Perry's chest. He couldn't wait to be gone. He didn't want to leave.

A stagecoach emerged from the Golden Cross, the passengers seated on the roof ducking their heads as the carriage passed beneath the arch. "Make way! Make way!" the guard shouted.

The commotion shook Perry from his abstraction. He headed in the direction of Hanover Square, striding briskly. He had a uniform to purchase, a sword, a brace of pistols. Thank heavens he still had most of his gear: the duty bag and writing case, the pocket lamp and tinderbox, the toilet kit, the sewing kit, the canteens. He even had his pay book, wrapped in oiled cloth, its pages a record of his history in the army.

Lord Abbishaw's man of business counted out a gratifyingly large number of guineas. Double the amount agreed upon, which would pay for both his sword *and* his new uniform. He wouldn't have to apply to the regimental agent for a loan.

Truly, the gods were smiling upon him.

Perry trod down the steps to Hanover Square, whistling under his breath, and paused for a moment, undecided. Reddell in Jermyn Street for his sword or Buckmaster on Old Bond for his uniform?

The sun was high overhead, a blazing orb in a sky the color of forget-me-nots. Birds twittered in the garden in the middle of the square and the world seemed bright and golden, filled with beauty and hope and joy.

Perry decided that tomorrow was soon enough for swords and uniforms. He set off for Cavendish Square.

"It worked!" was the first thing Devereux said. He grabbed Perry and swung him into a wild jig. "Everyone knows! It's all over town!"

"Did you hear what happened at the Galpins' ball?" Perry asked, once Devereux had stopped spinning them around. "Thane gave him the cut direct, and he knocked over Lady Sefton in his hurry to leave."

"I heard!" Devereux looked almost manic with glee. "I wish I'd seen it."

Perry wished he had, too.

"What I don't understand is how Thane knew. It was early in the evening by all accounts. I'd barely told anyone."

"I might have had a word in someone's ear," Perry admitted.

"Whose? Thane's?"

Perry shook his head and changed the subject. "Saintbridge has left London. Did you hear?"

"I did! Good riddance, is what I say." Devereux's grin was wide and elated. He spun Perry around in another mad little jig. "Let's celebrate. I have a bottle of Haut-Brion that's just begging to be drunk!"

They celebrated over an early dinner, with not one bottle of Haut-Brion, but two.

"How's Giles taking it?" Perry asked.

"He's glad to see the back of Saint—not that he'd say it out loud, of course. Giles ain't one to speak ill of people."

"Is he a close friend of yours?"

Devereux shook his head. "Not really. Keeps to himself, very quiet, but a decent chap, you know? Kind-hearted. Best one out of the three of 'em. About time my uncle realized it."

Perry leaned back in his chair and sipped his wine. "Have you told anyone about the clocks?"

Devereux shook his head. "Giles asked me not to. He said it muddied an already muddied pond. I doubt m' uncle will tell anyone and Saint sure as hell won't. The baron's the only one who might, and if he does . . . so be it. I'm not ashamed of what I did." He went to pour them both more wine and discovered that the bottle was empty. "I'll send for another bottle."

"None for me, thanks. I want a clear head tonight."

Devereux's gaze sharpened with interest. "Your lady friend?"

"My lady friend."

Curiosity was vivid on Devereux's face and bright in his eyes. To ward off the inevitable questions, Perry said, "I resigned from Bow Street this morning. I'm off to India again."

That news quenched Devereux's curiosity. He grimaced and pushed his wineglass aside. "When?"

"Two weeks."

Devereux grimaced again and Perry was almost sorry that he'd told him; then Devereux leaned forward, his face alight with enthusiasm once more. "Come out to Richmond with me tomorrow! I'll mount you on one of my horses. We'll go for a good gallop."

Last week, Perry would have refused such an invitation—it would have felt too much like charity—but today he didn't hesitate to accept. If he only had a fortnight left in London, he wanted to spend as much time as he could with Devereux.

And with Lady Violet.

CHAPTER
FORTY-FIVE

*T*own was abuzz with the tale of Saintbridge's fall from grace. People paused to whisper between the bookshelves in Hatchards and they exclaimed to one another over ices at Gunter's. They discussed it while they browsed the prints at Ackermann's, selected ribbons and thread at the linen draper's, and chose their snuff at Fribourg & Treyer.

"*Such* a juicy scandal," Violet overheard one stately dowager declare to another as they emerged from a milliner's closely followed by their maids.

The gossipers only knew the half of it. Violet was bursting to tell Rhodes the whole story, but when she first went looking for him he was out riding, then he was at Manton's shooting at wafers with Oliver, and when she went in search of him in the afternoon, she discovered that, the breeze being too brisk for launching miniature hot air balloons, he'd taken the children to Astley's Amphitheatre instead.

Thwarted, she paid a visit to the Westfell mansion on Berkeley Square. She'd barely spoken two words to her sister since Primrose's return from Brighton, and while she couldn't tell her about the stolen clocks, she could at least show her the pamphlet Wintersmith had purchased. They could exclaim over the drawings and laugh at how ludicrous they were.

Primrose received her in a sunny parlor that looked out over the maple trees in Berkeley Square. A footman brought a tray piled with dainty chocolate confections, while another set a platter brimming with fruit from Oliver's succession houses on the table—plump apricots, rosy strawberries, succulent grapes.

Violet pondered her choice of refreshments, while at the same time debating the wisdom of showing Primrose the pamphlet. Would her sister laugh, or scold her for having it?

She selected several strawberries, half a dozen grapes, two chocolate bonbons—and decided that Primrose would laugh. Her sister *had* married Oliver, after all, and she laughed at all the outrageous things he said and did. "I've something to show you," Violet said, sliding the pamphlet from her reticule. "It's rather wicked. I think it will amuse you a great deal."

"Oh?"

Violet passed it to her, and not one second later a footman ushered Aster, Daphne, and Clematis into the room in a cloud of chatter and laughter and gauzy spring dresses.

Violet tried to retrieve the pamphlet, but it was too late. Primrose had already laid it on her lap.

"I thought you were buying hats?" Violet said, flapping her hand at Primrose in a surreptitious hide-it-quickly gesture.

The gesture was too surreptitious. Primrose didn't see it.

"We've bought hats. A bonnet apiece." Daphne flung herself down on the sofa beside Primrose. Her gaze landed on the trays of refreshments. "Ooh, just what I feel like. I'm ravenous!"

Violet sent Primrose a fierce warning glance while the girls piled their plates high with bonbons and fruit, but Primrose was apparently unable to distinguish warning glances from ordinary glances, for she opened the pamphlet.

Her eyes grew round with astonishment.

Violet checked that Daphne, Clematis, and Aster were engrossed in choosing the delicate morsels for their plates, then looked back in time to see Primrose turn a page. Her sister's lips parted in silent surprise.

Violet choked back a gleeful cackle of laughter. Primrose's reaction was precisely what she'd hoped for. She only wished that Aster, Clematis, and Daphne weren't there, so that she and Primrose might laugh aloud over the absurdities in the pamphlet.

She gestured again for Primrose to hide it, but her sister was transfixed by whatever picture was before her. She turned another page. Her eyes grew even rounder. "Good gracious!" she exclaimed.

Violet winced. Everyone else paused in mid-bite.

"What is it?" Clematis asked. "Let us see!"

"Absolutely not." Primrose turned sideways on the sofa, hunching her shoulders against prying eyes. She peeked at the open page and then threw Violet a sharp, quizzical glance. "Wherever did you get this?"

"From a friend."

"It's quite . . ." Primrose, who usually had no difficulty expressing herself, seemed bereft of words. She peeked at the pamphlet again, turned another page, and uttered a shocked little giggle. "I mustn't let Oliver see this!"

Violet blinked in surprise. Oliver didn't seem at all prudish to her. "He'd find it amusing, surely?"

"What he would find amusing is attempting to do all these impossible things!" Primrose informed her tartly.

"What impossible things?" Daphne asked, abandoning a half-eaten apricot and making a grab for the pamphlet.

Primrose snatched it out of reach. "None of your business."

"Oh, but—!"

"It's for Primrose's eyes only," Violet declared.

"And yours," Daphne pointed out.

"Because we're older than you," Violet said.

"Pooh! I'm not a child. I'm old enough to marry."

"So am I!" Clematis said. "Do show us, Prim!"

At that moment, the door opened. Her brother-in-law Oliver, the Duke of Westfell, strolled in. When he saw all five of them sitting there, he opened his arms in a flourish. "What a sight to behold! A veritable bouquet of flowers!"

Primrose hastily shoved the pamphlet behind a cushion.

Violet looked at her sister's expression and almost went into whoops of laughter.

Oliver stayed for twenty minutes, munching his way through almost all of the bonbons while entertaining them with the tale of wearing his ducal regalia for the very first time, which shouldn't have been funny but was, because if Oliver had one talent, it was that he could make almost anyone laugh.

Primrose sat stiffly throughout, her back ramrod straight. Violet imagined the pamphlet burning its way through the cushion behind her.

Finally, Oliver climbed to his feet, bade them a grandiloquent farewell, and headed off to Rundell & Bridge on what he termed "a quest for a toothpick case that will flatter all my notions of self-importance."

The room felt very empty after his departure.

Violet took one look at Primrose's face, and fell into helpless laughter.

"*Stop* laughing," Primrose hissed, and felt behind the cushion for the pamphlet. She frowned. "Where on earth is it?"

"Are they really that long?"

All eyes turned to where Daphne sat, clutching the open pamphlet, her eyes wide with shock.

Violet reached over and plucked the pamphlet from Daphne's grasp. It was open to the illustration of a circus performer whose appendage was nearly as long as his arm. "Of course not. They're only this long." She measured between her hands.

Everyone stared at her.

"What's that long?" Aster asked.

"How do you know?" said Daphne, her eyes narrowing.

Primrose's eyes were also narrow. Her expression, as she gazed at Violet, was three parts suspicion, one part alarm.

Clematis leaned close and peered at the pamphlet. "Goodness!"

"What is it?" Aster said, rising from her chair.

Violet closed the pamphlet firmly. "Nothing."

"Is that *real*?" Clematis said. "Can it really grow that big?"

"Can what grow that big?" Aster asked.

"It's nothing but nonsense," Violet said, coming to the belated conclusion that bringing the pamphlet with her had been a rather large mistake.

"Then why publish it?" Clematis asked.

"Because some people find it amusing."

"I want to see it again," Daphne declared.

"No," Primrose said, in a tone that brooked no argument. "It's not for young ladies."

"Pooh," Daphne said. "Violet's only a little older than me, and *she* looked at it."

"If you looked at these pictures it would give you a very wrong idea of things," Violet told her. "Why, the first time I saw drawings like this, I actually thought they were accurate!"

"All the more reason for us to see them then," Aster put in. "So we'll know what's real and what's not."

Aster's logic was irrefutable, as it usually was.

Violet exchanged a glance with Primrose. She had the feeling that Primrose was going to give her a severe scolding once the girls were gone. A scolding that she deserved. Bringing the pamphlet to Berkeley Square had been the opposite of wise.

"At least show me what Daffy and Clem saw," Aster said. "It's not fair otherwise."

Primrose could have pointed out that life wasn't fair, but she didn't. Violet took that as tacit consent to Aster's request. With a sigh, she opened the pamphlet to the offending drawing and laid it on the table so that they could all see.

Aster leaned forward, recoiled with a shocked "Oh," then leaned in for a closer look.

"You're certain it's not that big?" Daphne said, with a dubious frown.

"I'm certain," Violet and Primrose said at the same time.

She should have left the assurances to Primrose, because once again Violet found herself the object of everyone's scrutiny. Four pairs of eyes looked at her with varying degrees of speculation.

"Is there something we ought to know?" Daphne asked.

"No," Violet said, and then her conscience pricked her to say, "Possibly?"

She felt herself blush crimson under the weight of those stares—Primrose concerned, Aster worried, Clematis and Daphne avidly curious.

"Well, tell us!" Daphne said.

Violet felt that almost anything would be preferable to divulging her secret, but heaven only knew what wild flights of fancy Clematis and Daphne would conjure up or what dreadful scenarios Aster and Primrose would envisage. Anything they could imagine would doubtless be worse than the truth.

What was it Wintersmith had said about consequences? Well, this was a consequence, and it was entirely her own fault.

"You know how last night I told you that Saintbridge had killed Jasper Flint?"

They all nodded.

"Well, I knew because I helped a Bow Street Runner to solve the case." Much as she wished she had the nerve to say "We've become lovers," Violet found that she didn't quite dare. It sounded too rakish, too sinful. She gave a light little shrug, hoping her sisters and cousins would infer the truth without her having to state it.

Everyone made that leap of deduction. There was a stunned silence, and then "A Bow Street *Runner*?" Primrose had found her voice first, but they all looked equally appalled.

"He's a gentleman," Violet said hastily in Wintersmith's defense. "He was at school with Rhodes. And he was a captain in the army!"

"Are you in love?" Daphne asked, wide-eyed, at the same time that Primrose said, "How on earth did you meet him?" and Clematis said, "Tell us about the case! How did you solve it?"

"Are you going to marry him?" Aster asked, looking even more worried than she had before.

"No," Violet said, answering that last question first.

"Then why . . ." Aster made a helpless gesture to indicate the liaison with Wintersmith.

"Because we like each other," Violet said, her chin acquiring a slightly defiant tilt. "And because it's fun."

The alarm on Primrose's face was giving way to something rather more disapproving.

"We're being very discreet and I'm using my necklace, so it's none of your concern!" Violet bundled up the pamphlet and shoved it in her reticule. She stood.

"Don't go," Primrose said in what Violet had come to recognize as her duchess voice. "Aster, Daphne, Clem, thank you for your visit, but I must ask you to leave. I would like a private word with Violet."

Aster, Clematis, and Daphne recognized Primrose's duchess voice, too. They all three bade hasty farewells and filed out the door, darting wide-eyed glances back over their shoulders.

Violet wanted to storm out after them in affronted outrage, but that would have been childish and she was an adult—and about to have a very adult conversation with her older sister.

She huffed out an annoyed breath and sat. "This is none of your business, you know."

Her sister looked at her gravely. "Violet, do you know what you're doing?"

"Yes," she said firmly. "I do. I know you think that Bow Street Runners are all coarse, hurly-burly men with little education and few manners, but Wintersmith's not like that. He's a gentleman. He'd never do anything to harm me or my reputation, or our family! He's safe."

Primrose pressed her lips together. She didn't look convinced.

"If you met him, you wouldn't be so censorious! And I must say, I think you're being very hypocritical! You used your necklace before you were married."

"Who told you that?"

"No one. I guessed. But I'm right, aren't I? Otherwise Oliver wouldn't have made that joke about state beds and virgins."

Primrose's cheeks went pink. "You weren't supposed to hear that."

"Then he shouldn't have spoken so loudly."

Primrose didn't argue this truth; she said, "I only used my necklace with Oliver. Not with someone I didn't marry."

"Well, I'm not going to marry Wintersmith and I'm not ashamed of what I'm doing. I'm glad of it, because it's been the best week of my life!"

Primrose's eyebrows pinched together. "I thought you said you weren't in love with him?"

"I'm not. Nor he with me. And besides, he's leaving soon. He's rejoining his regiment." Saying that out loud made her feel rather glum.

Primrose didn't look glum. If anything, she looked relieved. "Well, then," she said, and then brushed her gown over her knees and looked as if she didn't know what to say next.

Violet rose. "I should go."

Primrose rose, too. "Yes."

They stood awkwardly for a moment, and then Violet said, grudgingly, "Would you like to borrow the pamphlet?"

Primrose looked disapproving again. "If this man gave you such a . . . a *publication*, it does cast doubt upon his character."

"No, it doesn't!" Violet flared. "Because he bought it at *my* request. I was curious. I wanted to see! Men look at such things all the time. *Gentlemen* look at them. Why shouldn't we?"

Primrose's eyebrows pinched together again.

"Good-bye!" Violet announced. She turned on her heel, preparing to depart in high dudgeon.

"I would like to borrow it," Primrose said to her back.

Violet halted. She opened her reticule, turned back, and handed Primrose the pamphlet. "I hope it makes you laugh," she said, and then she left in only a moderate dudgeon.

Violet marched back to St. James's Square, a footman in attendance, but her sense of outrage only lasted as far as Piccadilly, which wasn't very far. On the heels of outrage was the realization that if Daphne or Clematis or, heaven forbid, Aster, had made such a revelation, she would have been just as shocked, worried, and concerned as they'd been. And possibly she would have been a little censorious, too. She would want to know who the man was and to be certain that he wouldn't cause any harm.

As she crossed St. James's Square, the footman following dutifully behind, Violet decided that although the scene at Berkeley Square had been unpleasant, she was relieved it had happened.

The truth was out now. Her sisters and two of her cousins knew, and she wasn't ashamed, not even the tiniest bit. If anything, she was proud of herself. She wasn't sitting back while life passed her by; she was grabbing hold of it with both hands.

Violet begged off attending the opera that evening, but before retiring to her bedchamber she slipped into her brother's dressing room. Rhodes was frowning over the arrangement of his neckcloth. His valet hovered to one side, several more lengths of starched muslin draped over one arm.

"Monsieur Benoît? Would you give us a moment alone, please?"

The valet acknowledged her request with a bow and withdrew.

Violet waited until the door had snicked shut. "Wintersmith said I might tell you the whole story, but you must promise not to tell anyone else."

"Mmm." Rhodes peered more closely at the mirror and tweaked his neckcloth.

"Are you listening to me?"

Rhodes made no reply. He frowned at his reflection.

"Rhodes!"

He started, and half-turned from the mirror. "What are you doing in here?"

"Telling you the rest of the Abbishaw story, if you wish to hear it."

"Of course I do," her brother said, but his gaze went back to the mirror. One hand rose to his throat.

"Lord Abbishaw collects lewd automatous clocks."

Rhodes stopped adjusting his neckcloth. "He what?"

"Collects lewd automatous clocks."

Rhodes turned to face her. "Abbishaw? Lewd clocks?"

"Extremely lewd clocks," Violet confirmed, and plunged into the story.

Rhodes leaned against his dressing table, arms folded over his chest. His eyes grew huge as he listened. "Saintbridge played false witness against *both* his brothers? That's beyond infamous!"

Violet nodded gravely. "It is. But you mustn't tell anyone about the clocks, or what Devereux did or Giles's tiepin and cuff link or any of that! It's not public knowledge."

"I shan't. You have my word." Rhodes hesitated, and then said, "I haven't liked your involvement with Wintersmith, but if you had a hand in uncovering this, then I'm proud of you. You did well. You and Wintersmith, both."

Violet felt herself flush with pleasure. "Thank you."

"I suppose you're seeing him tonight? That's why you're not coming to the opera?"

"Yes."

"Rooftops?"

"Yes."

Now would be the time to tell him that she was doing more with Wintersmith than running along rooftops, but Violet found that she didn't have the courage. She hoped Wintersmith would be gone before her brother discovered the truth. Or better yet, that he never found out.

Rhodes looked as if he wanted to tell her to be careful, but he didn't. His lips pressed together; then he turned back to the mirror. "Send in Benoît, will you?"

Wintersmith had the harness laid out and ready when she landed outside his window. He also had a small satchel, the contents of which he refused to divulge. Around his waist was a broad leather belt with two small, sturdy leather loops threaded onto it, one at each hip. "They're for you to hold onto," he said. "It should make it easier to go up walls."

It did.

They roamed London's rooftops for more than an hour, Wintersmith leaping over chimneys and soaring across streets and alleyways. When they finally approached the British Museum, the handles attached to his belt made scaling the building ridiculously easy. Violet gripped the loops and rose upwards. Wintersmith went up the side of the museum with the ease of a bird hopping up a tree, touching a window ledge with his fingertips here, pushing off with a toe there. In a matter of seconds they were on the roof, both of them panting, both of them laughing. They stripped off the harness and then Wintersmith swung her off her feet in an exuberant embrace. "That was capital!" he said, kissing her soundly.

They made love on the roof of the British Museum, and afterwards Wintersmith opened his satchel—his duty bag, he called it—and presented her with two Banbury cakes that he'd purchased from a street vendor in Holborn.

Violet was a duke's daughter. She had grown up eating the finest food that the finest chefs could create using the finest ingredients, but half-penny Banbury cakes turned out to be the best things she'd ever eaten.

"I've never tasted anything so delicious!" she declared, licking her fingers. A cheeky little breeze tugged at the blanket around her shoulders.

"It's the rum," Wintersmith said.

"Rum?"

"The best Banbury cakes have rum in them."

They made love again. The first time had been laughing and energetic; this time was slow and sweet, gentle, tender, beautiful. Afterwards, they lay wrapped around one another, snug in the nest of blankets. Wintersmith told her about his day.

"You're leaving in two weeks?"

"Yes."

Violet felt a pang of dismay. "That's soon."

"Mmm." His next exhalation sounded like a sigh, but his voice, when he spoke, was cheerful: "Devereux and I are going out to Richmond tomorrow."

"Devereux Abbishaw?"

"Yes. We were friends at school. Chums."

"Oh. When are you going? Morning or afternoon?" She tried to see his face, but couldn't make out his features.

"Noon-ish."

"Oh," Violet said again.

Richmond. At noon.

She thought about it while they dressed, and while they packed everything up, and while they buckled themselves into the harness. She thought about it when she bade Wintersmith goodnight in his room above a narrow lane in Holborn. She thought about it as she lay in her bed later that night, with its soft pillows and cool sheets and high canopy.

First thing the next morning, she paid a visit to Berkeley Square. Her sister was in the breakfast parlor with her plate pushed to one side and a book laid out in front of her. "I'd like to ride out to Richmond Park today. Will you come with me?"

Primrose looked up from the book and wrinkled her nose. "In all honesty, Vi, I'd rather—"

"My Bow Street Runner's going to be there."

Primrose's eyebrows twitched together. "An assignation?"

Violet shook her head. "No. He doesn't know I'll be there. But I've never spent time with him in daylight, so *please* will you come with me, so that I may?" She pressed her hands together prayer-like. "You'll get to meet him and you'll see that he's not at all what you think he is!"

Primrose closed the book without marking her place. "I should like to meet this Bow Street Runner of yours. When do we leave?"

CHAPTER
FORTY-SIX

*T*hey set out at noon from London, not only Violet and Primrose, but Aster, Daphne, and Clematis, plus two grooms with picnic hampers attached to their saddles.

Violet almost balked when she saw the size of the party. Any excursion that included both Daphne and Clematis would not allow for quiet *tête-à-têtes*.

"I extended the invitation," Primrose said, a statement of the blatantly obvious. "I thought it would look less particular."

Look less like a tryst, was what Primrose meant. And perhaps she was right. Violet might *want* a daylight tryst with Wintersmith, but she didn't dare actually have one, not if she wished to keep her family safe from gossip.

Richmond lay nine miles from London. It was past one o'clock by the time they reached the high brick wall that enclosed the expanse of parkland. Violet wanted to ask the gatekeeper whether he'd seen Wintersmith and Devereux Abbishaw, but that would have necessitated describing them, something that Daphne, Clematis, and Aster would hardly fail to notice.

She shifted in her sidesaddle and fidgeted with the reins, conscious of a nervous excitement. "King Henry's Mound?" she suggested, once they'd passed through the gate.

"Yes, let's!" Daphne cried, setting off at a trot that quickly became a canter, which in turn became a race between Daphne and Clematis to see who could reach the mound first.

Violet joined in, arriving at the celebrated viewpoint in a mad gallop. It was rather breezy at the top, little gusts of wind plucking at her hat and stirring the long folds of her riding habit. Violet shaded her eyes with her hand and looked eagerly around. She saw barouches and landaulets trundling along the avenues. Deer grazed near one of the ponds. Riders cantered along the bridle paths, three in one party, four in another, tiny figures on horseback.

Was Wintersmith one of those riders?

Violet was suddenly conscious of just how large Richmond Park was. More than two thousand acres of woodland and meadow. She could spend all afternoon riding along one path after another and fail to find Wintersmith.

Her eagerness folded in on itself and reshaped into something rather like anxiety.

"Is that one of the Abbishaws down there?" Primrose said.

Violet's cousins immediately began jostling one another to see. "Is it Saint?" Daphne cried. "I'm astonished he dare show his face in public!" And then, "Oh, it's only Devil."

Violet followed the direction of Primrose's pointing finger. Two riders trotted leisurely along a bridle path. One was Devereux Abbishaw, recognizable both by his lankiness and by the blood bay he rode. Her gaze latched eagerly onto the man alongside him. He had a military alertness that contrasted with Devil's laidback slouch in the saddle.

Her heart gave a joyful little skip. "Let's say hello!"

Violet went down the hillside so fast that it almost felt as if she was flying. She galloped across a meadow like a hoyden, butterflies and songbirds scattering in her path, and came up behind the two horsemen. "I say! Hello! Mr. Abbishaw!"

The two men checked their horses and looked around.

Wintersmith looked quite astonished. He opened his mouth as if to greet her by name, then closed it abruptly.

Violet brought her horse to a halt, feeling oddly breathless. "I thought it was you, Mr. Abbishaw. We saw you from the mound."

"Lady Violet," Devereux said, bowing in the saddle. "What a delightful surprise."

Violet, who hadn't felt shy in years, suddenly found herself feeling rather bashful. "I'm here with my sisters and cousins. Do you mind if we ride with you?"

"Not at all," Devereux said. "Allow me to present my friend, Mr. Wintersmith."

Their two parties merged after a round of introductions. If Wintersmith felt awkward in the company of a duchess, he concealed it well. As they moved off along the bridle path, he dropped back to ride beside Violet.

"This is a surprise," he murmured.

"Do you mind?" Violet asked, equally quietly.

"No." He glanced at her, a tiny smile turning his lips up at the corners.

Their gazes caught and held. Blood rushed to Violet's cheeks. She felt breathless again.

"Mr. Wintersmith," Primrose said, her voice cool and tart. She'd fallen back, too, and was on his other side.

Wintersmith turned his attention to her. "Your Grace."

Primrose launched into a conversation that sounded rather like an interrogation. She swiftly established that Wintersmith had served in India. "My husband did, too. Perhaps you knew him? Oliver Dasenby?"

It was a question that required a simple yes or no answer, but Wintersmith said: "He wasn't in my regiment, ma'am."

Violet recognized that as an evasion. She inferred that Wintersmith did indeed know Oliver.

Primrose failed to notice that her question had been side-stepped. She embarked on another line of inquiry.

Violet perched tensely on her saddle, gripping her reins tightly, ready to interrupt should her sister's questions become too intrusive, her tongue too tart, but Wintersmith's years as a soldier had clearly given him practice at being interrogated by persons of higher rank. He was unruffled by the questions. The longer the conversation endured, the more Wintersmith proved that he wasn't a crude, brutish thief-catcher, but rather a man of good sense and good breeding.

Violet stopped worrying about protecting Wintersmith from her sister and began wishing instead that she could interrogate Primrose.

What did Primrose think of him?

Did she think he was dull and nondescript?

Was she wondering why on earth Violet liked him?

After fifteen minutes, Primrose abandoned her interrogation and trotted ahead to ride with Aster and Devereux Abbishaw, leaving Violet in sole possession of Wintersmith.

She took that as a mark of approval.

At last, she was alone with Wintersmith. In daylight. Or rather, as alone as one could be in a public park, with two sisters and a gentleman riding ahead, two cousins riding behind, and two grooms bringing up the rear.

"I apologize for my sister. She can be rather nosy."

Wintersmith's lips twitched as if he was suppressing a smile. "A family trait?" he suggested.

Violet blushed and laughed at the same time. "Possibly."

She'd seen Wintersmith in lamplight and candlelight, moonlight and starlight, but this felt different. More real, less dream-like. Less private, less intimate, yet also more serious, as if by riding alongside him, talking with him, she was making a statement to the world. *I value this man. He is important to me.*

He looked the same as he always did—brown hair, gray eyes—and yet he also looked different. The sunshine showed him to her more clearly. His eyes were still gray, but also ever so slightly blue, and the creases at the corners were more pronounced, hinting at gravitas and humor at the same time.

He was familiar, but at the same time he was almost a stranger. Violet felt oddly flustered. She searched for something witty to say, failed to find anything, and instead said, "I love coming out to Richmond, don't you?" a trite, commonplace little remark that she mentally kicked herself for.

"I haven't here since I was a boy," Wintersmith replied.

"But . . . surely you've visited since coming back to England?"

He shook his head. "I haven't had the opportunity."

"But—" Violet bit her tongue on what she'd been about to say: that visiting Richmond was so easy that anyone could do it. The chasm between her life and his suddenly seemed vast. She could come here on a whim, had horses and carriages and grooms at her beck and call, had the leisure to spend a whole day doing nothing more than riding and picnicking.

Wintersmith didn't.

"Then we must go around the whole park. There are some lovely views. You must see them all."

But she didn't just want to show him the park; she wanted to show him her daytime self, the Violet her friends and family knew. She wanted him to think that Violet was worth knowing, she wanted him to *like* that Violet, and she wanted to see his daytime self, too, but she didn't know where to start. Didn't know how to start.

She glanced at Primrose and Aster up ahead and then back at him, and her wits spilled out her ears and she couldn't think of anything droll or amusing to say, anything clever or entertaining. The only thing on her tongue was a silly comment about the weather.

Wintersmith was looking at her, with eyes that were gray but also a tiny bit blue.

Violet's cheeks grew warm. Her heart began to beat faster than it needed to.

Dimly, she heard the jangle of a carriage harness as a barouche passed by on one of the avenues, heard Daphne and Clematis bickering amiably, heard Devil Abbishaw laugh, but those sounds were distant and inconsequential, as if the people who made them existed in another world. In *her* world, Richmond Park was empty and it was just herself and Wintersmith, riding side by side, staring at one another.

She wasn't certain how long they stared without speaking. A gallop of hooves passed them and a shouted, "Race you around the pond!" and it took her several seconds to realize that everyone else in their party was thundering off across a meadow as if a troop of French hussars was after them.

Except for the two grooms, who were waiting at a respectful distance.

"Shall we gallop?" Violet suggested, aware that grooms had eyes and ears and tongues that could spread gossip.

"Why not?"

So they galloped for a bit, and then they rode to the top of King Henry's Mound again, so that Wintersmith might see the view, and then they picnicked together, all seven of them, on a grassy sunlit slope out of the worst of the wind, and it was easy and relaxed and perfect. They ate cheese and bread and cold meats, a raised chicken pie, apple pastries and *macarons*, grapes and apricots.

The men removed their hats and gloves. Wintersmith's hair was fairer than it seemed by candlelight, his brown locks threaded through with blond strands that gleamed brightly in the sunshine.

Conversation ranged widely but came, inevitably, to the latest *ton* scandal. "Saint has left town for the season," Devereux confirmed, plucking several grapes from one of the bunches. "So has my uncle."

"Lord Abbishaw's gone?" Violet said, surprised by this new information.

"Left this morning. The house on Hanover Square is being closed as we speak, everything put under Holland covers." Devereux tossed a grape high and caught it. "And as for Saint, the lease on his house has been let go. He won't be back in London for a long time. If ever." His smile was razor sharp.

"But what about Giles?" Aster asked, concern wrinkling her brow. "Where will he live? Must he leave London too?"

"No." Devereux leaned back on one elbow. His smile lost its sharp edge. "His allowance has been increased to match what Saint's was. He's taken a set of rooms in Portugal Street, near Hyde Park."

The street where his lover resided.

Violet glanced at Wintersmith. They exchanged a secret smile.

"And what of Wilton?" Primrose inquired, pouring herself more lemonade.

"Been summoned back to England."

"And so justice prevails!" Daphne exclaimed. "How lucky."

"Yes," Devereux said, but Violet knew the truth. It hadn't been luck. Justice had prevailed because of Devereux's determination to bring his cousin to reckoning. Perhaps his method had been underhand, perhaps even criminal, but it had also been a little heroic.

Violet wished she could tell him that she knew what he'd done, and that she approved of it, but she couldn't. Instead, she took the last apricot and nibbled on it.

Birds twittered and bees hummed and a breeze rustled its way through the grass. The picnic was in disarray. A spread that would have been overly generous for five ladies had perfectly accommodated the addition of two gentlemen.

Daphne ate the last *macaron*, Primrose the last grape, Devereux the last slice of pie. The grooms packed everything back into the hampers and then, unfortunately, it was time to go home. Violet's sisters and both of her cousins were going to a ball that she herself would have been eager to attend—if she hadn't been planning to traverse London's roofs with a former Bow Street Runner and then do something exceedingly naughty with him on top of the colonnade at Burlington House.

Devil Abbishaw was going to the ball, of course.

Violet expressed the hope that they could all ride back

to town together, but Primrose scotched that by saying, "We mustn't take up any more of Mr. Abbishaw and his friend's time. I'm sure they didn't come all this way just to spend the afternoon with a gaggle of females."

"Only because we didn't think we'd be so fortunate," Devereux assured her, but he didn't offer to accompany them back to town, which meant that Primrose was correct, and he wanted to spend time with Wintersmith.

Violet felt rather guilty. She hadn't meant to monopolize Wintersmith's attention. Devereux had as much claim to it as she did. More, perhaps, given that their friendship was of long standing.

She cast Devereux an apologetic glance, and found herself the object of a disconcertingly speculative perusal—which told her that perhaps she had made her interest in Wintersmith rather too obvious.

They parted ways in a flurry of good-byes. Their party rode out through the gate onto Sheen Common. Scarcely had they left the high brick walls behind than Primrose came up alongside Violet.

Violet bit her tongue against the urge to say *What did you think of him?* She didn't care what her sister thought of Wintersmith; her own opinion was the only one that mattered.

Except that she *did* care what Primrose thought. She wanted her to have seen Wintersmith's good qualities. To perhaps not like him, but to at least respect him.

"Well? What do you think?" she demanded.

Primrose checked that no one was within earshot. "He's not at all what I expected. Quite unlike your usual flirts."

"He's not one of my flirts!" Violet said indignantly.

"No, that's obvious."

Violet huffed out a breath. "Pray tell me, what are my usual flirts like?"

"Dashing," Primrose said with annoying alacrity. "Devil-may-care, high spirited. Rattles and gadabouts and blades on the strut."

None of those terms could be applied to Wintersmith.

"He's not dull," Violet said defensively. "And he's not bland and nondescript either. Or boring!"

"I didn't say that he was. Merely that he's rather more . . . ordinary than your usual flirts."

"He's not ordinary!" Ordinary men didn't run across London's rooftops, laughing as they leaped over chimneys and alleyways.

Primrose looked amused. "That wasn't an insult."

Violet huffed again. "Well, it sounded like one."

"Your Mr. Wintersmith appears to be a man of good sense," her sister said, and then tempered this praise with: "Although that's doubtful."

"It's not doubtful! He's a man of *very* good sense. He thinks things through, and he considers consequences, and he knows how to balance recklessness with caution."

"Does he?" Primrose's voice was dry, her expression more than a little sardonic.

Belatedly, Violet understood what her sister meant by good sense. "We're being very careful."

Primrose's lips tucked in at the corners, but not in a smile. "I hope so, Vi. I truly do."

Chapter Forty-Seven

"So . . . you and Lady Violet?" Devereux remarked, as they rode back over the Putney bridge.

"I don't know what you mean," Perry said evasively.

Devereux smirked. "Don't you?"

"Of course not!"

"The pair of you made sheep's eyes at each other all afternoon. If she's not your inconvenient, I'll eat my hat."

"Well, she's not!" Unfortunately, his denial sounded so false that even Perry heard the lie.

Devereux crowed with laughter. "I knew it!"

Perry felt his cheeks redden with chagrin. "Were we that obvious?"

"Well, *I* could see it, and I'm fairly certain the duchess could, too."

Perry was absolutely certain that the duchess had known beforehand. It was the only explanation for the rather rigorous cross-examination she'd subjected him to.

"You're a brave man," Devereux said. "And a dashed lucky one. Lady Violet's a diamond of the first water. How the devil did you meet?"

"You wouldn't believe me if I told you," Perry said truthfully.

They parted ways at the stable yard off Wigmore Street where Devereux kept his horses. Perry found himself whistling as he walked the mile and a half home to Holborn. He purchased some Banbury cakes, let himself into the lodging house with his latchkey, and ran up the stairs, still whistling. Today had been the best day he'd had since returning to England. The best day he'd had in years.

Lady Violet, when she appeared not long after dark, shared his ebullience. They ran from one side of London to the other, further than they'd been before. Perry was airborne between each step, so close to flying that it felt as if he possessed magic, too.

The blankets were on top of the colonnade at Burlington House. They made love, muffling laughter and gasps of pleasure against each other's skin, while pedestrians and carriages passed by on Piccadilly, not thirty feet below. Afterwards, they sat munching on Banbury cakes, talking in low voices.

"What did you think of Richmond Park?" Lady Violet asked once the pastries were gone. She lay back on the blankets and tugged him down alongside her, curling into him, laying her head on his chest.

"I liked it," Perry said.

The moment felt perfect, as some moments did—Lady Violet nestled in his arms, cool air feathering over his skin, stars shining above—which was probably what made Perry reveal part of himself that he hadn't meant to. "It's the first time I've felt happy to be back in England."

There was a moment of startled silence, and then, "You don't like England?"

"I do like England. It's just . . ."

"Just?"

Perry stared up at the sky. He remembered the bleak days after his father had died, the sick knowledge that they were ruined, his mother's inconsolable despair.

Lady Violet didn't repeat her question. She waited for him to speak.

Perry blew out a breath and tried to articulate something that he wasn't entirely certain that he understood himself. "I think it's because of Father. It was all so awful after he died, and it wasn't much better when I came back, because Endymion and Alexander were dead, and Mother was ill. England just felt wrong. It's felt wrong this whole time. But today, in Richmond Park, it actually felt right for a few hours." It was more than the idyllic setting; it was Devereux's company, Lady Violet's, even her formidable older sister. For an afternoon, England had felt as golden as it was in his memories.

"You miss your brothers a lot?" Lady Violet asked softly.

"Yes." But it wasn't only that. "I think . . . what I miss most is how it was before Father died." The halcyon days of his childhood, when he'd been safe and loved and unburdened by the worries of adulthood. "But that's by the by! For heaven's sake, don't pity me, for I'm perfectly happy!"

Although hadn't he just told her otherwise?

"I don't pity you," Lady Violet said. "But I am sad you have no family. I wish I could share mine with you." She slipped her fingers between his, lacing their hands together.

"The regiment's my family. I'll be back with them soon enough." Perry's voice was cheerful, but his mood no longer was. The buoyant ebullience had evaporated. In its place was something that felt rather melancholy.

Her thumb stroked his skin lightly, then she said, "You know Oliver, don't you? When Primrose asked, you didn't say no."

"Oliver Dasenby? Yes. We were friends." Perry hesitated, and then said, "I didn't tell him I'm back in England."

Lady Violet didn't ask why. She knew as well as he did that dukes couldn't be friends with people who lived in attics in Holborn.

The melancholy was still with him when he woke the next morning. Perry shaved and dressed and headed downstairs, planning the day in his head. The tailor first, to get fitted for his uniform, then he'd see about a new sword. He stepped out into the lane, avoiding the open gutter.

He was wondering whether it was worth his while to go to Enfield, where he'd pawned his pistols eight months ago, when a curt voice hailed him. "Wintersmith!"

The Marquis of Thane stalked towards him, his expression savage. He'd clearly found out that his sister's relationship with Perry had progressed beyond friendship.

Perry halted.

There was no doubt in his mind what would happen next. The marquis would mill him down, thrash him, perhaps even horsewhip him—and it would be no less than he deserved.

He braced himself for what was to come. Whatever Thane did, he'd take it. He wouldn't raise a hand against Violet's brother.

Thane halted. His eyebrows were knotted together. His mouth was a grim line.

Perry steeled himself for the first blow, his muscles tightening in unhappy anticipation.

"We need to talk," the marquis said brusquely.

"Talk?"

"Yes. That coffeehouse."

❦

At such an early hour, the coffeehouse had few patrons. It looked shabby, dingy, neglected.

"What the devil do you think you're doing?" Thane demanded, once they'd been served. He looked as if he hadn't entirely ruled out thrashing Perry within an inch of his life.

There were many ways Perry could answer that question,

but it all boiled down to one thing: "I'm doing what Violet wants."

Rage flared in Thane's eyes. He inhaled sharply and opened his mouth to utter what would undoubtedly be a blistering assessment of Perry's character.

"Has she told you about the case? I know she intended to." Thane was on the brink of speech, but Perry barreled on: "She found a stash of pornographic drawings. Hidden in a bandbox."

This revelation deflected Thane from what he'd been about to say. He scowled. "She didn't tell me that."

"I tried to keep her from seeing them, but Violet's not . . ." He searched for the correct word. "Biddable. She does what she wants—which is to be expected. She's an adult, after all."

Thane's scowl deepened.

"She saw the drawings and naturally she was curious."

"Curious, yes, but you didn't have to damned well tumble her!" Thane said in a low, furious voice.

"If not me, then it would have been someone else."

Thane's nostrils flared. He looked ready to lunge across the table at Perry.

"She asked me," Perry said bluntly. "She wanted to know what it was like, so she asked me to show her. And do you know why she asked me and not someone else? Because I'm safe. Of all the men in England, I'm the safest, and your sister had the sense to recognize that, so be grateful it's me and not someone who's in the brothels every other night, like Frederick Stanhope."

Thane's upper lip curled. "Am I supposed to thank you for your altruism?"

The caustic tone made Perry flush. Thane was being a prick. But given the circumstances, he had every right to be one.

"It's not altruism. I like your sister very much, but whatever my feelings for her, you must believe that I wouldn't have embarked on this path if she hadn't asked. Or if she hadn't had that charm."

Thane's eyes narrowed. "How much do you like her?"

"Don't worry," Perry said. "I'm not going to propose." He picked up his cup and took a big gulp. The coffee burned his tongue, burned his throat.

"Why not? An honorable man would."

Perry uttered a bitter laugh. "No, an honorable man would walk away. Which is what I shall do. We both know I'm not worthy of her."

Thane scowled his agreement. He picked up his cup, drank, grimaced. His cup clattered in its saucer when he put it down. "Are you in love with her?"

Perry's first impulse was to tell him it was none of his damned business, but it was Thane's business. Everything to do with keeping the Garland family safe was Thane's business. "Yes, I have been for quite some time. But I know she doesn't return my feelings—and even if she did, I'm not the husband for her. Your sister deserves someone wealthy, someone who moves in the first circles."

"You were born into the first circles, and if you marry Violet you'd be wealthy."

Perry put his cup down so hard that coffee sloshed over the sides. "I'm not a damned fortune hunter!"

Thane laughed, a short, surprised sound. Then his face twisted. Perry was shocked to see tears spring to his eyes.

"What?" he said uncertainly.

Thane shook his head and wiped his eyes roughly.

Perry looked down at his cup. The saucer was filled with coffee. He tipped it back into the cup, then glanced across the table. Thane had regained his composure.

Perry didn't speak. He waited, wondering which direction the conversation would take now.

The answer was, no direction. Thane sipped his coffee silently.

Perry gave an internal shrug and sipped his coffee, too.

"You looked just like Endymion then," Thane said abruptly. "Sounded just like him, too. He said those exact words to me ten years ago. Same tone. Same look on his face." Thane's mouth compressed. He shook his head. "I thought you weren't like him at all, but you are."

Perry looked down at his half-empty cup.

They sat without speaking for almost a full minute, and then Thane said, "I'm sorry they both died."

Perry nodded, and then—damn it—had to dab at his own eyes. "Thank you for the letters you sent," he said, still looking at his coffee cup. "They meant a lot."

"I sent one after your mother's death, too."

Perry glanced up. "It's probably on its way back from India."

"Probably." Thane shrugged, and drank a mouthful of coffee.

Perry drank, too, then put down his cup. "You're wasting your time worrying about me. Once I've gone, that's when you need to start worrying."

Thane cocked an eyebrow. "Oh?"

"If Violet looks to replace me, she may choose the wrong person."

Thane choked on his coffee.

"She should be married," Perry said bluntly. "She needs a husband, not a lover. Someone worthy of her."

Thane mastered his breathing and set his cup down. "There aren't that many unmarried dukes around, or dukes' sons for that matter—and Violet doesn't want to marry any of 'em."

"That's not what I mean by worthy."

"What then?"

"Someone with an adventurous spirit. Someone who won't try to tame her, who'll let her be who she is. But he needs to be steady. Sensible. Able to keep her safe. Not a Frederick Stanhope or a Wilton Abbishaw." He paused, and then said, "Devereux Abbishaw might do. Your sister seems to like him a lot."

"Not enough to marry," Thane said.

"Someone else, then. You need to start looking."

312

"You think I haven't been?" Thane said, with asperity. "Violet's been out for seven years. She knows every man in the *ton*. She's flirted with half of them, been proposed to by half of 'em, too, but she doesn't want to marry any of them. No one's ever taken her fancy."

The words "before you" hung unspoken in the air between them.

"Well, you need to look harder." Perry picked up his cup and put it down without drinking. "Now that Violet knows what it's like between a man and a woman, maybe she'll consider marriage more seriously." He hesitated, then forced himself to say: "I think you could trust Devereux with your family's secret."

Thane didn't look convinced.

"He might have been wild when he was up at Oxford, but he's not wild now."

"He's not exactly steady, though, is he? There was more than one way to handle the issue with Saintbridge. Devereux didn't pick the best one."

Perry wanted to ask how Thane would have handled it, but it was a conversational detour he didn't have time to get lost down. "She deserves a husband. Someone who'll make her happy. Now more than ever."

Thane's lips thinned. "I wish to God you hadn't—"

"Would you rather she'd asked someone else? Because she would have."

Thane grimaced, which Perry took as a *No*. He gulped the last of his coffee, set the cup in its saucer, and pushed it to one side, indicating that the conversation was over. "If you'll excuse me, I must see a tailor about my uniform."

CHAPTER
FORTY-EIGHT

*H*is business with the tailor concluded, Perry's next task was to purchase a sword and pistols. He'd brought his sword back with him from India for sentimental reasons and his pistols as a means of defense on the journey—and sold them when it became obvious that he needed money more than he needed mementos of his military career. It was doubtful the pawnbroker still had them, but the day was warm and sunny and he had the time, so he set out for Enfield, ten miles north of London.

A ha'penny bought him a ride on a passing cart as far as Tottenham. From there, he walked the last four miles to Enfield. Meadows stretched on either side of the road, dotted with thickets of trees. Livestock grazed and birds sang overhead. Perry lifted his face to the sky. The air was fresh, clean, smelling of wildflowers and grass, horse dung and cowpats. Carts and carriages passed him, smart post-chaises, ponderous wagons, a mail coach. Perry found himself whistling as he walked, found himself feeling glad to be in England for the second time in two days.

He stopped whistling when he reached Enfield. It was a pleasant enough town, but it was where his mother had come after they'd tumbled into ruin. To him, Enfield was his mother's grief and despair, her sickbed, her death.

The pawnbroker's shop looked exactly as it had eight months ago, its windows crammed with a miscellany of items: vases and snuff boxes, candlesticks and clocks, chess sets, tea sets, pocket watches and toothpick holders, rings and brooches and trinkets of all descriptions. It proclaimed itself a silversmith's, but there was no mistaking it for what it was: a place where the unfortunate divested themselves of their possessions in exchange for money.

The last time Perry had entered the shop, he'd felt sick at heart, defeated. His life had been shrinking around him, becoming smaller, narrower, duller. Now, his life was widening again. He had a direction, a destination, a reason for being.

He stepped inside, into a crowded, stuffy space where even more items were on display. He looked around for his sword, for his pistols.

"Can I help you, sir?"

Perry explained his purpose to the proprietor, trying not to hope too much—it had been eight months, after all—but it seemed that he had held out hope, because when the man shook his head and said, "I sold those pistols long ago," he felt rather cast down.

"Thank you." He turned away. Pistols were only pistols, after all. A sword was only a sword.

"The sword, I still have."

"You do?" Perry swung back, feeling his heart lighten.

The proprietor presented a sheathed sword, laying it on the counter for him to see.

It looked like Perry's sword. The belt was showing wear in the exact same places, the tassel was sun-faded, the chape at the end of the scabbard slightly dented. "May I?" he said, reaching for it.

The proprietor nodded.

Even if he were blind, Perry's hand would have known the sword for his. The weight, the balance, the worn ridges on the grip—everything was familiar. The hilt was cold, though. It sent a sharp, icy shiver up his arm, up the back of his neck, up over his scalp. The shiver felt like a portent of doom, a warning not to become a soldier again, but Perry knew that it wasn't. The metal was cold, was all.

"I'll take it," he said.

Three minutes later, he stepped out onto the street, lighter in his pocket, but lighter in his heart, too. The shiver still lingered uneasily at the nape of his neck, but he paid it no heed.

Perry visited the churchyard before returning to London. He wandered among the graves until he found his mother's, with its small, plain headstone.

He knelt, laying the sword alongside him on the grass. "You wanted me to be safe, Mother, but I'd rather be happy than safe, so I'm going back. I know I promised not to, but I need to do what's best for me. I'm sorry."

There was no sense that she was there, no sense that she heard his words. Grass blades stirred in the breeze, bees hummed, a horse clopped past on the street.

Perry stayed there for a while, and it was quiet and peaceful, and then he headed back to London with his sword.

CHAPTER
FORTY-NINE

*V*iolet went hunting for Rhodes after luncheon. He had his own suite of rooms at Sevenash House, complete with a sitting room and study. She found him in the study, glowering at a letter he was composing.

Violet tapped on the doorframe. "Rhodes?"

Her brother lifted his head and glared at her. The glare was so fierce that Violet almost stepped back. "Is something wrong?"

His lips compressed until they almost vanished. Violet took that to be a *Yes*. She stepped into the room and closed the door. "What's wrong?"

Rhodes flung down his quill, spattering ink across the letter. "You're having an affair with Wintersmith. Don't try to deny it; I've already spoken with him."

Violet froze, just inside the door. Dismay flooded through her, and on its heels was a heart-clenching fear. "Did you call him out?"

Rhodes scowled and screwed up the ruined letter. "No."

Violet inhaled a relieved breath.

"Damn it, Vi! What the devil do you think you're doing?"

"Living my life."

Rhodes snorted, a contemptuous sound.

Violet advanced to the desk. "I'm living my life," she repeated. "And it's none of your business."

"Of course it's my damned business! Everything that happens in this family is my business!"

"No. This isn't. It's my business, mine and Wintersmith's, and no one else's."

Rhodes opened his mouth to disagree with her, but Violet plowed on: "If you were to have an affair, it wouldn't be my business, or Prim's or Aster's, or even Mother and Father's. It would only be your business. And don't tell me that it's different for men and for women, because Mother gave us all charms when we turned twenty-one, so it's not as if I can fall pregnant!"

Rhodes grimaced and looked away. Violet inferred that he didn't want to think about her having sex. Which was fair enough, because she didn't want to think about him having sex either.

"I'm an adult, Rhodes. Mother trusted me enough to give me that charm. You need to trust me to use it discreetly. I shan't damage our family's reputation. I give you my word."

His lips pinched together. He looked back at her and she saw the worry beneath the anger.

"We're a family with a great many secrets. Trust me to keep this one hidden, too."

Rhodes rubbed his brow so hard that his fingertips went white. Did he find all those secrets a burden? The various magics in the family? Magic that he didn't possess himself.

"Who told you?" Violet asked. "Was it Prim?"

"I overheard her talking with Aster last night. I thought I'd misunderstood, but . . ." He lowered his hand and gave her a black look. "You told me you'd keep me apprised of what was happening!" There was accusation in his glare, accusation in his voice.

"I told you what was happening with the case. My personal relationship with Wintersmith is no one's business but my own."

"You told Aster and Prim," he snapped.

"I didn't mean for them to find out."

Rhodes breathed out audibly through his nose. If he was a dragon, that breath would have been a scorching plume of fire. He was not happy with her.

Or with Wintersmith.

"Did you hit him?" Violet asked apprehensively.

"No." He looked as if he'd wanted to, though. As if he still wanted to.

"Thank you," Violet said. "Now, I came to find you because there's not a breath of wind and the children would like to fly the balloons."

Her brother exhaled another dragonish breath. He wanted to hold on to his rage—she saw it in the set of his eyebrows, the set of his jaw—but Rhodes had never been one to sulk or to wallow in ill temper. He rubbed his face with both hands, then blew out a less dragonish breath and stood. "All right."

He didn't immediately head for the door, though. He halted in front of her. They exchanged a long stare, two adults taking one another's measure.

"For God's sake, be careful, Vi."

"I will. I promise."

Not all of the houses on St. James's Square were mansions, and not all of the mansions had private gardens, but Sevenash House was one of the mansions that did. It had beds of flowers and strips of lawn and two fountains. At the far end was a gate into the mews.

They set up at the top of the garden, with the balloons and

a chafing dish filled with charcoal and a bucket of water from one of the fountains in case of accidents.

The children wanted to send all six balloons aloft at once, but Rhodes demurred. "Let's see what happens with one first."

They inflated the balloon over the chafing dish. When fully distended it was nearly three feet tall. It looked like an upside-down pear, wide at the top, narrow at the bottom. At its opening were two cross wires. Violet and Aster held the balloon steady while Rhodes attached cotton wool soaked in spirits of wine to the cross wires. He lit a twist of paper from the chafing dish and carefully set the wool alight.

The children squealed with delight to see the balloon rise in the air. It floated upwards surprisingly fast. Soon it was as high as the rooftops. The children laughed gleefully, and Violet laughed, too . . . until she realized that while there might not have been a breath of wind down in the garden, there was definitely a breeze higher up. A breeze that was causing the balloon to drift towards the end of the garden—and the mews beyond.

She stopped laughing. What if the balloon came down in the mews? What if it set fire to the hay there? What if the stables started to burn?

If it had been dark, she could have flown up and retrieved the balloon, but in broad daylight she didn't dare. Violet exchanged a horrified glance with Rhodes. "Stay with your aunts," he told the children. He snatched up the bucket and headed for the gate into the mews at a run.

Violet caught Jessamy's hand and watched the balloon sail on the breeze. The children were still laughing, still squealing, their delight spilling over into the gardens on either side, but her own tongue was frozen with horror, her mouth dry. Dread clutched in her chest—but as Rhodes neared the gate, the balloon began to deflate. It sank swiftly, plummeting to the ground in a matter of seconds, landing almost at her brother's feet.

"Thank heavens," Aster breathed.

Rhodes brought the balloon back, looking rather green. The cotton wool had burned to a charred wisp. He caught Violet's eye and pulled a face that said *That was nearly a disaster of catastrophic proportions.* The children didn't notice. They were clamoring for the balloon to be relaunched. "Again! Again!" Hyacinth cried, jumping up and down.

"I think that's enough for today," Rhodes said.

"But I want to fly *my* balloon," young Jessamy said, with a pout that signaled tears were imminent.

"Let's all go to Gunter's and get some ices!" Aster suggested brightly.

Jessamy's lower lip wobbled ominously. So did Hyacinth's.

"What a grand idea!" Violet said, swinging Hyacinth up on her hip. "I'd love an ice right now. I think I'll have strawberry. What about you, Melrose? Jessamy? What would you like?"

It hung in the balance for a moment, and then Melrose declared, "Chocolate."

"Chocolate!" said Jessamy, too.

"Strawbee!" Hyacinth cried.

Rhodes met her eyes over the top of the children's heads and mouthed *Thank you.*

CHAPTER FIFTY

It started raining while they were at Gunter's. It rained all that night and the next day. And the next. And the next, until Violet was ready to burst with frustration. She wanted to see Wintersmith, wanted to run along the roofs with him, wanted to talk with him and laugh with him and make love with him. But she couldn't, not while the rain beat down so heavily.

She would have gone mad if not for the children.

On the first rainy day, she helped them build a fortress out of furniture, with tunnels and hidey-holes and a roof made of blankets. They all picnicked inside, even Rhodes and Aster, and it was capital fun.

On the second rainy day, they played hide-and-seek throughout the house, adults and children alike. Violet found Jessamy in her window seat, and later that afternoon, Melrose. She was thankful she no longer had anything concealed there. Freddy Stanhope's bandbox was back in its hiding place, Wintersmith had the harness, and she'd stashed the blankets in the steeple of St. James's Church, where they were dry and out of sight and inaccessible to anyone but her.

On the third day, they painted pictures together, and then they piled onto the sofa in the nursery, all of them tumbled together like puppies, and Rhodes read nursery rhymes. Hyacinth dozed off, snuggled on Aster's lap, lulled to sleep by her father's comforting baritone. Violet fell asleep, too.

On the fourth day, when they were anticipating the duke and duchess's return from Surrey, they instead received a letter by express. The duke had broken a bone in his foot. He and the duchess would stay another week in Surrey, until he could walk more easily.

That dampened everyone's mood. Rhodes looked at the glum faces and said, "I have an idea. Let's fly the balloons inside."

Violet exchanged a dubious glance with her sister. "Inside?"

"Yes, in the entrance hall."

"But—"

"No cotton wool," Rhodes said. "Just hot air."

A footman was sent to Berkeley Square with an invitation for Primrose and Oliver, and another to Grosvenor Square, where their aunt and uncle and cousins lived. Everyone came, even Violet's cousin Lily, who usually preferred to be alone.

The entrance hall was a cavernous space with a sweeping double staircase and a domed ceiling painted with flowers and songbirds.

Rhodes laid out six chafing dishes on the marble floor, one for each of the paper balloons. Each chafing dish had charcoal inside, and a lid to cover it. "Adults only near the dishes," he instructed, but the children were too excited to argue this stricture. They sat on the bottom step with their nursemaids, pink-cheeked and bright-eyed and jiggling with excitement.

With no burning cotton wool to fuel them, the balloons didn't stay aloft long, but that only added to the fun. It was wildly entertaining, ridiculously exciting. Shrieks and laughter echoed in the great entrance hall. Even Lily laughed until her face was flushed.

Balloons bumped against the domed ceiling. They drifted off course. They plummeted and were re-inflated and plummeted again, and eventually they disintegrated.

As dusk fell, the rain tapered to a drizzle and then finally stopped. Violet's aunt and uncle and cousins stayed to dine with them, but much as she loved her family, there was someone she wanted to see more. Someone she was desperate to spend time with. Someone who was leaving England very soon.

CHAPTER
FIFTY-ONE

*T*ime had passed with painful slowness when Perry was a secretary; now the days flew by almost too fast. He and Devereux rode out to Hampstead Heath and Finchley Common, Greenwich and Dartford, Richmond Park and beyond to Hampton Court. When they weren't riding, they played chess, played cards, talked, laughed, everything easy and relaxed between them, the way it had been when they were boys.

The nights were for Lady Violet.

Perry had a new mask now, one that she'd sewn for him. They were a matched pair, the two of them, dressed from head to toe in black. Together, they explored the city. They looked down from the dome of St. Paul's Cathedral. They crossed the Thames on Westminster Bridge and came back again on London Bridge. They ran further than they had before, north, south, east, west.

Perry brought his duty bag with him each night, stocked with tidbits for Lady Violet to try, food he'd purchased from the street vendors in Holborn. Pickled whelks and eel pies.

Roasted potatoes. Roasted apples. Currant tarts and treacle tarts and rhubarb tarts.

But the running, the almost-flying, the exploring, the eating, were only part of it. Each night they made love, lost in a small, intimate world of blankets and starlight and cool breezes whispering across naked skin, a world of soft touches and soft laughter, soft conversations.

After they parted, Perry was never able to determine whether the best part of the evening had been the lovemaking or the laughter, the running or the conversations.

He did know that every night he fell more in love with Violet Garland. He'd never been so eager for the sun to rise each morning, or so eager for it to set each evening, but he also knew that this wasn't real life. Or rather, it wasn't real life for the Periander Wintersmiths of the world.

Real life was sitting behind a desk all day. Or it was putting on a uniform and sailing to India. What he was living right now was an interlude, magical and carefree and fleeting.

He knew he had to enjoy every minute spent with Devereux, every second spent with Lady Violet, because time was running out, and once he left England he'd probably never see either of them again.

On his last Thursday in London, Perry picked up his uniform from the tailor, then went riding with Devereux. "You should come to the Worthingtons' ball tomorrow," Devereux said. "It's a masquerade. One of the highlights of the season. Quite a wild affair."

"I can't."

"You could dance with your inconvenient," Devereux said slyly.

"I can't," Perry repeated.

But that evening, as he lay in a tangle of blankets on top of Northumberland House, Lady Violet said the same thing: "Come to the Worthingtons' masquerade tomorrow. We can dance together!"

Perry's skin was cooling after what had been a rather energetic bout of lovemaking. He tugged the blankets up. "A masquerade?" he said dubiously.

"Yes. If you wear a mask no one will know who you are!"

Perry was silent. He heard a carriage rattle across the cobblestones below. In spending her evenings with him, Lady Violet had missed out on many entertainments. "Would you like it if I went?"

"Yes. Very much."

"I'll come then."

"Capital!" She sat up, spilling the blankets around them, letting in cool air. "We'll dance together a dozen times and no one will know. You can come as pirate or—I know—a legionnaire!"

"Or I could just wear a domino and a loo mask."

"Dominoes are so boring."

Perry laughed at the censure in her voice. "Very well, I'll come in costume."

"Excellent!" She planted a kiss on his cheek. "Where's your satchel? I'm starving. What did you bring tonight?"

"Do you have a costume?" Perry asked, sitting up. He handed her his duty bag.

"No. Usually I do, of course, but this year I didn't think I'd be going. I'll wear one of Primrose's old ones. Or Aster's. Ooh, it smells like Banbury cakes!"

"It is."

"With rum?"

"With rum."

"My favorite!"

Perry knew that. It was why he'd brought them tonight.

They ate Banbury cakes beneath the looming shape of the huge stone lion. "This is so, so, so good," Lady Violet said, biting into her second one, and then, "Oh, no! I dropped it."

They both peered over the parapet. Charing Cross lay far below. Two flambeaux burned, one on either side of the entranceway to Northumberland House. Perry thought he could just make out the shape of a Banbury cake, lying off to the right.

Lady Violet muttered something under her breath.

Perry blinked, and then looked at her. "What did you say?"

"Bollocks," Lady Violet repeated in a very small voice.

Perry absorbed this information and then laughed, a great whoop that rang out over Charing Cross. He put his arm around her bare shoulders and pulled her close and kissed her soundly. "Don't ever change. Promise me."

"You don't mind that I said it?"

"Not in the slightest. Although I didn't think dukes' daughters knew such words."

"I'm not like other dukes' daughters," Lady Violet said, a statement that was so blatantly true that Perry laughed again, and then kissed her again.

"Here," he said, handing her his second Banbury cake. "Take mine."

"Are you certain you don't want it?"

"I'm certain."

She gave him half back, though, and they ate in companionable silence, and then, after she'd licked her fingers, Lady Violet said, "What are bollocks? It's plural, isn't it? Or is it one bollocks?"

"You don't know?"

"No. It's something Rhodes said once. He didn't know I heard."

"I should rather think not!"

"Is it very bad? Will you tell me what it means?"

"Given that you've seen my bollocks, I don't see why I shouldn't tell you."

"Oh! You mean . . . bollocks are . . . ?"

"A man's balls. Or any animal's balls, for that matter. Bollocks, balls, baubles —it all means the same thing."

"Oh." There was a moment of reflective silence, and then Lady Violet said, "Have you finished eating?"

"Yes."

"Do you wish to go home now?"

"No."

They stayed another hour on top of Northumberland House, talking and laughing and making love beneath the great stone lion.

CHAPTER
FIFTY-TWO

*R*ed Riding Hoods at masquerade balls tended to stand out on account of their bright red cloaks. Shepherdesses, on the other hand, didn't draw the eye quite so much, especially when their bodices were as modest as the bodice of the costume Primrose had worn two years ago. An added bonus to Primrose's old costume was the wig, with its profusion of pale blonde ringlets. With that bodice and that wig, and with the most concealing mask she could find, Violet knew she'd be unrecognizable. Just another shepherdess among a flock of ladies wearing costumes.

Which meant that she could dance every dance with Wintersmith without anyone knowing who she was.

Except Primrose, of course, who would recognize the costume as her own. And Rhodes, who would probably recognize it, too.

And Aster.

And possibly Daphne and Clematis.

But other than her family, no one would know that the shepherdess who danced every single dance with the same man was a Garland.

There would be no scandal. No sullying of the family name.

"Thank you for lending me the costume," Violet said, tucking the shepherdess's straw bonnet into the bandbox.

"Would you like the crook as well?"

Violet had no intention of carrying an unwieldy crook around with her all evening. "No, thank you. I should put it down somewhere and then forget it."

Primrose shrugged, and put the crook to one side.

"What are you going as?" Violet asked her.

"A Faerie godmother."

Violet stared at her, awed. "As Baletongue?"

"The opposite of Baletongue. A benevolent godmother, like the one in Cendrillon."

"Oh," Violet said, disappointed. "What about Oliver? What's he going as?"

Primrose pursed her lips in a frown. "He wants to be a Viking. He says he's going to throw me over his shoulder and carry me around the ballroom."

Violet uttered a squeak of shocked laughter. "He's not!"

"He most certainly is *not*. I told him that if he does that, he'll be sleeping in an empty bed for the rest of the month."

Violet wished her brother-in-law would dare to toss Primrose over his shoulder in the middle of a ballroom. She'd give anything to see it.

Primrose was still frowning, but the set of her mouth suggested that she was suppressing a smile. Did she, too, wish that Oliver would do something so scandalous?

They were a strange match, Oliver and Primrose, one gregarious and lighthearted, the other tart and bookish.

A perfect match, though. They were clearly in love, clearly happy.

"Prim? How did you know that you wanted to marry Oliver? What was it about him?"

Primrose lost her frown. Her expression became thoughtful. She was silent for almost a full minute. "He knows the real me, and he likes that person. And I know the real him. We can be ourselves with each other." Her smile became fond. "And he makes me laugh, great jingle-brained fool that he is. He brightens my world."

"You brighten his world, too."

"I hope so."

"You do. Anyone can see that."

Primrose's smile was still soft, still fond—then her gaze sharpened. "Why do you ask?"

"No reason. I was curious, is all." Violet laid the wig on top of the bonnet and closed the bandbox. "I'll see you at the ball tonight."

Five hours later, she was dressed as a shepherdess. The bodice and skirt were pale pink, a color that suited Primrose, but that Violet never wore. She preferred stronger colors, bolder colors. But the pink was yet another reason she wouldn't be recognized.

She surveyed herself in the mirror. Pink dancing slippers. White stockings. A full pink skirt with layer upon layer of frothy white petticoats underneath. A gauzy apron embroidered with pink flowers. A pink bodice criss-crossed with pink lacing. A chemise whose ruffles entirely obscured her *décolletage* and whose puffed sleeves went all the way down to her elbows. A pink ribbon around her throat. A wig of blonde ringlets. And to crown it all, a flower-bedecked bonnet.

Violet tied the mask in place. It was pale pink, too. It covered her from upper lip to hairline, hiding the darkness of her eyebrows.

I don't look like myself at all, she thought, staring at the mirror. The costume was too pink to be anything she'd ever wear, too demure.

"You look very pretty, miss," Violet's maid said dubiously.

"I look very *dull*," Violet said. But dull was what she needed to avert scandal tonight.

She ran upstairs to show the children her costume. Rhodes was already there. He was dressed as a footman, with black and green livery and a white horsehair wig. "Aster," he said. "I thought you were going as Cendrillon."

"I changed my mind," Violet replied, and then crowed with laughter at her brother's double take.

"Violet? Is that you?"

"No one will recognize me, don't you think?" she said, giving a little twirl.

"I should think not," Rhodes said, still gaping at her. "Wherever did you get that costume?"

"It's Primrose's."

They stayed with the children for fifteen minutes, then went downstairs to wait for the carriage. Aster passed them in a rush on the stairs, dressed as Cendrillon, in a robe of tattered rags over her ballgown. Her slippers weren't glass, but they were studded with sparkling silver sequins, as was her gown. Diamonds were wound through her hair. "I'll be five minutes," she said. "I just want to show the children."

"No rush," Rhodes said. "Take your time." In the drawing room he sprawled on one of the sofas, legs stretched out, an arm slung along its gilded back. He looked vastly out of place, a footman lounging on a duke's sofa.

"You'll confuse people, dressed like that," Violet told him.

"So will you. I've never seen you look so . . . pink."

"I wish to be unrecognizable."

"You've succeeded," Rhodes told her, with dry amusement.

Violet sat opposite him. She arranged the monstrosity that was her skirt. She sincerely doubted that shepherdesses had ever worn skirts like it. And if they had, they definitely hadn't worn a dozen frothy petticoats underneath.

When she glanced back at Rhodes, the amusement was gone from his face. His expression was pensive.

She remembered suddenly that Rhodes's wife, Evelyn,

had gone to the Worthingtons' ball as a shepherdess one year. Rhodes had worn a matching shepherd's costume.

They'd gone as Robin Hood and Maid Marion another year. Paris and Helen of Troy. Red Riding Hood and the Huntsman. Always with costumes that matched and eyes only for each other.

Violet's throat tightened. She looked down at her lap. The gauzy apron was embroidered with flowers and trimmed with lace and seed pearls. No shepherdess had ever worn an apron so wispy and insubstantial, so lavish, so impractical.

She glanced at her brother again. If he was already thinking about Evelyn, perhaps he wouldn't mind talking about her?

"Rhodes?"

"Hmm?"

"How did you know Evelyn was the one for you?"

Her brother's face stiffened. He seemed to flinch on the sofa.

"I'm sorry! Forget I asked!" Violet jumped to her feet. "I'll just see how long Aster's going to be."

She was halfway to the door when Rhodes said, "Don't go."

Violet halted. She bit her lip and turned back uncertainly.

Her brother's expression was solemn, but he didn't look angry or upset. "Sit down, Vi," he said, and his voice was . . . kind?

Violet walked slowly back and sat, perching on the very edge of the seat, paying no heed to the state of her ruffles.

Rhodes didn't immediately speak. His gaze rested on her for a long moment, and then he said, "Evelyn wasn't on the hunt for a marquis or a duke. She was so shy she could barely talk to me. That was why I noticed her, but I married her for her character. She had such sweetness of temper. We never argued. Not once."

Violet nodded. Her sister-in-law had been everything that was gentle and warm-hearted. Evelyn would no more have picked a quarrel with Rhodes than she would have tied her garter in public.

She'd been sweet and sunny-natured, and she had suited Rhodes perfectly. He'd loved her and she had loved him.

"But I don't think such a spouse would do for you," Rhodes said. "You need someone with more fire, more strength of character."

"Evelyn had strength of character," Violet said, defending her dead sister-in-law instinctively.

"She did, but she would never have dreamed of arguing with me. You need someone who will. Someone who'll stand up to you, who won't always yield."

"I'm ready!" Aster cried from the doorway. "And the carriage has just pulled up."

The Worthingtons' residence was near Islington Spa, two miles from St. James's Square—which gave Violet ample time to ponder her brother's words.

The thought of an amiable, compliant husband made her shudder. When she married, it would be to someone strong-minded. A man who had edges she could clash off. Someone with whom she could have heated exchanges of opinion without descending into bitter acrimony. Someone who saw her as an equal, who'd let her make her own decisions, or at least have as much say in them as he did.

And she wanted someone who would brighten her world, as Oliver brightened Primrose's. Someone she could argue with *and* laugh with. A man who saw her for who she was, who didn't care that her father was a duke and that her brother would one day be one. Someone to whom her name and fortune were irrelevant.

Violet wasn't certain that such a person existed.

Her family's status could never be irrelevant. It was right there in her name: *Lady* Violet. That honorific would follow her to the grave. Regardless of who she married, even if he were a mere mister, she would *always* be Lady Violet.

And no man could know her for who she truly was. Not when she hid so much of herself. And yet she couldn't *not* hide it. If her family's secret were ever exposed, it would be a disaster beyond anything. When she married—if she married—she would tell her husband about Baletongue. But not before then.

Rhodes hadn't told Evelyn.

Primrose *had* told Oliver.

Violet wished she'd thought to ask her sister how that conversation had gone. Had Oliver been fearful? Disbelieving? Intrigued?

It was daunting to imagine revealing her secret. What if knowing it changed her husband's opinion of her? What if he was angry that she hadn't told him earlier? Or jealous of her magic? Afraid of it?

She wished she could marry someone like Wintersmith, who already knew.

The carriage lurched as the wheels went over a pothole. Violet nearly pitched off her seat. Not because of the pothole, but because of the epiphany she'd just had.

She could marry Wintersmith.

He already knew her secret.

He argued with her, even though she was a duke's daughter.

He made her laugh, made her cross, challenged her, disagreed with her, ran along rooftops with her, brought her Banbury cakes, made love to her beneath the stars. He was brave and daring and reckless—and yet also sensible and prudent and responsible. Her life was infinitely better with him in it. He brightened her world as much as Oliver brightened Primrose's.

He was the perfect husband.

The perfect husband for *her.*

Except that he'd stated, quite emphatically, that she was the last woman he'd ever wish to marry.

But that was before they'd become friends. Before they'd run along rooftops and kissed. It was likely Wintersmith's opinion of her had changed. Her opinion of him certainly had.

Violet chewed on her lip. Did she want to marry Wintersmith? Marriage was irrevocable. It was forever. A decision as enormous as the one she'd made about which magical gift to wish for—and she'd debated *that* with herself for months.

She didn't have months to consider whether or not to marry Wintersmith. She had only a few nights.

One of which was tonight.

CHAPTER
FIFTY-THREE

*T*here was a long line of carriages at the Worthingtons'. Violet wanted to leap down and navigate the last hundred yards on foot, but Aster's sequin-studded dancing shoes were too delicate for that.

She sat restlessly, changing her mind every few seconds. She did want to marry Wintersmith.

No, she didn't.

She did.

She didn't.

Finally, a footman opened the carriage door and let down the steps. They descended one by one, trod across a red carpet laid over the gravel, and climbed marble stairs between blazing flambeaux. Music tickled her ears, the opening notes to a quadrille.

The vast ballroom was at the back of the house, opening out onto a terrace and gardens. The room was already thronged with people. Violet turned on her heel, searching eagerly for Wintersmith. He'd refused to tell her what costume he'd be wearing.

She abandoned her brother and sister, diving into the crowd. A circuit of the ballroom failed to find Wintersmith. Violet paused to take stock. The quadrille was less sedate than quadrilles usually were, but dances at the Worthingtons' masquerades were always like that. This was no ball for the prudish and the straitlaced, the easily shocked, and it was definitely no ball for demure little débutantes.

She stood on tiptoe and scanned the room. The dancers skipped through their steps and there, behind them, entering the ballroom, was Devil Abbishaw. His height was unmistakable, his lankiness—which meant that the gentleman alongside him was most likely Wintersmith.

Violet crossed the ballroom faster than she'd ever crossed a ballroom before.

Devil and his companion paused and surveyed the room. Devil was dressed in a checkered harlequin costume. The man alongside him had come as Robin Hood.

Violet halted in front of them and curtsied. "Mr. Abbishaw. Mr. Wintersmith."

Devil's brow furrowed above his colorful mask. He looked her up and down. ". . . Lady Violet?"

"Oh, no," Violet said primly. "You have me mistaken."

Devil looked her up and down a second time, his brow even more perplexed.

Violet grinned at him, and turned her attention to Wintersmith.

As costumes went, Robin Hood's was rather a subdued one—dark green shirt, dark brown breeches, leather vest and wrist guards—but it suited Wintersmith superbly. The cut of the vest drew attention to his shoulders and the clinging breeches emphasized his muscular thighs. He looked inconspicuous and dangerous at the same time. The quintessential Robin Hood.

Violet stared at him. *Do I want to marry you?*

"May I have the next dance?" Wintersmith asked.

"You may have them all." Violet took his elbow and tugged

him into the crowd. It was bold behavior—scandalous behavior—but nobody knew who she was. Not even Devereux had been completely certain.

She found a footman with a tray, divested him of two crystal goblets filled with punch, and handed one to Wintersmith.

The punch was very pink. Wintersmith eyed it dubiously.

"It's a Worthington tradition," Violet told him. "Drink!"

Wintersmith's first sip was tentative. His second was not. His eyebrows arched above the rim of his mask.

Violet laughed, and took a sip of her own. The punch was tart, sweet, effervescent, potent. It sparkled on her tongue, tasting of champagne and citrus and rum.

They strolled arm in arm, watching the dancers, admiring the costumes. There were sailors and gypsies, pirates and priests, nymphs, goddesses, ladies' maids, nursemaids, chimneysweeps and night watchmen, Persians and Turks, a Queen Elizabeth, a Cleopatra, a Roman empress. There were also two other Robin Hoods and half a dozen shepherdesses.

Oliver *had* come as a Viking. Violet hoped he'd throw Primrose over his shoulder, and that she'd be there to witness it if he did.

The musicians struck up another dance. The ball was still in its infancy, but already there was a wildness to it, a giddiness. But the Worthingtons' masked balls were always rather rowdy—and if one stayed past the fireworks display, more than a little scandalous.

Or so she'd heard. Violet had always gone home after the fireworks. And truth be told, she'd always found the Worthingtons' balls rather scandalous *before* the fireworks.

"Shall we dance?" she asked Wintersmith.

They danced together. Not one dance, but five, one after the other. Each dance was merrier than the last, more frolicsome, people prancing and capering, laughing as they misstepped. No one noticed that Violet was dancing with the same man. No one cared. The music grew faster, wilder. Faces were flushed, eyes shining, laughter shrill.

If Violet had drunk more punch, she had no doubt that her face would be flushed and her laughter shrill. But she didn't drink more punch. Dancing with Wintersmith was intoxicating enough. Being with him in public was almost as exciting as skimming across the rooftops with him. She was holding hands with her lover, matching her steps to his, in front of half the *ton*.

They were one of the few sober couples on the dance floor. All around them, people flirted madly with one another.

Violet didn't flirt. She'd attended hundreds of balls since she'd made her début, and at those balls she'd danced with a great number of men. She'd also flirted with many of them. Flirting was playful and meaningless, something one could do with men one didn't want to marry. But with Wintersmith, flirting was impossible. She could only clutch his hands a little too tightly and revel in the madness of the ball, her brain working as fast as her feet—skip, twirl, pirouette. Did she want to marry him? Yes, no, maybe.

Her skin was growing hot with exertion, a little damp. Wintersmith's was, too. The forest-green shirt was open at his collarbone, loosely laced with leather cord. His throat was bare, a light sheen of perspiration gleaming in the glare cast by the chandeliers.

Violet had licked that gleaming skin last night, kissed him there, tasted the salt, nipped her way up his throat to his ear, made him gasp and shudder. And he'd done the same to her. They had made love together, laughed together. And after that, they'd held each other and talked for a long time, and after that they'd simply been silent, lying with their arms around one another, and the talking and the being silent had been as wonderful as the lovemaking, a memory to treasure for the rest of her life.

In that moment, Violet knew that she didn't want Wintersmith to leave England.

She wanted him to stay. Forever.

She wanted to be able to dance with him in public.

She wanted to talk with him and argue with him, laugh with him, make love with him, lie silently in bed with him— and wake up in the morning and do it all again.

Yes, her feet told her as they skipped.

Yes, as they twirled.

Yes.

The dance ended. They were both out of breath. "A drink?" Wintersmith asked.

"Yes, but not punch." She needed her wits about her tonight.

They drank lemonade, cool and astringent, by one of the tall French doors that opened onto the terrace. No breeze wafted in from outside; the press of air in the ballroom was too thick, too warm. All around was a roar of noise. People talked and laughed; dancing shoes slapped on the floor. The musicians labored strenuously, the giddy tune of a reel skipping across the ceiling and down the walls.

Violet felt rather giddy herself, a little off balance, even though she was standing still. She sipped her lemonade and listened to her heart, and her heart said *Yes*.

She looked at Wintersmith over the rim of her glass.

He was steady, daring, sensible, reckless, prudent, intrepid. Someone who didn't back down from an argument. Someone who liked to laugh. A man who was safe and exciting at the same time.

He was like his costume: unremarkable, until one realized that the shirt and breeches concealed a fighter's muscles. The leather wrist guards made him look dangerous. Which he was.

Violet finished her lemonade, glanced around for somewhere to set the glass down, and came face to face with Rhodes.

He looked past her, at Wintersmith. "I should have known you'd be here." His voice was grim.

"Thane," Wintersmith said. His voice wasn't grim. Rather, it was . . . wary?

Violet couldn't see much of Rhodes's face, but she saw

muscles work in his jaw. She looked down at his hands and discovered they were clenched.

She glanced at Wintersmith's hands. They weren't clenched. He was tense, though, poised for . . . what?

"If you challenge him to a duel, I swear I'll shoot you myself," Violet told her brother in a low, fierce voice.

Rhodes's lips tightened, and then twisted into something close to a snarl. He turned on his heel and stalked away.

Violet stared after him, caught between anger and dismay.

"I would delope," Wintersmith said quietly. "Your brother has the right of it."

Violet had always thought it would be rather exciting to have men duel over one. She discovered now that it would be horrible.

She imagined Wintersmith dying, lying on dew-damp grass at dawn, while his blood soaked into the soil. A fighter who wouldn't fight, because his opponent was in the right.

It was a terrible image. It made her feel physically ill.

"Let's go outside. I need some fresh air."

Flambeaux burned on the broad terrace and lamps flickered in the gardens below. They went down the steps and wandered along ghostly white marble-chip paths surrounded by shadows and lamplight and foliage. Wild, lilting music slipped from the ballroom and whispered on the breeze. It was beautiful, magical, enchanted, as if they'd stepped beyond the everyday world into another realm.

They came to a gazebo. Candles were lit inside, casting a golden glow. Columns rose tall, crowned with stone acanthus leaves. The roof was high above them, indiscernible against the dark sky.

"Let's watch the fireworks from up there," Violet said.

"Fireworks?"

"Yes, there's always a display. Unless . . . would you prefer to stay down here?"

Wintersmith gazed upwards. She knew he was gauging the height, the lack of a harness, the risk of being seen. "All right," he said. "Let's do it."

They walked around to the back of the gazebo, the marble chips crunching secretively beneath their shoes. Violet put her arms around Wintersmith and took firm hold of his clothing, a fistful of shirt, a fistful of belt. "I won't drop you. I promise."

"I know." He locked his arms around her.

Violet lifted them both off the ground. The roof was high and Wintersmith was heavy, and it was more than a little dangerous, but it was over in a moment. Their feet found purchase, they crouched low, caught their balance, laughed a little breathlessly, a little giddily.

The roof of the gazebo was pan-tiled, with a shallow parapet all around. It was definitely the least comfortable rooftop they'd been on together, and also the smallest, but it felt as if it was the most secret. The garden was far below, all shadows and darkness and clandestine pools of lamplight, and beyond that was the vast bulk of the house, its windows brightly lit. Half-heard strains of music teased at her ears. London was distant. The sky was wide and dark overhead. The feeling that she and Wintersmith were in a world separate from everyone else grew stronger.

Violet removed her shepherdess's bonnet. Wintersmith removed his jaunty Robin Hood hat. She took off her mask. He took off his. She could barely see him, but the pale blur of his face was achingly familiar. This was how she'd seen him the most: a phantom perched alongside her on a rooftop, indistinct in the darkness.

A cool breeze touched her cheeks, whispered music in her ears, ruffled her shepherdess's ringlets. They had no blankets on this roof, but Violet didn't care if the tiles were uncomfortable or dirty. Such things were irrelevant when one was in a magical little space off to the side of the real world. "Let's lie down," she said, tugging on Wintersmith's shirt.

They lay down on the bumpy tiles, feet towards the parapet, heads towards the roof's peak. Wintersmith put an arm around her and shifted until they were nestled close. "How long until the fireworks?" he asked.

"Maybe half an hour. An hour?" Violet pressed her lips to his.

They kissed for an eternity, gently, unhurriedly, their mouths dancing together to distant, barely-heard music. Violet felt as if she was in a dream, but she knew it wasn't a dream. It was real life, and Wintersmith was leaving in a few days, and she had a huge decision to make.

Except that she had already made it. In the ballroom. And lying up here on the gazebo only reinforced it. The rightness of it sank into her bones. This was the future she wanted: rooftops with Wintersmith.

The decision was as terrifying as it was thrilling. When should she tell him? How should she tell him?

Wintersmith rolled onto his back, taking her with him. Their noses bumped. They laughed against each other's lips. Violet lay on top of him and he was warm and solid and much more comfortable than a pan-tiled roof.

"What would you like to do?" Wintersmith asked, his hands resting at her waist.

There was more than one answer to that question, more than one thing she wanted to do.

Violet sat up, her knees on either side of his hips, her petticoats voluminous around them. She wanted to make love like this, astride him, but she also wanted to talk with him. "What I would like is . . ."

The night seemed to hold its breath. No breeze stirred, no music played, everything was still and silent. Her decision loomed overhead, as huge and vast as the galaxy, terrifying and thrilling at the same time.

"Marry me," Violet said.

CHAPTER
FIFTY-FOUR

*T*here was a shocked silence, and then Wintersmith said, "I beg your pardon?"

"Marry me," Violet said again. It was easier to say the second time. Words bubbled from her, excited and exuberant: "That's what I want. I don't want you to go. I want you to stay. Think how much fun we'd have together! We're the perfect match, don't you think?"

Instead of speaking, Wintersmith sighed, and after he'd sighed he lifted her off him and set her alongside him on the roof.

"Periander? What is it?"

He sat up. "I can't marry you," he said, very gently.

"Of course you can!"

"My circumstances—"

"Tosh! If I don't care about your circumstances, I don't see why anyone else should."

"Well, you should care. Your brother certainly will, and so will your parents."

"They might at first, but once they see how well-matched we are, they'll be happy for us. I know they will!"

"We're not well-matched."

"Of course we are! How can you think that we're not?" She stared at his shadowy shape, hurt and bewildered. "Have you not enjoyed our nights together?"

"Of course I've enjoyed them, but Violet, if we were together day in and out, you'd soon become bored with me."

"No, I wouldn't!"

"I'm a stick-in-the-mud, remember?"

Violet huffed out a short, annoyed breath. "You know I didn't mean it."

"You did mean it, and you were right; compared to you I *am* a stick-in-the-mud." He took one of her hands between both of his. "There's someone else out there for you, Violet. Someone better than I am."

"There's no one better. You're safe *and* exciting, and that's what I want."

"I'm only exciting because of how we've spent our time together. Marriage wouldn't be like that. It would be uneventful and ordinary. If you married me, you'd soon find me safe and *boring*."

"No, I wouldn't," she said stubbornly.

Wintersmith sighed again. "Violet, I like you very much. You make me feel more alive than anyone I've ever met. But I can't marry you. You and I, we're suited for nighttime and secrecy, not for daytime. Not for marriage."

She jerked her hand free. "You're wrong."

Something exploded overhead, shockingly loud, shockingly bright.

Violet flinched. Wintersmith did more than flinch. He shoved her down on the tiles, swift and forceful, and covered her with his body.

Another loud *crack* sounded above them. Sparks lit the sky. Wintersmith was taut, tense, braced for action. Did he think it was musketfire? Cannonfire?

"It's the fireworks," Violet wheezed, crushed beneath him.

Wintersmith's weight eased slightly off her. It became easier to breathe.

347

More fireworks detonated, loud, bright, harmless. Winter-smith rolled to one side and sat up.

Violet sat up, too.

Guests thronged on the distant terrace. *Oh*, they cried as another rocket burst high above.

"I'm sorry," he said. "I thought—"

"No, thank you." It had been brave of him to protect her from what he thought was gunfire. More than brave: heroic.

Soon it would be real muskets he faced, not fireworks.

Violet clutched his sleeve. "Please don't go to India."

"I'm sorry," Wintersmith said. He leaned close and kissed her cheek.

Violet recognized that kiss. It was good-bye.

Half a dozen fireworks burst overhead, exuberant and joyful, sparks cartwheeling and cascading. In the lingering glow, she saw Wintersmith retie his mask and don the jaunty Robin Hood cap.

"Let's go down," he said, his words almost lost beneath the noise in the sky and the cries of the guests on the terrace.

Violet wanted to refuse, wanted to sit on top of the gazebo until she'd argued him into changing his mind. But she also knew that if she had to convince Wintersmith to marry her, then that wasn't the marriage she wanted.

Violet fumbled to put on her mask and bonnet. Tears stung her nose and blurred her eyes.

They embraced awkwardly, stiffly, not holding each other tightly enough. Violet almost dropped him on the way down. He landed with a jarring thud.

"Are you all right?"

"Yes."

They made their way briskly to the terrace and merged with the guests there. People were beginning to drift back towards the ballroom. Spirits were high, laughter loud. "We always go home after the fireworks," Violet said, pitching her voice to be heard beneath the hubbub. "It gets rather wild. Or so I've been told."

In previous years she'd been tempted to stay and find out just how raucous the ball could become. Tonight, she wanted to go home.

"I'll help you find your brother."

"I see him," Violet said, and she did, solid and dependable, standing off to the left, scanning the guests, no doubt looking for her and Aster.

"Then I shall bid you good-night."

"Good night."

It was too formal a parting for them, too wrong, but Violet didn't know how to make it right. She didn't know how to make anything right, so she headed for Rhodes and home.

CHAPTER
FIFTY-FIVE

Violet hadn't argued with Wintersmith on the gazebo roof, but she spent most of the rest of the night arguing with him in her head. She *wouldn't* come to think him boring. He was wrong and she was right, but she couldn't find the words to articulate why. It was a feeling, a conviction, but not one that she could defend with any real evidence. Evidence would accrue over time, and proof that she was right would come at the end, when they were old and gray-haired and sitting side by side with blankets over their knees. She'd poke his no-doubt-bony ribs with her no-doubt-bony elbow and say, *See, I was right.* And she *was* right. She knew it. But she didn't know how to convince Wintersmith of it.

It was dawn before Violet fell asleep and past midday when she woke. She threw back the covers and crossed to the window, opening the curtains.

It was rather dull outside, gray clouds hinting at rain.

Wintersmith thought that she'd find him dull if she married him.

Violet dressed without noticing what she was wearing and

ate without noticing what she was eating. The day grew duller, the sky grayer.

At four o'clock, it started to drizzle. Violet nibbled on one fingertip and stared out at the damp square and told herself that one night of rain would be all right. It might even be a good thing, because it gave her more time to marshal an irresistible and unassailable argument. An argument that would convince Wintersmith that she was right and he was wrong.

But what if it rained for days? What if it rained until Wintersmith left for India? What if—

An elegant traveling chaise drew to a halt outside. A very familiar footman jumped down from the box seat and let down the steps.

Violet ran down the stairs like a hoyden, calling out to Aster and Rhodes. "Mother and Father are home!"

The drizzle became rain, which in turn became a downpour. Violet was relieved. It meant that she didn't need to choose between staying at home with her parents or arguing with Wintersmith until he agreed with her.

They dined together as a family. Primrose and Oliver braved the deluge and joined them. Afterwards they all sat in the smallest and coziest of the parlors, while rain drummed against the windowpanes. A fire burned in the grate and candles cast a soft, golden glow over everything.

Violet hadn't realized how much she'd missed moments like this, all of them gathered together. Dinner parties were fun, and balls and masquerades, soirées and theater parties, evenings at the opera and at Vauxhall, but times like this were even better, quiet hours spent with her family, no one wearing diamonds or fine silks, no one on their best manners. Ordinary evenings, when one could wear gowns that were comfortable rather than fashionable and sit with one's feet tucked up under one. Or in her father's case, with a foot propped up on an ottoman.

These were the important evenings in her life. They anchored her, gave her a deep-rooted sense of happiness.

Nights didn't have to be thrilling. It was nice when some of them were, but evenings spent quietly in the company of people one loved were more important. Evenings that were ordinary and unexciting, but also satisfying and precious.

Wintersmith was wrong. She needed steady and ordinary just as much as she needed excitement—more, even—because the steady and the ordinary were what made one able to enjoy the exciting.

Life was a balance. Marriage was a balance, too. Her parents balanced one another. Primrose and Oliver balanced one another. Rhodes and Evelyn had balanced one another.

Wintersmith would balance me, she thought.

Violet became aware that someone was speaking to her. "I beg your pardon, Mother?"

"I said, that's a very serious expression you're wearing, my love."

There was so much Violet wanted to tell her parents—about Bow Street Runners and investigations and about finding someone who liked to run along rooftops, but most of all, she wanted their advice about marriage.

But her parents had spent six hours in a carriage today. They were both weary. "I have things to tell you, but it can wait until tomorrow."

The duchess cocked her head. "What sort of things?"

Violet pressed her lips together. Now was not the time, but her mother's expression was so open, so warm, so inviting.

"I asked someone to marry me last night, but he said no."

She spoke the words too loudly. The quiet conversations taking place in the parlor stopped. Heads turned. Everyone stared at her.

Primrose broke the silence. "You asked him to marry you?"

Violet nodded.

"He said no?" A frown was gathering on Rhodes's face.

"Yes. And he said that you'd be right to challenge him to a duel. And that if you did, he'd delope!" Her voice was sharp, angry, but Violet didn't know who she was angry with—Rhodes or Wintersmith—or whether perhaps she was angry with both of them.

"Who are we talking about?" her father asked.

"Periander Wintersmith," Rhodes said. "Endymion's youngest brother."

Her father frowned. "I thought he died in India, too."

"Periander's in England?" Oliver said. "When did he get back?"

"It was Alexander who died, not Periander," Rhodes told their father, while at the same time Primrose turned to Oliver and said, "You know him? But he was in a different regiment to you."

"Of course I know him," Oliver said. "He's a capital fellow. One of the best!"

"Duel?" Violet's mother inquired, a note of alarm in her voice.

"Rhodes doesn't like him," Violet said.

"I do like him, actually. He reminds me of Endymion. But I *don't* like the risks the pair of you have been taking."

Rhodes hadn't said outright that they were having an affair, but the inference was clear. Violet's father looked stern; her mother looked worried.

"I like him, too," Primrose put in. "But I'm not sure why you like him so much, Vi. He's not dashing at all."

"He doesn't have to be dashing!" Violet said hotly. "Oliver's not dashing, and Evelyn wasn't, and Mother and Father aren't either!" Her voice was too sharp again, too loud. She took a short breath and continued more calmly: "I like him because he argues with me, and because he listens to me, and because he's daring *and* cautious. He balances me, the way Oliver balances you and Mother balances Father. But he thinks I'll find him too boring, so he won't marry me."

353

Her parents exchanged a glance. "I think we need to meet this young man," her father said.

CHAPTER
FIFTY-SIX

*I*t was midday by the time Perry returned from the emporium in Cheapside with a package that contained tooth powder and toothbrushes, boot blacking, handkerchiefs, and two new pairs of stockings.

He turned into the lane, rooted in his pocket for the latchkey—and found a highly polished footman loitering outside his lodging house.

"Mr. Wintersmith?" the footman inquired, when Perry halted at the door.

"Yes."

The footman produced a letter.

Perry accepted it warily. It was either from Lady Violet informing him that he'd broken her heart or from the Marquis of Thane threatening to horsewhip him.

Whichever it was, he wasn't going to read it in front of the footman.

"Thank you," he said, and unlocked the door.

"I've been directed to wait for a reply, sir."

Perry looked at the letter again. Probably not Lady Violet, then. Thane, perhaps? Demanding a meeting of honor?

But one didn't challenge someone to a duel by letter.

Perry broke open the seal and unfolded the paper—and discovered that he was requested to present himself at St. James's Square that afternoon, to partake of tea with the Duke and Duchess of Sevenash.

Perry arrived at Sevenash House precisely on the hour. His neckcloth and shirt were fresh back from the laundress, his boots polished, his tailcoat meticulously brushed, but he knew that he looked like a clerk. Everything he wore was plain, sober, and well-worn. His neckcloth and collar points might be newly starched, but they weren't as crisp as they could be and the polish on his boots was thruppenny blacking.

A butler admitted him into a vast entrance foyer paved with white, gray, and black marble.

Perry relinquished his hat and followed the butler up a majestic double staircase. He had a sense of gathering doom, thunderheads piling high on his horizon.

They walked along a corridor and paused at a door. The butler opened it. "Mr. Wintersmith," he announced.

Perry wished that Devereux were with him. Devereux would whistle a few jaunty notes under his breath and Perry would murmur, "Time to face the music," and they'd walk through the door, shoulder to shoulder, and endure whatever came next.

He inhaled a short breath and entered the room—and the sense of doom quadrupled. His inquisitors weren't merely the Duke and Duchess of Sevenash, but also their two eldest children, the Marquis of Thane and the Duchess of Westfell. His horrified gaze jerked from person to person—and halted, caught on one achingly familiar face.

Lady Violet.

He couldn't look away.

He'd spent a lot of time with her during the past few weeks, but very little of it had been in daylight, and during those few times she'd never worn that particular gown. The cut was unexceptional—demure neckline, puff sleeves—but the color wasn't. No débutante would dare to wear that shade of red. Perry didn't know what to call it. Turkish red? Peony? All he knew was that it set off her creamy skin and dark eyes and black hair to perfection.

She was ravishing.

Someone cleared their throat. "Wintersmith? May I present you to my parents?"

Perry jerked his gaze back to Thane, and from him to the Duke and Duchess of Sevenash. He made his bows to them.

Thane indicated a seat.

Perry took it.

Lady Violet's sister, the Duchess of Westfell, poured tea.

Perry accepted his cup.

Everyone was looking at him, which was only to be expected. Their expressions weren't what he'd anticipated, though. Thane didn't look as if he was on the verge of challenging him to a duel and Lady Violet didn't look as if she was about to leap to her feet and slap his face, or worse, burst into tears. And as for the Duke and Duchess of Sevenash, they were regarding him less with censure and disapproval than with frowning curiosity, as if he was a puzzle they were trying to solve.

Perry didn't dare drink his tea. He knew he would choke on it.

"I understand that you caught my daughter flying," the duke said abruptly.

"Yes, Your Grace."

"You were working as a Bow Street Runner?"

Perry felt no urge to inform the duke that the correct term was Principal Officer. "Yes, sir."

"You and my daughter solved a case?"

"Yes, sir."

The duke had one foot propped up on an ottoman. On it, he wore a sock instead of a shoe. Despite that sock, he was remarkably intimidating. He reminded Perry of a general, stern and authoritative, able to destroy a career with a single word.

"Our daughter has told us much of what happened, but I would like to hear it from you."

"Some of it isn't public knowledge, sir."

The duke accepted this with a curt nod. "My family is good at keeping secrets."

Perry took a moment to marshal his thoughts, then launched into the story, telling it from the very beginning, when Sir Mortimer had first brought the case to him.

His audience listened without interruption for the most part. Once the Duchess of Sevenash interposed a question, and twice the duke did. Perry's throat grew dry. He drained his teacup three times before the tale was told. Almost the whole tale. The only thing he left out was that Giles Abbishaw's lover was a man.

When he finished, Lady Violet's sister poured him a fourth cup of tea. Perry accepted it gratefully, even though the tea was now only lukewarm. He sipped, while Thane described the events of the Galpins' ball—Saintbridge's entrance, his reception, his furious departure. Thane then wrapped up everything succinctly: "As I understand it, Wilton has been recalled from America, Giles has been granted a comfortable independence, and Saintbridge has departed London indefinitely. The lease has been let go on his house."

Perry confirmed this with a nod, and set down his empty teacup. He'd been here nearly an hour, but Lady Violet hadn't uttered a single word, which was most unlike her.

He risked a glance at her, trying to decipher her expression.

"My daughter says that the pair of you go running on rooftops."

Perry's gaze snapped back to the duke. Lady Violet's

expression might be indecipherable, but Sevenash's was dauntingly severe. "Yes, sir. But no one's seen us, I assure you. We've been extremely careful."

The duke's frown didn't abate.

"We use a harness," Perry hastened to add. "It's quite safe. I would never do anything to risk your daughter's life."

There was a beat of silence. Now was the time for Thane to leap to his feet and accuse him of risking Lady Violet's reputation, but it wasn't Thane who broke the silence; it was the Duchess of Sevenash: "I'm glad that Violet's had company."

Perry wasn't the only person who was startled by that pronouncement. Everyone looked surprised, even Lady Violet.

"You're always alone when you fly, my love," the duchess said, reaching across to pat her daughter's knee. "It worries me sometimes. Not your safety, but . . . some people are happiest when they're alone, but you're not one of them. I'm glad you've been able to share your flying with someone."

Perry glanced at Thane. He knew the marquis wasn't glad Violet had been spending time with him—but still Thane said nothing.

The Duchess of Sevenash turned her attention to him. "I'm curious as to how you knew my daughter was following you. You said you sensed it before you saw her?"

"I felt it, yes. It runs in my family."

That prompted more questions. Perry found himself telling them about his grandmother and her insistence that she could sense when ghosts were near, and how he himself had never sensed any ghosts but that twice his scalp had informed him that he was riding into an ambush, and that it also told him when footpads were following him and when Lady Violet was overhead.

"Is it magic?" the Duchess of Sevenash mused. "Or intuition?"

"Intuition, I think. If it is magic, it's nothing like your family's. I don't have a Faerie godmother."

The mood in the parlor suddenly changed, from curiosity to a stiff wariness.

359

"I won't tell anyone," Perry said hastily. "Ever. I give you my word of honor."

The duke folded his lips together in a frown. He studied Perry for a long moment, and then said, "You're leaving London shortly?"

"In two days, yes."

"Why?"

"To rejoin my regiment."

The duke surveyed him through narrowed eyes. "I understand that my daughter wishes to marry you."

Lady Violet had told her father that? Perry glanced at her in shock, and then swiftly back at the duke. "I haven't asked her to marry me, Your Grace. I know I'm not worthy of her."

"Are you not Lord Wintersmith's nephew?"

"Yes, but my uncle washed his hands of us when my father was ruined."

"Are you a gambler?" the Duchess of Sevenash inquired.

"No, ma'am. I'm not."

"But your father's gambling makes you an unworthy match?"

"I have less than a hundred pounds to my name," Perry told the duke and duchess bluntly. "I'm in no position to offer for your daughter. Or for anyone."

"*Is* there someone else?" Lady Violet's sister asked.

"Of course not!"

The Duchess of Westfell didn't appear offended by his sharp tone. She gave a small, pleased smile.

The conversation wasn't progressing at all how it should. Perry tried to steer it back on track, something that Thane was patently failing to do. "Dukes' daughters don't marry penniless younger sons," he said. "And they especially don't marry penniless younger sons who've been Bow Street Runners."

"Principal Officers," Lady Violet corrected him.

Perry cast her a sharp, disbelieving glance. She was choosing *now*, of all times, to enter the conversation?

"Dukes' daughters who're over the age of twenty-one may

marry whomever they wish," the Duchess of Sevenash said mildly. "As may any woman in England."

"Well, they ought not to! Not if it will damage their families' reputations."

"I believe our family's reputation can survive marriage to a former Bow Street Runner."

"*And* a fortune hunter, for you know that's what people would think!"

"Then you'll just have to prove that you're not one by having a long and happy marriage, won't you?" The duchess smiled sweetly, but Perry was beginning to suspect that she wasn't as sweet as she looked.

He glanced to Thane for help. Why wasn't the marquis enumerating all the reasons that Lady Violet shouldn't marry him?

"It seems to me," the Duchess of Sevenash continued, "that the most important issue is not your reputation, Mr. Wintersmith, or my family's reputation, but whether you and Violet will be happy together."

Perry looked back at her. Her gaze was direct, astute, challenging.

He came to the belated realization that she was as much a general as her husband was.

"Do you love my daughter?" the duchess asked.

Perry's throat closed. He glanced at Lady Violet, and then away. "Very much," he managed to say. "But she deserves a better husband."

"Do you mean someone richer?" Lady Violet asked, in a tone that his ears recognized as being rather dangerous. "Or someone less ordinary?"

Perry met her gaze. "Both."

"I disagree," she said.

"I disagree, too," Thane said mildly.

Perry did a double take, then stared at the marquis.

"I think the two of you balance one another remarkably well," Thane said.

"So do I," Lady Violet's sister said, leaning over to pour Perry another cup of lukewarm tea.

He stared at her, too, struck speechless.

"You said that I make you feel more alive than anyone you've ever met," Lady Violet said.

His gaze jerked back to her.

"Did you mean that?"

Perry swallowed, found his voice, said, "Yes."

"Well, you make me feel happier than anyone I've ever met. You see me. The real me. The person no one outside my family knows."

For some reason that statement struck Perry as unbearably sad. Lady Violet shouldn't have to hide so much of herself.

"I don't want a wealthy husband," she declared. "Or an exciting one. I want someone who'll argue with me and buy me Banbury cakes and eat them on rooftops with me. I want someone who's adventurous and cautious. Someone who'll fly with me and anchor me." She paused, and then said, "I want you."

Perry stared at her, unable to speak. His throat was too tight.

"Violet has told us what she wants. I believe the time has come for you to tell us what you want."

Perry reluctantly stopped looking at Lady Violet and returned his gaze to her mother. She smiled at him, sweet and steely. "The truth, Mr. Wintersmith."

The truth.

The truth was . . .

His heartbeat measured the seconds until the words burst from him, anguished: "I want Violet, but it's too unequal a match!"

The duchess didn't look displeased by his outburst. She glanced at her husband. "Perhaps we ought to discuss money now."

"There's nothing to discuss," Perry said bitterly. "A husband ought to be able to provide for his wife and I can't!"

"It bothers you," the duchess said. It was a statement, not a question.

Perry pressed his lips together and gave a curt nod.

"The disparity between your fortune and my daughter's is rather large," the duke said. "But that can easily be remedied."

"I don't want Violet's money!"

Perry's tone was far too hot for addressing dukes, but Sevenash didn't appear to be offended. He ignored the interruption. "We've discussed this, and we think it's best if Violet's fortune is split equally between the two of you."

Perry opened his mouth to protest, and then shut it again. Half a fortune was abhorrent and repugnant, but also surprisingly sensible. "I don't want Violet's money," he repeated, less hotly.

"Do you believe that a man's worth is measured by how much money he has?" Violet's sister inquired, a tart edge to her voice.

Part of him did believe it. But the rest of him . . .

"No," Perry admitted reluctantly.

Thane leaned forward in his chair. "Forget your pride, Wintersmith. It has no place in this decision."

Thane was correct. The only thing that mattered was Violet. Her future. Her happiness.

Perry looked at her. She was vibrant and bold, daring, inquisitive, spirited, persistent. She questioned his decisions and argued as often as not, but he liked that about her. Loved it, in fact.

Loved her.

He would never love anyone as much as he loved Violet Garland. It was impossible, because there was no one else like her in the world.

Could he make her happy?

Violet thought so, and she was no milk-and-water miss. She knew her own mind. She also knew every eligible man in the ton . . . and yet she'd chosen him.

If he married her, they'd be together day and night, in public and in private. Year after year. Forever.

Was that what he wanted?

Perry's heartbeat was loud in his ears. He held Violet's gaze. "Will you marry me?"

"Yes!"

She was on her feet and he was on his and they were holding each other tightly. Violet was laughing and crying at the same time and he was, too. Someone in the room whooped. Perry's ears told him the sound came from Thane, however unlikely that seemed.

Perry looked across at the duke. Sevenash was smiling. His wife was smiling, too, and dabbing at her eyes, and Violet's sister was beaming widely.

"Welcome to the family," Sevenash said.

For some reason the word "family" made Perry's throat close. "Thank you, Your Grace," he managed to say.

"Sevenash," the duke corrected him. "There are too many Your Graces in this family."

Perry's throat constricted further. The reality of his situation was beginning to sink in. This man was to be his father-in-law.

"Banns or special license?" the duke asked.

"Special license!" Violet said, without hesitation. "We can marry tomorrow!"

"You may marry next week," the duke said firmly. "Wintersmith needs to settle things with his regimental agent first, and the marriage articles have to be drawn up. It'll also give the pair of you time to find a house you'd like to hire . . . unless you prefer to live here for the rest of the Season? You're most welcome to do so."

Perry and Violet exchanged a glance. "Our own house," she said, and he nodded agreement.

A house with windows they could climb out of and a bed they could sleep in together.

Perry's throat grew even tighter. He was afraid he was going to have to pull out his handkerchief and dab at his eyes like his soon-to-be mother-in-law.

But the duchess was currently tucking away her handkerchief. "I hope you'll stay to dine with us tonight, Mr. Wintersmith, but right now, I think that you and my daughter need some time to talk with one another."

Perry exchanged another glance with Lady Violet. There was a great deal he wished to say to her, but not in front of an audience.

"The garden parlor," Violet announced. She stepped out of his embrace and took his hand, tugging him towards the door.

Half a minute later, Perry found himself in a parlor that looked out over a flower-filled garden. He felt rather off balance, faintly bewildered. How had his life changed so much so quickly?

Violet released his hand and turned to face him. Her brow creased. She bit her lip. She looked uncharacteristically hesitant. "I didn't bully you into that, did I? You do wish to marry me?"

Perry took both of her hands in his. "There is nothing I want more in this world than to marry you."

"Truly?"

"Truly." He dipped his head to kiss her briefly, then drew back so that she could see his face. "I apologize for what I said on the gazebo. I was wrong. Night or day, it doesn't matter. We suit one another."

Tears filled her eyes. Her mouth turned up in a small, wobbly smile.

"You make me happy to be alive," Perry told her. "You're not like anyone I've ever met."

"You're not like anyone I've ever met either."

"Then we make a good pair." It was true, Perry realized as he uttered the words. They did make a good pair. A good team. "There's no one I'd rather marry than you."

Her smile trembled and grew wider. Her eyes were bright with tears and joy.

"I love you, Violet."

She made a sound that was half sob, half laugh. "I love you, too."

Perry caught her up in an embrace. His feet might have been on the floor, but his heart was so full that it felt as if he was flying.

$\mathcal{A}$FTERWARDS

$\mathcal{T}$he first time Violet had seen her husband had been at the Montlakes' ball. He'd stood off to one side, practically invisible. They were in that same ballroom now, but there was no dancing this time, just music and mingling, a soirée to mark the final days of the Season.

Periander stood near the center of the room, talking with Rhodes and Oliver. As Violet watched, he said something that made them all laugh.

It seemed impossible that she'd ever thought him non-descript, that she'd compared him to a piece of furniture and labeled him Mr. Bland. Violet huffed to herself, a scolding little sound. How blind she'd been. How wrong-headed.

Rhodes said something. Oliver chimed in, gesticulating with his glass. The three men laughed again.

Devereux Abbishaw joined them. Whatever he had to say made the men stop laughing. Violet saw surprise on their faces. Periander looked around, locating her with unerring accuracy. He always knew where she was in a room, just as she always knew where he was. He tilted his head, a silent *You need to hear this.*

Violet crossed to him, weaving her way through the throng. Chandeliers shone like small suns overhead and all around her was music and laughter. Everything was bright and merry and gay, but she was already looking forward to afterwards, to quiet rooftops and a dark night sky and time alone with her husband.

She joined the cluster of menfolk, stepping close to Periander's side. His hand came to rest in the small of her back, a warmth that was as thrilling as it was steadying.

"Lady Violet!" Devereux exclaimed. "I received a letter from Wilton today. He's not coming back. He says he prefers America to England. The pioneer spirit suits him."

Violet felt her eyes grow wide with astonishment, but by the time she left the soirée, two hours later, she was no longer astonished. England was too mannered and sedate for someone as wild as Wilton Abbishaw. America—young, raw, untamed—was a better fit for him.

In their house on Halfmoon Street, with their fine clothes put away, the rooftops beckoned. Periander laid the harness out on the floor and crouched, examining the straps and buckles, something he did every time they used it. Violet watched him. Dressed all in black, he looked mysterious, a little dangerous.

"Perry? How would you like to try flying? Truly flying."

He looked up. "How?"

"A new harness. One that binds us together at shoulders, hips, and ankles. You wouldn't be able to run, but we could fly."

She watched him think about it, watched him consider the risks.

"I'd like to do that," he said. "But we'd need to test the harness first."

It was exactly the answer Violet had expected. The answer she'd been hoping for. Tonight they would run across London's roofs, but sometime in the future—next week, next month—she would take him up to that cool, empty, eerie space that was hers alone and they'd look down at the world far below.

She had never thought she'd be able to do that with anyone.

Periander finished checking the harness. He rose to his

feet. "Ready?"

"Ready."

He didn't always bring his duty bag on their nighttime excursions, but tonight he slung it across his chest.

"What's in there?"

"What do you think?"

"Banbury cakes!" Violet bounced up on her toes and kissed him.

Periander laughed and lifted her off her feet and swung her around; then he set her down again.

Together, they put on the harness.

Together, they climbed out the window and up onto the roof.

They set off. Periander was her legs and she was his wings. Together, they were one.

$\mathcal{A}$UTHOR'S $\mathcal{N}$OTE

'Bow Street Runner' was the colloquial term for a Bow Street Principal Officer. Six to eight such officers worked out of Bow Street, traveling around England (and occasionally abroad) if needed. Principal Officers wore plain clothes and carried a short tipstaff with a brass crown at one end.

Policing was rather different to what it is now. In most instances it was up to the victim to instigate legal action. Someone who'd been burgled could pay for an investigation; equally, he (or she) could refuse to prosecute the culprit.

Automatous clocks with erotic scenes painted on them really did exist. Few examples remain, but occasionally they come up for auction. Pornographic illustrations were readily available and Holywell Street was the place to go if you wished to purchase them. Check out *The Amorous Illustrations of Thomas Rowlandson*, by G. Schiff, if you'd like to see some of the drawings that Violet found in Freddy Stanhope's collection.

There were many private banks in England, one of which was Coutts & Co. on the Strand. Banknotes in Regency times were numbered. There weren't many notes in circulation, though, as the denominations were larger than most people needed.

Silver paper was the Regency equivalent of tissue paper.

People did indeed use it to make miniature hot air balloons! At least one encyclopedia contained instructions on how to do so.

With regard to architecture, building regulations changed after the Great Fire swept through London in 1666. Houses had to be constructed of brick or stone, thatching was forbidden, eaves could no longer project over the street, and parapets were required at roof level.

London has undergone many changes in its history and a number of places mentioned in this novel no longer exist. There was a Portugal Street near Hyde Park, just as there was a Northumberland House at Charing Cross. You can follow Violet and Perry's journeys on either Horwood's or Wallis's *Plan of the Cities of London and Westminster*. Both maps are available online and are extremely detailed.

Sadly, Northumberland House was demolished in 1874. The stone lion was saved and now stands atop Syon House in Hounslow. If you have the chance, go see him. He's rather magnificent!

$\mathcal{T}$HANK $\mathcal{Y}$OU

Thanks for reading *Violet and the Bow Street Runner*. I hope you enjoyed it!

If you'd like to be notified whenever I release a new book, please join my Readers' Group, which you can find at www.emilylarkin.com/newsletter.

I welcome all honest reviews. Reviews and word of mouth help other readers to find books, so please consider taking a few moments to leave a review on Goodreads or elsewhere.

Violet and the Bow Street Runner is part of the Baleful Godmother series. I'm currently giving free digital copies of the series prequel, *The Fey Quartet*, and the first novel in the original series, *Unmasking Miss Appleby*, to anyone who joins my Readers' Group. Here's the link: www.emilylarkin.com/starter-library.

The Garland Cousins series runs concurrently with the Pryor Cousins series. The first Pryor novel, *Octavius and the Perfect Governess*, features a governess in jeopardy and the marquis's son who goes undercover as a housemaid to protect her.

If you'd like to read the first chapter of *Octavius and the Perfect Governess*, please turn the page . . .

OCTAVIUS
and the

Perfect Governess

CHAPTER ONE

*O*ctavius Pryor should have won the race. It wasn't difficult. The empty ballroom at his grandfather-the-duke's house was eighty yards long, he'd lined one hundred and twenty chairs up in a row across the polished wooden floorboards, and making his way from one side of the room to the other without touching the floor was easy. His cousin Nonus Pryor—Ned—also had one hundred and twenty chairs to scramble over, but Ned was as clumsy as an ox and Octavius knew he could make it across the ballroom first, which was exactly what he was doing—until his foot went right through the seat of one of the delicate giltwood chairs. He was going too fast to catch his balance. Both he and the chair crashed to the floor. And that was him out of the race.

His cousin Dex—Decimus Pryor—hooted loudly.

Octavius ignored the hooting and sat up. The good news was that he didn't appear to have broken anything except the chair. The bad news was that Ned, who'd been at least twenty chairs behind him, was now almost guaranteed to win.

Ned slowed to a swagger—as best as a man could swagger while clambering along a row of giltwood chairs.

Octavius gritted his teeth and watched his cousin navigate the last few dozen chairs. Ned glanced back at Octavius, smirked, and then slowly reached out and touched the wall with one fingertip.

Dex hooted again.

Octavius bent his attention to extracting his leg from the chair. Fortunately, he hadn't ruined his stockings. He climbed to his feet and watched warily as Ned stepped down from the final chair and sauntered towards him.

"Well?" Dex said. "What's Otto's forfeit to be?"

Ned's smirk widened. "His forfeit is that he goes to Vauxhall Gardens tomorrow night . . . as a woman."

There was a moment's silence. The game they had of creating embarrassing forfeits for each other was long-established, but this forfeit was unprecedented.

Dex gave a loud whoop. "Excellent!" he said, his face alight with glee. "I can't *wait* to see this."

When Ned said that Octavius was going to Vauxhall Gardens as a woman, he meant it quite literally. Not as a man dressed in woman's clothing, but as a woman dressed in woman's clothing. Because Octavius could change his shape. That was the gift he'd chosen when his Faerie godmother had visited him on his twenty-fifth birthday.

Ned had chosen invisibility when it was his turn, which was the stupidest use of a wish that Octavius could think of. Ned was the loudest, clumsiest brute in all England. He walked with the stealth of a rampaging elephant. He was terrible at being invisible. So terrible, in fact, that their grandfather-the-duke had placed strict conditions on Ned's use of his gift.

Ned had grumbled, but he'd obeyed. He might be a

blockhead, but he wasn't such a blockhead as to risk revealing the family secret. No one wanted to find out what would happen if it became common knowledge that one of England's most aristocratic families actually had a Faerie godmother.

Octavius, who could walk stealthily when he wanted to, hadn't chosen invisibility; he'd chosen metamorphosis, which meant that he could become any creature he wished. In the two years he'd had this ability, he'd been pretty much every animal he could think of. He'd even taken the shape of another person a few times. Once, he'd pretended to be his cousin, Dex. There he'd sat, drinking brandy and discussing horse-flesh with his brother and his cousins, all of them thinking he was Dex—and then Dex had walked into the room. The expressions on everyone's faces had been priceless. Lord, the expression on *Dex's* face . . .

Octavius had laughed so hard that he'd cried.

But one shape he'd never been tempted to try was that of a woman.

Why would he want to?

He was a man. And not just any man, but a good-looking, wealthy, and extremely well-born man. Why, when he had all those advantages, would he want to see what it was like to be a woman?

But that was the forfeit Ned had chosen and so here Octavius was, in his bedchamber, eyeing a pile of women's clothing, while far too many people clustered around him—not just Ned and Dex, but his own brother, Quintus, and Ned's brother, Sextus.

Quintus and Sextus usually held themselves distant from high jinks and tomfoolery, Quintus because he was an earl and he took his responsibilities extremely seriously and Sextus because he was an aloof sort of fellow—and yet here they both were in Octavius's bedchamber.

Octavius didn't mind making a fool of himself in front of a muttonhead like Ned and a rattle like Dex, but in front of his oh-so-sober brother and his stand-offish older cousin?

He felt more self-conscious than he had in years, even a little embarrassed.

"Whose clothes are they?" he asked.

"Lydia's," Ned said.

Octavius tried to look as if it didn't bother him that he was going to be wearing Ned's mistress's clothes, but it did. Lydia was extremely buxom, which meant that *he* was going to have to be extremely buxom or the gown would fall right off him.

He almost balked, but he'd never backed down from a forfeit before, so he gritted his teeth and unwound his neckcloth.

Octavius stripped to his drawers, made them all turn their backs, then removed the drawers, too. He pictured what he wanted to look like: Lydia's figure, but not Lydia's face—brown ringlets instead of blonde, and brown eyes, too—and with a silent *God damn it*, he changed shape. Magic tickled across his skin and itched inside his bones. He gave an involuntary shiver—and then it was done. He was a woman.

Octavius didn't examine his new body. He hastily dragged on the chemise, keeping his gaze averted from the mirror. "All right," he said, in a voice that was light and feminine and sounded utterly wrong coming from his mouth. "You can turn around."

His brother and cousins turned around and stared at him. It was oddly unsettling to be standing in front of them in the shape of a woman, wearing only a thin chemise. In fact, it was almost intimidating. Octavius crossed his arms defensively over his ample bosom, then uncrossed them and put his hands on his hips, another defensive stance, made himself stop doing that, too, and gestured at the pile of women's clothing on the bed. "Well, who's going to help me with the stays?"

No one volunteered. No one cracked any jokes, either. It appeared that he wasn't the only one who was unsettled. His brother, Quintus, had a particularly stuffed expression on his face, Sextus looked faintly pained, and Ned and Dex, both of whom he expected to be smirking, weren't.

"The stays," Octavius said again. "Come on, you clods.

Help me to dress." And then, because he was damned if he was going to let them see how uncomfortable he felt, he fluttered his eyelashes coquettishly.

Quintus winced, and turned his back. "Curse it, Otto, don't do that."

Octavius laughed. The feeling of being almost intimidated disappeared. In its place was the realization that if he played this right, he could make them all so uncomfortable that none of them would ever repeat this forfeit. He picked up the stays and dangled the garment in front of Ned. "You chose this forfeit; *you* help me dress."

⚬⚬⚭⚬⚬

It took quite a while to dress, because Ned was the world's worst lady's maid. He wrestled with the stays for almost a quarter of an hour, then put the petticoat on back to front. The gown consisted of a long sarcenet slip with a shorter lace robe on top of that. Ned flatly refused to arrange the decorative ribbons at Octavius's bosom or to help him fasten the silk stockings above his knees. Octavius hid his amusement. Oh, yes, Ned was *never* going to repeat this forfeit.

Lydia had provided several pretty ribbons, but after Ned had failed three times to thread them through Octavius's ringlets, Dex stepped forward. His attempt at styling hair wasn't sophisticated, but it was passable.

Finally, Octavius was fully dressed—and the oddest thing was that he actually felt *un*dressed. His throat was bare. He had no high shirt-points, no snug, starched neckcloth. His upper chest was bare, too, as were his upper arms. But worst of all, he was wearing no drawers, and that made him feel uncomfortably naked. True, most women didn't wear drawers and he was a woman tonight, but if his own drawers had fitted him he would have insisted on wearing them.

Octavius smoothed the gloves over his wrists and stared at himself in the mirror. He didn't like what he saw. It didn't just feel a little bit wrong, it felt a *lot* wrong. He wasn't a woman. This wasn't him. He didn't have those soft, pouting lips or those rounded hips and that slender waist, and he most definitely did *not* have those full, ripe breasts.

Octavius smoothed the gloves again, trying not to let the others see how uncomfortable he was.

Ned nudged his older brother, Sextus. "He's even prettier than you, Narcissus."

Everybody laughed, and Sextus gave that reserved, coolly amused smile that he always gave when his brother called him Narcissus.

Octavius looked at them in the mirror, himself and Sextus, and it *was* true: he was prettier than Sextus.

Funny, Sextus's smile no longer looked coolly amused. In fact, his expression, seen in the mirror, was the exact opposite of amused.

"Here." Dex draped a silk shawl around Octavius's shoulders. "And a fan. Ready?"

Octavius looked at himself in the mirror and felt the wrongness of the shape he was inhabiting. He took a deep breath and said, "Yes."

They went to Vauxhall by carriage rather than crossing the Thames in a scull, to Octavius's relief. He wasn't sure he would have been able to get into and out of a boat wearing a gown. As it was, even climbing into the carriage was a challenge. He nearly tripped on his hem.

The drive across town, over Westminster Bridge and down Kennington Lane, gave him ample time to torment his brother and cousins. If there was one lesson he wanted them to learn tonight—even Quintus and Sextus, who rarely played the forfeit game—it was to never choose this forfeit for him again.

Although, to tell the truth, he was rather enjoying himself now. It was wonderful to watch Ned squirm whenever Octavius fluttered his eyelashes and flirted at him with the pretty brisé fan. Even more wonderful was that when he uttered a coquettish laugh and said, "Oh, Nonny, you are so droll," Ned didn't thump him, as he ordinarily would have done, but instead went red and glowered at him.

It had been years since Octavius had dared to call Nonus anything other than Ned, so he basked in the triumph of the moment and resolved to call his cousin "Nonny" as many times as he possibly could that evening.

Next, he turned his attention to his brother, simpering and saying, "Quinnie, darling, you look so handsome tonight."

It wasn't often one saw an earl cringe.

Dex, prick that he was, didn't squirm or cringe or go red when Octavius tried the same trick on him; he just cackled with laughter.

Octavius gave up on Dex for the time being and turned his attention to Sextus. He wasn't squirming or cringing, but neither was he cackling. He lounged in the far corner of the carriage, an expression of mild amusement on his face. When Octavius fluttered the fan at him and cooed, "You look so delicious, darling. I could swoon from just looking at you," Sextus merely raised his eyebrows fractionally and gave Octavius a look that told him he knew exactly what Octavius was trying to do. But Sextus had always been the smartest of them all.

They reached Vauxhall, and Octavius managed to descend from the carriage without tripping over his dress. "Who's going to pay my three shillings and sixpence?" he asked, with a flutter of both the fan and his eyelashes. His heart was beating rather fast now that they'd arrived and his hands were sweating inside the evening gloves. It was one thing to play this game with his brother and cousins, another thing entirely to act the lady in public. Especially when he wasn't wearing drawers.

But he wouldn't let them see his nervousness. He turned to his brother and simpered up at him. "Quinnie, darling, you'll pay for li'l old me, won't you?"

Quintus cringed with his whole body again. "God damn it, Otto, stop that," he hissed under his breath.

"No?" Octavius pouted, and turned his gaze to Ned. "Say you'll be my beau tonight, Nonny."

Ned looked daggers at him for that "Nonny" so Octavius blew him a kiss—then nearly laughed aloud at Ned's expression of appalled revulsion.

Dex did laugh out loud. "Your idea, Ned; you pay," he said, grinning.

Ned paid for them all, and they entered the famous pleasure gardens. Octavius took Dex's arm once they were through the gate, because Dex was enjoying this far too much and if Octavius couldn't find a way to make his cousin squirm then he might find himself repeating this forfeit in the future—and heaven forbid that that should ever happen.

Octavius had been to Vauxhall Gardens more times than he could remember. Nothing had changed—the pavilion, the musicians, the supper boxes, the groves of trees and the walkways—and yet it had changed, because visiting Vauxhall Gardens as a woman was a vastly different experience from visiting Vauxhall Gardens as a man. The gown undoubtedly had something to do with it. It was no demure débutante's gown; Lydia was a courtesan—a very expensive courtesan—and the gown was cut to display her charms to best advantage. Octavius was uncomfortably aware of men ogling him—looking at his mouth, his breasts, his hips, and imagining him naked in their beds. That was bad enough, but what made it worse was that he knew some of those men. They were his friends—and now they were undressing him with their eyes.

Octavius simpered and fluttered his fan and tried to hide

his discomfit, while Ned went to see about procuring a box and supper. Quintus paused to speak with a friend, and two minutes later so did Sextus. Dex and Octavius were alone—or rather, as alone as one could be in such a public setting as Vauxhall.

Octavius nudged Dex away from the busy walkway, towards a quieter path. Vauxhall Gardens sprawled over several acres, and for every wide and well-lit path there was a shadowy one with windings and turnings and secluded nooks.

A trio of drunken young bucks swaggered past, clearly on the prowl for amatory adventures. One of them gave a low whistle of appreciation and pinched Octavius on his derrière.

Octavius swiped at him with the fan.

The man laughed. So did his companions. So did Dex.

"He pinched me," Octavius said, indignantly.

Dex, son of a bitch that he was, laughed again and made no move to reprimand the buck; he merely kept strolling.

Octavius, perforce, kept strolling, too. Outrage seethed in his bosom. "You wouldn't laugh if someone pinched Phoebe," he said tartly. "You'd knock him down."

"You're not my sister," Dex said. "And besides, if you're going to wear a gown like that one, you should expect to be pinched."

Octavius almost hit Dex with the fan. He gritted his teeth and resolved to make his cousin regret making that comment before the night was over. He racked his brain as they turned down an even more shadowy path, the lamps casting golden pools of light in the gloom. When was the last time he'd seen Dex embarrassed? Not faintly embarrassed, but truly, deeply embarrassed.

A memory stirred in the recesses of his brain and he remembered, with a little jolt of recollection, that Dex had a middle name—Stallyon—and he also remembered what had happened when the other boys at school had found out.

Dex Stallyon had become . . . Sex Stallion.

It had taken Dex a week to shut that nickname

down—Pryors were built large and they never lost a school-yard battle—but what Octavius most remembered about that week wasn't the fighting, it was Dex's red-faced mortification and fuming rage.

Of course, Dex was a sex stallion now, so maybe the nickname wouldn't bother him?

They turned onto a slightly more populated path. Octavius waited for a suitable audience to approach, which it soon did: Misters Feltham and Wardell, both of whom had been to school with Dex.

"You're my favorite of all my beaus," Octavius confided loudly as they passed. "Dex Stallyon, my sex stallion. You let me ride you all night long." He uttered a beatific sigh, and watched with satisfaction as Dex flushed bright red.

Feltham and Wardell laughed. Dex laughed, too, uncomfortably, and hustled Octavius away, and then pinched him hard on his plump, dimpled arm.

"Ouch," Octavius said, rubbing his arm. "That hurt."

"Serves you bloody right," Dex hissed. "I can't believe you said I let you ride me!"

Now that was interesting: it was the reference to being ridden that Dex objected to, not the nickname.

Octavius resolved to make good use of that little fact.

He talked loudly about riding Dex when they passed Lord Belchamber and his cronies, and again when they encountered the Hogarth brothers.

Both times, Dex dished out more of those sharp, admonitory pinches, but Octavius was undeterred; he was enjoying himself again. It was fun ribbing Dex within earshot of men they both knew and watching his cousin go red at the gills.

He held his silence as two courting couples strolled past, and then swallowed a grin when he spied a trio of fellows sauntering towards them. All three of them were members of the same gentleman's club that Dex frequented.

Dex spied them, too, and changed direction abruptly, hauling Octavius into a dimly lit walkway to avoid them.

Octavius tried to turn his laugh into a cough, and failed.

"You're a damned swine," Dex said. It sounded as if he was gritting his teeth.

"I think you mean bitch," Octavius said.

Dex made a noise remarkably like a growl. He set off at a fast pace, his hand clamped around Octavius's wrist.

Ordinarily, Octavius would have had no difficulty keeping up with Dex—he was an inch taller than his cousin—but right now he was a whole foot shorter, plus he was hampered by his dress. He couldn't stride unless he hiked the wretched thing up to his knees, which he wasn't going to do; he was already showing far too much of his person. "Slow down," he said. "I've got short legs."

Dex made the growling sound again, but he did slow down and ease his grip on Octavius's wrist.

Along came a gentleman whom Octavius didn't recognize, one of the nouveau riche judging from his brashly expensive garb. The man ogled Octavius overtly and even went so far as to blow him a kiss. Instead of ignoring that overture, Octavius fluttered his eyelashes and gave a little giggle. "Another time, dear sir. I have my favorite beau with me tonight." He patted Dex's arm. "I call him my sex stallion because he lets me ride him all night long."

Dex pinched him again, hard, and dragged him away from the admiring gentleman so fast that Octavius almost tripped over his hem.

"Stop telling everyone that you ride me!" Dex said, once they were out of earshot.

"Don't you like it?" Octavius asked ingenuously. "Why not? Does it not sound virile enough?"

Dex ignored those questions. He made the growling sound again. "I swear to God, Otto, if you say that one more time, I'm abandoning you."

Which meant that Octavius had won. He opened the brisé fan and hid a triumphant smile behind it.

Dex released his wrist. Octavius refrained from rubbing

it; he didn't want to give Dex the satisfaction of knowing that it hurt. Instead, he walked in demure silence alongside his cousin, savoring his victory . . . and then lo, who should he see coming towards them but that old lecher, Baron Rumpole.

"I warn you, Otto," Dex said, as Rumpole approached. "Don't you dare."

Rumpole all but stripped Octavius with his gaze, and then he had the vulgarity to say aloud to Dex, "I see someone's getting lucky tonight."

The opening was too perfect to resist. Warning or not, Octavius didn't hesitate. "That would be me getting lucky," he said, with a coy giggle. "He's my favorite beau because he lets me ride—"

"You want her? She's yours." Dex shoved Octavius at the baron and strode off.

Octavius almost laughed out loud—it wasn't often that he managed to get the better of Dex—but then Rumpole stepped towards him and the urge to laugh snuffed out.

He took a step back, away from the baron, but Rumpole crowded closer. He might be in his late fifties, but he was a bull-like man, thickset and bulky—and considerably larger and stronger than Octavius currently was.

Octavius tried to go around him to the left, but Rumpole blocked him.

He tried to go around him to the right. Rumpole blocked him again.

Dex was long gone, swallowed up by the shadows.

"Let me past," Octavius demanded.

"I will, for a kiss."

Octavius didn't deign to reply to this. He picked up his skirts and tried to push past Rumpole, but the man's hand shot out, catching his upper arm, and if he'd thought Dex's grip was punishingly tight, then the baron's was twice as bad. Octavius uttered a grunt of pain and tried to jerk free.

Rumpole's fingers dug in, almost to the bone. "No, you don't. I want my kiss first." He hauled Octavius towards him and bent his head.

Octavius punched him.

If he'd been in his own shape, the punch would have laid Rumpole out on the ground. As it was, the baron rocked slightly on his feet and released Octavius's arm.

Octavius shoved the man aside. He marched down the path, his steps fast and angry. How dare Rumpole try to force a kiss on him!

Behind him, Rumpole uttered an oath. Footsteps crunched in the gravel. The baron was giving chase.

Octavius was tempted to stand his ground and fight, but common sense asserted itself. If he were a man right now he'd crush Rumpole, but he wasn't a man and Rumpole outweighed him by at least a hundred pounds. Retreat was called for.

Octavius picked up his skirts and ran, even though what he really wanted to do was pummel the baron to the ground. Fury gave his feet wings. He rounded a bend in the path. The shadows drew back and he saw a glowing lamp and two people.

The baron stopped running. Octavius didn't, not until he reached the lamp casting its safe, golden luminescence.

He'd lost his fan somewhere. He was panting. And while rage was his predominant emotion, underneath the rage was a prickle of uneasiness—and that made him even angrier. Was he, Octavius Pryor, afraid of Baron Rumpole?

"The devil I am," he muttered under his breath.

He glanced over his shoulder. Rumpole had halted a dozen yards back, glowering. He looked even more bull-like, head lowered and nostrils flaring.

The prickle of unease became a little stronger. Discretion is the better part of valor, Octavius reminded himself. He picked up his skirts again and strode towards the people he'd spied, whose dark shapes resolved into two young sprigs with the nipped-in waists, padded shoulders, and high shirt-points of dandies. "Could you escort me to the pavilion, kind sirs? I'm afraid I've lost my way."

The sprigs looked him up and down, their gazes lingering on the lush expanse of his breasts.

Octavius gritted his teeth and smiled at them. "Please? I'm all alone and this darkness makes me a little nervous."

"Of course, darling," one of the sprigs said, and then he had the audacity to put his arm around Octavius's waist and give him a squeeze.

Octavius managed not to utter an indignant squawk. He ground his teeth together and submitted to that squeeze, because a squeeze from a sprig was a thousand times better than a kiss from Baron Rumpole. "The pavilion," he said again. "Please?"

The man released his waist. "Impatient little thing, aren't you?" he said with a laugh. He offered Octavius his arm and began walking in the direction of the pavilion. The second sprig stepped close on Octavius's other side, too close, but Octavius set his jaw and endured it. The pavilion was only five minutes' walk. He could suffer these men for five minutes. They were, after all, rescuing him.

Except that the first sprig was now turning left, drawing Octavius down one of the darker paths . . .

Octavius balked, but the second sprig had an arm around his waist and was urging him along that shadowy path. "I don't like the dark," Octavius protested.

Both men laughed. "We'll be with you, my dear," one of them said, and now, in addition to an arm around Octavius's waist, there was a sly hand sidling towards his breasts.

Octavius wrenched himself free. Outrage heated his face. His hands were clenched into fists. He wanted nothing more than to mill both men down, but he was outweighed and outnumbered and the chances of him winning this fight were slim. "I shall walk by myself," he declared haughtily, turning his back on the sprigs and heading for the lamplight.

Behind him, he heard the sprigs laughing.

Octavius gritted his teeth. A plague on all men!

He reached the slightly wider walkway, with its lamp, and glanced around. Fortunately, he didn't see Baron Rumpole. Unfortunately, he couldn't see anyone. He wished he'd not steered Dex towards these out-of-the-way paths, wished they'd kept to the busier promenades, wished there were people around. He picked up his skirts and headed briskly for the pavilion, but the path didn't feel as safe as it once had. The lamplight didn't extend far and soon he was in shadows again. He heard the distant sound of music, and closer, the soft crunch of footsteps.

They weren't his footsteps.

He glanced around. Baron Rumpole was following him.

Octavius began to walk more rapidly.

The footsteps crunched faster behind him.

Octavius abandoned any pretense of walking and began to run, but his skirts restricted his strides and the baron caught him within half a dozen paces, grabbing his arm and hauling him into the dark mouth of yet another pathway.

"Let go of me!" Octavius punched and kicked, but he was only five foot two and the blows had little effect.

"Think too highly of yourself, don't you?" Rumpole said, dragging Octavius deeper into the dark shrubbery. Rough fingers groped his breasts. There was a ripping sound as his bodice gave way. Octavius opened his mouth to shout, but the baron clapped a hand over it.

Octavius bit that hand, punched Rumpole on the nose as hard as he could, and tried to knee the man in the groin. He was only partly successful, but Rumpole gave a grunt and released him.

Octavius ran back the way he'd come. There were wings on his feet again, but this time he wasn't fueled solely by rage, there was a sting of fear in the mix, and damn it, he refused to be afraid of Rumpole.

The path was still too dark—but it wasn't empty anymore. There, in the distance, was Sextus.

Sextus was frowning and looking about, as if searching for someone, then his head turned and he saw Octavius and came striding towards him.

Octavius headed for him, clutching the ripped bodice with

one hand, holding up his skirts with the other. He heard fast, angry footsteps behind him and knew it was Rumpole.

The baron reached him first. He grabbed Octavius's arm and tried to pull him towards a dark and shadowy nook.

Octavius dug his heels in. "No."

"Stupid bitch," Rumpole snarled, but Octavius was no longer paying him any attention. He was watching Sextus approach.

His cousin's stride slowed to an arrogant, aristocratic stroll. His expression, as he covered the last few yards, was one that Sextus had perfected years ago: haughty, aloof, looking down his nose at the world. "Rumpole," he drawled.

The baron swung to face him, his grip tight on Octavius's arm. "Pryor."

Sextus glanced at Octavius. He saw the torn bodice, but his expression didn't alter by so much as a flicker of a muscle. "I must ask you to unhand the lady."

Rumpole snorted. "She's no lady. She's a piece of mutton."

"Always so crass, Rumpole. You never disappoint." There was no heat in Sextus's voice, just boredom. His tone, his words, were so perfectly insulting that Octavius almost crowed with laughter.

Beneath that instinctive laughter was an equally instinctive sense of shock. Had Sextus actually said that to a baron?

Rumpole flushed brick red. "She's mine."

"No," Sextus corrected him coolly. "The lady is a guest of my brother tonight."

"Lady?" The baron gave an ugly laugh. "This thing? She has no breeding at all."

"Neither, it appears, do you." Again, Sextus's tone was perfect: the boredom, the hint of dismissive disdain.

Octavius's admiration for his cousin rose. Damn, but Sextus had balls.

Rumpole's flush deepened. He released Octavius. His hands clenched into fists.

"I believe that's Miss Smith's shawl you're holding," Sextus said, and indeed, Octavius's shawl was dangling from one meaty fist, trailing in the dirt.

Rumpole cast the shawl aside, a violent movement, and took a step towards Sextus.

Sextus was the shortest of the Pryors, but that didn't mean he was short. He stood six feet tall, eye to eye with Rumpole, but whereas the baron was beefy, Sextus was lean. He looked slender compared to Rumpole.

Octavius found himself holding his breath, but Sextus gave no hint of fear. He returned the baron's stare with all the slightly bored arrogance of a duke's grandson.

For a moment the threat of violence hung in the air, then the baron muttered something under his breath that sounded like "Fucking Pryor," turned on his heel, and stalked off.

Sextus picked up the shawl, shook it out, and put it around Octavius's shoulders. "You all right, Otto?"

Octavius wrapped the shawl more tightly around himself, hiding the ripped bodice. "You were just like grandfather, then. All you needed was a quizzing glass to wither him through."

Sextus ignored this comment. "Did he hurt you?"

Octavius shook his head, even though his arm ached as if a horse had kicked it. Damn Rumpole and his giant-like hands. "It's a shame you're not the heir. You'd make a damned good duke."

"Heaven forbid," Sextus said, which was exactly how Octavius felt about his own ducal prospects: heaven forbid that he should ever become a duke. It was little wonder Quintus was so stuffy, with that multitude of responsibilities hanging over him.

"Come on," Sextus said. "Let's get you home." He took Octavius by the elbow, matching his stride to Octavius's shorter legs.

They were almost at the Kennington gate when someone called out: "Sextus!" It was Dex. He reached them, out of breath. "You found him! He all right?"

"Rumpole practically ripped his dress off," Sextus told

him. "What the devil were you doing, leaving him like that?"

Dex looked shamefaced. "Sorry, I didn't think."

"That is patently clear," Sextus said, a bite in his voice. "Tell the others I'm taking him home."

Dex obeyed without argument, heading back towards the pavilion.

"It was my fault," Octavius confessed, once they were through the gate and out in Kennington Lane. "I pushed Dex too far."

Sextus glanced at him, but said nothing. He still looked angry, or rather, as angry as Sextus ever looked. He was damned good at hiding his emotions.

Several hackneys waited in the lane. Sextus handed Octavius up into one and gave the jarvey instructions.

"It *was* my fault," Octavius said again, settling onto the squab seat.

"What? It's your fault that Rumpole almost raped you?" A shaft of lamplight entered the carriage, illuminating Sextus's face for an instant. Octavius was surprised by the anger he saw there.

"He didn't almost rape me," he said, as the carriage turned out of Kennington Lane and headed towards Westminster Bridge. "And honestly, it *was* as much my fault as Dex's. Neither of us thought Rumpole was dangerous. I didn't realize until too late just how puny I am." He remembered the baron forcing him into the dark shrubbery and gave an involuntary shiver. And then he remembered Sextus facing Rumpole down. "I can't believe you spoke to him like that. He'd have been within his rights to call you out."

Sextus just shrugged.

The carriage rattled over Westminster Bridge. When they reached the other side, Octavius said, "When I was fourteen, Father and Grandfather had a talk with me about sex. Did your father . . . ?"

"We all had that lecture," Sextus said.

Octavius was silent for several minutes, remembering that

long-ago conversation. He'd given his word of honor to never force any woman into bestowing sexual favors, regardless of her station in life. "I'd wager Rumpole didn't have a talk like that with his father."

"No wager there," Sextus said dryly.

They sat in silence while the carriage trundled through the streets. Octavius had given his word all those years ago—and kept it. He'd never forced women into his bed, but he had ogled the ladybirds, snatched kisses, playfully pinched a time or two. It had seemed harmless, flirtatious fun.

Harmless to *him*. But perhaps those women had disliked it as much as he'd disliked it tonight?

Octavius chewed on that thought while the carriage rattled its way towards Mayfair.

Like to read the rest?
Octavius and the Perfect Governess is available now.

ACKNOWLEDGMENTS

A number of people helped to make this book what it is. Foremost among them is my developmental editor, Laura Cifelli Stibich, but I also owe many thanks to my copyeditor, Maria Fairchild, and proofreader, Martin O'Hearn.

The series logo was designed by Kim Killion, of the Killion Group. The cover and the print formatting are the work of Jane D. Smith. Thank you, Jane!

Emily Larkin grew up in a house full of books. Her mother was a librarian and her father a novelist, so perhaps it's not surprising that she became a writer.

Emily has studied a number of subjects, including geology and geophysics, canine behavior, and ancient Greek. Her varied career includes stints as a field assistant in Antarctica and a waitress on the Isle of Skye, as well as five vintages in New Zealand's wine industry.

She loves to travel and has lived in Sweden, backpacked in Europe and North America, and traveled overland in the Middle East, China, and North Africa.

She enjoys climbing hills, reading, and watching reruns of *Buffy the Vampire Slayer* and *Firefly*.

Emily writes historical romances as Emily Larkin and fantasy novels as Emily Gee. Her websites are www.emilylarkin.com and www.emilygee.com.

Never miss a new Emily Larkin book. Join her Readers' Group at www.emilylarkin.com/newsletter and receive free digital copies of *The Fey Quartet* and *Unmasking Miss Appleby*.

OTHER WORKS

THE BALEFUL GODMOTHER SERIES

Prequel
The Fey Quartet novella collection:
Maythorn's Wish
Hazel's Promise
Ivy's Choice
Larkspur's Quest

Original Series
Unmasking Miss Appleby
Resisting Miss Merryweather
Trusting Miss Trentham
Claiming Mister Kemp
Ruining Miss Wrotham
Discovering Miss Dalrymple

Garland Cousins
Primrose and the Dreadful Duke
Violet and the Bow Street Runner

Pryor Cousins
Octavius and the Perfect Governess

OTHER HISTORICAL ROMANCES

The Earl's Dilemma
My Lady Thief
Lady Isabella's Ogre
Lieutenant Mayhew's Catastrophes

The Midnight Quill Trio
The Countess's Groom
The Spinster's Secret
The Baronet's Bride

FANTASY NOVELS
(Written as Emily Gee)

Thief With No Shadow
The Laurentine Spy

The Cursed Kingdoms Trilogy
The Sentinel Mage
The Fire Prince
The Blood Curse